THE
REFLECTION
OF
EVIL

THE
REFLECTION
OF
EVIL

BY

A. T. NICHOLAS

To order additional copies of this book, contact:
Xlibris Corporation
1-888-795-4274
www.Xlibris.com
Orders@Xlibris.com
24908

Special Thanks to God and the Lord Jesus Christ who always had good advice. My wife Anita for her patience, understanding, and love.

Special Note: To my parents, thank you for always being there for me and for always being a great example throughout my life. Your words taught me well, but your actions and the way you lived your lives was the greatest teacher, and it made all the difference. I love you both very much.

To my brother, Bill, no one could have a better brother, friend, and the occasional substitute father when Dad was hard at work. I want you to know I'm grateful for the sacrifices you made for me, and that I love you. Thank you.

I would like to thank William D. Van Wie at District Creative Printing for all his help.

Others to thank: My family and friends that helped and encouraged me. Jane Johnson, Scott MacDonald, Ed Zimmerman, Clint Cassa for ironing out the rough spots. Also, Mike S., Danny C., John T., Jim H., Robert J., and Mike T., Joe E., Danny S. Thanks.

I also would like Diane D. for taking out all the speed bumps and potholes.

I would also like to thank AMAZON.COM for spreading the word.

"Thou hast outraged, not insulted me, sir; but for that I ask thee not to beware of Starbuck; though wouldst but laught; but let thee Ahab beware of Ahab; beware of thyself, old man."

Moby Dick by Herman Melville

———————————————

"Hypocrite! First remove the plank from your own eye, and then you will see clearly to remove the speck from your brother's eye."
Sermon on the Mount by Jesus Christ

———————————————

"Not all that glitters is gold."

Characters

Allen Pyrit .... Evangelist

Mary Jopuez .... Private investigator,
ex-FBI agent

Kelsey Anderson .... FBI analysis

Sam Dent (Uncle Sam) .... ex-CIA, Kelsey's uncle

Gregory Orfordis .... Theologian

Jordan Iblis .... Secretary General of the
United Nations

Art Hanson .... Private investigator

Derrick Moore .... President of the United States

Shelly Deanster .... Vice President

Walter Web .... Speaker of the House

Alfred Buckler .... Archaeologist

Sean Carbon .... President of Golden Calf
Enterprises

James .... The voice

Chapter 1

Jerusalem, Summer, 1962
Archaeological Site # COT-001

Alfred Buckler, head archaeologist for the team of Americans on the dig site, stood at the summit of the hill and conversed with two men who were dressed like high-powered lawyers. They had "secret government operative" written all over them.

Behind them, he saw a young Israeli boy race across the desert and up the rocky embankment toward the restricted archaeological site on which they stood. The boy's brown face and shirtless body glistened with sweat; his frightened eyes locked onto them. Out of breath, he got to within a few yards of them when the operatives spun around and drew their handguns. They took aim at the boy and prepared to fire.

"Stop!" Buckler shouted, becoming a human shield. "He's just a boy."

One of the operatives waved his gun. "Send him away."

Buckler glared at the operatives and mumbled a few choice words in their direction before he escorted the young boy away from the covert area. "You must not do that again," he said looking down at the boy. "You'll get yourself killed. Understand?"

"But, Mr. Buck, they are coming." His tone was filled with worry.

"Who?"

The boy was frightened. "The soldiers."

"When?"

"Now."

He leaned down, face to face with the boy. "What else do you know?"

The boy swallowed hard. "They want what you found."

"We had a deal," Buckler mumbled, glancing at the site.

"Deal?" the boy asked, apparently not understanding the word.

Israeli officials had granted permission to four countries to excavate, with the condition that all discoveries would be shared with the Israeli government. But there was a secret agreement between the Israeli and American governments concerning a particular discovery. If or when that discovery was made, the American government would seize authority over the archaeological site. That particular discovery had been made yesterday, and now it appeared the Israelis had changed their minds.

Buckler removed his thin-rimmed glasses. "Was there anything else?"

The boy shook his head and glanced over his shoulder.

A large cloud of dust swelled on the orange and indigo eastern horizon. Buckler straightened to obtain a better view across the russet canvas of sand and rock. "I want you to get out of here. Hurry now." He gave the boy a light shove, then trotted back to the site.

The cloud of dust approached like a sandstorm. He spoke briefly to the group of archaeologists and scientists on his team. They scattered and rushed in organized panic to gather papers and files, attempting to conceal them in carrying cases. The two government operatives approached and he explained the bad news with a point of his finger at the ominous military vehicle convoy.

The Israeli military vehicles reached the site, and heavily armed soldiers circled the freshly excavated discovery. The laborers, scientists, and archaeologists from other countries stepped out of their dusty tents, yawning and scratching the night out of their bodies, only to be greeted with automatic weapons shoved in their faces. They raised their hands in surrender, and joined Buckler and his team. The group of uniformed Americans and the two operatives stood with their weapons by their sides, ready.

The Israeli jeep skidded to a halt, digging its front tires into the sand. A soldier stepped out, slow and confident. He came into focus as the dust settled to the ground around him. Judging by the markings on his uniform he was a high-ranking officer. He removed his sunglasses and surveyed the situation like a predator sizing up his next meal. He stared with empty brown eyes, his sun-beaten face expressionless. His lips were tightly sealed beneath his thick, black mustache. He demanded in English that they leave the site immediately.

One of the American government operatives lifted his weapon to an offensive position, and the rest of his team joined him in the lock and load position. The Israeli soldiers responded in the same manner. The tension and temperature rose by the second. The opposing soldiers stood with an eerie stillness, weapons aimed at each other, waiting for an amicable solution, or death.

Buckler wasn't a religious man, but he closed his eyes for a moment and prayed for someone or something to intervene. The other archaeologists, scientists, and workers stared nervously, sweating.

Three T-62 Israeli tanks roared over the sand embankment like metal monsters from the depths of hell. Their fifty tons of armor came to a halt, positioned behind the Israeli soldiers. The egg-shape turret centered on one tank's base rotated its long main gun at the government operatives and their team. The idle roar of the diesel engines kept a steady and intimidating hum. Buckler squinted at the machine guns and the antiaircraft DShK machine guns mounted at the loader's hatch position, but those weapons paled in comparison to the large, open mouth of the 115mm main gun staring at him. He stepped to the side, attempting to get out of direct fire, but like a well-painted portrait, the black eye of the gun followed him. He shook his head and glanced down at the sand, thinking this was where he was going to die.

An Israeli soldier from each tank emerged from a hatch on the turret and armed the mounted machine guns with cool eagerness. Buckler caught the scent of diesel fuel permeating the air, another reminder of the tanks and those big guns peering at him with bad intentions. He thought of the artifact in the tomb and what it signified; he whispered a short prayer to whomever might listening.

After a long, uneasy minute, one of the government men, showing no emotion, threw his weapon to the desert floor. The rest of the team followed suit. The muscles in Buckler's body finally relaxed. He wanted to scream for joy, but all he could manage was a sigh. He was going to live. He felt the sudden urge to relieve his bowels.

Chapter 2

Israel: 1963

The dark, glass-like surface of the Mediterranean Sea was broken by the cautious emergence of sixteen mystical forms. The black hooded and goggled heads glided effortlessly across the face of the sea. The scout swimmer gave a hand gesture, signaling the shoreline was at 'threat level zero.' The team of sixteen commandos proceeded forward and settled beneath a wooden pier, where they stripped off their goggles, flippers, and scuba tanks, allowing the equipment to sink to the sandy bottom before advancing over a stone retaining wall.

The city streets of Tel Aviv were dark and quiet with the exception of the sound of water lapping against small bobbing boats and the pier. The nearby port town of Yafo slept peacefully in the cool, early morning hours under a moonless sky and the strong odor of salt water and raw seafood. The team, led by Lieutenant Gill, silently moved throughout the shadows of the streets, maneuvering into an alley. The white-washed buildings had cooled from the long summer sun's pounding, while clothing still remained lifelessly hung from the small iron balconies. The cobblestone streets were abandoned, but with the arrival of dawn, hundreds of vendors and shoppers would once again fill the streets, repeating three thousand years of life in Yafo.

The commandos had been hand-selected by a group of suits that hid behind their desks somewhere in Washington, D.C., playing war games with the lives of others. Forty-eight hours before, the team was in the jungles of Vietnam destroying enemy shipping and harbor facilities. Now their orders were to infiltrate the

Museum of Antiquities in the small Israeli port town on the southern coast of Tel Aviv and extract a relic.

Gill scanned the harbor port and surrounding streets. *What the hell are we doing here?* he thought. His team had been assembled in 1961 and officially became one of the two SEAL units in 1962, compliments of President Kennedy, who himself was largely responsible for the development of the two Special Forces. *I don't think this is what Mr. Kennedy had in mind for us,* Gill thought of the pointless mission. He yanked on his lucky nylon H-harness with magazine pouches and K-bar knife.

Still dripping with salt water, he glanced at one of the team members crouched across from him, counting the magazines on his vest for the AR-15/M16 rifle. The moderately new weapon was proposed, developed and introduced by President Kennedy himself. Gill recalled the day he tested the new weapon for the president. It was a privilege and honor he would never forget. He turned his attention back to his own vest and continued through his mental and physical checklist. Seated at one o'clock from him was another lieutenant, a big Italian named Rustlin, who was checking his own equipment. Gill cracked a smile beneath his camouflage-painted face while he watched one of the young team members diligently inspect his mosquito repellent. When the young soldier was finally satisfied that he was well-prepared to combat the attack of an army of mosquitoes, he moved on to check his rations and canteen. The young soldier had his priorities in order: bugs, food and drink.

Gill had been briefed concerning the artifact before he was airlifted out of Vietnam; he in turn briefed three team members on the helicopter before they were dropped into the Mediterranean Sea. He, three of his men, and a handful of others in Washington were the only people on earth who knew the true objective of the mission.

The team moved along the alley undetected. Parked on a remote street was a pale gray, two and a half ton 6x6 cargo truck with canopy. It had been left there for them earlier in the evening by a military operative, where it would be unnoticed for days. One of the commandos slid in behind the steering wheel. He pulled a single key from one of his many vest pockets and started the unmarked truck's diesel engine while the rest of the team climbed into the back and let down the coal-colored tarpaulin flaps. The team changed into dry, black camouflage uniforms.

The truck rolled slowly through Yafo heading for the museum. The driver followed a well-mapped route of the streets and alleys he had memorized, cunningly maneuvered throughout the town, avoiding the main roads of Yefet and Yehuda ha-Yamit. Once at the museum he parked beneath a group of low-lying trees against a windowless building.

The team unloaded into the alley and split into two groups of eight. Rustlin led his team around the museum for reconnaissance and surveillance. Gill and his men quickly reached the museum's walls. There the team split into two groups of four, called fire teams. Gill and his three men squatted in the shadows beneath a tree, waiting. One soldier was positioned across the alley within view of the truck. Two others watched the entrance of the alley. The fourth member of the team was busy clipping electrical wires that powered the security system. Within five seconds after he opened the power box, he gave the thumbs up.

Nylon ropes with grappling hooks were thrown to the roof of the museum where they hooked to a foot high limestone wall bordering the building. Gill scaled the wall in ten seconds, followed by the other three team members. One of them unwrapped a black leather case with a vial, which contained clear liquid developed at the Department of Defense, and a six-inch metal syringe. He inserted the short, stubby needle of the syringe into the vial and exacted the liquid acid, then carefully squeezed the liquid out along the outer rubber and limestone seams of the skylight. The liquid sizzled and smoked with a burning odor; forty seconds later the team was lifting the square, two-inch-thick glass skylight off its metal base.

A rope was dropped through the square that the skylight once occupied. The bottom of the rope disappeared into a black emptiness. Gill descended the rope into the darkness; his rubber soled boots landed quietly on the museum's marble floor. The room felt cool and was dimly lit with small studio lights. He scanned the room with quick glances, then gestured to the young commando waiting above, who immediately slid down the rope to join him. The other commandos remained on the roof, keeping watch for any surprises in the alleys or streets below.

Gill and Double B worked their way through a tall, narrow corridor lined with skylights and marble pedestals where ancient pottery was perched. They entered a huge room, large enough to house twenty-foot statues and thousands of other ancient artifacts discovered at archaeological sites throughout the country. The room was softly lit. Similar lighting illuminated the large glass-enclosed cabinets exhibiting pottery, gold relic pieces and other artifacts.

Gill glanced around the room, confused. *Where the hell am I?* Double B continued to scan the room with his weapon. Gill unfolded and studied a laminated floor plan of the museum; he turned the map, examining it from different perspectives.

Double B gave him a look that asked, 'Are you lost?' Gill gave him a wink and walked over to a wooden display case. He pulled it away from the wall, exposing an unmarked, knobless, white wooden door. He slid his crowbar into the seam between the door and frame, prying the door open. He pulled his 9mm out of the holster and entered the room with his flashlight leading the way.

The beam revealed what appeared to be a storage room. He pulled a string dangling from above, lighting a space the size of a family room. There were hundreds of pieces of stone, marble, and clay pottery with small paper tags tied to them, labeling the pieces with letters and numbers. The shelves were full of artifacts and they covered all four walls and ran from floor to ceiling. Gill moved to a file cabinet and three wooden crates that also had labels with letters and numbers. He spotted a small wooden crate the size of a computer monitor.

"M.A.T.-27-29. "Bingo," he whispered. He holstered his weapon and took a quick glance at a piece of paper from his pocket. The markings matched; he smiled.

He knew that the information on that piece of paper had traveled an amazing path. It changed hands many times, only to return full circle to its birthplace. It began here in the museum with a storage clerk, who was bribed handsomely for the information, then passed on to an operative, who transmitted the data to the proper ears in Washington, D.C. It was relayed agency to agency like a relay team at a track meet, finally reaching his hand on the aircraft carrier, USS Enterprise, in the Atlantic Ocean. From there a helicopter trip to the shores of Tel Aviv, then a short swim and truck ride to the museum. He removed the lid of the wooden crate with the crowbar, his eyes wide with anticipation. With great care, he pushed away the shredded paper, revealing the two-thousand-year-old artifact. He had never been a religious man, nor had he ever subscribed to any belief system, with the exception of the United States Marine Corps, but the artifact's historic past and what it represented to millions around the world, coupled with its crude, painful appearance, left him mesmerized.

Double B took a peek over the Lieutenant's shoulder. "Is that what I think it is?"

"Yeah," he answered, never taking his eyes off the artifact.

"Sweet Mother of God," Double B whispered, and made the sign of the cross.

They'd stared at the artifact too long. "We've got to go."

Double B backed away. "Yeah, yeah, sure," he said still staring at the artifact.

Gill had a 12x12x6 inch black waterproof box made from hard shell plastic. He carefully placed the artifact with shredded paper in the black box and returned it to his backpack. Then they were down the corridor, up the rope, and off the roof in minutes. The rest of the team gathered at the truck for a final head count.

The cool and peaceful night was shattered by a woman's shriek echoing through the alley. She was yelling in Arabic that someone was breaking into the museum.

That terminated any notions of a quiet withdrawal. The driver had already started the truck and the rest of the team jumped in the back. The woman continued to yell and point from the balcony fifty meters down the street. A commando lifted his weapon and took careful aim at the woman; his finger gently started to squeeze the trigger.

Gill slapped the barrel of the weapon toward the sky. The woman on the balcony would never know she was a tenth of a second from having a bullet pass through her head. Security lamps inundated the alley with light. Little square golden lights of curiosity appeared in the white-washed homes around the museum. In the distance, the unmistakable sound of approaching sirens was heard.

That was quick, Gill thought, somewhat impressed with the Israeli military police's response time to the burglary. He leaped into the back of the truck and yelled, "Go! Go! Go!"

The truck sped down the narrow cobblestone alley toward an intersection. Suddenly from one of the many alleys an Israeli police vehicle emerged and followed in a heated pursuit. The passenger of the vehicle leaned out his window firing an Uzi sub-machine gun into the tailgate, thumping the metal frame of the truck with lead. Two commandos returned fire, putting half-inch holes in the Israeli vehicle's windshield and grill. A black and gray cloud of smoke poured out of the engine and into the interior of the jeep, blinding the driver. It scraped to a halt against the alley wall, nearly disappearing beneath a heap of trash. The truck continued toward the mouth of the alley—also the destination of a half dozen speeding Israeli military vehicles. Another police car entered the alley a hundred meters directly ahead, speeding straight for the truck.

"Yee haa!" Big John, the driver of their truck cried. "A game of chicken, just like back home!" The military vehicle and the truck closed the gap. Big John flashed the headlights in warning, but the vehicle continued to approach, unfazed by the oncoming two and a half tons of metal.

Another Israeli police vehicle closed in from the rear. A commando took aim at the driver, but his weapon misfired. Gill pushed him aside and grabbed his bloop gun, the M79 grenade launcher. He snapped the weapon at the breech and loaded a single spin-stabilized 40mm grenade and fired. With one shot, he catapulted the police vehicle fifteen meters into the air. The car became a roadblock of distorted metal engulfed in a blaze.

The driver of the military vehicle that approached from the front slammed on the brakes. Big John had no intention of stopping. An Israeli soldier stood in the passenger seat and fired his weapon over the windshield. The alley was too narrow to turn around nor was there time. The Israeli driver ripped the gears into reverse and started to retreat out of the alley. The passenger continued to spray the truck and the alley with a barrage of bullets.

From the rear of the truck, Gill could see that a bullet slammed into the man seated next to Big John, jolting his body upward before he slumped. Big John pulled his Browning 9mm semiautomatic pistol and emptied the clip on the retreating Israeli vehicle. He popped holes in the hood and smashed the windshield into thousands of pieces and forced the police officer to duck for cover behind the dashboard. The police vehicle spun out of the alley. Two other police jeeps blocked the entrance of the alley in an attempt to trap the truck. Five military police positioned themselves behind the vehicle barricade. The truck gained speed on the slight decline of the alley, leaving a swirl of trash in its wake. In the back of the truck Lieutenant Rustlin was bleeding to death from a stray bullet in the stomach.

A commando pulled the dead man from the front seat, and climbed into the cab with Big John, but a bullet penetrated his skull, killing him instantly. Big John glanced at the dead body and yelled. "Nooooo!" He turned his attention to the roadblock and the truck sped forward. With one hand, he squeezed off a round from his grenade launcher, sending a shocking explosion of glaring orange through the alley. The military jeeps overturned and caught fire. Burning bodies were scattered throughout the street. Out from the metal debris and glowing flames, a lone Israeli soldier stepped into the alley with his sub-machine gun. He showered the truck cabin with ricocheting bullets. The alley walls were dotted with sparks like fireflies in the night.

Big John took a bullet in the shoulder and a piece of glass from what remained of the windshield in the eye. He lost control of the truck, smashing and scraping against the alley wall. A commando from the back grabbed the steering wheel and pulled the truck away from the wall. More bullets flew into the truck, clipped off the top of Big John's ear, followed by a fatal shot in the neck.

The spray of blood covered the interior of the truck, not sparing the commando now pulling the lifeless body of Big John out of the driver's seat. Gill could see the new driver was Hank Jackson, a short, muscular, black man from Baltimore. He aimed the truck toward the Israeli soldier who shot Big John.

"You're dead meat," Hank shouted, seconds before a bullet burned into his bicep. He jerked the steering wheel, bounced off the wall once, but remained in control of the truck. The soldier in the alley was reloading his machine gun; blood streamed from a wound in his thigh. "You're mine," Hank growled. He clamped down on the steering wheel and slammed the gas pedal to the floor. The Israeli soldier lifted the machine gun with his burnt and bloody hands and took aim at Hank's head, but the machine gun didn't fire. A misfire! Hank had a death lock on the steering wheel. The extra second it took for the soldier to recover from the shock of the misfire of his weapon cost him his life.

"This is for Big John!" Hank yelled. The front of the truck met the Israeli soldier with a sickening sound of flesh and bones ripping and breaking. The truck roared through the burning, convoluted remains of the jeeps, leaving an unrecognizable body in the alley.

"Shalom," Hank hissed in Hebrew.

He drove the truck down two more alleys, and then sped down one of the main roadways. A local police car pulled out in the middle of the road attempting to stop the truck at the intersection of Yefet and Yahuda ha-Yomit. The truck outweighed the car by three thousand pounds, and the police were about to discover that the hard way. Hank swerved to avoid a direct collision, but intentionally plowed through the back of the police car. The truck never faltered in its path to freedom, leaving the two occupants of the police car burning to death in a fiery explosion. He avoided any other encounters with local law enforcement, but sirens of other military police vehicles were approaching quickly. Hank took the truck down Nemal Yafo toward the Yafo Port, where two UH-1 Huey slicks from the U.S. Army's 9th Infantry would be waiting; at least that was the plan. He brought the truck to a skidding halt near the pier.

"Where the hell are they?" Hank screamed. He leaped out of the truck and searched the sky.

Gill barked out orders. The team spread throughout the port, prepared for a shootout, and checked the horizon desperately for the helicopters. The sirens drew near, and the flashing of the blue and red lights from military vehicles appeared five hundred meters away. One commando counted the headlights. Over twenty military police vehicles, he informed them. "Where the hell are the helos?"

An Israeli military police boat appeared on the water. Gill pulled a flare from his vest, prepared to destroy the artifact, when a sudden explosion erupted on the water behind the team. The Israeli military boat was gone; in its place was floating pieces of boat and a shower of burning debris. A streak of light whistled overhead toward the approaching military convoy. A violent, vibrating, orange and bright yellow explosion lit up the sky and the city streets of Tel Aviv. Six military vehicles were engulfed in flames. A cheer from the team followed.

Two UH-1 Huey gunship helicopters appeared from out of the darkness. The team quickly loaded their dead and wounded onto the helicopter, while the other Huey unleashed a storm of rounds from the mounted gun on portside. Then, 2.75 inch rockets were sent down the street, hurtling vehicles and humans into the air under a fireball of exploding heat. The M-60 rendered the rest of the military vehicles useless. The team was loaded and the Huey lifted from the rendezvous spot. Vehicles exploded randomly as leaking fuel discovered fire. The helicopters turned gracefully and disappeared into the darkness over the Mediterranean Sea, leaving an orange glow of destruction behind.

Chapter 3

Arlington, Virginia: 1968

I n the center of the windowless laboratory under cold surgical lamps was a metal table draped with a dull, teal-colored laparotomy sheet. On the table was a woman unconscious from general anesthesia; she was in the supine position with her feet in the stirrups. Earlier, she had been injected with the anesthetic-methohexital—through the intravenous line inserted in her arm. She was fitted with a blood pressure cuff, oxygen sensor and electrocardiograph monitoring electrodes. The machines near the table housed the oxygen and nitrous oxide that led to a mask.

Next to the anesthesia cart was a stack of electrosurgical equipment that beeped, blinked, registered, and monitored every bodily activity. Isolated on a cart was a monitor the size of a nineteen-inch television. Five men with white surgical smocks and masks surrounded the woman on the table. Doctor Howard Larson lifted a small scalpel from a tray and glanced at the protruding balcony fifteen feet overhead. It circled the entire room in an amphitheater design, which allowed observers to witness a surgery from above. Half of this balcony was enclosed behind a tinted glass enclosure, the type of tinted glass one may see out of, but not in. Ten men stood behind the glass. The group consisted of military personnel, scientists, and others from Washington. A man with a black suit told an operator to start filming. The 16mm camera suspended over the operating table started recording.

With scalpel in hand, Doctor Larson waited and stared at the tinted glass. "Proceed," a voice said finally over an intercom. Larson glanced down at the woman; a dark green cloth covered her body except in the area of the abdomen where it had been cut away into a circle. He looked at the anesthesiologist seated on a stool beside the woman's head.

The anesthesiologist checked the oxygen analyzer, the pulse oximeter and the electrocardiograph, and then studied the tidal carbon dioxide monitor for a moment before he examined the woman's temperature, color, and chest excursion. Once he was satisfied, he gave Doctor Larson a nod.

Larson made three incisions, one in the navel, one near the pelvic bone, and one in between the pelvic bones below the navel. He inserted an experimental thin, flexible camera rod in through the navel, then inserted instruments in the other incisions. The abdomen was inflated with gas to separate the organs from one another. Larson observed the black, white and gray image of the uterus on the monitor's screen. After a close examination of the inner wall of the uterus, he turned his attention to an incubator placed beside him.

A quiet conversation from the observation deck filtered through on the intercom, and Larson recognized the voice of the man in the black suit. "Were there any problems with this batch of embryos?"

One of the scientists quickly answered. "No. The oocytes were perfect. The embryonic samples achieved the sixty-four cell stage." There was a tone of respect in the scientist's voice toward the man in the black suit. Larson realized it was the type of respect created from fear.

The man in the black suit spoke again. "Were there any problems extracting new samples from the artifact?"

"No," the scientist answered. "Everything went smoothly. The DNA fragments were undamaged."

Larson stared at the incubator; the temperature read thirty-seven degrees Celcius. He lifted the glass lid and exposed the container with zona pellucida, protein and polysaccharide membrane that protected and provided the necessary nutrients for the submerged embryos floating within. He transferred the embryo from the incubator to a small flexible catheter, then gazed for a long moment at the catheter, contemplating his actions for the two-hundredth and thirteenth time.

How did my life's work lead to this? He felt the stinging question of ethics for the millionth time; numerous other questions plagued his mind and bounced around in his head uncontrollably. He thought about the two-hundred and twelve miscarriages, infertile oocytes, deformed stillborns, and worse, the deformed live births that were rushed away immediately after delivery, never to be seen again. The results had been nothing less than futile. He could feel his assistant's eyes fixed on him; he could feel the cold stares from above that peered down on him from behind the tinted glass room. He also felt an additional pair of eyes watching him, and those eyes were bearing down on him from higher above.

"Doctor Larson, are you all right?" an assistant asked.

"Yes, I'm fine," he answered, positioning himself between the stirrups. A weighted speculum had been placed in the vaginal vault and the cervix was grasped with a tenaculum. The catheter had been fitted with a tiny flexible camera rod and penlight. He guided the tip of the catheter through the cervical canal into the uterine cavity by watching the monitor screen. He maneuvered the instrument and inserted the point of the catheter firmly but gently against the endometrium of the uterus, where the embryos would encapsulate. For a fleeting moment he believed the two hundred and thirteenth *in vivo* implantation attempt had a chance.

Behind the tinted glass window there was optimism and urgency. After the pats-on-the-back, the handshakes, the congratulations and the optimistic predictions, the conversation turned to a much different subject.

"I heard there were some difficulties obtaining the artifact," someone said, pulling a handkerchief out and cleaning his thin-rimmed glasses.

"There was a slight ripple in the plans," the man in the black suit said. "An unforeseen occurrence," he added dryly.

"A woman suffering from insomnia is difficult to plan for," the stout voice said from the back of the room. The dimness of light concealed the details of the man's attributes; however, a large outline of a figure and the reflection of a gold crucifix and a white collar were evident.

"Yes, it would be very difficult to plan for," another man agreed.

The corpulent figure of the man sat in the shadows of the room. "Regardless, it had a happy ending," General Pike said.

An important government official turned slightly toward the back of the room. His face hardened. "Lives were lost. There were many casualties," he said, bordering on disrespect.

"The objective was obtained," the general said sharply.

"I heard a very high ranking Israeli military officer was killed at the museum," someone said, obviously attempting to confirm the rumors.

The general shifted his large body. The metal stars on his shoulders caught the light. "That's what military men do," he said bluntly.

"What?" the government official asked.

"Kill and get killed," General Pike said, with decades of military hardness in his blood.

"This particular officer was the son of a Middle East Prime Minister," the important government official shot back.

A silence fell over the room; the men in suits and the scientists stared into darkness at the large, motionless figure.

The general leaned partially out of the shadows, exposing his large, broad shoulders and head. His eyes pierced out from beneath the bill of his hat. With a cold glare in his eyes he said, "He shouldn't have stood in front of a speeding truck."

Chapter 4

Washington, D.C.: The Present.

The fresh snow crunched beneath Allen Pyrit's boots. He stopped for a moment in the middle of the street to admire the beauty of the snowflakes drifting down peacefully through the glow of streetlight above him. He often stopped and admired the beauty of life around him; it was something he had started in childhood. His mother had always said he had a great awareness and an appreciation for life.

He watched the snow fall with a sense of peace, forgetting for a moment where he was going and what awaited him, until a cold gust of wind rudely reminded him. He shoved his hands deeper into his pockets and tucked his head lower into the turned up collar of his coat. He turned the corner and stopped before a black iron gate that spanned thirty-five feet across and reached twelve feet in height. Like weapons of primeval days the spike-like rods of the gate stabbed upward at the sky. The crude points of the rods stepped down gradually away from where the two swinging halves met. The gate was an intimidating iron barrier.

He pushed a small button after he brushed the snow from the intercom. A voice crackled over the speaker and asked emotionlessly, "Yes?" He leaned toward the panel and said his first name. The motor of the gate growled as the two halves separated, pushing the snow like a plow. As he walked the hundred-yard long driveway, he occasionally glanced at the tire tracks that were nearly filled in with freshly fallen snow. The tire marks reminded him of his abandoned car stuck in the snow on the roadside. The driveway was lined with immense oak trees and old-fashioned lampposts dating back to the 1920's. The tunnel of trees had the appearance of old, white, crooked witch fingers reaching out with a haunting desire. He never did like those trees as a child in the winter; he still didn't like them.

Once out of the tunnel of oaks, the twelve thousand square foot gray stone house appeared tremendously large on the crest of the hill beyond the granite fountain. He climbed the gray marble stairs leading to the mahogany French doors, where he stood for a moment staring down at the welcome mat that read, "Merry Christmas." He stared at it as if it were something out of place. He gave the numerals of the address a slap of his glove, removing the snow, then reminiscently ran his hand across the numbers. Just for a moment, it was a cool spring day and he was a little boy helping his father nail up the numerals that showed the house's address. His father was proud of him that day, and so was he of himself. That was a good day—he and his father, a team, working together. Oh, how he missed those days—the days before everything changed—before everything got bad.

The memory faded quickly as the wind rushed through his bones, snapping him back to the present. He stood before the door and bowed his head in silent prayer, praying for strength. He opened the door and entered without knocking. The first thing he encountered was the aroma of incense. It reminded him of Sunday morning in church. Slowly his eyes adjusted to the candle-lit room. A short, petite woman with brown hair and chocolate eyes approached him from across the room and greeted him with a hug and a soft kiss on the cheek.

"You look sick," Joan said in a concerned tone.

"I feel sick," he responded.

"Why are you so wet?"

"I walked." He pulled his damp coat off.

"Where's your car?"

"Stuck in the snow."

"I've missed you."

"I've missed you, too." He forced a shadow of a smile.

"Father's upstairs with the priest," she said glancing up at the top of the stairs. "He's been waiting for you."

"Priest?" he asked, surprised. "A certified atheist on his death bed, with a priest at his side. That's probably killing him more than the cancer."

"He asked for the priest," she said solemnly. "He's gone through some changes over the last couple of weeks."

"Dying will do that to a person." The words came out colder then he expected. He glanced to the top of the staircase, regretting his remark.

"You're being a little hard aren't you?"

Allen looked at her callously. He could count on one hand the times he had spoken to his father in last twelve years. "Maybe," he answered eventually. "How long does he have?"

"They don't know."

"It must be close, for them to allow me here." His eyes shifted toward the relatives gathered in the living room. They stared unemotionally at him from the dark.

"It was father who wanted you to come," she said softly.

He looked at her skeptically.

"It's true."

The cynicism slowly left him. He climbed the dark oak staircase to the poorly lit hallway. He opened the door and entered a room that was warmly lit with many candles. Lying peacefully in the bed was a pale, elderly man with his eyes closed. Allen stared at his father's balding head and thin face. Regardless of the cancer ravaging his body, he remained distinguished and handsome. His arms were outside the blankets and his hands were interlocked across his stomach.

Standing close to the bed, halfway in the shadows of the room, was a priest holding a prayer book, praying in a low voice. The priest and Allen locked eyes for a moment, long enough to acknowledge each other's presence. Allen knelt at the side of the bed. A million memories rushed through his mind, simply from the sight of his father's face.

"Father, I'm here," he said quietly. "It's Allen, your son. Can you hear me?"

His father's eyes opened slowly and he tilted his head toward him. He labored to smile and reached for his hand. Allen met his hand and held it tenderly. "You were right," his father whispered.

Allen nodded and squeezed his father's hand gently, not sure what he meant. He discarded the thought and focused on his father's face.

"Your mother wanted you to know something about yourself," he said, struggling to be heard. "She always wanted you to know."

Allen waited; the hardness in his heart started to soften. The sight of his father on his deathbed had mellowed his hate to sadness.

"She loved you very much." His eyes filled with tears. "As I do."

A single tear streaked down Allen's cheek. He thought he had stopped loving his father years ago. He was wrong. A memory of his mother passed through his thoughts. He missed her so much.

"Your mother felt that you should know the truth."

Allen waited, not understanding what he was talking about. He thought he might be blathering from the medication.

He tightened his grip around Allen's hand. "You were adopted," he confessed with a whisper.

His father's painful words reached his mind like an echoing distant gunshot through the mountains. Allen looked at him with a blank, numb stare; the word 'adopted' kept stabbing at him like a long steel dagger. Then, pain and more pain, wave after wave of hurt crashed down on him, draped in bewilderment.

He finally realized his father's hand had fallen away from his grip. Death had come and taken hold.

Chapter 5

Mary Jopuez was slouched in the driver's seat of her old Honda, cradling the long lens high-speed Minolta camera she used in her work as a private investigator. Hired by a suspicious wife who desperately wanted to be wrong about her husband, Mary had followed the husband, whom she sardonically named 'Mr. Pig,' to a motel. There she'd sat in her car for the last twenty-eight hours, her Washington Redskins cap pulled low, waiting for the happy couple to emerge from their love nest. She had watched the snow turn to sleet to rain to sun—typical Maryland weather. *Why in the hell do people get married?* she thought. *It just doesn't work as long as men are involved.* Of course, at the moment she wasn't the most impartial person on the subject, since she was coming off a fresh break-up, which wasn't the smoothest or prettiest of partings. She sipped her coffee and thought about the case, the fourth adultery case in two months. The good news in this particular case was there were no children involved, otherwise the wife would be forever connected to the cheating pig.

"Love," she blurted out sarcastically. "Isn't it grand?" Maybe she was being too hard on marriage and Mr. Pig. This was the third time she had followed him and had yet to catch him with another woman. Maybe he wasn't cheating; maybe there was a logical explanation for his behavior. Maybe he just likes hotels; maybe it was a coincidence, a misunderstanding . . . maybe.

She perked up and grabbed her camera. She took aim and peered through the 75-300 Macro Zoom lens, and focused until a hundred yards became a few feet. It was Mr. Pig and he was checking out at the front desk, alone. He exited the front doors and entered his car. She took a few snap shots for the file. He drove off and she lowered the camera. He checked in alone, he checked out alone. Damn. Nothing again. But, wait a minute.

She saw a figure in the lobby, quickly brought the camera to her eye and attempted to focus on the subject, but she couldn't get a clean shot. The figure exited the motel. She clicked off a half a dozen shots of a man in a gray business suit. She kept him in the frame, continually shooting photographs until he entered a black BMW. She focused and snapped a shot of the license plate. He drove off and disappeared around the corner. She lowered her camera and stared curiously at the motel.

"Possible. Maybe the other woman is a man. I think I got you, Mr. Pig," she said smiling, and pulled off into the early morning light.

Chapter 6

The marine helicopter hovered above the White House grounds, churning the snow outward into powdery, white circles. Secret Service agents jogged toward the helicopter. Their sunglasses reflected the glare of the sun and their trench coats flapped in the wind as they hurried across the lawn. The helicopter touched down and the doors opened. A small set of steps descended to the ground. Two Secret Service agents stepped out followed by a woman in a long, black, wool coat—Shelly Deanster, the Vice President of the United States. She was escorted to the double doors beneath the stone canopy of the West Side entrance. Once inside, the pace slowed down and became more relaxed. A White House aide helped her out of her coat and disappeared around a corner. Her personal aide, Miss Harrison, stepped from a room to meet her. She had a note pad and an organizer cradled in her arms. The two women walked side-by-side down the red-carpeted hall.

"So, how was lunch?" Harrison asked, insinuating something with a sly grin.

"It was good," Shelly answered.

"Good? Just good?"

She smiled sheepishly. "It was great," she whispered.

They laughed like two schoolgirls talking about dirty joke, then hushed each other as they approached a Secret Service agent posted at the front of her office door.

The agent stepped aside and opened the door for the two women. "Good afternoon, Vice President Deanster."

"Good afternoon, Ben."

"Hey, Ben," Harrison said, passing him with an over-friendly smile.

"Good afternoon, Miss Harrison," he said, returning a smile as the door closed.

"So, where did you and Mr. Iblis have lunch?" Miss Harrison asked.

"We met in Annapolis," Shelly answered, while searching through papers on her desk. "We ate at the Chart House."

She and Iblis, the Secretary General of the United Nations, had been the media's favorite story since they became an item six months ago.

"How long is he staying this time?"

"A couple of days. He has to go back to the Middle East."

"What in the world is going on over there?"

"He said the peace talks broke down again, but they agreed to return to the table. He needs to talk to Derrick and the U.S. Protocol team about scheduling a return date as soon as possible."

"It must be frustrating for him," Harrison said. "Every time they get close to completing the peace talks, something goes wrong."

"He deals with it surprisingly well."

"President Moore didn't handle the headlines too well this morning," Miss Harrison said. "He had that look."

Shelly looked at the Washington Post on her desk that read, 'U.S. Breaches 2001 Arms Agreement. Peace Talks Break Down.'

"The ice pick between the eyes look?" Shelly asked.

Miss Harrison nodded.

She let out a sigh. "He takes it so hard."

"President Moore has been working on the peace treaty for over a year. It's everything to him."

She turned and stared out of her office window. "Did he call a press conference?" she asked, knowing Derrick would address the false accusations immediately.

Miss Harrison checked her watch. "He should be speaking to them at this very moment."

*   *   *

"Is it true that the peace talks are off?" a reporter asked. "And if so, is it because the U.S. breached the Arms Treaty?"

"Yes, the peace talks have stalled," President Derrick Moore responded wearily. "And no," he added, his face and voice becoming stern. "The United States did not breach the Arms Agreement of 2001 in any way."

"Why the breakdown?" another reporter asked.

The president paused for a moment. "Palestinian officials maintain that we have broken the arms agreement but that is not true."

"Why are they saying that?"

"Palestinian officials believe that we have offensive warheads in Israel, which is simply untrue. All that remain are defense missiles and the personnel to operate the equipment."

"So, why the communication breakdown?" a reporter asked smugly.

"Someone is leaking false information and the Palestinians choose to believe it," Moore said, frustrated. "Or they're simply looking for an excuse not to sign the disarmament agreement."

"Do you know who the leak is?" a reporter yelled.

Moore stared with raised eyebrows and a dumbfounded expression. "Any more questions?" he asked.

"Now what happens?"

"We've sent a proposal to the Palestinians and their allies, and we've also arranged a tour of the facilities with the United Nations inspectors in an attempt to disprove the accusations," the president explained. "The media will be invited," he added with a smile.

*   *   *

Professor Gregory Orfordis stood alone in the cemetery in front of a headstone that read,

JAMES T. ROOD
A RIGHTEOUS MAN, WHO PUT THE SOULS
OF OTHERS BEFORE HIS OWN LIFE

James Rood had given his life protecting the future president of the United States, Derrick Moore, from an assassin's bullet. Greg had been a close friend of James'. They only knew one another for a brief period, but the short time they had spent together felt like a lifetime. Buried next to James' grave was his wife, Faith, who had been the sister of Derrick Moore. A reporter for the Washington Post, she knew too much about a criminal figure and had been murdered.

Greg placed his flowers at the base of the headstone, joining the numerous other flowers, thank you cards, and well wishes from visitors.

James' courageous actions had made him a national hero; his name would be in the history books, and his gravesite had become a stop for sightseers visiting the nation's capital.

Greg noticed three white roses in between the headstones, an indication President Moore had visited the gravesite recently. Derrick had placed the three roses in remembrance of James, Faith, and their unborn child. Greg knelt in silent prayer, then stood and glanced up at the gray sky as if he were watching the prayers float to heaven.

"Professor Orfordis?"

He heard the voice of a man who had smoked since birth. Greg turned. "Yes."

"I'm Art Hanson." The big man shifted the cigar in his mouth and reached out his meaty hand.

Greg smiled. "Yes, the private investigator."

"I just missed you at the church," Art explained. "They told me you were coming here. I hope you don't mind."

"No, of course not."

A cool March breeze cut through the cemetery grounds. Art pulled his trench coat together attempting to protect his bulky belly from the cold.

"Friends of yours?" Art asked glancing at the headstones.

"Very good friends."

"He's the one who saved Derrick Moore," Art said, recognizing the name.

Greg nodded.

"I remember the day." He puffed a cloud of cigar smoke into the air. "Wasn't there another guy who took a bullet? What was his name?"

"Charles Malefic."

"I remember thinking those two guys were the two biggest heroes I'd ever seen, or two damn fools." He smiled with the cigar in his mouth. "I still can't make up my mind."

Greg grinned. Something about Art Hanson reminded him of a character from a 1940's Humphrey Bogart movie. Maybe it was his trench coat and fedora, or the cigar and his manner of speech. He studied the brown suit and shoes, also forties attire, something his father wore when he was a child, sixty-plus years ago. Art probably wasn't a day past forty-five, but his bushy sideburns, thick gray mustache, and aged eyes gave him an older appearance. Greg sent the waiting taxi on its way and rode back to the church in Art's old Cadillac. What else would he be driving?

*   *   *

Greg talked to him during the entire ride about his counselor position and the clinic he operated at the church and about the large garden he tended to. He spoke of his travels throughout the Middle East and his interests of archaeology, theology, etymology, and his love of linguistics.

Art had done a little background check on the professor; it was an old habit. He liked to know who he was dealing with, get a feel for the potential client before actually meeting him. He already knew everything the professor told him in the car and he also knew the professor was an acclaimed theologian. He had been summoned from around the world because of his renowned knowledge and accomplishments in the theological field. He knew of the many books Orfordis had written on spiritual warfare, which he had read and found interesting, but weird and a little creepy. He also knew the professor lost his wife and kid in a fire forty-odd years ago.

They walked down a corridor of the church. Before today, he hadn't stepped a foot in a church for at least twenty years; now it was twice in one day. This event he would regard as an act of God. That was, of course, if he believed in God.

"So, professor, what do you need me for?"

"I need you to follow a man."

They passed through a door and climbed down a set of old wooden stairs, which Art wasn't sure would hold up under his two hundred and fifty pounds. The old steps sounded like they were being pushed to their limit. To his relief, his feet finally hit solid concrete. Greg led him through the dimly lit cellar to a section with file cabinets, bookshelves, and an antique oak desk covered with papers. Art thought this must be where he wrote all those creepy books.

"Who's the guy?" he asked, leaning against a file cabinet.

Greg handed him a photograph and he studied the picture. The face was familiar, someone popular, he thought. He flipped the photo over and read the writing on the back. "Jordan Iblis, Secretary General of the United Nations." He laughed. "You want me to follow the Secretary General? That should be easy in my private jet."

"Do the best you can, Mr. Hanson."

"Call me Art," he said studying the picture again, entertained by the thought of the case. "Do you mind telling me why?"

"I don't believe he is who he says he is," Greg answered.

"Who do you think he is?"

"Are you taking the case?"

Art studied the picture, then Greg's face. There, deep in the old man's blue eyes, was a grim, unspoken thought. Art could feel the importance in his stare. "Sure, professor, I'll check him out for you."

Chapter 7

Landover, Maryland

Allen watched the large crowd streamed into the enormous amphitheater church, filling the eight thousand seats on the local news channel. "Thirty-eight countries around the world would view or listen to the broadcast live," the reporter said. "And the center of attention was Allen Pyrit, who *Time* magazine called the "Great Liberator." Other dominant publications had called him the spiritual pulse of the world. Allen was the founding father of the new multi-religion known as The New Faith Order," the reporter continued to explain. "The movement had swept nearly a billion people under its influence, proclaiming a "One Destination By Many Paths" message, standing on the decree that all faiths lead to the same Creator. The thought of "one destination by many roads" had been widely embraced throughout the world, and its numbers were growing."

Allen changed the channel. "The movement's critics had labeled the new denomination a watered-down religion with loose requirements and questionable practices. It had also been called a cult. The doctrine was simple: try to lead a peaceful life and don't harm others, and you're on the road to paradise. Oh yeah, don't forget to send money," the reporter added grinning. "This impartial and neutral tenet was very appealing to many, a billion's worth and still counting. This declaration was evident in the church's architectural design, built with a single thought in mind—not to single out one faith as more important than any other. There were no religious statues, paintings, or icons of any sort in the building. The seats were dark blue, the carpet was white, and the walls were light blue that gradually darkened to a night sky full of stars, an image so realistic it was impossible to tell the difference between the real cosmic sky and the painting. Allen Pyrit had worked hard to demonstrate to the world that all people pay homage to the same Creator in one form or another, and that everyone wanted the same thing—unity."

Allen turned the TV off and listened to the radio for a minute. "He had been declared by many of his peers and scores of world governments to be one of history's greatest philosophers, spiritual leaders, and philanthropists," the voice on the radio declared. "His message to put aside religious differences and narrow viewpoints for the welfare of all people had been welcomed with open arms by millions who had been waiting for something, or more importantly, someone to believe in. Allen's message asked people to sacrifice their selfish belief systems for the betterment of the world. One sixth of the world's population had adopted Allen Pyrit's message of sacrifice, and it was predicted that half of the world would be a part of The New Faith Order within the next two years.

The ancient and established religions argued the phenomenon of the New Faith Order had a dark side; Allen Pyrit and the movement was attempting to replace God with a hollow, apathetic belief of blind tolerance. A battle line between the traditional and the more fundamental religions of the world was drawn a year ago when the New Faith Order openly criticized the organized world religions, stating they were wrong, self-absorbed, and only continued to create separation among the world population. Religions around the globe believed they were under attack and felt their existence was threatened by the New Faith Order. Old religions were struggling to maintain their congregations and for some churches that meant declining financial support."

Allen Pyrit sat alone in his dressing room staring into the mirror, wondering who he was. Lying before him was a thick file full of his medical, educational and other personal records, which did nothing to help him discover his biological parents or any other information concerning his past. The man who so many looked to for guidance and direction had become spiritually and emotionally lost himself. An entire life shrouded by a lie had left him drowning in an abyss of doubt. Allen Pyrit was in a desperate search for his true identity.

*   *   *

Mary Jopuez entered her small apartment in Georgetown; all she could think about was sleep. Following Mr. Pig and waiting twenty plus hours for him to show his face had taken a toll on her. She wanted to sleep for a couple of days. She tossed her keys on the table next to a picture of her parents, who now were living in Puerto Rico. Every time she saw the photo, a longing washed over her, reminding her how much she missed them. She had only visited them twice since they'd moved back to Puerto Rico two years ago, and with that thought came a guilt trip, but she was so tired, it quickly passed. She hit the playback button on her answering machine. She grabbed a Corona out of the refrigerator and stuffed a lime down the neck of the bottle.

"Hey, Mary. It's Kelsy," a vivacious voice said. "Where are you? Call me. See ya."

Kelsy was Mary's good friend; they had plans to meet for drinks tonight. She'd forgotten. The message made her more tired, if that was possible.

The machine announced the time of day, and then beeped. "Ms. Jopuez, this is Jake Plummer from the MVA returning your call concerning the information on that license plate number. I have it and I'll be available tomorrow morning between eight and eleven."

The answering machine beeped three times in between three hang-ups. Then there was silence, but Mary could tell there was someone on the line.

"Mare," a voice said finally, barely audible. "It's Allen. I need to see you. I'll be at the church tonight." A lingering silence continued to be recorded on the machine, then a sharp click and an announcement of the time followed.

Mary stared at the answering machine; concern had replaced the tiredness.

*   *   *

Landover, Maryland

"Two minutes," a voice announced.

"Thank you," Allen said. He finished the chapter of *Moby Dick,* then set the book on the table. He reflected on Melville's character, Elijah. He was the prophet of doom who warned Ishmael and Queequeg of the ship, Pequod, and the ship's captain, Ahab, casting a mood of gloom on the voyage. But Ishmael and Queequeg ignored the prophet's warning and sat sail for the open seas of the world on the Pequod.

Allen looked into the mirror at the dark circles under his weary blue eyes. *Who am I?* He ran his hands across his thick, well-groomed black hair and stood. His usual tanned Mediterranean facial characteristics had become pale. *Who am I?*

He exited the dressing room and walked along the dimly lit, blue-carpeted corridor. He reached a large archway with a white curtain. *Who am I?* a voice in his head asked. His name was announced over an intercom. He split the curtains and stepped onto the stage to the thunderous applause of the congregation. He stood at the pulpit and observed the crowd of eight thousand people before him and waited for the applause to stop. The television cameras focused on him, sending his image to the millions all over the world. *Who am I?,* continued to repeat in his mind. He stood emotionless as the applause slowly came to a stop.

"I have something that I would like to say tonight," he said softly. "I'm sure you've heard by now of my father's death, and I would like to thank everyone for the flowers and cards and the warm condolences." He smiled slightly. "We all know he's better off than we are now."

The crowd said, "Amen" in unison.

"I would like to speak to you about feeling lost," he said as if he were experiencing that very pain. He had always been able to bring raw emotion to the stage and make people feel his words. He truly had a gift.

He never wrote out his sermons; he ad-libbed all of his material. The bigwigs at the TV station used to panic during every show, but they finally got used to his style.

"Feeling lost can lead one to many dark places. Places of doubt, places of fear and loneliness. And when that darkness falls over the path of light, it can be so cold and empty you feel like you'll never see the end." His voice strengthened and he knew the crowd could feel him rising to a higher energy. They fed off him with every word. The choir started to sing softly behind him, and the band played a low, steady beat, building the mood.

"This period of darkness is like many gray, overcast days in a row, but we know the sun is coming back, we know the sun will shine again. And we'll appreciate the sun even more; we'll have a greater joy when the darkness has past." The crowd nodded with agreement and 'Amens' were shouted.

"But, we will question ourselves in the moment of darkness because it's human nature to do so . . . but what is important is what we do in the time of darkness." He glanced around the room with a burning glare. "It's not the action, but the reaction that matters. Bad things happen to everyone, but not everyone handles the dark times the same. How one responds to tragedy is a reflection of what is in the soul."

He lowered his head for a moment. "Right now, my life is dark and overcast. It's pouring down hard on me. I'm caught in a thunderstorm! No! I'm caught in a hurricane! It's trying to beat me down!" The crowd was building emotionally with him. "I stand here before you in my darkest days." He stared in silence for effect, then gave them a determined look. "But-I-am-standing. I-am-standing!"

The eight thousand people in the church leapt to their feet and erupted in a deafening roar of cheers and applause.

*   *   *

Mary parked at the back entrance to the church and listened to Allen's sermon on the radio. She and Allen had been the best of friends since grade school and had continued to be best friends to this day. Some would call their connection a kinship, the kind of bond found between brother and sister. She could hear the pain in his voice. She wasn't fooled by his optimistic and confident speech; she could hear the whisper for help. Allen had always been there for her. He was there for the broken bones and the broken hearts. Now, for the first time, he needed her.

She listened as the service went on. A number of people approached the stage; they came from every part of the world so Allen could lay hands on them and heal their illnesses. First, an elderly woman suffering from arthritis approached and was apparently healed with a single touch of Allen's hand, then a chronic back pain sufferer was escorted to the stage and touched by Allen. One ailing soul after another marched onto the stage suffering from some sort of pain and exited miraculously healed.

Mary's eyes closed and she slipped into a hazy daydream, back to another time in her life.

"I got him," a young Mary said to Allen.

"Who?" Allen asked, from across the café table.

"The guy who has been selling government secrets."

"Espionage?"

She hushed him. "Yeah. He's double dealing the government."

She was a young FBI agent on the verge of exposing a huge espionage ring. She was on her way to the big time. Was.

Her daydream faded and her eyes refocused on the raindrops hitting her windshield. Allen's voice was still on the radio. "Come on, Al," she said. "Wrap it up."

*   *   *

A young boy of about seven approached the stage from one of the aisles. His mother walked beside him, her arm interlocked with his.

"Who's that?" the program director asked.

Two assistants skimmed through a list of names. Another programmer radioed to a programmer on the floor.

"Well?" the program director asked.

"We don't know," one assistant answered.

"Where's Robert?" he asked. "Get him on the phone."

The boy and his mother neared the stage and Allen.

"Call the floor," the program director ordered. "Stop that kid and that lady."

The camera zoomed on the boy and the mother.

"Who the hell is on them?" the program director yelled. "Get the camera off them."

"Oh my God," one of the assistants mumbled looking at the monitor.

"What?" everyone in the room asked.

"The kid is blind."

The room hummed with silence.

"Don't let that kid get on stage," the program director screamed.

The boy and his mother reached the stage and stood before Allen.

"Too late," an assistant grumbled.

"Go to a break, go to break," the program director yelled.

"I'm trying," the board operator said. "Nothing happens." He was pushing buttons, but the control board didn't respond.

"You were born blind?" Allen asked the boy.

"Yes, sir," the boy answered softly.

The program director covered his face with his hands. "Great."

Allen reached out and put his hands over the boy's eyes.

Robert Ward, Allen's personal advisor and public relations agent, rushed into the control booth. "What the hell is going on? Who's that on stage with Allen?"

"We don't know." The program director never looked up from his hands. "We're hoping you'd know."

"I've never seen him before." Robert said. "How did he get up there?"

"He slipped through."

"Why aren't we at commercial? Why are the cameras on them?"

"We've been cut off."

"We sent someone down there, but it was too late, as you can see," the assistant said.

Robert looked down at the stage helplessly. "What's wrong with him?"

One of the assistants mumbled, "He's blind."

"Blind!" Robert nearly jumped out of the booth. "Bloody hell."

Allen removed his hands from the boy's eyes.

Everyone in the control booth waited for the hammer to fall, with the exception of the program director who continued to hold his face in his hands.

"Come on, Allen," Robert said under his breath. "Tell the world it just isn't God's will for the boy to see. Come on. Tell them."

The camera zoomed in on the boy's eyes. "Oh, hell," Robert sobbed.

The program director rubbed his temples. "Great."

"It isn't God's will," Robert repeated. "It isn't God's will, tell them."

The boy blinked as if he were attempting to remove something from his eyes. He turned to his mother with a sweet smile. "You have beautiful blue eyes, Mom."

The mother embraced him, tears streaming down her cheeks. The crowd exploded with applause.

"He did it!" Robert yelled. "The kid can see!"

"I can't believe it!" an assistant yelled.

"Did you have something to do with this?" the program director asked, suspiciously.

"No," Robert answered. "I swear."

"It's not some sick joke of yours?"

"No, I had nothing to do with it."

"Good Lord A'mighty," an assistant blurted out. "Did we just see Allen heal a blind boy? I mean, really heal a blind boy?"

The program director looked down at Allen, who appeared to be embarrassed about the incident. "Damn, he's good," he said, still in shock.

*   *   *

Mary drifted into a daydream again, slipping back into the past. It was a cold, wet night at a warehouse near a harbor in

Baltimore. She was positioned outside on a roof across from a plain, gray cinderblock warehouse, where she watched the building with infrared binoculars and a listening device. She was listening and recording the conversation between two men in the warehouse. Her partner, Ed, was positioned down on the street with a camera, taking photographs through a broken window. The two men were discussing the terms of an agreement. Government secrets and millions of dollars were about to be exchanged. She spotted a third suspect approaching the scene, walking up on her partner. The man had a gun. She grabbed her transmitter to warn Ed, but his radio was turned off. Without hesitation she pulled her weapon and aimed at the armed suspect.

There was a rapid sound, then a flash of light. Someone was knocking on the driver's side window of her car, abruptly ending her flashback. She pressed a button and the window glided halfway down. It was Allen standing in the rain. A burst of lightening illuminated the sky above his head, revealing desperation in his eyes.

"Get in, Al," she said, and unlocked the doors. She returned her gun to its holster before Allen got into the car. She didn't remember pulling her weapon out; it was an involuntary reflex.

Allen sat quietly, staring out the window as the rain tapped on the roof of the car.

"You don't look good,"

"I don't feel good," he mumbled.

She looked at her watch. "Can we talk on the way downtown to meet my friend? I couldn't reach her to cancel."

"Sure."

She started the car and drove. "Are you all right?"

"I'm fine."

Of course, she didn't believe him. He would talk about whatever it is when he was ready. They rode in silence for a few miles.

"They weren't my parents," he finally said.

She glanced over. "What?"

"I was adopted."

She stared at him, dumbfounded.

"Red light," Allen said.

"What?"

"Red light," he repeated, pointing ahead.

She looked at the stoplight and the heavy traffic crossing the intersection and slammed on the brakes. The car skidded to a stop a few feet from an eighteen-wheeler crossing in front of her car.

"How do you know?"

"He told me before he died." He stared out the passenger side window.

She looked at him blankly, not knowing what to say next.

"That's why I called," Allen said, turning to her.

"To find your biological parents."

"Green light."

"What?"

"Green light," he said, pointing at the traffic light.

*　　*　　*

Twenty minutes later Mary pulled into a parking garage in Georgetown.

They walked up the ramp out of the garage. "It's bothering the hell out of you, isn't it?"Allen didn't say anything, but he didn't need to. "It would bother me, too," she said quietly.

The restaurant and bar crowds were at full force. They pushed through the crowd, maneuvering toward the bar and a woman in her early thirties, with dark strawberry blond hair laying an inch or more past her shoulders.

"Kelsy," Mary said, touching her shoulder.

Kelsy turned around with a smile. "You're late as usual. Did you get caught in traffic?"

"No, I had to meet someone," she said turning to Allen. "Allen, Kelsy, Kelsy, Allen."

Allen reached out and gently shook her hand. "Nice to meet you."

"So, this is the other best friend," Kelsy said, pretending to be jealous of Allen. She stared for a moment. "I know you." She pointed a finger. "You're Allen Pyrit, the evangelist."

A man seated on the barstool next to them turned to look at Allen, then lifted his drink in a toast and told Allen, 'Good job, Preacher." He turned back, resuming to his business of drinking.

"Why didn't you tell me you were friends with Allen Pyrit?" Kelsy asked, looking him up and down as if he were a movie star.

"I don't know." Mary shrugged. "It didn't seem important."

"You're unbelievable sometimes," Kelsy said shaking her head. "He's one of the most influential people on the planet."

"Says who?"

"*Newsweek, Time, Rolling Stone, People, . . .*"

"Yeah, yeah, I heard," Mary said, unimpressed. "Can I get a drink?" she asked, raising her hand, attempting to get the attention of the bartender.

"I don't listen to the program as much as I use to," Kelsy admitted. "But I do read the weekly newsletter about the revival movement. I'm amazed by the hands-on healing of the sick and the nice miracle stories from people all over the world. I must confess I don't understand the 'slain in the spirit' phenomenon."

"I'm not sure if I comprehend it myself," Allen said with a slight smile.

Mary rolled her eyes.

"What can I get you?" the bartender asked.

Mary ordered a Tom Collins for Kelsy and an iced tea for Allen, knowing what her friends liked to drink. She ordered herself a rum and pineapple.

"Leaded or unleaded on the iced tea?" the bartender asked.

"Unleaded," Mary answered. Allen didn't drink alcohol with the exception of a glass of wine from time to time.

"What's your problem?" Kelsy asked.

"What?" Mary asked acting oblivious.

"I saw you roll your eyes."

"I didn't roll my eyes," Mary said defensively glancing at her drink.

"What's her problem?" Kelsy asked Allen.

"She doesn't like talking about my . . . ,"

"No," Mary interrupted. "We agreed we wouldn't talk about your work and the stuff that goes along with it."

"Why?" Kelsy asked looking at the both of them.

Allen looked at Mary as she sipped her drink, ignoring the question.

"Why?" Kelsy asked again.

"Mary doesn't believe," Allen said quietly.

Kelsy shook her head with a smile.

"Don't shake your head at me," Mary said. "I just don't think the Almighty is healing the ill on TV. And I have a hard time with people falling down all over the place in church, rolling around like crazed fools." She gave Kelsy a push on the forehead with the palm of her hand. "Be healed," she said in a mocking southern accent.

Allen shook his head with a grin.

"I can respect that," Kelsy said. "I simply can't believe you made an agreement not to talk about it. You, of all people. You love a good debate. Good Lord, you were on the debate team in college."

"Not about this."

"Do you think it's fake?" Kelsy asked.

"I don't want to talk about it," Mary said.

Kelsy started to say something, but Allen shook his head, indicating not to pursue the subject.

"How about those Redskins?" Kelsy asked sarcastically.

Allen smiled and put his arm around Mary. "Let me get you another rum and pineapple."

She had finished her drink already.

"I need a favor, Kelsy," Mary said.

"Sure."

"Maybe you can help me find some information."

"I'll do what I can."

"I'll talk to you about it later."

"All right. Excuse me, I have go to the little girls room. I need to get this paw print off my forehead." Kelsy excused herself and walked to the restrooms.

"Will she be able to help us?" Allen asked.

"She has access to a lot of information."

"Where does she work?"

"FBI."

Chapter 8

College Park, MD
University of Maryland Campus

G reg Orfordis listened to the summation of the second to the last speaker on World Religions.

"Chinese religions have many lessons for us today," the Asian man said, "beginning with loyalty and cooperation within the families and the strong sense of being responsible for the order of society. This social concern is the basis for an important form of immortality in China. This immortality of influence in practice means to live right while on earth so that one leaves behind a fragrance for a hundred generations. Chinese hold to the belief that what counts in an individual's life is their contribution to the family and society, through education, hard work, and ethical integrity. Society continues after we die, so strengthening it with our own influences leaves one with the feeling that we have not lived in vain." He bowed slightly with the conclusion of his speech.

The students politely applauded.

The instructor in charge of the lectures stepped out onto the stage from the wings. "Last but not least, we will be hearing from Professor Gregory Orfordis. He will lecture on Christianity," the man read from a piece of paper. "Please welcome Professor Orfordis."

The halfhearted applause welcomed Greg to the podium. He couldn't really blame them for their lack of enthusiasm—they had sat through three hours of six different world religions.

Greg smiled. "I promise I'll make it short."

The students cheered and whistled loudly with appreciation.

"Today, I speak to you about Christianity," Greg began. "The simple definition of Christianity is, those who believe in Jesus Christ as the Lord and Savior of the world. But if you remember only one thing I say to you today, let it be this: the cornerstone of the Christian faith is centered around one single event; the bodily resurrection of Jesus Christ. His return from the dead and His victory over death and sin." He spoke for twenty minutes more.

"In closing, there are three major points to retain. The incarnation of God, meaning, God personified with flesh and dwelling on earth with humans as the man known as Jesus Christ, and secondly, the crucifixion, which is the sacrifice for man's sins and the act of restoring the lost relationship between God and man. Last, but most important is the resurrection, the redeeming act of the Christ for man, meaning victory over death and sin." He removed his glasses and smiled. "I see I'm beginning to wear out my welcome." There was laughter from the students. "I would like to sum up my lecture this way. 'For God so loved the world that He gave His only begotten Son, that whoever believes in Him should never perish, but have everlasting life.' Thank you, and God bless."

The students gave him a quick, polite applause while leaping from their seats and heading for the exits.

He sat at a table by himself organizing his notes. A sheet of paper slipped onto the table from one of his folders and he read the words.

"A time will come when the dark Trinity will form and the spiritual and physical realms align. A battle will be felt on earth and in the heavens." He believed that time was now. He thought of his friend, James Rood. He remembered the conversations they'd had concerning spiritual warfare and the difficulty James had believing there was a spiritual war. He remembered the special bond formed between himself and James. It was a bond formed between two people who struggled through hell together to reach a common goal and some kind of understanding and purpose in life. A bond formed in this manner was unbreakable even in death. He missed his friend.

Two students approached him from across the lecture hall. "Professor Orfordis," one of the students said.

"Yes," he answered, coming out of his thoughts.

"Would you please sign my book?" she asked holding it out.

The book was entitled, *Spiritual Warfare—What Color Is Your Soul?* The title was metallic red and the cover design resembled a black and white jigsaw puzzle with some of the pieces missing.

Greg signed the inside cover, "Every soul has a purpose and a destination. Greg Orfordis." "Here you are young lady." He handed the book back to her.

"Could you please sign mine, too, Mr. Orfordis?" the second student asked.

The young lady spoke up. "Professor, can I ask you something?"

"Of course."

"Do you really believe there's a spiritual war going on around us and the forces of good and evil are fighting for our souls?"

He grinned. "Are you asking me if my book is fiction or nonfiction?"

The students laughed. "Did you really see those things you wrote about?"

"Every one of us is part of a plan," he explained. "There are great forces working to make it good, but there are also forces equally great working to destroy it. Sometimes those forces manifest and become visible in the physical realm. When that occurs, supernatural events begin to appear."

"Why wouldn't they show themselves all the time?" one of the students asked.

"I don't know," Greg answered. "I wish they would. It would make my job easier."

"What about the part in your book that says our souls are like pieces of a puzzle?" the student asked.

"Our souls are the pieces that make the plan what it is," he said.

"Every soul is black or white and when all the pieces are put together one color will dominate the puzzle," the other student said perceptively. "Influencing the spiritual balance of the world."

Greg stood and gathered his notes. "That's correct." He loved to talk about spiritual warfare; it was his business and his pleasure. Studying, lecturing, and preaching to the world about the struggles between the forces of good and evil was the essence of his life; his purpose. "I believe it's time for me to be on my way." He felt the need to get to work on his project at the church. "I need a nap," he said smiling. "When you're my age, naps are more important than food."

The students thanked him and disappeared around a corner.

He could still see the jigsaw puzzle of his book cover floating before his eyes. "Sometimes some of the white pieces are a little bigger and brighter than the others," he whispered to himself, thinking of James Rood again.

*   *   *

Mary sat in her car flipping through the file she had put together about the suspicious wife's husband. An odd thought crossed her mind. She had been working on the case for practically three weeks and had never met the suspicious wife in person. The wife contacted her by mail, telephone, or e-mail. It was the first time she hadn't met a client face-to-face in eleven adultery cases. Of course, she had been absorbed with Allen's problem and the suspicious wife could easily be consumed with her everyday life, leaving neither one of them time to meet. Plus there was no rule saying that they had to meet in person.

With that in mind, she brushed the thought off and glanced at the coffee shop across the street where Mr. Pig was having a gourmet coffee. She pulled a sheet of paper out of the file. "Donald Herman, Communications and Networks Consultant, fifty-four years old, six feet two inches tall, and two hundred and forty pounds," the information on the page read. He had two government positions that dealt with communications, but there were no specifics. But she didn't need his life's history to catch him cheating on his wife. She shoved the page back into the file and glanced at the coffee shop again; Mr. Pig was stepping out onto the sidewalk. He had a tailored dark blue suit, a thick but well-trimmed gray beard and gray hair to match, and he also wore dark glasses. He ducked into a taxicab. She followed the cab over the Francis Scott Key Bridge to the George Washington Parkway, then to 495. She continued on the Capital Beltway, staying a few car lengths behind Mr. Pig's taxicab.

A stray thought drifted into her mind, a distant memory when she was at the FBI Academy in Quantico training to be an agent. She smiled when she remembered the first time she met Kelsy. They were drill partners in a self-defense training exercise. Mary kicked a little too hard and a little too high and her foot found Kelsy's head, nearly knocking her unconscious. Kelsy did pay her back. Her grin broadened with the thought of Kelsy's method of retaliation. The next day in training class Mary's breast shield was mysteriously full of itching powder. The memory of her ripping off her jacket, breast shield, and shirt made her laugh out loud. The two of them had many great memories together.

Kelsy came from a wealthy family and a sheltered upbringing; her parents were having a difficult time dealing with their little princess' career choice. It didn't help matters when Kelsy showed up at one of the family's galas with a black eye and went on to explain to her parents about the sixteen weeks of intensive programs and the 654 hours of training, which she was enjoying immensely. The thought of their little girl handling firearms and being thrown about in a physical training and defense tactics course didn't sit well with them. It showed clearly on Mommy and Daddy's faces.

Her parent's hadn't taken a shine to Mary either. They found her to be quite odd. They referred to her as the girl who kept scratching her breasts.

A car horn sounded, erasing her jovial thoughts, only to be replaced by dark memories from a cold night—a bloody night from her last days as an FBI agent. Those dark memories always lurked in her mind, waiting, pining for her attention. She could control them most of the time; most of the time. "Damn," she said. "This guy travels a lot."

The taxicab was on the Dulles access road heading toward the Washington Dulles International Airport. It stopped in front of the British Airlines terminal. Mr. Pig strolled to the counter and within minutes he was heading to the departure gates. Mary made a few notes on a pad, then headed back to Washington and tried not to think about anything.

Chapter 9

Mecca, Saudi Arabia

In a whitewashed building in the city of Mecca, the chief negotiators of six countries sat at a large, round, oak table, discussing the final details of the removal of biological warheads from their countries. Every man and woman in the room was equipped with an ear piece that was linked to a computer, called ITS, which stood for Immediate Translation System. As the name suggested, the headset immediately translated all languages to the wearer's indigenous language, or any language the person programmed into the system. Also, there were small monitor screens placed before each of the members of the committee for visual confirmation.

Walking toward the conference room wearing a tailor-fitted, white suit was Jordan Iblis, the Secretary General of the United Nations. He had arrived to collect signatures for the nuclear disarmament agreement from the head negotiators.

The conference had already been in session for hours and from the reports he had received, disagreements dominated the conversations, again. This was the third peace summit in thirteen months, the third attempt for disarmament, the third quarreling time, possibly the third failure to reach an agreement.

He stepped into the conference room and the chaotic dialogue between the nations stopped. He stood quietly for a moment scrutinizing the room like a teacher returning to a classroom full of fourth graders who had been acting up during his absence. He circled the table, greeting each leader in his or her native language without the aid of ITS. He shook their hands and hugged them and asked about their families. He knew each leader's language, customs and beliefs as if they were his own; he spoke to them not as a chief officer from the UN, but more like a member of the family. A trusting and respectful relationship had developed between him and the leaders at the disarmament meeting; they considered him their friend.

He took his seat at the head chair. He could feel the discouragement and annoyance in the air. "I have read each one of your disarmament proposals." He threw a stack of papers on the table. "I like none of them."

The mumbles, groans and upset expressions turned over in the room like a bad odor.

"Gentlemen and ladies," he said softly.

The room fell silent and the members of the committee shifted their attention to him again.

"The problem with your proposals is that they lack trust," he said with a grin. "Where's the trust?"

"That's not true," one of the leaders from North Korea said defensively.

Jordan looked at him with an unconvinced stare until the Korean man's eyes conceded to him.

Some of the other members attempted to conceal their sheepish grins.

"Would anyone else like to deny my statement for the record?" he asked.

The committee members remained quiet, finding it useless to refute the obvious.

He continued with a smile. "I have here something that will ease your minds," he said tapping a piece of paper with a pen. A young lady passed out a single sheet of paper to each person seated at the table. "This piece of paper says that there will be no disarmament of any weapons until the United Nations tours, inspects, and documents the findings on every site in each country." His smile disappeared.

"Why?"

"These peace talks and disarmament agreements were unsuccessful due to lack of trust and fear of breach of agreement," Jordan stated.

"We have, for one reason or another, failed to come to an agreement. In the document before you is the plan that will solve the problem. In short, the United Nations inspectors will be at every site at the same time, ready to begin the shut down process once a date is agreed to."

"The entire disarmament will be executed simultaneously?" one of the leaders asked.

"Yes, by the United Nations," Jordan answered.

"What about the United States weapons facility in Israel?" one of the Libyan leaders asked. "Did they not breach the agreement of 2001? Where are they today?"

The other nations at the table joined in with the Libyan leader, demanding answers.

Jordan raised his hands. "I have spoken to the president of the United States myself and I have his full cooperation on the matter. And the Israeli government also agreed on the UN's terms. Okay. So, please, one problem at a time."

The leader from Iran signed the document and handed the sheet of paper to Jordan. Jordan stood and the Iranian leader bid him goodbye. He walked out the door followed by his entourage.

Jordan smiled. "One down, six to go."

After another thirty minutes of explaining and pampering, the remaining leaders left their signatures in the conference room before leaving Mecca, with the exception of Libya, who signed a tentative agreement. The third time was the charm.

Libya was going to be a difficult customer, Jordan thought. They were the latest to join the countries with nuclear technology. No one was certain how far along they were, but it appeared they had reached respectability. The same way one would respect a crazy fool with a gun that had one bullet. They could hurt someone before everyone jumped all over them. And it appeared Libya still had a grudge against the US. Then again, who didn't?

Iblis walked down the corridor holding a black leather briefcase with the six coveted signatures; he was pleased with the success of the conference. He was also pleased with himself. It had been a long thirteen months of work, but finally the disarmament would proceed and the UN would have total access to all the nuclear housing facilities; his true intention from the very beginning.

He passed a number of men armed with automatic weapons and security metal detectors every hundred yards. Uniformed men waved hand held devices that beeped and registered information to a portable screen displayed on their helmet visor. The security in Mecca had been tripled thanks to his strong insistence and that of the UN. It was important to have a terrorist-free weekend.

A man in a black military uniform carrying an automatic weapon stopped him. "Mr. Iblis, can you step into the room?" he asked, glancing toward a door that had an armed guard standing in front of it.

Jordan walked over without saying a word. He was allowed into the room by the armed guard. The door closed behind him and automatically locked. Unaffected by the odd request, he stood in the center of the poorly lit room. It contained one small bare desk and a lone wooden chair. There was no other furniture, and the walls were stark white and windowless. On his right was a second door without a doorknob, from which a man in a gray suit entered. He had a brown sweaty complexion and dark greasy hair. Jordan recognized him as one of the security agents for the Libyan government.

"What can I do for you, Slim Jim?" Jordan asked in Arabic.

"My name is Shimhim." He leaned against the small desk. "The people I represent would like to have the same arrangement. They prefer the same officials to tour their facilities as before."

"I will prepare my demands," Jordan said in perfect Arabic dialect. "Is there something else?"

"There's military movement on our borders. What are the Americans up to?"

"The rumor is that there are two American journalists being held against their will there," Jordan answered.

"There are no American journalists being held prisoner there," Shimhim snorted defensively.

He smiled. "If you say so."

"We are not holding anyone."

"I have a plane to catch."

"The Americans are delaying the tour of their weapons facilities in Israel and are moving military forces because of a rumor?" Shimhim asked.

"The inspections of the facilities are delayed because the peace talks broke down. I know nothing of the military movement outside of the rumor. I believe even if the rumor were true, the Americans would not mobilize their military because of two journalists." Jordan grinned and walked toward the door. "You guys need to relax."

"I believe you know more." A wide, toothy grin appeared on his sweaty face. "You're the vice president's boyfriend," he said, sound degrading. "You are . . . how do you say it? Buddies with the American president."

Jordan stood at the door and waited for it to open.

"I believe you should tell me what you know."

Jordan turned with a steel and ghostly glare. He walked to Shimhim and slammed his briefcase onto the desk. Shimhim jumped back from the desk, startled, looking unsure of what to do next.

Jordan unsnapped the latches on the briefcase as he stared into Shimhim's eyes. "Do you know why I deal with you?" he asked coldly.

Shimhim pulled his weapon out of the holster from beneath his jacket, fearing Jordan had somehow smuggled a weapon into the building.

"Because you have strings." Jordan answered his own question.

"What are you talking about?"

He pulled out an envelope and threw it on the desk. He shut the briefcase and walked to the door. "They cut off your hands for stealing in some parts of the world," he said with his back turned to Shimhim.

He heard Shimhim reach into the envelope and pull out the photographs of him and another man's wife bumping bellies. The woman in the photo was married to a very important official in the Saudi Arabian government.

"Imagine what they will cut off you. Do you have anything else that you would like to discuss, Slim Jim?" Jordan asked, glancing over his shoulder with a sinister stare.

Shimhim pushed a remote control in his pocket and the door unlocked. He collapsed into the chair, dazed by the photographs, the life knocked out of him like a boxer on his worst night.

"Have a good day." Jordan disappeared through the door.

*   *   *

Jordan entered the airplane whistling cheerfully. The Shimhim incident added to his already great mood; it was a perfect conclusion to a perfect day. *Yes, the Shimhim meeting was a pleasant surprise,* he thought. He took his seat in first class after carefully placing his briefcase in the compartment above.

An elderly Chinese man sat next to him and looked at him curiously. "Don't I know you?" he asked in broken English.

"That may be possible," Jordan responded in Chinese.

"What is your business?" the elderly man asked, this time in his own language.

"I work for the United Nations."

He looked at Jordan with a contemplating stare. "That isn't it," the man said with a slight hint of frustration in his tone.

Jordan laughed and leaned in close to the man and whispered. "I'm the secretary general."

"Oh yes, of course. But you remind me of some else."

Jordan closed his eyes. "You let me know when you figured it out, Mr. Sung."

"How do you know my name?"

"I heard the flight attendant welcome you," he said, his eyes still shut.

"You were an informant for Mao Zedong and his Red Army. You betrayed Chang Kuo T'ao and the Nationalist movement," the old man said, disbelief in his voice. "But how could that be? That was over fifty years ago."

"I would've had to been born well before 1949 when the Communist rule was established in China under Mao's leadership." Jordan grinned and opened his eyes. "Quite impossible, wouldn't you say?"

The man gaped at him as if he were a ghost. "Yes," he mumbled. "Of course, you're too young to be him." He continued to stare with amazement. "The resemblance is uncanny."

"Who was this man I remind you of?"

"His name was Luke Lusian. He was the personal advisor of Chang Kuo T'ao, the leader of the Nationalist troops. Lusian mysteriously vanished, only to reappear as Mao Zedong's advisor a year later. Soon after, Mao Zedong and the Communists crushed the Nationalist resistance."

Jordan fluffed his pillow. "Communism has some nice qualities," he said closing his eyes again.

*   *   *

Art Hanson watched Jordan Iblis depart the plane and enter a limousine. He followed the car out of Dulles and back to Washington. Art had also watched Jordan three days ago. Jordan had met a woman who strongly resembled Shelly Deanster, the vice president, but it hadn't been her. The woman and Jordan had a lengthy conversation, but Jordan did all the talking. It appeared that he was explaining something or giving instructions of some kind. It certainly wasn't a romantic chat or a business meeting. At the end of the conversation the two parted uneventfully. Jordan had made his way to his terminal for Mecca, and she to hers, which was the departure terminal for the Caymans.

*   *   *

Two men entered the eight thousand seat church and walked down the ramp toward the stage. They gazed upward and around at the church, apparently amazed by its enormous size.

"Hello," a man yelled from the stage, waving his hand to get their attention. "Come on down." He did his best Bob Barker impersonation, which wasn't very good. He held his hand out. "Hi. I'm Robert Ward, Allen Pyrit's public relations manager."

"I thought God was Pyrit's public relations manager," one man said, grinning.

"No, He's the promoter," Robert replied.

"I'm Clint Wilkins from *Time* magazine and this is Dewayne Preston. He's going to film the interview for a possible documentary." His partner was busy setting up the equipment.

"That's fine."

Clint glanced down at his watch. "Is Pyrit going to be here soon?"

Robert looked at his watch. "He should arrive any moment." The reality of it was, Robert had no idea of Allen's whereabouts, and he was having a nervous breakdown because of it. It had taken him months to set up this interview.

Clint looked over some of his notes while Dewayne arranged wires for the equipment.

"If you want something to eat or drink, you can help yourself to the buffet table," Robert offered. "I need to check on another matter; please excuse me."

Clint and Dewayne looked over at the table spread of shrimp, salmon, crab, and lobster fare. Every fruit and vegetable known to man was provided on fancy display dishes. There were also six different types of meats available and the dessert choices were endless. The two men glanced at one another with grins that reached from ear-to-ear.

"Do you think this is all for us?" Clint asked.

"Looks like they're trying to butter us up," Dewayne said.

"I don't mind a little buttering."

*   *   *

A taxicab pulled up to the church and Allen stepped out onto the wet sidewalk. He tucked his umbrella under his arm and pulled his wallet out.

"No, Mr. Pyrit," the cab driver insisted. "I don't want your money."

"You have to take something," Allen implored, holding a ten-dollar bill.

"Your advice and help, Mr. Pyrit, is payment enough."

"Make sure you call the number I gave you. They'll get you started in the right direction," Allen said, shaking the driver's hand. He smiled sincerely. "I'll be checking up on you."

"Thank you, Mr. Pyrit. Thank you so much."

The taxi pulled away. Allen had dropped the ten dollar bill in the driver's lap when he hadn't been paying attention.

Robert Ward opened the large wooden doors of the church and walked toward Allen. He wasn't a happy camper.

"Hello, Robert. Is the journalist here?"

"What are you doing?" Robert fussed over him like a worried hen.

"What?"

"Why did you take a cab?"

"Why not?" Allen asked as they walked along the sidewalk.

"We have limos. What if something were to happen to you? There are crazies out there."

"Nothing is going to happen to me. You need a day off." He climbed the steps to the entrance.

"A day off?" Robert asked, running his hand through his thinning hair. "Allen, please next time . . ."

"It's all right, Robert," he interrupted, and left him standing outside staring at the church doors.

Once inside the church, Allen took a deep breath. The quiet and peacefulness soothed him right away. He saw a few of the security guards walking the corridors and he and the guards acknowledged each other with a wave. He approached the stage where two men sat on the floor surrounded by large amounts of food.

"Did you save any for me?" he asked, smiling down at the two men.

They looked up from their elaborate picnic, startled and embarrassed.

"Mr. Pyrit," one said with his mouth full of food. "I'm Clint Wilkins, reporter for *Time*. How are you?"

"Fine, thank you."

"I'm Dewayne Preston, photographer. Shrimp?" he asked, holding one up to him.

"Thank you," Allen said. "Any cocktail sauce?"

Clint handed the cocktail sauce to Dewayne, who offered it to him. He dipped the shrimp and took a bite. "Thanks," he said. "Have you tried the crab dip? I heard it was great."

"I don't think there's anything we haven't tried," Clint said under his breath.

Allen started to dip the remainder of his shrimp, but stopped suddenly.

"Something wrong, Mr. Pyrit?" Dewayne asked.

He smiled. "No double dipping," he said, tossing the rest of the shrimp into his mouth. "Shall we begin the interview?"

Clint prepared the chairs and the microphones. Dewayne adjusted his camera.

Allen fixed himself a soda. "Can I get you guys anything?"

"We've had our fill of everything, thank you," Dewayne said.

Allen took a seat and connected his microphone.

Clint pulled his notes out. "Are you ready, Mr. Pyrit?"

"Whenever you are. You have a little sauce on your chin."

Clint wiped his chin with his forearm. "Thanks." He read from a note card. "Have the constant investigations and scrutinizing of your religious practices affected you in any way?"

Allen stared for a moment. "What investigations?" he finally asked.

"The investigations concerning the healings," Clint said.

He put his drink down. "I know nothing about that."

"They're saying the healings were faked, that there were payoffs involved. They're also saying church officials put pressure and great expectations on some of the followers. Others are saying the power of suggestion made them react. Some people in the congregation said they were put in an altered state of consciousness."

"Who is saying this?"

"The media. Other religions."

He was truly confused. "And their proof is?"

"Interviews with the people who were allegedly healed," Clint said. "The individuals who experienced the 'slain in the spirit' and others who spoke in tongues claim the whole thing was bogus. These people confessed during interviews that they faked it."

"I don't know what to say," Allen said. "I didn't create those events and I certainly didn't in any way participate in any mind games."

"Could the entire thing have been staged without your knowledge?"

"I guess so, if what you are saying is true," Allen said disconnecting his microphone and standing. "You have to understand, my job is to preach, encourage people to find God."

"Then, you wouldn't know about the negative press on one of your biggest sponsors, and who your church is affiliated with."

"Which one?"

"Golden Calf Enterprises."

"Sean Carbon's Internet Company?"

"Yes."

"GCE gives Biblical advice via computer all over the world," Allen said. "They also provide Bibles on the Net to countries that can't get them."

"That's true," Clint said. "But they also deal with astrology, psychic readings, tarot cards, and predictions of the future. They have claimed to have prophets. GCE claims you endorse their practices."

"Really," Allen said staring up at the large cosmic painted ceiling. "Does Robert have any idea what this interview was about?"

"We never discussed the story." Clint stood. "You don't appear to be very informed on the operations of your church."

Allen looked at the large amounts of food on the buffet table and then back to Clint. "Can you do me a favor?"

"If I can."

"Don't write this story," Allen said.

Clint stared at Allen as if he misunderstood him.

"I need some time," Allen said.

"For what?"

"Something very wrong is going on, and it has to be brought out in the open, but in a proper manner."

"How long do you need?" Dewayne asked.

Clint looked at Dewayne inquisitively.

"As long as it takes for us to find the truth."

"I have a deadline, Mr. Pyrit," Clint said.

"I'll tell you what," Allen said. "You find out the truth, and you get the exclusive with me no matter which way the story goes."

Clint and Dewayne grinned at one another. "You have a deal, Mr, Pyrit," they answered.

Chapter 10

The workday ended for many in the nation's capital, but Kelsy Anderson continued to work into the night; not as an FBI analyst, but as a friend. Staying late wasn't anything new for her, but doing personal business at work was. She was not one to exploit her special privileges as an employee of the bureau for personal use, but Mary was her best friend, and for her to ask a favor, it must be very important. At least that was what Kelsy convinced herself to believe before abusing her FBI accesses. Plus, deep down she thought it would be cool to do something for Allen Pyrit. To her, Allen was a celebrity; she felt important aiding someone as famous as Allen. It had been a little slow at work anyway. The truth was, it had been downright boring and she could use a little excitement. If she got caught, maybe they would just fire her. She had a clean record and it would be her first offense. Hell, they wouldn't put her in jail for trying to find Allen Pyrit's biological parents, would they?

She sat at her desk looking over a file belonging to Allen. She contacted Allen's childhood physicians and the records department at Columbia Hospital. The physicians were a dead end. The records department at the hospital had a file on Allen, but required Allen to personally pick it up and sign a release form. She typed on the keyboard gaining access to information from the FBI's national database. She entered her code number and typed in Allen's name, but before she was able to activate the database, her computer crashed.

"What the . . . ?" She stared at the blank screen as if she had been betrayed.

"What's wrong?" a voice asked from a cubical away.

"Bob, is that you?" Of course, it was him. He always worked late. He was a geek who had no life. Different from her, who was a geek who thought she had a life.

"Yeah," he answered, popping his head up like a prairie dog with thick black-rimmed glasses.

She attempted to boot the system, but the screen remained blank. She tried a few other things, but with no success. She walked over to Bob's desk. "Can I use your computer?"

"Sure," he said, offering her his chair. "What's wrong with yours?"

"I don't know."

"I'll check it out for you."

He dashed over to her desk. She knew Bob had a crush on her, so he loved every minute of interaction between the two of them. She had given him a chance to be a hero and fix her computer.

She typed on his keyboard. "Are you already coded into the database?"

"Yeah!" he yelled from her cubical.

She tapped in Allen's name and the information she was requesting. She waited patiently, but something was wrong. The computer never took this long. She typed again, but the screen remained unaffected. Finally, a message appeared on the screen: "REQUEST DENIED." That was odd, she had full access. There was a series of numbers below the message. She recognized them as a Pentagon security code. Her stomach tightened; not what she wanted to see. It was like swimming in the ocean and seeing a dorsal fin glide by. She wrote the number down on a piece of notepaper, and then typed the Pentagon security code in the access space and pressed "enter," not sure what to expect. Maybe the dorsal fin belonged to a dolphin. "REQUEST DENIED, the screen read again.

Suddenly, a new screen message appeared, this time a warning. "IT IS A FEDERAL OFFENSE TO ATTEMPT TO ACCESS INFORMATION FROM THIS DOCUMENT. THIS IS A SECURED FILE. THIS IS A CLASSIFIED DOCUMENT" Shark!

She immediately cleared the message from the screen and exited the national database. She walked over and grabbed her coat, glancing once at the computer as if someone were watching her from the screen.

"I'll see you later, Bob." She hurried out of the office.

"See ya, Kelsy," he said tapping away on her keyboard. A few seconds later, she heard a celebrating whoop. "I fixed it," he yelled.

"Thanks," Kelsy yelled back. "I owe you one."

*   *   *

Seated in the corner of McGarvey's restaurant at the Annapolis harbor, Jordan Iblis and Shelly Deanster were having cold beer and a bucket of mussels. Hot seafood and cold beer, an Annapolis pastime. Seated near the important twosome was a peculiar couple. This couple wore listening devices in their ears and carried automatic weapons. They didn't eat, they watched. Everything. There was an identical pair seated across the room.

"Why is Moore mobilizing military forces along the borders of Libya?" Jordan asked as he picked the meat out of a black-shelled mussel.

Shelly took a sip of her beer. "It's not a military operation."

"What's going on?"

"Foreign aid. It's part of the NATO relief troops."

"Foreign aid?" he asked with a suspicious grin.

"The Egyptian President requested aid after the earthquake. You did hear about the earthquake?"

"What earthquake?"

"There was an earthquake. You didn't hear about it?"

Jordan grinned. "Oh really."

Shelly took another sip of her beer, trying to hide her grin.

"And Chad, Algeria, and Tunisia, are they also requesting aid?"

"No, but the governments of Chad and Algeria are participating with the aid effort, and our assistance was requested." She put the soft meat of the mussel on a saltine cracker with cocktail sauce.

"So, as you can see, there would be American personnel along the borders of Libya."

"I see," Jordan said, raising his hand to get the waiter's attention. "Two more Heinekens, please."

"Are you trying to get me drunk?"

He smiled seductively. "And a plate of oysters," he ordered.

"I've heard that oysters were an aphrodisiac," she said, eyeing him like a temptress.

"Make that two plates," he yelled to the waiter.

*   *   *

Washington, D.C.

Art Hanson climbed down the old rickety stairs to the church cellar, knowing the prehistoric wooden steps were going to be the death of him one day. He reached the bottom stair in one piece and avoided any head trauma from the low crossbeams.

"Professor O, You down here?"

"Over here, Mr. Hanson," Greg answered.

"You can call me Art," he told him for the hundredth time.

Greg sat behind his desk studying ancient scrolls under the golden glow of candlelight. Spread across his desk were more scroll fragments sealed in tinted glass casings to protect the brittle paper from the elements.

"You need to get some rest, professor," he recommended, noticing the dark bags beneath Greg's eyes.

"Yes, I believe you are correct, Mr. Hanson," he agreed, removing his reading glasses. "I've been deciphering ancient manuscripts for seven hours nonstop."

"You can call me Art," he requested, for the one hundredth and first time. "What are you working on?"

Greg told him about the ancient manuscripts named the Mount Sinai scrolls. He told him how he had come upon them many years ago in the foothills of Mount Sinai during one of his many expeditions, and how he had smuggled them into the United States and hid them in the church's cellar for over forty years.

He had a difficult time imagining the professor breaking any law, let alone smuggling.

Greg explained there was a mysterious group attempting to obtain the scrolls to destroy them. He asked the "who and why" questions, but Greg told him it was a long and extraordinary story and he would love to tell it, but not now, and he left it at that. Art didn't bother pursuing the matter any further.

He caught a glimpse of a large chalkboard off to the side of the room. Written with red capital letters across the top were the words, "Demonic Trinity." Beneath those were the words, "The Four Horsemen of the Apocalypse."

"I guess that's not the Horsemen of Notre Dame?" he joked.

Greg smiled. "No, those gentlemen didn't play football. Especially at a Catholic school."

He pulled out a cigar and chewed on it while examining the chalkboard. "I'm curious, professor," he said, pointing with his cigar. "What's the deal with the color horses?"

"Have you heard of the book of Revelation?"

"It's a Bible thing, right?" His religious education of any sort was pretty limited.

Greg laughed. "Yes, it's a Bible thing. To be more precise, it's a section within the Bible. In Revelation there are many signs, and the four horsemen are one of those signs."

"Signs for what?"

"Some are warnings, some are predictions of things to come."

"For what?"

"The end of time. The second coming of Jesus Christ." Greg smiled. "He's a big part of that Bible thing."

"I think I've heard of him," he joked.

"For believers like myself, the signs are also warnings to protect us against the Antichrist, the false prophets and Satan himself," Greg explained. "For the rest of the world, the signs are more like an invitation."

"Invitation?"

"There will come a time when the world will witness incredible events," Greg explained. "The world will want answers, answers found only in the Bible."

"So, I see here," he said, pointing to the chalkboard. "It looks like some of the signs have already happened." He was looking at the date July 4, 1776. "The first seal, the white horse sign is connected to the Declaration of Independence?"

Greg stood. "Yes, I believe the first seal was broken with the signing of that document."

"When you say seal, what do you mean?"

"When the Bible speaks of a seal being broken, it's a symbolic image of the beginning of an event." He quickly explained how in the book of Revelation there were seven seals, seven trumpets, and seven bowls, also symbolic starting points in the book.

"I still don't get it. What's the deal with the white horse and the United States?"

"I believe the rider of the white horse symbolizes the Antichrist and his kingdom."

"Antichrist," Art said. "I'm assuming he's the bad guy."

"One of the baddest," Greg replied.

They both laughed at Greg's usage of the word baddest. Art was starting to really like the professor. He was a little corny, he thought, but in a good way. Like *Star Wars,* KISS, or the *Wizard of Oz.*

"Wouldn't that make him pretty old?"

"I believe the Antichrist manifested recently," Greg said. "Within the past forty years."

"America, the home of the Antichrist. France had Napoleon, Italy had Mussolini, Mongolia had Genghis Khan, Germany had Hitler, and America will have the Antichrist." He was actually finding the subject interesting, which surprised him. "What makes you think the U.S. is the white horse sign thing?"

"This passage here says." Greg pointed to an open book on his desk. "The first seal of seven is a white horse; its rider holds a bow and wears a crown, and he rides out to conquer as a conqueror. The rider's bow is a symbolic sign of military power, but he is without an arrow, which indicates he not only will conquer with military force, he will also conquer with diplomacy. America throughout her history has defeated many a foe with both military might and diplomacy. Immediately after America won her independence, the new world power crowned a leader, George Washington, who rode down the streets of New York on a white horse, celebrating the conquest. A new world power was born, and I believe from this new kingdom will rise the Antichrist."

He stared, somewhat dazed with the idea. He didn't believe in any of it, but Greg's conviction had him defiantly intrigued.

"What about this?" Art asked, pointing to the chalkboard. "The Antichrist's nationality. Mediterranean, Roman lineage, Jewish ancestry," he read. "Roman-Grecian-Jew. He's going to be all of these?"

"The Bible suggests the Antichrist will be all of these nationalities, which is another reason I believe America is where he will rise from. America is a composite of all people of the earth."

He pointed to a name beneath the red horse sign. "Who's Archduke Franz Ferdinand?"

"I believe he was the breaking of the second seal. The red horse of war." Greg read the passage out of the Bible. "The rider was given a large sword to take peace from earth, and to make men slay each other. He will stand for that destructive strife which sets man against man and nation against nation."

"Hasn't that happened a lot throughout history?"

"There has never been more bloodshed and more countries involved with war on a world level worse than the time period between 1914 to 1945."

He noticed on the chalkboard the year 1914 was the beginning of World War I and 1945 was the end of World War II. Greg also had highlighted the years of the revolutions of Russia and China that were within the 1914-1945 time frame. "So, who's this guy Ferdinand? What's his connection to the wars and the second seal?"

"Ferdinand was a principal figure in Austria in 1914, who was assassinated by Serbian nationalists. His death prompted Austria-

Hungary to invade Serbia, precipitating the start of World War I. And like a domino effect, wars spread throughout the world."

Greg explained the third seal, the black horse. Famine. He talked about the pair of scales the rider carried and the quart of wheat and three quarts of barley for a day's wage. He explained how the scales and the measurements of food were symbolic of the hardships during the famine and a day's pay will be just enough to survive.

"I can see that in some countries," he responded. "But it seems to me the richer countries are doing fine."

"The third seal isn't simply about starving children in third world countries. Not all famines are physical."

"You lost me, professor."

"How many people do you know who make a good living, but seem to be always living paycheck to paycheck. It doesn't seem to matter how much money people make, it never seems to be quite enough. It's a famine from within."

"What about the part that says not to damage the oil and wine?" he asked.

"I believe that suggests the wealthy will not be affected like the common people. In the scriptures, oil and wine was associated with the rich."

"Oh good, I'm safe," he said laughing.

Greg flipped through the Bible and read another passage. "When the Lamb opened the fourth seal, I heard the voice of the fourth living creature say, 'Come!' I looked, and there before me was a pale horse! Its rider was named Death, and Hades was following close behind him."

"The pale horse looks like a butt kicker, and then some," he joked. "The rider was given power to kill with famine, plagues, wild beast, and by the sword. This guy's hell on wheels."

"That's true, but I'm not certain the fourth seal has been broken. As for the fifth, sixth, and seventh."

"What are the rest?" He noticed the other seals weren't on the chalkboard.

"The fifth is the persecution of the Christian church and people, the sixth seal is catastrophes on a global scale never seen before, and the seventh is the beginning of the seven trumpet judgments."

"What are the trumpet judgments?"

"More signs and hardships for the world," Greg said. "Aren't you bored with this religious stuff?"

"No, not really. Let me ask you something, professor. Why do this? Why try to figure out the signs and identify the . . ." He stopped and glanced at the chalkboard. "Demonic Trinity? What's the point?"

Greg stared at him for a moment, almost making him uncomfortable. "Once I know who they are, I can stop them."

For a fleeting moment, he thought Greg had to be out of his mind, stone cold crazy. This man was waging war against things that didn't exist. But, many brilliant men are loony, why not him?

"What about Jordan Iblis?" Greg asked, snapping him out of his thoughts.

"Sorry, I drifted for a second." He almost felt embarrassed, as if Greg could read his mind. Maybe his eyes gave him away; maybe his eyes were saying, "Sorry, professor, you're a brilliant man, but you're off your nut. The cheese has slipped off your cracker."

"Do you have any information on Jordan Iblis?"

Art told him about Jordan's meeting with the woman at the airport who resembled the Vice President, and another meeting that took place after hours in a restaurant with a scientist who had arrived from a government facility located in New Mexico. He also told him about Jordan's lunch date with Shelly Deanster and the Speaker of the House, Walter Web. "This guy knows everybody," Art said, impressed.

Greg glanced at the headlines across the *Washington Post* on his desk. UN NEGOTIATES ARMS TREATY. Art had seen the article earlier. It stated how Jordan Iblis, had brought the promise of peace to the world, and how he and Derrick Moore had single-handedly negotiated the disarmament of mass-destructive nuclear weapons between ten nations.

"He seems to be a decent guy," Art said.

Greg looked at him. "I need you to continue to follow him."

"Sure, professor." He headed for the stairs. "I'll keep in touch," he said carefully stepping onto the first step.

*   *   *

After Art had gone, Greg sat at his desk with the Mount Sinai scrolls before him and examined them meticulously into the night. His painstaking and conscientious efforts had revealed another passage.

> "Behold, witness the beast from the sea;
> The world will marvel at his healed scar from a mortal wound.
> Behold, witness the beast from the earth;
> begotten from arrogance and pride, who deceives with great signs.
> Behold, witness the rise of the great dragon;
> who shall embrace the beasts, and they shall become three in one."

"The forming of the Demonic Trinity," he said staring at the scroll. "The Antichrist, the False Prophet and Satan together to become one evil force." The passage was very similar to the passages found in Revelation 13 concerning the beasts from the sea and land. The Bible warned of a beast from the sea that would heal from a mortal wound, causing the world to marvel. Also, there would be a beast from the land, who would make the world worship the beast from the sea. He leaned back into the chair and rested his eyes. He sensed the spiritual and the physical realms were on another collision course—the type of clash that altered human history toward the path of light or down the road of darkness. He felt himself being called upon again to do battle with the intangible forces that lurked in the flesh of man.

Chapter 11

J. Edgar Hoover Building. Washington, D.C.

K elsy strode from the metro to the FBI building's entrance. She shook the excess sleet from her umbrella and walked through the security post. It appeared to be a typical morning until she discovered the lobby was crowded with coworkers. They stood around in little groups whispering to one another. Men in black suits with hands-free radio equipment were posted in front of all the elevators and stairwells. That couldn't be good. The scene gave her a sick feeling in her gut; she had a strong suspicion this had something to do with last night. She cursed herself for poking around the database for personal motives.

She approached a group of five coworkers whispering among themselves. "What's going on?" she asked, hoping it had nothing to do with last night.

"I don't know," one of them answered. "They won't let us up to our offices."

Maybe it was a leaky pipe or a fire drill. Maybe someone accidentally sprayed pepper mace. Wishful thinking. "Where's Richardson?"

"Over there," the coworker said, pointing.

She made her way to him through the crowd. "What's going on, Mr. Richardson?"

"I'll let you know when I know," Richardson said. Richardson was the director in her department, but the guys in the black suits had apparently treated him like a mail boy, and it hadn't set well with him.

She went back to one of her friends and glanced around the room. "Hey, Sid, have you seen Bob?"

"No, I haven't." Sid also looked around looking for him. "Do you know what's going on?"

"No." Bob was never late. She was scared, but didn't know exactly why.

The elevator doors finally slid open and a man wearing a black trench coat stepped out. Two more men emerged carrying two cardboard boxes full of files. They left the building without saying a word to anyone.

Richardson instructed his people to return to their offices. Kelsy and her coworkers reached their floor and spread out to their own desks, glancing around suspiciously.

"Kelsy," a coworker said quietly. She directed Kelsy's attention toward Bob's desk with a nod.

"What in the world?" Kelsy said hurrying across the floor.

Bob's station had been cleared of all his personal things and his work files, including his floppy and compact disks. She noticed his computer had been opened and the hard drive had been removed.

"What the hell is going on?"

Richardson walked out of his office holding a piece of paper. "I need your attention, please."

Everyone in the office turned to face him. Kelsy didn't like the sound of his voice and the poignant expression on his face.

"Bob died last night," Richardson said, his voice somewhere in between sad and professional.

There was a collective gasp followed by murmuring.

"He was found shot to death in his car outside his house. The authorities believe it was a robbery. That's all I have." He disappeared into his office.

The room full of people was stunned to silence.

Kelsy stared into space with disbelief. Why did they take his things? Who took his things? For the rest of the day, questions leaped at her from every corner of her mind. She constantly glanced at the elevators in fear of those men in black trench coats coming back, but this time to get her. Rumors flooded the office the entire day about Bob being involved in espionage. Endless stories circulated the building about him selling government secrets to the Russians and Chinese, and last night must have been a deal gone bad.

She somehow made it through the day. Of course, she accomplished nothing to do with work. To add to her anxiety she had been unable to reach Mary. She headed for the exit, nerves on edge, wondering what waited for her out there.

"I'm sorry to hear about your coworker," a voice said from behind her.

She turned around. It was Anthony, the security officer at the front desk. "Thanks," she said with a glassy stare. She started to leave, but stopped. "Anthony, who was that in our offices this morning?" He usually had the inside poop in the building.

"I don't know. No one knows."

"Unbelievable! A group of guys dressed like vampires could stroll into the FBI building, take an agent's personal property and rip out his computer without identifying or explaining themselves."

He leaned forward. "NSA," he whispered. "That's my guess."

She tried to convince herself the entire day that it wasn't NSA. She also tried to convince herself that the manner in which Bob's files and possessions were seized was routine practice and she simply wasn't aware of the security procedures that were taken in the occurrence of the sudden death of a federal agent.

She stepped out into the cold, wet streets of the city, making her way along the sidewalk with a thousand thoughts pounding in her head. She glanced over her shoulder off and on, feeling paranoid. Her thoughts ultimately led her to the night before. Last night she had been attempting to access confidential documents off the Bureau's database on Allen Pyrit, using Bob's computer, using his access code number. Now, he was dead. Her mind spun with thoughts of the Pentagon, the NSA, and Bob's death. But one insane thought screamed above the rest in her head. Bob was murdered because she attempted to access restricted data from a confidential document on his computer. No, that couldn't be. For a moment she persuaded herself Bob's death was a coincidence. It was a mugging that went horribly bad. Hell, they lived and worked in the murder capital of the world. It was bound to happen to someone you know, if not yourself. Maybe the rumors were true, he was selling government secrets. It had happened in the past, why couldn't it be someone like Bob? He was smart, a loner, and he most certainly had the opportunity.

His death had nothing to do with last night, she kept telling herself. Why would one government agency murder someone from another agency over a TV evangelist's file? "They wouldn't," she said out loud. Her own voice surprised her. Passers-by on the sidewalk looked at her as if she were a nut case. The thought of the NSA confiscating his personal things, his hard drive and his files, continued to drip on her mind like a leaky faucet, no matter how hard she tried to turn it off. And the insane idea of the NSA's involvement with Bob's death kept coming back like Niagara Falls. She took a seat on the metro and her mind went numb; the guilt of Bob's death hung on her like a five hundred pound backpack.

*   *   *

Allen unlocked the front door and stepped into the dark house. It was the first time he had been back since the night his father died. The room felt cold on his face and an odd smell hung in the air. The smell of nothingness—no food aromas, no lingering fragrance of incense, not even the musky odor of a vacant house was present. *The smell of cold, dark emptiness,* he thought. He hit a switch and the room brightened, but the house still felt dark. He placed his keys on a table along with a document that made his sister and himself the sole owners of the estate. He searched the house for anything that might help him find his biological parents. He stopped before his father's office door and stood in the very spot where he overheard the many arguments between his parents when he was a child. Their fights were always about him.

He thought about the last time he and his father had spoken, which wasn't a conversation at all, but more of a shouting match. It was the same argument time and again. Allen had found his calling. He was going to study theology and eventually become an evangelist. His father detested every aspect of it. He believed Allen was wasting his mind and his time on such nonsense. Deep in his heart, Allen felt the need to please his father and desired his approval. But his attempts to speak to his father about his decision only drove him further away. His father had forbidden any talk about his so-called "calling" in his house again. Allen's rejoinder was if they couldn't talk about his passion and what he planned to do for the rest of his life, then they need not speak about anything. His father had agreed. They hadn't spoken to one another again until nearly eleven years later, the night his father died. That's why pride was one of the seven deadly sins.

He searched the drawers of his father's office desk and found two small keys in a little copper box. He unlocked the bottom drawer with one of the keys, and to his amazement he found a pile of articles and videotapes of his evangelical career. His father had been following his achievements the entire time. Within the collection of tapes and papers were two congratulation cards he never sent. His father had been proud of his accomplishments. He stared at the cards and thought about the eleven years they hadn't spoken to one another. He felt sick to his stomach.

He remembered finding his mother crying one day in the greenhouse. She and his father had just had an argument. "Your father loves you very much," she said attempting to sound strong.

"I love you, Mom," he'd said, touching her cheek. "Don't worry about me and Dad. You don't have to defend me from him. He'll learn to accept my decision."

"You have to keep trying to talk to him. He just wants the best for you."

"He won't listen. As far back as I can remember he wanted one thing for me, to be president of the United States. It's like some sick obsession with him. He's been grooming me for politics since I was three. Why? Why is it so damn important to him?"

"Your father believes you're special." She smiled through the tears. "We believe you have a gift, a gift that can change the world."

"I can still use my gift, but I'll be an evangelist instead of a president. I'll still reach people."

He would never forget the deep love for him in her eyes. That day in the greenhouse he also saw something else in her eyes. She had wanted to tell him something, but she couldn't bring herself to say it. She had seemed to be struggling with something important. Whatever it was, she took it to the grave with her. She had killed herself shortly after. She'd overdosed on sleeping pills; that was what he'd been told. A sudden, overwhelming feeling of nausea and paranoia hit him. Had his mother been murdered because she wanted to tell him the truth? Was there more to the adoption? What kind of secret was worth her life?

He sat on the floor for a long time, crying and thinking about his mother, before he finally threw the videotapes and clippings back into the drawer and climbed the dark oak staircase to his old bedroom. He looked out of his window at the twilight creeping in; only the brightest stars were shining. Night was coming. From his window he was able to see the finely landscaped property and the large pond carved into the five acres of rolling knolls. The estate rested quietly in the center of a thick grove of trees. Below his window, there were several gardens and a swimming pool with a guesthouse that hadn't been used in years.

He recalled the time he had been walking along one of the cobblestone walkways when he was ten years old. He had come across a beautiful red cardinal on the ground by the greenhouse. He reached down and cupped it carefully in both hands, still warm but lifeless. "Don't be dead," he breathed. Unexpectedly, the cardinal stood up in his palms. He had pushed his hands away from his body in fear, surprised by the sudden life in the bird. The cardinal hopped in his palms for a moment before flying off into one of the trees in the garden. As he stood there in the yard bewildered by what had happened, he felt an exhilarated surge of energy rush through his body. He felt his blood flow through him like a current of electricity.

He had told the story to his mother, and she had explained that sometimes birds fly into closed windows, or into a glass wall of a greenhouse and knock themselves unconscious; within a few moments they regain consciousness and fly off. His mother always took the time to explain life's little events to him. She also reminded him not to pick up animals off the ground.

The memory faded, but the surge of energy he'd felt in the garden that long ago afternoon lingered within him still to this day. When he was young, he'd believed the flood of energy he'd experienced was the force of life, something pure and good, and that was what brought the bird back from unconsciousness or maybe even death.

"What are you looking at?" Mary asked. He spun around, jolted out of his memories. For a moment, Mary sounded like his mother. "Nothing. I was daydreaming."

She ran a finger across a dusty dresser and looked around. "I haven't been up here in years. I kicked your butt almost everyday in Stratego up here."

He laughed and rolled his eyes. "Oh, please."

"Any day, any time," she challenged. She pulled her keys out of her pocket. On her key chain was a gold-painted Stratego piece, the piece with the number '1' on it. She dangled it in his face.

"I can't believe you still have that," he said shaking his head, attempting not to be bothered by it.

"I am the champion." She grinned proudly. "And the champion gets to keep the trophy. Loser," she mumbled. He sat on his bed and smirked. He bent over and slid the game of Stratego out from beneath the bed. "Let's do it."

Mary threw off her coat and pulled the dusty sheet away from the desk. They placed their pieces on the board with canny and calculating concentration. After the last pieces were in place, they glared at each other like two heavyweight fighters about to do battle for the championship title belt.

"I want that trophy back," he demanded.

"Come and get it," she said, motioning with her hands invitingly. Allen made his move.

*   *   *

There was a knock at the door.

"Yes," Derrick said.

The Oval Office door opened. "Mr. President," the staff aide said, "The Secretary General is here."

"Please, send him in." He took one more look at the remaining minutes of twilight through the French doors

"Another beautiful day in paradise," Jordan Iblis said.

He turned around. "This is a pleasant surprise. Nice to see you again, Jordan." He crossed the room to shake hands.

"It's good to see you again, Mr. President." Jordan shook his hand and patted him on the back. "I'm sorry to hear about the peace talks."

"So am I. I got them to agree on a cease fire until your inspectors finish with the facility."

"The official statement is scheduled for next week," Jordan said. He gave Derrick a wink. "You've been cleared of all accusations. There's nothing in those warehouses that constitutes an infringement of the arms agreement."

"Great. I believe congratulations are in order. I heard the solution for the disarmament was agreed upon," he said fixing them drinks.

"Not everyone is aboard."

He handed Jordan a drink. "Who's not signing on?"

"Libya." He took a sip. "You make an excellent Martini, Mr. President." They clinked their glasses together.

"Thank you," Derrick said, enjoying his lemonade. "Why aren't they signing on? Is it the UN resolution I filed against them?" He knew they had an excuse. They always did.

"No, they didn't mention the inspection demands you made on their weapons facilities. They're saying they need more time to read over the proposal concerning the disarmament agreement.,"

"You sound unconvinced."

Jordan grinned. "I believe it has something to do with the two American journalists who disappeared from their prison over the weekend."

"How could two American journalists disappear from their prison when allegedly there were never two American journalists imprisoned there in the first place?"

"Good question." Jordan raised his glass again. "And the military was overseas simply for foreign aid," he added with a laugh.

"We're there to help."

"I saw Lieutenant Decker in Chad with the foreign aid teams," Jordan mentioned casually. "If I recall correctly, he's a SEAL."

He suppressed a smile. "Retired SEAL."

Jordan stirred his drink. "Does he know that?"

"Is the journalists thing the reason you're here?" he asked.

"Sort of." Jordan pulled a sheet of paper from a file. "I told the Libyans that I would investigate the situation."

"Is this official UN business?"

"This is an official UN questionnaire, so it must be official." The grin on Jordan's face suggested otherwise.

He glanced at the phone. "Do I need to call anyone?"

"No, I don't think so," Jordan said. "Let's just get started and see how it goes. First, did the United States conduct a military rescue mission in Libyan territory?"

Derrick wondered if he should call the attorney general.

"No," Jordan answered for him and jotted down the answer on the form. "Thank you, Mr. President for your time. I declare this investigation officially closed."

"I'm glad I could be of help."

They both smiled as Jordan returned the document to the file.

"Now, what needs to be done to get them to sign?"

"I'll pamper the bruised egos," Jordan said, "and we'll get back on schedule."

"Great. Let me know if you need anything from me."

"For starters, I wouldn't vacation in Libya," Jordan laughed. "I'll schedule a conference with the Libyans. We'll be ready to go by the end of the week."

Jordan left the president and headed for the vice president's office. "Let's get some lunch," he said, poking his head into her office.

"It's three o'clock in the afternoon," Shelly reminded him. She walked over and gave him a hug.

He gave her a wink and a suggestive grin. "You must be a little hungry."

"Well, I think I could have something," she said, blushing.

They walked down the hall.

"I just finished speaking with your boss," he said. "He's a very smart man." There was an undertone of admiration in his voice.

"I personally believe he's the best president this country has ever had. No president has done more for the American people. He started the disarmament agreement proposal that you so wonderfully handled." She touched his cheek affectionately. "He has the Israelis and the Palestinians talking peace. Real peace." she said as if she had the evidence to back up her statement.

"He's a little too goody-goody for me," Jordan said grinning.

They disappeared into the Lincoln room.

*   *   *

Allen was in the basement of the house searching through his father's file cabinets. The basement had become a cluttered storage place since he moved out. A noise at the window distracted him for a moment. Someone could be watching him and he wouldn't be able to tell because of the light in the room reflecting into the glass. He stared at the black square, wondering if someone was there, watching. A shiver ran through his body. He forced himself to ignore the window and the feeling of being watched.

He found his adoption papers and birth certificate. There was also a letter stating the final arrangements of the adoption. One of the stipulations was that he was never to see his birth mother again. His heart raced. The address of the adoption agency was on the letter, but more importantly, a woman's name appeared on all the documents; a name he heard his father mention on the telephone a number of times when he was a child. A noise at the basement window again brought him out of his thoughts. He stared at the blackness in the window, feeling again as if someone were watching him. He convinced himself it was just his imagination, but he decided to find Mary. She was upstairs in the den.

"I found a letter from an adoption agency," she said.

"So did I. Is there a woman's name on yours?"

"No."

"I found this document in the basement." He held it out. "It has a woman's name on it. We need to find her."

"It's in pretty bad shape."

"I can make out the name," he said tilting the document toward the light. "Sarah L. Rosenberg."

"I'll check the name and agency out tomorrow," Mary said, yawning and glancing at her watch. "It's after midnight. I need to get home."

"Do you want to crash here?"

"No, I need to get some things done. I'll talk to you tomorrow."

He walked her to the door.

"You're going to stay here tonight?" she asked.

"Yes."

"Turn on the alarm. I'll call you tomorrow."

"Goodnight."

"Goodnight." She walked down the stairs.

"Loser," he mumbled.

"I heard that."

He started to sing a modified melody from a song by the rock group, "Queen." "I am the champion, I am the champion, of the world."

"Very funny," she yelled before she ducked into her car.

He dangled the gold Stratego piece above his head so she could see it clearly before she pulled off down the driveway.

Chapter 12

Greg sat at his kitchen table having breakfast when he noticed the headline across his morning paper. In bold block letters the words read, "The Prophecy of Death." "When two Egyptian rulers visit the eagle's nest, and in the month when darkness equals light, a world leader, a man of God will fall."

One and a half billion computers had this prediction posted across their screens last night. Sean Carbon's Golden Calf Enterprises, the largest Internet portal in the world was responsible for the grim forecast. He read the GCE prediction in its entirety. He felt the prediction was important to him. Was he supposed to decipher it? No, it was a ploy, a publicity stunt, he believed. It was just another self-promoting gimmick by Carbon and GCE. But why did it feel ominous? Why did it feel like an omen? Why did he feel like the prediction was relevant to the president, his good friend Derrick?

*   *   *

Shelly Deanster marched down the hall toward the Oval Office, anger chiseled across her face. She ignored the morning greetings of several Secret Service agents as she breezed through the Oval Office entrance.

"Good morning, Shelly," Derrick welcomed.

She threw a newspaper on his desk. "What are we going to do about this?"

"About what?"

"About this." She pointed to the headline.

The headline read, "A Great Nation Mourns The Death of Its Leader" with a subtitle that read, "But, Who? And When?"

"I didn't see that one," Derrick said, picking up the paper. He smiled and threw it on a pile of other newspapers beside the wastebasket. "Freedom of speech and the press." He shook his head. "What a waste of ink and paper."

She looked down at the accumulating stack of newspapers. They all had similar headlines, but some predicted the leader to die would be an influential religious person. "This is a direct threat to the president of the United States," she fumed. "Something has to be done."

"We have our people looking into it as we speak," he said, flipping pages of a document on his desk. "These guys live for this kind of thing."

"Carbon and Golden Calf Enterprises must be crazy if they think they can make a prediction like this and get away with it."

"You need to relax, Shelly, before you pop an artery. GCE sales have been slow, so Carbon puts something like this out there on the net to boost profits. The media picks up on it and just like magic the sales pick up. It's hard to beat free advertising."

A knock on the door stopped Shelly's flow of exasperation. Derrick was handed a printout by one of his aides.

"What is it?" she asked.

"We have a hostage situation." His words were heavy with anxiety. He handed the printout to her.

"Oh my God." She took seat. "Libya."

A second aide entered with a file.

Derrick sighed. "It's a warehouse with missiles. UN inspectors also found chemical and biological weapons." He turned to an aide. "Get everyone in here."

Forty-five minutes later the Oval Office was crowded with the Chief of Staff, the Secretary of State, the Secretary of Defense, the director of the CIA, the president's NSA advisor and a handful of foreign and military advisors.

"Any demands coming out of Libya?" he asked.

"Not yet," the Chief of Staff said, working the telephones.

Derrick's face remained calm, but Shelly knew he grieved inside with every turn of events.

The Secretary of Defense hung up the phone. "Intelligence says they have reason to believe shots were fired in the building. And there may be three dead UN inspectors."

Shelly shook her head. "It's going bad fast. The peace talks have stalled, this idiot Carbon makes an assassination prediction which everyone knows is about you, and now a hostage situation in Libya, in a nuclear weapons facility."

Derrick sat down next to her. "How are you and Jordan getting along?

She glanced at him with a vacant stare. "What?"

"How are you and Jordan getting along?"

Her face relaxed and she smiled. "Good."

"See, it's not all bad."

*   *   *

Kelsy poured sugar into her coffee. "Thanks for meeting me."

"No problem," Mary said. She looked at the Naval Academy across Spa Creek. "I like this place."

Kelsy poured three more packets of sugar into her coffee. "I need to ask Allen a few questions or you can ask him for me."

"Are you all right?" she asked, noticing Kelsy had poured nearly ten packets of sugar in her coffee. "You sounded funny on the phone."

"Bob was murdered," Kelsy said, looking down at her coffee. "Shot in the head."

"Bob Joshski?"

Kelsy nodded.

"Damn, I'm sorry. What happened?"

"They said it was a robbery." Kelsy looked up from her coffee with uncertainty. "Something weird happened the day after."

"What?"

"NSA cleaned out his desk and computer files." Her tone was unmistakably full of fear and suspicion.

Mary gave her one of her famous stares of skepticism. "NSA cleaned out Bob's desk."

Kelsy nodded again, then glanced around the room and whispered. "There's something going on, Mary. It started with the investigation of Allen's file. I think someone doesn't want us snooping around in his past."

"Like the NSA?"

"Yes."

She gave her the look again. "Why?"

"I don't know," Kelsy said, irritated.

"So, what would Bob's death have to do with it?"

Kelsy took a drink of water and leaned in toward her. "My computer went down, so I used Bob's computer and his clearance number to get into the department's national data base to pull information up on Allen."

"Bob's death is a coincidence, and the NSA . . . well who the hell knows what they are up to? They're so paranoid they don't trust themselves. You're letting your imagination get the best of you."

"No, you don't understand. There's more. I asked William Daniels to look up a security code attached to Allen's file."

"The self-defense trainer from the Bureau?"

"He went to work for the Defense Department in tech security. I asked him to check the security code out. He died in a fire the next day. They said there was a gas leak in his house." Her eyes started to tear. "His wife and child were in the house."

"I'm sorry, Kelsy. I know the two of you were good friends." Kelsy had lost a coworker and a good friend within a week's time. She had every right to be shaken, but there was something else in her eyes Mary couldn't ignore—fear, bordering on terror. The fact that there was a security code from the Pentagon attached to Allen's file struck Mary as odd, but then again, she shouldn't be surprised by anything the Pentagon did.

A loud crash of plates and glass breaking across the floor filled the dining room. Kelsy nearly jumped out of her seat.

"Hey, it's all right. A waiter dropped some glasses."

Kelsy's blue eyes were unblinking. Intense fear swirled in the irises of her eyes. Mary had never seen her friend in this condition.

"Calm down," she said. "You need to relax."

"Someone broke into my apartment a couple of days ago, too. My so-called, 'guard-at-the-desk-high-security' apartment complex," she mumbled sarcastically.

"I want you to come and stay with me for a little while," Mary insisted.

"Do you think it's another coincidence?" Kelsy asked.

Mary didn't believe it was a coincidence, but she kept her thoughts to herself. "I think it's been a pretty crappy week for you."

*   *   *

Well after midnight, a small crowd remained in the jazz club tucked away in an alley in Georgetown. The smoky atmosphere had a blue tint from the stage lights. Seated in one of the dark corners were two men dressed in suits.

A man at the bar leaned in toward the bartender. "Isn't that Walter Web, the Speaker of the House?"

The bartender wiped the bar surface down with a rag. "Yup," he answered, never looking up.

"Cool. Is he a jazz fan?"

"He's in here at least once a week."

The man at the bar stood.

"I wouldn't do that," the bartender warned.

"Why?"

The bartender shot a glance at the wall behind the Speaker's table. Barely noticeable, two men stood watching like black panthers waiting to pounce on their prey from the shadows. "They don't like uninvited guests."

"I'm cool," the man said walking over. "I just want to say, 'what's up.'"

From the shadows a six foot three, two hundred twenty pound figure blocked his path. "Can I help you?" he rumbled.

"I just want to say 'hi' to the Speaker of the House. We're from the same state," he said, looking up at the Secret Service agent.

"I'll be happy to tell him for you."

He realized there was no chance in hell he was going to talk to the Speaker of the House, so he returned to his barstool.

"I told you," the bartender said.

The agent whispered into Walter Web's ear. The Speaker gave the man at the bar a smile and a wave.

The man waved back. "Cool," he said pleased.

The bartender shook his head.

Walter pulled out a cigarette. The man seated across from him lit it with a wooden matchstick that he made appear out of nowhere.

"You have to teach me that trick one day, Jordan."

"Sure, Walter." Jordan's face flickered with a golden glow from the burning match.

Speaker of the House Walter Web and the UN Secretary General, Jordan Iblis were the best of friends. Two years ago at a political fundraiser they met and discovered that they were both jazz fanatics. Ever since, they'd attempted to get together every other week to listen to some music.

"How's your girlfriend?"

Jordan extinguished the match with his fingers. "Good, for now. How's your boyfriend?"

"Hey, keep it down," Walter hushed him.

Jordan laughed. "Be proud, Walter. It's the twenty-first century."

"Very funny." He took a drag from his cigarette. "If that self-righteous Moore and the rest of those conservative zealots get wind of my private life, they'll find a way to get rid of me for sure."

"Your secret is safe with me," Jordan said grinning. He handed him a file. "Take a look at this for me, and tell me what you think."

"What is it?"

"Some ideas on how to run a more efficient government and a couple of foreign policy concepts."

"Why?"

"I'm writing a proposal of sorts, and I respect your opinion on these matters."

"Sure, Jordan," he said, feeling flattered.

Jordan reached into his coat pocket and pulled out a stainless steel cigar holder. It held four cigars and had a humidification system built in to keep them fresh. "Put that cigarette out and smoke something good," Jordan said, handing him a cigar.

He sniffed the cigar. "Very nice. Partagas 150, Signature Series."

Jordan smiled. "Cameroon wrapper," he said passing the cigar under his nose. "Aged for eighteen years. Rolled by Ramon Cifuentes in Santiago."

"You sure know how to treat a date," Walter said laughing.

"Tony. Doug." Jordan waved the Secret Service agents over. "Here," he said offering them the remaining two cigars.

The men looked at Walter, waiting for permission. He nodded, giving his consent.

"Thank you, Mr. Iblis," the agents said.

Tony pulled out a silver, soft-touch cigar cutter and clipped the ends of the four cigars.

"You guys are prepared," Jordan said.

"The government trains us to be ready for anything," Doug replied.

Jordan made a burning matchstick appear out of nowhere again.

"I love that trick," Walter said.

The two agents returned to their positions. The glowing orange tips of their cigars pierced the shadows.

"Thank you, Jordan," Walter said leaning back in his chair. "This is the best damn cigar I've ever had."

"Anytime, Walter."

Chapter 13

Allen was on his second glass of red wine. The document he'd discovered in the basement hadn't left his sight. He held, stared, and sometimes subconsciously rubbed the document like a magic lamp, hoping it might reveal hidden answers from his past. Sarah L. Rosenberg. Who was she? His birth mother? If so, why did she give him up? Did she have to? He thought about his mother; the one who raised him; the one who was always there; the one who loved him. The one he loved more than anyone. He leaned back on the wooden bench and gazed up through the glass ceiling of the conservatory.

The conservatory was the size of a modest single family home adjoined to the main house. The ceiling, east, west, and south walls were entirely constructed of glass, nearly three stories in height. It was one of his favorite places as a kid. It was great for playing hide and seek. Growing in the conservatory were mature dogwoods, blue spruces, pines, and three Japanese maples. The once finely manicured shrubs had grown wild, along with hundreds of ordinary and tropical plants, but somehow most had survived the years of neglect. Most likely, Jim the gardener had been sneaking in and tending to the plants. The half dozen waterfalls that once spilled into the ponds were dry and the tropical birds that harmonized with the cascading waters were gone. The serene peace of nature that once filled this room was now just empty silence. He could see himself as a young boy playing around the swimming pool with Mary and a group of other friends from the neighborhood. He missed those times; he missed his friends. He remembered a friend named Frank Sedona in particular. Frank was first generation American; his parents crossed over via freighter from Italy in the late fifties.

His eyes fixed on a marble birdbath near one of the maples and he slowly drifted back into the past. He was fourteen and he was riding his bike to Frank's house. He knocked on the screen door and a woman's voice invited him to enter, but he was already in.

"Frank will be down in a second, Allen. Would you like some Kool-Aid?" Frank's mother asked from the kitchen.

"Yes, please," he said, taking a seat on the couch.

She brought a glass of red Kool-Aid. "Here you go, Allen," she said with a tearful glance.

"Thanks, Mrs. Sedona. Are you all right?" She smiled slightly. "Yes, I'm fine," she said turning away.

He took a sip of his drink and a drop dripped on the floor. Staring at the tiny red dot on the tan carpet reminded him of something his mother always said. She was convinced a carpet cleaning company must have created Kool-Aid. He sat quietly on the couch watching Mrs. Sedona in the kitchen, rinsing the same glass continuously. The glass had cartoon figures painted on it.

Frank ran down the stairs and yelled to his mother. "I'm going out."

Allen thanked Mrs. Sedona, but she never looked up from the glass.

He and Frank rode their bikes side by side down the street under the canopy of hundred-year-old oaks.

"What's wrong with your Mom?"

"My sister's in the hospital," Frank answered. "She's really sick."

"What's wrong with her?"

"They don't know."

Allen's memories took him back to the hospital. He stood outside of Frank's little sister's hospital room, looking through a glass barrier at her. The pain and suffering on Frank's parents' faces flashed into his mind like an old heartache. He recalled Frank telling him about the experimental drugs the doctors used, but his sister wasn't responding as they'd hoped. He and Frank entered the room, Frank's hundredth painful time. He quietly thanked Allen for coming with him. Allen looked at the little five-year-old girl. She appeared tiny on the large white bed encircled with medical equipment. It was an awful sight seeing her little body surrounded by tubes and wires. The monitors and screens beeped and blinked with a dull, steady pulse.

Frank pulled out a thin, colorful book and started to read it aloud. It was *Cinderella,* her favorite book and Walt Disney movie. "Hang in there little Sis," he said after finishing the story. Before he left he touched her hand. "I'm tired of feeding your dumb goldfish, so hurry up and get better." His eyes filled with tears.

Before Allen followed Frank out of the room, he leaned against the bed and lowered his head in a praying manner. He gently held the little girl's hand. After a half a minute he stood and whispered into her ear. No sooner did the last word leave his lips than the alarms sounded. Nurses and doctors rushed into the little girl's room. Her signs started to improve dramatically. The color of her skin became healthy within seconds. She opened her eyes like a child waking from a pleasant nap. Frank's parents broke through the circle of medical personnel with tears of joy. Allen moved away from the crowd surrounding the little girl's bed and the clamor of optimism.

Frank stared astonished at the transformation in his little sister. When the shock finally wore off he walked over to Allen. "What did you say to her?"

"Get well," he said quietly. "Why?"

Frank looked for a moment at his sister, who appeared to have never been ill. "Man, if I ever get sick, make sure you tell me to get well," he said, laughing. He pushed through the crowd of nurses and doctors to welcome his little sister back to the world of the living.

Allen stood off to the side watching the joyous scene. He overheard one of the doctors say that the medication must have finally started to work. The memory faded.

"Allen, what are you doing?" Mary asked, walking into the conservatory.

"Thinking about Frank Sedona and his little sister."

"What in the world made you think about them?"

"I don't know. Have you seen Frank or Amy lately?"

"I saw Amy last year," Mary said. "She's a surgeon at Prince George's Hospital."

"How about Frank?"

"Haven't seen him."

"I wonder what he's up to?" She threw some papers onto a black cast-iron table next to Allen. "I need you to sign these, so I can get your records from the hospital."

He glanced up at her. "I already got them. They're on the dining room table, but they were no help."

"The adoption agency on the document we found never existed."

"What does that mean?" he asked.

"That there was a mistake on the information, or the document is a fake."

He shook his head, his disappointment, deep.

Mary sat next to him on the bench. "I'll keep checking it out. I do have some good news. I have an appointment with Sarah L. Rosenberg."

That made him more optimistic. "How did you find her?" She looked at him. "That's what I do." She sounded offended.

"Where is she?"

"Florida."

"Perfect. I was invited to speak at a convention in Pensacola on Sunday. We can stop on the way back home."

"Great," she said sarcastically.

*   *   *

A horn from a distant passing car blared, but Kelsy heard it clearly because she was wide-awake. She had been unable to sleep for days. Maybe she should have taken Mary up on the invitation to stay at her place. Mary had insisted that the death of her friends, the break-in at her apartment, and the other suspicious occurrences were all coincidences. But Kelsy could feel in her gut that there was something bad happening, something real bad. The telephone rang and she nearly jumped out of her skin.

"Hello," she answered, eyes wide and alert.

"Kelsy Anderson?" The caller almost whispered.

The glowing green numerals on the clock that read 2:15 A.M "Yes, who is this?".

"A friend."

"Who is this?" she demanded.

"That's not important."

"It's customary that friends know each other's names."

"You can call me . . ." The caller hesitated. "Call me James."

Could this be a childish prank or was it connected to the conspiracy? Or was it just another coincidence for the list?

"You have or you will have in your possession something that will put your life in danger." James sounded dead serious.

She sat up in bed. "What?"

"Something they will kill for. But you all ready know that, don't you?"

She didn't say anything for a moment while she gathered her thoughts. "Bob and William were murdered because they knew something. Is that what you're saying?"

"I'm not one who believes in coincidences."

"Who broke into my house?"

"I have to go," he said hurriedly.

"Why?"

"They may be listening."

She got out of bed. "How do you know?"

"Check your phone."

"Wait," she said urgently. "Who are, 'they'?" She glanced out her sixth floor apartment window.

"Don't trust anyone," James warned.

"Does that include you?"

"Trust no one."

The telephone clicked, followed by a dial tone. She stared at her phone. She examined it carefully, then slid the cover off where the batteries were installed. There was a tiny black device the size of a pencil eraser stuck to the inside. Her stomach tightened with the thought of someone listening to her conversations. She felt sick. She pulled the tiny device out, laid it on the desk, and picked up a paperweight. It was a smooth, beautiful river stone with an inscription on it that read, "The Lord is my rock and my fortress and my deliverer. She delivered a crushing blow to the device, sending pieces in every direction. Someone out there got an ear load of smack. She bent one of the horizontal blinds and peeked at the street below. It may have been a mistake to destroy the device. Now they would know she was on to them, whoever the hell "they" was. She couldn't see anyone on the street, but she could feel someone watching her. But they weren't listening anymore. She returned to bed, but not before she went to the closet and dusted off her gun. She pulled the weapon from its holster and placed it beneath the extra pillow beside her.

Chapter 14

Mary sat in the Caffeine Bean Café in Georgetown, observing Mr. Pig eating his breakfast in a diner across the street. *This guy's a heart attack in the making,* she thought, watching him devour a plate laden with cholesterol and grease.

Yesterday, she had reported to the suspicious wife that she hadn't been able to gather any hard evidence concerning another woman. The wife gave her an optimistic pep-talk and encouraged her to carry on with the investigation. She considered telling her about the other *man,* but decided against it, feeling it wasn't the right time to drop the gay husband theory on her.

She neatly folded her *USA Today,* which she hadn't read a word of, and placed it on the table. She'd hid behind it most of the morning, pretending to be deeply engrossed. She took a sip of her regular, everyday plain coffee. The café had sixty-eight types of coffee to choose from; she stuck to the standard bean, and drank it black with a couple hits of sugar. She continued to watch out of the large plate glass window. She remembered the hundreds of times before when she sat, watched, and waited for suspects to make a move. Many of those times were spent with a partner.

She thought back to when she was an FBI agent and Edward Holt was her partner. A six-foot bulky cowboy raised in south Texas who loved anything barbecued, he was a good man, a family man, and one hell of an agent.

"We got him," Ed had said, taking pictures of two men having a conversation.

The man she and Ed were interested in was Jack Copper; that was the name he was using this week. He was average height, average weight, and plain-faced. He blended into a crowd with ease, a perfect asset in his line of work. Espionage. He was a double operative working both sides of the pond. Copper was having a tête-à-tête with a man who wore an over-priced suit and appeared to be from the Middle East. Mary was confident he had a large checkbook, too.

"They're making it easy for us," she said.

"This bust should get us some major brownie points with the director," Ed said, grinning as he snapped more shots from a hundred yards away.

"Arrogant. Right in the open, in the middle of the day."

Ed smiled. "That's why he's going to jail."

Three weeks later on a rainy night, she was on a roof with a listening device, four floors above the alley, prepared to monitor a transaction in a warehouse. Ed was down on the street taking pictures through a broken window, perfectly positioned between two large green dumpsters. She glanced at her watch. "Where the hell are you Copper, I have a schedule to keep." They had been on surveillance for five hours and she was beginning to get antsy. No sooner did the thought pass, than headlights flooded the far side of the warehouse.

"Show time," she said into her transmitter. Ed gave her a wave, acknowledging her transmission. She noticed a figure in the shadows approaching him from the south. It was Jack Copper. Why in the hell was he coming down the alley? Damn, had he been tipped off? Her thoughts raced; her heart skipped a beat and her eyes darted back and forth from Ed to Copper. It seemed Copper hadn't seen him yet. She tried to contact Ed, but he must have turned off his radio or the rain had fouled up the transmission. Copper pulled something out from beneath his trench coat. She drew her weapon and yelled Ed's name, trying to get him to turn around. Ed heard the footsteps behind him; he spun and drew his gun in one fluid movement, but it was too late. A single twelve-gauge slug blasted into his chest, catapulting him off his feet and onto his back.

Mary unloaded her 9mm at Copper, catching him twice in the shoulder before he fell behind a dumpster. She wanted him alive. She dropped the empty clip and reloaded. Copper had started down the alley with her bullets closely trailing. She needed him alive; she needed to put a bullet in one of his legs, but he disappeared around a corner before collecting any more lead in his body. From four floors above she looked down at the horrifying sight. Under the streetlight, the blood oozed out like black oil from beneath Ed's body, circling him in death. Two men exited the warehouse and one grabbed Ed's camera. She took aim and yelled, identifying herself as FBI. The two men ran and fired at her. She returned fire; bullets sparked against the pavement and shots echoed off the concrete buildings. When the smoke cleared, one man lay motionless a few yards from Ed's body. The other man had fled down the alley. She stood numbed with dismay, stunned by the nightmare that had unfolded before her eyes.

The siren of a police car on M Street snapped her out of her thoughts. Mr. Pig finished his heart attack special at the diner and a couple hours later he was having lunch in Baltimore with an Asian gentleman. He had another cardiac favorite, the type of meal that flowed through the arteries like Beltway traffic at five-thirty in the afternoon. After a long lunch he returned to D.C. at 4:10 and disappeared into a telecommunications company owned by the government. She parked a block away and waited through an uneventful forty minutes before calling it a day.

She threw her keys onto the table in her apartment and headed for the kitchen. She stuffed a slice of lime into her beer and hit the answering machine before collapsing on the couch. The machine played a message from the suspicious wife seeking new information on her husband. She tossed her logbook on the floor. She would tell the wife later about the breakfast in Georgetown and the lunch date in Baltimore with a man he'd encountered twice before. The machine continued. The next message was from Kelsy. She claimed she was doing fine and she would call back later, but she was unable to mask the stress in her voice. She made a mental note to call Kelsy as soon as possible. She wondered about Allen and why he hadn't called.

She debated whether to tell the suspicious wife about Mr. Pig's relationship with the other man. After a couple of beers, she decided against it; she would wait and get more physical evidence.

She could be wrong. It was his job to meet with people. In motels with the same man though? *Don't think so.* She noted in the logbook that Mr. Pig's name wasn't checking out with her background search. She wrote herself a reminder to ask a friend at the Bureau to search the name and to ask the suspicious wife for more information on her husband. She threw the logbook onto the floor again and grabbed the remote control.

"Welcome to the show, Mr. Carbon." The host greeted him with a smile. "It's a pleasure to have you here today."

An African-American man appeared on Mary's television screen. He was athletically built with a shaved head, tightly groomed goatee, and wore a very expensive suit. He was a good-looking man who appeared comfortable in front of the cameras.

Mary shook her head and rolled her eyes at the sight of him.

"Thank you for having me," Carbon said with a millionaire's smile.

The host talked about how Carbon had lost his parents at an early age and was raised by an aunt in Baltimore, how he had no formal education but still managed to build the largest and most lucrative Internet portal on the planet, known as Golden Calf Enterprises.

"Nice ring," Carbon said.

The host of the program had a medium-width gold band on his finger, with "GCE" in gold, in a black setting. It was unpretentious and simple, but tastefully crafted. Each GCE member received a ring after a certain number of hours were logged in or a specific total of merchandise was purchased. But it was not unheard of for new members to receive a ring as a gift, simply for signing on to the service.

The host smiled. "I've been on-line since the beginning."

"Great."

The host tugged on his Armani suit toward the camera. "Thirty percent off from GCE."

Carbon laughed. "Nice suit. And I appreciate the plug for the company."

Mary was anxious to change the channel, but as were the other million or so viewers watching the program, she wanted to hear what Carbon was going to say about the prediction. Predicting the death of a nation's leader had made him headline news, and Mr. Notorious.

The host became serious. "I understand this is your sixteenth talk show in three days. Has the prediction hurt Golden Calf Enterprises?"

"No, it hasn't."

"Is Golden Calf Enterprises bankrupt?"

"I assure you, GCE is far from being bankrupt."

"Is GCE being investigated for criminal activity?"

"No."

"Rumors say that the Platinum Club is a drug ring and the FBI and the ATF are investigating it. Is here any truth to that?" The host fired question after question.

Carbon crossed his legs, knee over knee and smiled. "They haven't contacted me."

"What about the accusations concerning your Empire Mall," the host asked, reading from his card, "the virtual reality shopping mall on the Internet that has been accused of supplying virtual reality prostitution?"

Carbon grinned. "I do say we sell everything. It appears that I'm not going to be able to say that anymore."

"May I read something to you?"

"It's your show."

"'We believe that there's a secret membership within Gold Calf Enterprise, and those members are offered a virtual reality body suit that was made specifically for the prostitution experience.' That is a direct quote from an article in the *Washington Post*. The reporter was interviewing a federal agent," the host said.

"A VR body suit?" Carbon asked amazed.

"Yes. With this suit on one can experience the realism of touch all over his or her body."

Carbon's eyebrows arched. "I have heard of something like that before, but I know we at GCE don't have a VR body suit. But I'll start working on it," he added smirking. "Of course, we will use it for other forms of entertainment."

"So, it's not true?" the host asked.

"Sorry, not true."

"Is the government investigating you because of the prediction?"

"Yes. They believe the prediction GCE made was directed at the president of the United States."

"Was it?"

"No."

"He is a leader of a great nation."

"True."

"That would make him a target."

"He qualifies."

"So, it could be directed at President Moore?" the host badgered.

"Sure."

"What if the prediction doesn't come true? That you're wrong."

"That would be fine with me. I've been wrong before."

"The Y2K debacle?"

"Yes." For the first time a hint of discomfort settled into Carbon's posture. He became sincere. "If being wrong saves a life, then I pray that I'm wrong."

"Thank you, Mr. Carbon for clearing up some of the rumors."

"My pleasure."

Mary threw the remote control to the floor. "Give me a break."

*　　*　　*

The White House

Derrick put the phone down and spun his chair around to look out at the White House grounds, hoping the scenery would ease the sinking feeling in his gut. The call informed him the hostage situation had taken a turn for the worse. Intelligence believed there were biological and offensive warheads in the warehouse, but that was yet to be confirmed. He was determined not to allow himself to panic. The Libyan government was blaming an underground Afghani group, who splintered from the main government body, for the hostage situation, but no terrorist group or government had claimed responsibility. His heart pounded in his chest. He couldn't escape the thought of a disastrous conclusion to the hostage situation. If biological weapons were there, what would they do with them? And what do they want? The questions continued to pound away.

The Secretary of Defense and a CIA analyst entered the Oval Office holding a file Derrick had been waiting anxiously for. The information in the file would help determine the level of devastation the hostage situation could have on the world. He was about to discover if he had a possible international panic of nuclear proportions on his hands.

"This is the chain of events up to this point." The Secretary of Defense started to read. "During the inspection of one of the Libyan facilities, a nuclear device was discovered; fifteen nuclear warheads." The Secretary looked up at him. "One homemade dirty bomb. May be chemical or biological. Specifications unknown."

His eyes closed and his shoulders sagged with the confirmation.

The Secretary of Defense continued mechanically. "A group of men impersonating warehouse workers and UN inspectors immediately seized the facility. All exits and means of communications from the building were secured. Intelligence estimates twenty-four to twenty-six bodies in the building, six United Nations inspectors, three American inspectors, ten warehouse laborers and five to seven unidentified persons. Latest satellite photographs confirmed warheads and twenty-six live bodies. Unofficially."

"How in the hell did this happen?" Derrick simmered with disbelief and exasperation. "I thought we were watching?"

"I don't know, sir."

He threw an invoice sheet on the desk. "We knew about the two MIM-14s for high altitude and long-range intercepting, and twenty Patriots to defend against ballistic missiles and anti-aircraft weapons," he read from the invoice printout. He leaned back into his chair and studied the aerial photographs of the warehouse taken from a satellite. The infrared images of blues, reds, blacks, and greens revealed twenty-six bodies in the warehouse. The red glow from the occupant's body heat confirmed the count. The next set of photos corroborated the data of nuclear warheads in the warehouse. He was unable to refute their existence, and the potential destruction on his hands. "We've been watching them with everything we've got." He mumbled like a man who had just witnessed the most amazing magical trick. "Is there any communication between the terrorists and the arbitrators?"

"None, as of the last hour," the CIA analyst answered.

"Are we mobile?"

"We're monitoring the skies."

"And the Israelis?'

"They're aware of the situation."

How is this thing going to end? jumped into his head like a sudden migraine.

The mood in the room had become rigid and tense.

"What do they want?" he asked.

"Sir," the CIA analyst said tentatively. "I believe you were correct in your earlier assumption. It may be a ploy to further disrupt the UN's inspection tours."

"Then they've succeeded." He was renowned for his patience and composed temperament, but now he had been forced into a military position.

An NSA advisor rushed into the office holding a printout. "The Libyan negotiators claim that they were informed by a correspondent that there was gun fire in the warehouse and a hostage was killed. They also say they intercepted a transmission from the facility. They believe the terrorists are working with an outside party." He handed the printout to Derrick. "The terrorists and the outside party spoke to one another in Russian."

"Russian?" the Secretary of Defense said. "What the hell are they doing in this?"

"We were unable to pinpoint the outside party's transmission location," the NSA advisor said.

"Do we know who was shot?" Derrick asked.

"No."

"What was the conversation about?"

The NSA advisor took a breath. "Coordinates."

"Coordinates for what?" the Secretary of Defense blurted out.
"Israel."

"Christ," the analyst mumbled.

Derrick's head filled with more questions. Were they bluffing? Was it a trick? Were they attempting to turn us on the Russians? Were they trying to start a finger-pointing game? He felt the questions pounding him like hammers to the back of the head. He walked down the hall and knocked on the vice president's office door.

Shelly and Jordan were having coffee when he entered. They stood simultaneously, apparently surprised by the visit.

"Derrick, what's wrong?" Shelly asked.

"The offensive nuclear warheads were confirmed. There may also be a dirty bomb."

Shelly gasped and Jordan shook his head.

"May I ask you something, Jordan?"

"Of course, Mr. President."

"It's about the hostage situation. Have you heard anything negative from the Russians concerning our involvement with the UN's inspections?"

"No."

"What's going on?" Shelly asked, getting him a cup of coffee.

"The Libyan officials intercepted a transmission between the terrorists and an outside group."

"Who?" Shelly asked.

"We're not sure. The terrorists and the other party spoke in Russian."

"Russian?" Jordan asked with a calm, inquiring stare.

"What does that mean?" Shelly asked.

"Things are getting messy," Derrick said. He rubbed his temples. "Right in the middle of the Israeli-Palestinian peace treaty effort. I'm trying to re-establish the peace talks treaty. Now this."

"Could this be a diversion?" Jordan asked.

"Stage a hostage situation while you move and hide the real weapons," Derrick said.

"It's possible," Jordan agreed.

Chapter 15

Annapolis, Md.

Allen and Kelsy sat at a small table outside of Maria's, an Italian restaurant on the corner of Pinkney Street. The restaurant removed the tables from the sidewalk during the cold season, but the warm March day had made dining outdoors pleasant and irresistible. The red brick sidewalks of the City Dock were increasing with foot traffic with every rising degree, and next door, Middleton Tavern and McGarvey's were quickly filling up with lunch crowds.

The waiter arrived and placed bottled water and an iced tea on the green tablecloth. "Would you like to order, now?"

"We're waiting on a friend," Kelsy said.

The green and white striped canopy flapped in the unseasonably warm breeze. Allen took in a deep and fresh breath of air. "Nice day," he said gazing outward in the general direction from where Mary would be approaching.

"Beautiful," Kelsy agreed.

He ordered a glass of wine and a fresh calamari appetizer to help pass the time.

"Why haven't you and Mary ever dated?" Kelsy asked.

The question surprised him, but he maintained a poker face while he searched for a response.

"Sorry." Kelsy smiled. "Is the question too personal?"

"No." He reached for his glass of wine. "We're too close," he finally answered.

"Too close?"

"Too good of friends."

Kelsy stared with a shifty grin.

"What?"

"I find it strange that the two of you never hooked up."

"Men and women can be just friends."

"If the woman wants it that way."

He caught a glimpse of Mary approaching from Main Street. "Mary's coming," he announced with some relief, welcoming a subject change.

Mary pulled up one of the small metal chairs. "People cannot drive down here. They should make you pass a special test before you're allowed to drive in town."

Kelsy ignored her complaining. "Why haven't you and Allen ever dated?"

"We're too close," Mary answered nonchalantly, waving the waiter over. "Too good of friends."

"That's what I told her," Allen said.

"So, what's the problem?" Mary asked. She ordered a Corona. "Have you ordered yet?"

"No, we were waiting on you, *again*," Kelsy said.

Mary ordered first. "I'll have the linguini pomidore."

"I'll have a salad," Kelsy said when it was her turn.

He ordered the eggplant parmigiana.

Mary looked at Kelsy. "Are you on a diet again?"

"Again?"

"Yeah, again."

When women talk about their weight or age Allen's tenet had been to listen and then listen some more. Stay out of it at all cost.

"You're becoming obsessive about your weight," Mary said. "Always trying to lose those mysterious five pounds."

"That's not true."

"You're the only person I know who checks the fat and calorie count on toothpaste and Tylenol."

Allen laughed.

"You're a real piece of work," Kelsy said, tossing a balled-up napkin at her.

Mary looked at him. "She wouldn't take NyQuil one night because it didn't have the nutrition facts on the bottle. She was convinced it was too fattening."

"Very funny," Kelsy scoffed. "So, the two of you never dated because you're best friends," she pried, refusing to let it go. "You don't want to ruin your friendship, is that it?"

"We're not interested in each other that way." He glanced at Mary for concordance.

Kelsy gawked at Mary.

Mary studied her for a moment. "Kelsy, do you want to date Allen? Is that what this is all about?" He felt himself redden a bit.

"No," Kelsy answered.

Mary intensified her stare. "Are you sure?" It seemed she was attempting to make her a little more uncomfortable.

"Yes, I'm sure."

He attempted to hide his grin, knowing Mary's tactics well. She had an uncanny ability to turn the tables on anyone. She was the master cross-examiner.

"Because it's just fine with me," she continued. "If you want to date him."

Kelsy shifted uncomfortably in her chair.

"Are you feeling awkward yet?" Mary asked.

"You're so touchy lately," Kelsy mumbled.

"Lately?" Allen blurted out. "Since birth."

Kelsy changed the subject. "Why are you going to Florida?"

Mary handed her a piece of paper. "We're going to meet someone named Rosenberg. Apparently, she has something to do with Allen's birth and the adoption document we found at his parents' house."

Kelsy looked over the sheet of paper. "Do you want me to check it out, too?"

"See what you can find," Mary said. "And be careful. You were right. We did attract some attention. I'm pretty sure someone broke into my apartment."

"Strange," Allen said. "I think someone also broke into the house."

"They bugged my phone," Kelsy whispered.

"What?" Mary asked.

"Someone bugged my phone."

"How did you find out?"

"I got a call in the middle of the night from some guy who told me my phone was tapped."

"It was probably him who bugged it," Mary said suspiciously. "Trying to get your trust."

"That's what I think."

"What's going on?" he asked.

Kelsy gave Mary a look. "You didn't tell him?"

"Tell me what?" He could feel a dark undertone to the conversation.

Mary avoided eye contact for a moment. "I think two people were murdered because . . ." she hesitated. "Because we're checking out your past."

"What? Why?"

"That's what we're trying to find out." Kelsy took a long drink, finishing her water.

"Two people died because of me?" he said.

"We're not entirely sure yet. It could be a coincidence."

He wasn't taking the current development very well and realized Mary was trying to soften the blow.

Kelsy must have also realized it. "Mary's right, it may be a coincidence." She didn't sound very convincing or convinced.

"Someone breaks into our homes and your phone's bugged, that's no coincidence," he said. "All of our phones are probably bugged. Someone doesn't want us poking our noses in my past."

The waiter arrived with their food. "Buon appetito," he said before disappearing into the building.

Kelsy and Mary picked at their food aimlessly.

His mind had gone into computing mode, launching questions off in rapid fire. He focused on a white cross protruding over the buildings in the distance from a local chapel. *Was it a coincidence?* He hoped an all-knowing voice would answer "yes." *If they were killed, who murdered them?* The answer his mind provided terrified him.

Chapter 16

Jordan Iblis noticed the two Secret Service agents enter the restaurant. They scrutinized the room, then headed toward him at his isolated table in the rear of the restaurant.

"The vice president will be with you in a moment, Mr. Iblis," the agent said.

Jordan finished his second mixed drink and his sixth telephone conversation while waiting for Shelly. He had become accustomed to waiting for her, as she had with him. "She's out there campaigning again, isn't she?" he asked half-smiling.

The agent grinned. "Of course."

Two more agents had had already scanned the floor area for weapons with handheld devices that looked similar to Dust-Busters. It was a new device able to register gunpowder and other explosive material onto a readout screen. Jordan was familiar with it. More familiar than he wanted to be. The device itself was named the Explosives Detector, ED for short, but was warmly regarded by the agents as "Peeping Tom." When ED was aimed at an object or person, the band of electromagnetic radiation waves fed the gadget information, and it was quickly analyzed by crystal detectors in a scintillator. Within milliseconds the data was converted electronically into cross-sectional images onto the display screen. Information about the targeted material would register on the screen identifying the level of threat.

The agent near him pointed Peeping Tom at a young couple having lunch. The screen immediately registered hydrocarbons from the paraffin series. The substances were in the vicinity of the male subject's coat pocket. The information was instantaneously analyzed and the ED quickly determined there wasn't a substantial amount of material to be a threat. "Cigarette lighter," the agent whispered to him.

Another agent entered the restaurant followed by Shelly. She shook hands and smiled politely with people on her way to his table.

"Hello, Jordan," she said giving him a kiss on the cheek.

He slid the chair out for her. "I ordered you a glass of wine."

"Thank you."

An agent walked by with the Explosive Detector.

"I see Peeping Tom is hard at work," Jordan said.

"We don't leave home without him."

Suddenly, a high pitched sound came from the ED, warning the agent of potential danger.

"I'm sorry, Mr. Iblis," the agent said.

"Again?" Shelly asked, irritated.

"It's all right, honey."

One of the agents searched him.

"I don't understand it," the agent holding the device said. "ED goes crazy around Mr. Iblis."

The agent finished the search. "Thank you. Again, Mr. Iblis, I'm sorry."

"It's really all right."

Shelly gave the agent a weary look. "Get it fixed."

"Yes, ma'am."

"I'm in the mood for some crab dip. Would you like some?" she asked looking over the menu.

"I would love some," he said reaching for her hand. "How's the day going so far?"

"It's getting better by the minute." Her tone sweetened.

The waiter arrived and Jordan ordered for them. Shelly squinted her eyes attempting to see across the room. She put on her glasses and gawked at a man seated in the lobby of the restaurant.

"What is it?"

"That looks like Greg," she said excitedly.

"Greg who?"

"Professor Greg Orfordis."

He was pleasantly surprised. "Oh really?"

"Do you know him, too?"

"I know his work."

She instructed one of the agents to ask Greg to join them, and a few moments later, he did.

"Shelly, how are you?" he asked, taking hold of her hands.

"Fine." She turned to Jordan. "Jordan, I'd like you to meet a very good friend of mine. This is Professor Gregory Orfordis."

He stood and extended his hand. "Very nice to meet you."

"Greg, this is Jordan Iblis." She leaned in close to Greg. "My boyfriend," she whispered.

"It's nice to meet you, Mr. Iblis."

"Please, join us," Jordan said.

"Here you go, Greg." Shelly pulled out a chair.

"I'm meeting a friend for lunch."

"You can sit with us until your lunch companion shows," Shelly suggested.

"Thank you." He gave Shelly a warm smile. "The two of you have become quite the media darlings."

Shelly blushed. "They turned it into a soap opera."

"I enjoyed your last book, Professor," Jordan said.

"Thank you."

"A lot of people thought you were crazy. You put your reputation on the line."

"What men think of my reputation doesn't concern me," Greg said staring into his eyes.

Jordan grinned. "My favorite part is your theory on spiritual evilness and its hands-on involvement in corrupting the world," he said with a genuine interest in the subject. "Your hypothesis on the devil cloaking himself in human flesh and interacting in the physical realm is fascinating."

"What do you think Mr. Iblis," Greg asked. "Is the devil among us?"

He laughed. "Oh, I feel I'm not qualified to comment on such matters."

"Please, Mr. Iblis," Greg urged. "I'm confident your opinion is no less worthy of any other view I've heard."

Jordan took a long sip from his drink. "Promise not to laugh. I believe the devil and evil have become a scapegoat of sorts. A reason, an excuse, or an explanation for what is human nature. Humanity is unable to accept the horrendous acts that it does to one another, so they attempt to shift the blame." His smooth, rational and rhythmic tone was hypnotic. "Mankind has always had a difficult time accepting their human nature. So, humanity blames an intangible being or force for their behavior. 'The devil made me do it' mentality."

It was Shelly who replied. "This is a side of you I've never seen before. If you believe the devil doesn't exist, you must not believe God exists."

"Not true, honey," he answered.

"I certainly believe God exists. He created everything, including us, and we screwed it up. It's just in our nature; we're greedy, territorial, selfish, and deceptive. We can't help it. It's not totally our fault. All of these wonderful attributes are human, part of our blueprint." A slight hint of sarcasm passed his lips. "We love war; hate and prejudice comes naturally, and we try to control everything. It's what we are."

"What about the love, hope, and compassion in us?" Shelly asked.

"That's the influence of God in us," Jordan answered. "We know God, we just don't know we know God."

Greg spoke up. "When you say we can't help ourselves, we can't control our actions, are you saying there's no free will? That we're a product of our genetic makeup? Preprogrammed?"

"Some call it predestined, fate, or destiny, but that's not what I'm talking about." Jordan continued. "We think we have free will, but we don't. We lust, hoard, and covet materialist wealth. We don't choose to be that way, it's just in our nature. Things like love, compassion, tolerance, and sympathy are instilled in us when we're young. Reprogramming. We have to be taught to share and be polite. We're brainwashed to feel guilty if we're not charitable and help the needy. In reality, we're naturally self-serving. We're a survival-of-the-fittest kind of species."

Shelly had a shell-shocked expression.

"Don't worry, honey." Jordan took hold of her hand. "God will straighten us all out one day," he said as if he truly believed it. "For now, we can enjoy the pleasures of humanity."

His optimistic attitude returned a smile to her face. She needed it.

"That's true, Shelly," Greg said, staring at Jordan. "God will straighten us all out. Some more than others."

"One of the secret service agents approached the table. "Professor Orfordis, your lunch companion called and said she's going to be late."

"Thank you." Greg called a waiter and ordered a salad.

"What do you think of this Carbon character?" Jordan asked, changing the subject.

"I think he's a very powerful and influential man," Greg answered.

"I think he should be arrested," Shelly snapped.

"Now, now, Shelly," Jordan said. "He hasn't broken any laws."

"Threatening the president isn't a crime?"

"That's your interpretation," he said with a smile. "What do think of his prediction, Professor?"

"I believe it's going to sell many newspapers and memberships."

Jordan smiled. "He says it's a warning. It may save a leader's life."

"Right!" Shelly said cynically.

"I'm not sure what he's up to," Greg said. "But I'm sure it's self serving."

"What about Golden Calf Enterprises?" Jordan asked.

"I think his Internet business is a technological marvel and a great leap forward for the communication industry."

"And the cons?" Jordan asked, sensing the indecision of Greg's previous answer and feeling Greg also had a negative opinion on the subject.

"It has created a greater form of neglect."

"What do you mean?" Shelly asked.

"The program of GCE is a time-consuming activity," Greg explained, "which in turn means the user is sacrificing something else to be on the GCE program. That something could be time from family and friends. People could easily begin to neglect duties concerning school, home and employment because they've become absorbed in the virtual reality world of GCE. The program could create a hermetical generation. A generation living and working in cyberspace, creating a secluded existence with no human contact, living in a world with no real physical stimulation. I believe that is a dangerous path."

"The population rate would certainly drop," Shelly said.

"No real physical stimulation." Jordan gave her an erotic glance. "I don't like that."

"The program could become one's addiction," Greg said. "A person could lose touch with reality."

"I see your point," he said. "But there are many beneficial facets to consider. There would be less traffic on the roads, which means fewer accidents, a cut back on insurance, less fuel used, easing the demand on oil, and of course, less air pollution. When a customer shops at the virtual reality mall there are no parking problems, no fear of being robbed, no crowds to fight through, and the prices are always discounted, so the average consumer saves money. That adds up to more spending, creating a healthy economy."

"Don't forget road rage and stress in general would lower," Shelly said. "But, like everything, moderation is the key."

"I'll drink to that," Jordan said. "And to good old-fashioned stimulation." He raised his glass.

Greg saw his friend entering the restaurant and excused himself from the table. "It was very nice to meet you, Mr. Iblis." They shook hands again.

He smiled crookedly. "I look forward to seeing you again, Professor."

"You will." Greg grinned back. "Very soon."

The two men locked eyes, acknowledging the rivalry between them, very much like two heavyweight boxers touching gloves in the center of the ring before going toe-to-toe.

Greg turned to Shelly and hugged her. "I'll call you soon."

Chapter 17

"Flight 201 to Orlando is now boarding at gate six," the voice over the intercom announced.

Mary downed her second mixed drink and grabbed her carry-on bag. It was unheard of for her to drink early in the morning, but Allen kept his thoughts to himself. They headed down the terminal and found their seats on the plane. She sat quietly and fidgeted with a folded map of Orlando in her lap but her tension was evident.

"Are you all right?" he finally asked.

She shrugged her shoulders. "Yeah," she mumbled, looking around the airplane.

"What's up?"

She shook her head, suggesting she would rather not talk about it.

He gave her a half smile. "Come on, I'm your buddy," he said nudging her shoulder with his own.

After a minute of playful harassment she eventually broke down. "I have this thing about flying," she said avoiding eye contact.

"Since when?"

She didn't answer.

"Is it the terrorist thing?"

She hesitated for a long time. "No," she eventually answered.

"Then what?"

"All those plane crash specials." She sounded almost embarrassed.

He realized she was talking about the programs on the Learning Channel that attempted to explain why airplanes crashed, or reenacted past tragedies. Recently, a plane had gone down in Europe killing two hundred and fifty people. The educational channels immediately followed the catastrophe with plane crash specials all day and night. Mary, like so many others, was addicted to the History Channel, the Discovery Channel, and any other channel of that nature. In most cases, that was not a bad thing, but there was a drawback: over-education. In some cases, "What you don't know can't hurt you" was golden. And that held true when it came to sharks, insects, diseases, and plane crashes. The less you knew, the better off you were. Especially the many types of bugs that lived in beds. That was in the "didn't need to know" category.

That explained her drinks early in the morning. He stared out at the uniformed men and women working on the airfield and around the airplanes.

"I think it's the taking off and landing part mostly," she said.

The more she talked the more obvious it was to him; she was scared of flying. Mary exhibiting fear and him witnessing it was a rare experience for both of them. The tough, hard-nosed, sarcastic ex-FBI agent had disappeared. In all the years he had known her, this was a first.

The plane slowly taxied along the runway preparing to depart. Mary showed no sign of relaxing.

"More people die from bee stings than plane crashes," he said, trying to lighten the mood and reassure her.

"I don't see any bees."

"Forty seven thousand people die a year in car-related accidents. It's much more dangerous than flying."

"Not from thirty thousand feet." She took a deep breath and exhaled.

He saw a brochure for Walt Disney World in the storage pocket in front of him. "Do you remember when we were thirteen and I went on vacation with you and your parents to Disney World?"

"Sure."

"Remember Space Mountain?"

She looked over at him and smiled as if she just opened an old photo album of good times. "You mean the time you puked?"

"You puked first," he said defensively.

"You puked longer," she added with a grin.

"And then," he said shaking his head, "we turned around and rode it another three times."

Mary laughed and he reminded her of the time they had talked her parents into riding Space Mountain. Mary's mother had cussed them out the entire ride, in two different languages. The story brought tears of laughter to their eyes and odd glances from the other passengers.

Allen wiped the tears away. "We had some great vacations," he said looking out the window at the puffy white clouds below them now. "It's so beautiful up here."

Mary glanced out the window, still grinning. He saw in her face an easiness that wasn't there before. The reminiscing of the past appeared to have occupied her mind; she had hardly noticed the plane taking off; or maybe the drinks had finally kicked-in.

*   *   *

Kelsy sank deep into the couch and watched the evening news. Her eyelids blinked heavily and the television screen became a flickering, blurry blotch.

"Renowned archaeologist Paul Russet died yesterday in his California home," the newscaster said with a photograph of a bald old man in the corner of the television screen. "The police were called by a neighbor after she hadn't seen Mr. Russet for three days. He died of a heart attack." The newscaster continued about Russet's achievements and international awards, while photographs of him flashed across the screen. "Mr. Russet was seventy two," the newscaster concluded.

The telephone rang. "Hello," she answered, half asleep.

"Hi, honey," a cheery voice said.

"Hi, Mom."

"How are you doing?" There had been concern in her mother's tone since the death of Kelsy's two friends.

"Okay."

"You sound tired, honey."

"Work's been a little stressful." Her voice was dragged down with fatigue.

"It's not easy when you lose friends, especially when they're so young," her mother said.

There was a lingering silence before Kelsy finally spoke again. "I need to get some rest, Mom."

"OK, honey. I called to tell you a package came here for you."

"I'll get it when I come over this weekend. I'll see you then, Mom. I love you."

"I love you, too."

"Mom, wait a minute!" Her intuition, gut feeling, or whatever it was, screamed at her. She suddenly remembered the conversation with the man named James. He had warned her she would receive something that some people would want. People who would want that something bad enough to kill for. "Mom, I want you to bring the package to our favorite restaurant. Don't tell anyone where you're going."

"What? Why?"

"Mom, please listen to me carefully. Go to our favorite restaurant, right now."

Her mother started to say the name of the restaurant but Kelsy cut her off.

"Don't say the name of the restaurant." She could tell her mother was stunned by the sudden and frantic turn of the conversation. "All right, Kelsy."

She heard the doorbell ring in the background. "Don't answer it! Go out the back door and over to Ms. Simmons' house. Go now Mom, hurry!" She hung up, then dialed 911 and reported a burglary in progress at her mother's address.

Moments later her phone rang. "Kelsy, it's me," her mom said.

"Are you all right?"

"Yes, I'm fine. I'm at Ms. Simmons' house. What's going on, honey? I saw a man with a gun run from the house."

Kelsy could tell she scared the hell out of her. "I'll explain it later. Wait there for me," she said heading for the door. "I'll be right over."

"What about the police out front of my house?"

"Don't worry about them. Just stay out of sight."

*   *   *

Kelsy picked up her mother and found the most crowded street and restaurant in Washington. The more witnesses the better.

"What's going on?" her mother asked, still shaken by the ordeal.

Kelsy touched the package that was inside her coat pocket.

"Is it the package?"

"I think so." Kelsy noticed the package had a Virginia postmark, but no return address. She wanted to open and examine the contents, but she didn't dare in public. 'Don't trust anyone,' rang in her ears. She patted the videocassette-sized package again to make sure it didn't magically disappear from her coat pocket. She nervously glanced toward the entrance of the restaurant.

"What is it?"

"I'm not sure, but I don't want you to concern yourself with it. You can't get involved," she said. "The less you know, the better," she added as she glanced around the room.

"Are you in danger? Does this have something to do with your work?"

"I don't know," Kelsy said standing. "Come on, Mom. I want you to stay at a hotel."

Outside the restaurant, she hailed a taxicab and closed the door behind her mother. She leaned in and gave her a kiss on the cheek. "I want you to go to the Grand Hotel," she instructed. She was worried to death about her mother, and couldn't think straight until she knew her mother was safe. "Then, I want you to call your brother Sam and tell him you need to stay with him, that you need witness protection. He'll understand."

"Please, be careful, sweetie," she said, unable to conceal the overwhelming fear in her eyes.

"I will. You can't go back to your house." She pulled a credit card out and handed it to her. "You can buy clothes when you get together with Uncle Sam."

Her mother took the card and nodded. "I love you." Her smiled looked forced.

"I love you, too," Kelsy said touching her cheek. She tapped the roof of the cab and told the driver to go.

Suddenly, an unmarked black van squealed around the corner and sped past Kelsy. The sliding door of the van glided open and man wearing a black jump suit and a black ski mask started firing an automatic weapon, dotting the side of the taxicab with bullet holes.

Kelsy ran hard toward the van with her gun drawn, a gun she hadn't carried, nor fired, since the academy. The taxi swerved into a parked car and came to crushing halt and the van skidded to a stop next to it. Pedestrians took cover wherever they could find shelter.

She approached the rear of the van and carefully poked her head around the side, surveying the situation. A man was leaning through the taxi window, searching her mother and the interior of he car. "FBI!" she screamed aiming her gun at the man. She was doing everything in her power not to allow the fear to overcome her, not to allow the gun to shake uncontrollably in her hand.

The man backed out of the window and turned to face her. She tried to remember if she had taken the safety off. She looked at the car riddled with bullet holes and shattered glass. The driver was draped over the steering wheel with blood pouring from a bullet wound in the back of the head. She glanced at her mother who was slumped to the side; the back of her head was soaked with dark, matted blood. A rush of pure fury hit Kelsy. "On the ground!" she yelled. Her fear had become rage and that rage was making its way to her trigger finger.

The man in the ski mask stood motionless. The sirens of the police cars and emergency vehicles could be heard in the distance. Time stood still; everything around her blurred and the sounds of life were gone. Her eyes locked onto the cold blue eyes peering out from the black ski mask, eyes that reminded her of the color of window cleaner. Windex, yes that was it; they were the color of Windex. Her mind clouded with numerous emotions, but she forced herself to focus. Then, like a piercing alarm in her head, the questions erupted. *Where was the driver? How many more of them were there? Where were they now?*

Windex's eyes shifted toward the sliding door of the van. She made a life-saving leap behind the taxi as bullets came spraying out of the van. Windex dashed for the van's sliding door. She popped up and fired five shots into Windex's partner's chest. He stumbled back into the van and filled the roof with a dozen bullet holes. The van sped away, leaving a reeking trail of burning tire rubber. A small fire ignited beneath the hood of the taxicab.

She pulled her mother out of the taxi to a safe distance and lay her down on the sidewalk. The taxi exploded, sending fragments and debris throughout the street. She wrapped a cloth around her mother's head, attempting to slow the oozing blood.

*   *   *

"And that's why George Washington and Thomas Jefferson regarded the Capitol building as the most important architectural part of the design of the city of Washington, D.C.," Speaker of the House, Walter Web, explained to a group of grade school children who had come to tour the U.S. Capitol.

Jordan had stood behind the group of children and listened attentively.

"What do you say to Mr. Web for the wonderful history lesson about the Capitol?" the teacher asked, prodding good manners out of the children.

The children and Jordan said, "Thank you, Mr. Web!" simultaneously.

"All right, children, let's get going." The teacher rounded up the group of children like a small herd of sheep and guided them up the Capitol steps.

"Thank you very much, Mr. Web," the teacher said as she passed.

"My pleasure."

Jordan grinned. "That was so educational, Walter."

"I'm happy you enjoyed it."

"Let me buy you lunch."

Walter pointed to a stand across the street. "How about a hotdog?"

"Whatever your heart desires."

The two men crossed the street with a half a dozen secret service agents, who kept their presence as inconspicuous as possible.

"Good day, Mr. Web," the vendor greeted. "A dog with everything," he said knowingly, handing him the prepared hotdog.

Jordan laughed.

"And for your friend?" the vendor asked with his two-packs-of-cigarettes-a-day voice.

"I'll have the same."

"Isn't that the Speaker of the House?" a tourist said, passing the hotdog stand.

"Yeah right," the other tourist said. "The Speaker of the House hangs out in front of hotdog stands. And that's the Secretary General with him."

Jordan and Walter walked toward the Capitol Reflecting Pool.

"What's going on with the hostage situation?" Walter asked.

"It's getting uglier by the day."

"And the peace talks?"

"We're meeting later this week to iron out a few misunderstandings," Jordan answered, disinterested. "What's going on with the President's Mexico proposal?"

Walter stopped for a moment to feed the pigeons pieces of bread. "Congress is looking it over."

"Do they like it?"

"I don't know. But Moore has a trip planned for Mexico."

"Do you know when?"

Walter wiped a stain off his tie. "No. He hasn't made an official announcement."

"What's the Mexican government think of Moore's proposal?"

"The word is they like it, but they want a few amendments. That's why he's flying down." Walter shook his head. "I know one thing, the people love him down there."

"I would think so. If Mexico agrees to accept statehood with the U.S. that would mean no less than ten million new jobs for their country."

"The first phase of the plan has over two thousand businesses signed and prepared to incorporate in Mexico. The second phase, the coastline resorts will begin construction immediately after the signing."

"What exactly is holding the proposal up?" he asked.

"The wording in the document concerning Mexico retaining their country status and continuing their system of government without U.S. involvement." Walter shrugged. "But I heard it wasn't anything that could stop the deal."

"Looks like Moore's going to pull it off."

"No one thought he could do it."

"I'm impressed," Jordan said, looking at the Washington Monument. "The commonwealth of Mexico. The fifty-first state, or is it the fifty-second? I've lost count."

"If he wasn't so damn conservative and self-righteous," Walter said. "I would like him."

"By the way," Jordan said, as if he just remembered something. "What did you think of my alterations for a more efficient government?"

"I thought you had some great ideas."

Jordan smiled. "Do you think it would work?"

"Sure. As I was reading your proposal, I realized that you and I think a lot alike."

He had hoped was true. "Did you know the Border Emendation Treaty in Yugoslavia was my proposal?"

"No, I didn't."

"I've been involved in many treaty conventions, but sadly, I have failed many times to accomplish peace. I don't have a very good record."

"If you get the peace talks next week to succeed, I believe that would put you on the upside," Walter said, climbing the steps of the Capitol.

"Big 'if.'"

"Thanks for lunch."

"Anytime." He patted Walter on the back. "You might want to get that mustard off your tie. I'll see you around, Walt."

*   *   *

Across the street on a park bench, Art watched Jordan and Walter part company. He noted that Jordan spent most of his free time with Walter Web. The rest was spent will Shelly Deanster. He also spent time with a scientist from a government facility in New Mexico, named Donald Linenski, and a woman who uncannily resembled the vice president. She looked so much like Shelly she could easily be her sister. From twenty yards away she could be her twin. Art hadn't a clue to who she was, or the connection between herself and Jordan. But it was only a matter of time before he did, he thought, blowing a stream of cigar smoke into the air.

Chapter 18

Orlando, Florida

Mary slid behind the steering wheel of the rented Jetta and gave the interior of the car a quick look over, familiarizing herself with the gadgets and the instruments.

"Nice car," Allen commented.

She revved the motor and gave him a mischievous grin. "We'll see."

Allen returned a composed glance but she knew it hid his apprehension. She had a reputation for being an aggressive driver. He had once teased her that when she got behind the wheel it was as if she became possessed, like in the movie *The Exorcist;* not by the devil, but by the late race car driver, Dale Earnhardt. Allen believed she must have bribed someone at the Motor Vehicle Association to have gotten her license.

He fastened his seat belt. "Remember, forty seven thousand people die a year in car related accidents."

She grinned.

They left the Orlando International Airport and traveled west. Thirty minutes later, they reached Saran Rosenberg's neighborhood in one piece, but she knew Allen nearly had a heart attack on the way. And she secretively loved it. Allen was an imperturbable individual; he rarely became excitable or ruffled, but she had a gift for finding new ways to rattle his calm demeanor. It had been that way between them since grade school.

"Make a right on Flamingo Fountains Boulevard," Allen said looking at the map. "Then, a left on Sherberth Road."

She could hear the tautness in Allen's voice caused by her driving. "All right," she said tight-lipped, hiding her pleasure.

"There it is," he said, pointing at a house. He sounded a little too eager to stop and get out.

She pulled over in front of the modest home. There was no car in the driveway. "It doesn't look like anybody is home."

He looked at his watch. "She said she would be here at four o'clock."

"Maybe bingo's running late."

"Maybe she doesn't drive." He double-checked the address written on the piece of paper. "Let's go knock on the door."

He stepped out of the car and she could almost swear he looked like he wanted to kiss the ground.

"The pictures you were looking at on the plane, are they from a case?" he asked.

"Some woman hired me to follow her husband."

"Is there another woman?"

"No, but there might be another man," she said grinning. "I'm not sure yet."

"It should be interesting to see where that case is going."

"It looks like to divorce court."

They stood on the front veranda waiting for Rosenberg to answer the doorbell.

"The entire case has a strange feel to it," she said. "I haven't even met the wife in person." She rang the doorbell again. "She contacts me by phone or e-mail and pays me in cash through the mail."

"Maybe she's a busy person like you or she's afraid the husband might discover she hired you."

"Maybe, but I think she just doesn't want to meet. I'm going to run a check on her, too."

Allen shook his head.

"What?"

"Everybody's hiding something, right?"

"Yup," she said turning to leave. "She's not home."

They started to head back to the car, but Allen stopped suddenly. "Did you hear that?"

"I didn't hear anything."

"I heard something," he insisted.

She walked to the window and peeked into the house, then dashed to the door and kicked it open.

Allen's eyes widened. "What are you doing?"

She darted into the house and he followed. She leaned over an elderly woman lying in the middle of living room and checked her pulse.

Allen hurried over. "Is she alive?"

"She's dead."

"Do you think she had a heart attack?"

"I don't know."

There was a noise in the back room. She went to draw her weapon, but it wasn't there; she'd left it at home. "Wait here," she whispered.

Allen reached for the telephone and called the police.

She crept along a poorly lit hall toward two bedroom doors at the end of the hallway. The wooden floor squeaked beneath her feet like a rusted hinge. So much for sneaking up on anyone. She slid along the hallway wall, prepared for an attack. She took a quick glance into the first bedroom, then scanned the other room while continually surveying the hall behind her. Her heart pounded against her chest. She used to love the anticipation, the unexpected; she wasn't feeling the love. Her mind worked hard to gain control of her emotions. She missed her gun.

She heard a noise in one of the bedrooms and rushed into the room. She found an opened window. She didn't see anyone running from the house. Her excitement and her adrenaline had caused her to make a fatal mistake. She didn't check the entire room bedroom before exposing her back. The window was a diversion and the intruder was behind her. She turned immediately, crouched in a defensive position. 'No one is there!' her mind exclaimed with relief. She turned back to the window. 'Where the hell did he go?'

A hand grabbed Mary's shoulder. "Hey."

Mary turned on the offensive and nearly ripped Allen's arm out of its socket.

Allen was built solid and athletically, but she knew he felt the move she used on him.

"It's me!" he said clutching his arm.

"Damn. Don't do that." The thought of nearly striking Allen with a neck blow terrified her.

A car started and she and Allen sprinted to the front door. A figure wearing a black suit and ski mask was behind the wheel of a gray Ford. She burst out of the front door, followed by Allen. The intruder sped away, as they got into their rented car, but the siren of an approaching police car forced him to turn around. He made a desperate u-turn and nearly collided into their car. He sped along Sherberth Road with them in pursuit. "A high speed chase," Allen said. "You must be in heaven." She looked in her rear view mirror. The police car stopped at Rosenberg's address with an ambulance right behind.

Mary, Allen and the intruder sped through Osceola County and entered Orange County, where the intruder abandoned his vehicle because of a Walt Disney Park security fence on Bear Island Road.

"We've got him, now!" Mary hooted. She glanced at Allen. He appeared cool under the circumstances, but his heart was probably racing from the pure rush of adrenaline. Driving a hundred miles an hour would do that to him.

With her and Allen following, the intruder ran through a dozen backyards, a small field, and a parking lot before he finally reached the outer limits of Walt Disney World's Animal Kingdom attraction. He zigzagged through the Disney property and climbed a tall, ivy-laced chain link fence. He jumped down and fought through a wall of shrubs.

Allen, breathing hard, caught her at the fence. "What are you doing?"

She started to climb, and he followed. They reached the top of the fifteen-foot fence at the same time a giraffe lifted its head. They were face-to-face with the beautiful animal eighteen feet above the ground. The giraffe curiously stared at them while chewing on foliage. Mary and Allen were frozen with disbelief. The giraffe walked away nonchalantly, not giving the two strange creatures perched on the fence a second thought. Still paralyzed, they watched the animal stroll from them, then they exchanged grins, neither believing what they just witnessed.

The landscape before them gave the impression that they had been transported to the dry plains of Africa. The appearance, the ambiance, and the smell were identical to the real African terrain. They would discover later that they had entered the Kilimanjaro Safari area of the Wild Animal Park of Disney World. The zebras, antelopes, and the other African wild life in the fields grazed on the grasslands and paid no attention to the two human invaders.

Mary's eyes were drawn from the animals to the man in black who was confiscating a tour vehicle by gunpoint. She and Allen climbed down the fence and ran across the open plain, dodging animals on their way to a second tour vehicle. The twenty some bewildered tourists in the brown and tan truck watched, photographed, and videoed the insane couple. Mary flashed her FBI badge at the driver and instructed her to follow the hijacked tour vehicle. The driver explained the masked man was on the Pangani Forest Exploration Trail heading to a service road leading to Magic Kingdom Park. Mary encouraged the driver to join the exploration. The young black tour driver appeared extremely happy to do so. She stomped on the gas pedal and the truck sprung forward, racing through the dusty fields and trails leaving a massive cloud of dust in its wake. The tour driver appeared to be enjoying the chase a little too much. The tourists' eyes bulged with fear as they clung to anything available. The exception was a small group of Asians, who were taking pictures at a rapid-fire pace and appeared to be quite excited with the entire experience. Maybe they thought this was a part of the ride.

They reached the hijacked tour vehicle abandoned at the outer limits of the Magic Kingdom Park. The twenty tourists from it were spread out across the ground. No one appeared harmed. Mary asked which way the masked hijacker had gone. Three frightened tourists pointed toward a service gate entrance to the Magic Kingdom Park. One of the tourists informed her that the gunman had taken his shirt and hat, apparently to change into.

She and Allen took off in the same direction and spotted someone pushing his way through the crowd. It was pure luck that they saw him at all in the mass of people. He gradually faded into the sea of colors, shapes, and figures swarming on the grounds.

"Damn," she said, knowing the chase was over.

They turned the corner and stared into the crowd with their faces flushed and their chests heaving.

"I don't see him," Allen wheezed. He was bent over, gasping for air.

She sat on a bench, panting.

"That was interesting," he said, barely able to speak.

"I'm out of shape," Mary admitted.

He took a seat on the bench next to her. He sniffed the air. "What's that horrible stench?"

She looked around, then down at her shoes. "Crap," she mumbled.

"Yes, it is," he laughed. "Zebra, I would guess."

She scraped the Animal Kingdom souvenir off her shoes.

"Let's ride it," Allen said.

"What?" She looked up, and shining in the Florida sun like an old friend was Space Mountain. She smiled.

Eight security guards suddenly appeared and surrounded them. She looked at Allen. "Looks like we're going on a different ride."

"Can you please come with us?" one of the guards asked politely.

Chapter 19

Greg and Art sat at the kitchen table in Greg's modest apartment overlooking the garden grounds of the church. The last of the sun's light spread across the white lace tablecloth. A tablecloth his mother gave him many years ago, which she received from her mother, making the tablecloth a hundred and ten years old. The two men enjoyed a glass of red wine and a bowl of Greek olives. The aroma of fresh bread and feta cheese circulated throughout the room.

"Professor," Art said, dropping an olive pit into a bowl, "what does that plaque mean?"

He had a silver plated plaque hanging in his kitchen that read, "Born once, die twice. Born twice, die once."

"Some believers," he explained," experience a born-again sensation. Basically, when you decide to become a Christian, you're beginning a new life. Therefore, these believers are born twice, and when a believer dies, he or she dies once, physically. A non-believer is born once, so he or she dies physically and, we believe, dies again spiritually."

Art grinned. "That would be a tough insurance policy to write up."

Greg laughed and took a sip of wine.

"I still like that sign over there best," Art said, pointing to a hand-stitched banner that read, "Everyone goes to heaven, but not everyone gets to stay."

"You do?" he asked.

"Before I met you," Art joked. "I didn't think I had chance to go to heaven. Now, at least I know I'll get to see it."

"It is possible you may stay."

"If there's a cigar section," Art said. "I'm there." He pulled a photo from a file and slid it across the table. "His name is Donald Linenski, he's a chemist Iblis meets with often. Great mug shot, don't you think?"

He studied the photograph for a moment before he concluded he had never seen the man before.

"Iblis and the chemist spent three days in town before flying out to New Mexico. I followed them to Los Alamos Atomic and Space Research Center and White Sands Missile Range. A day later I discovered Iblis was in Mexico City."

"Did you go to Mexico?"

"No, I was too late. I caught up to him in D.C. again with the woman he sent to the Caymans. Looks like she was going on another trip." Art slid another photo to him of Jordan and the woman. "I don't know why she goes down there yet, but I'll find out soon."

"I see the Speaker of the House is still meeting with Jordan," he said, pulling a third photograph from the pile.

Art spread a handful of photos across the table. "They've been more buddy-buddy of late."

"Interesting."

"I'll tell you what's interesting. Iblis goes from eating lobster lunches with big shots in members only clubs, to having a beer and pretzels in some rat hole with a dirt bag who has a rap sheet that reads like a crime novel."

"You're doing a superb job, Mr. Hanson."

"Thanks. I hope this stuff helps you out. You know, save the world from the devil and all," he grinned.

Greg smiled. "What happened to your hand, Mr. Hanson?"

Art sat his glass of wine on the table. "I think it's a rash. It's nothing." He slipped his trench coat on.

"You really should have it looked at," he urged.

"Sure, professor."

He knew Art didn't intend to have the rash checked out, and Art probably knew the Professor knew he wouldn't, so they left it at that.

"If I get anything else, I'll give you call. Thanks for lunch."

After Art left, he sat for a long time, thinking over what he'd learned about Jordan in the past few days. If Jordan was who Greg thought he was, then Jordan knew him from their past encounters. That day in the restaurant with Shelly, he had wanted to say, "I'm on to you, Jordan, and I'm watching." Greg had been pleased to notice, Art had been sitting at the bar, ever-vigilant in his watch on Jordan.

The conversation Greg and Jordan had had in the restaurant only served to convince him that Jordan was the devil in the flesh. He had deliberately baited Jordan by asking if he thought the devil was among them. If Jordan was the devil, he wouldn't be able to resist dropping hints of his true identity. It was the ultimate chess game, but it was played for souls.

*   *   *

Kelsy's mother lay in a coma, and Kelsy hadn't left her side since they'd arrived at the hospital. Her eyes were bloodshot from no sleep and the dark circles grew beneath her eyes with every passing hour. She ran her hand across her mother's soft, wrinkled face. "Hold on, Mom," she whispered.

The shoot out with the two men ran over and over in her mind like a scene from a cop movie, permeating a burning hatred that only hardened her heart with a revenge she had never experienced before. She was transforming.

Kelsy was resting her head on the bed when she heard someone enter. A large silhouette filled the doorway. She jerked up and stood, taking aim with her weapon at a large white man, who looked to be at least six foot four and close to three hundred pounds. And they didn't look like fat pounds. The man was built solid. But after her vision adjusted on the man's face, she lowered her gun and gave the large man a tight hug. "They shot her, Uncle Sam," she said beginning to cry.

"Who did, honey?" His voice had a soothing, deep, soulful tone that brought comfort.

She wasn't alone anymore. She looked up at his familiar, well-loved features; his shaven bald head and his closely cropped salt and pepper beard brought out his bluish-gray eyes. "I don't know," she said.

"Why would anyone shoot her?"

She released him and crossed the room to a chair. "Because of this," she said, pulling the videocassette-size package out of her coat.

"What is it?"

"Disks and CDs."

"What's on them?" He examined the outer package.

"I don't know." She gave the package an odious glare. "People are dying because of them," she said with a glance at her mother. Her voice was raw and melancholy.

"Who sent it to you?"

"I'm not sure, but I think it was a friend of mine who was doing me a favor. I asked him to search some information on a man and the following day . . ." She stopped and looked at the floor. "He was dead."

After a lingering silence, Sam finally said, "He must have known his life was in danger. That's why he sent it to you."

She felt a surge of guilt shiver beneath her skin. She felt responsible for the deaths of her coworker, Bob and her friend William Daniels; and for her mother's condition. Guilt could feed on one's soul like a cancer and she could feel it eating her alive from the inside out.

She watched Sam walk to the bed and take hold of his little sister's hand. He and his sister had been close growing up, only a year apart in age. They remained close over the fifty plus years. He leaned down close to her head and whispered into her ear. "Kathy, it's Sammy." His voice cracked slightly. "You listen, Kat. You need to wake up and make me some of those famous one inch thick pancakes that you stuff with syrup and blueberries." After a long minute of staring into her peaceful blank face, he stood and exhaled.

"First thing we need to do is find out what's on those disks. Maybe that will tell us who did this to her." His voice hardened.

He was all business now. He'd spent twenty-three years in the CIA and had reached a high level of clearance; he still had all his connections. He glanced back at his sister. "And then . . ." he growled, "we're going to get some payback."

Chapter 20

Pensacola, Florida:

U nder the brilliant twilight sky, tens of thousands of people crowded into the newly built cathedral. The pews, aisles, and the balconies were packed with worshipers brimming with anticipation. A hundred network television cameras lined the rear of the church like a firing squad. Six eminent religious personalities including Allen, had been invited as guest speakers for the blessing of the latest New Faith Order place of worship. The six religious leaders were named by spiritual community as the spearhead of the greatest revival in human history. They had spread their teachings worldwide, starting congregations in over eighty countries.

Standing out front of the enormous building were thousands more followers, who felt the calling to be a part of the holy event in some manner. A few hundred feet from the entrance to the church was a structure that would project the ceremonial events on a fifty by forty-foot projection screen. The building and church grounds were heavily patrolled by police officers on foot and horseback, plus hundreds of other uniformed security personnel. The safety of the religious speakers was top priority, but security would be busier containing small conflicts between the many diverse groups gathered for the event.

Mary watched a live interview on one of the screens. "April Val reporting live from the New Faith Order ceremonial blessing. I have here with me, Joy Geris of the Church of Christ from Jacksonville." The camera shot widened and a thin, short woman with dark hair and thick glasses appeared next to the heavily made-up reporter. "Why have you and your congregation isolated yourselves from the main assembly?"

Joy Geris remained blank-faced. "This is a great apostasy," she said into the camera.

"Then, why are you here?"

"We're here to pray for them," Joy said as if she truly meant it. "The people have been misled by these so-called religious leaders." A tone and an expression of dislike suddenly appeared with the words, 'religious leaders.' "They employ peer pressure and socio-psychological manipulation tactics on their followers, leading them to unbiblical teachings and away from the truth."

"But they have brought so many people to God," the reporter said, fueling the fire.

"What god?! Not my god!" A chorus of "amens" sounded in the background. "What god has his followers rolling around on the floor laughing uncontrollably and roaring like animals? They're intoxicated with power."

"Are you saying that these religious leaders gathered here today are false teachers?" The reporter knew that was a loaded question. Good television, she thought.

"I'm saying that this is a counterfeit revival." Another chorus of supportive "amens" followed her statement. "These men are preaching spiritual deception and false experiences under the banner of God. Some in the name of Jesus Christ." She pointed her finger judgmentally at the building. "They don't know the Truth; and the Truth will not know them."

"What is the truth?"

"Knowledge. Read for yourself. Learn the Word. Protect yourself from the father of lies," she preached.

"Thank you, Ms. Geris," the reporter said. The camera zoomed in on the reporter. "I'm April Val, reporting live from the New Faith Order ceremonies." The light dimmed with a quick fade out. The reporter thanked Ms. Geris again off camera, and then turned to her crew and rolled her eyes. "A bunch of nuts, all of them," she mumbled.

Allen concluded his sermon on being well equipped in the faith and to remain open minded and spirited in God. His ideology as always was to beware of the enemy within, the wolf in sheep's clothing. Watchful of the evil forces working to keep you from God. Allen's teachings scrutinized false teachers and prophets, and questionable practices in all religions including his childhood religion, Catholicism. He warned against false worship and idol worshiping.

But within many Christian faiths a dramatic shift had taken place. Many large Christian groups have taken a stance against Allen and his peers, believing their teachings had strayed from the fundamentals of the Bible and God. Now, he was the one who was the false teacher in numerous Christian circles. He was the very thing he preached against.

Allen finished his sermon and took a seat next to the other evangelists. It took a full minute for the long, roaring applause to taper off. He had become one of the most popular of the six.

Mary sat in the very back of the building, near the exit. Her attendance was a favor to Allen; otherwise, she would have never associated with this movement. She was raised by Christian parents who led by example, not by force; who allowed her to find God on her own, which she did. And her God didn't heal the sick on television every week, where they lined up like some drive-through fast food place and ordered a "Super Size Healing Meal" to go. This revival, this great awakening, was not of God, but of man, she believed. She knew a con when she saw one, and this was the mother of all cons. What pained her the most was that her best friend was one of the prominent leaders of the movement.

A man draped with gold jewelry and an extravagant white suit stood to speak to the congregation. His name was Steven Postiche, a chubby, middle-aged evangelist from Baton Rouge. In his strong Louisiana accent he told a story about how the Holy Spirit visited him at night and provided him with inspirational sermons. Suddenly, he started speaking in a babbling language no one understood. Mary realized he was "speaking in tongues," as the religious community called it. Another evangelist leaped to his feet and began speaking to Postiche in the same babbling gibberish. The two men seemed oblivious of their surroundings, simply carrying on a conversation between the two of them. They were laughing back and forth as if they were telling each other jokes. The congregation started to giggle and laugh, and it quickly spread through the church. Mary watched on the big screens set up so that the thousands of worshipers could have a clear view of everything. A woman in the front pew fell to the floor and quivered and jerked, followed by two more worshipers, then five, then ten more.

Mary looked at Allen, but he remained seated and watched the phenomenon unfold before his eyes. He looked very uncomfortable. People continued to dance, jerk, sing, pray, yell, and fall to the floor throughout the building. One of the screens showed the view from a camera outside. The crowd there also started to laugh and yell, "The Holy Spirit is at work."

The inside cameras that showed the crowd, focused on a thin, pale-faced man with dark, messy hair, who was walking toward the stage, tapping the floor before him with his white cane. His face was rough with a week's worth of growth and his eyes were covered with dark glasses; a long, black coat was tightly wrapped around his body.

The crowd settled down and cheered the blind man on. Everyone was probably aware of Allen's miraculous healing of the blind boy at his church and the anticipation of another dramatic healing built. Healing the blind boy had made Allen a renowned religious figure, but the sudden fame had brought intense scrutiny from nonbelievers and most of the well-established faiths.

Mary sensed something wrong when she saw the blind man. A warning went off in her head. Allen had always called her warnings, "well-honed paranoia." The man had a newspaper in his coat pocket. What was a blind man doing with a newspaper? Why was he wearing a long coat in hot, steamy Florida? The more she thought about it the less blind he appeared to her. While she tossed those thoughts around in her head, she headed toward the stage. The man stopped before the stage and thousands of people hushed and stared.

Steven Postiche still stood encircled in a golden spotlight, his white suit beaming and his jewelry sparkling before the blind man like a god preparing to lift him to heaven. He waved the security officers away from the man and asked, "What can I do for you, my brother?"

The blind man dropped his cane and slowly removed his glasses, revealing to the close-up cameras dark brown eyes with endless depth. "I have a message from God," he said, as dark as his eyes. He opened his coat to reveal what was beneath it, and Mary recognized a sawed-off Remington 870 pump-action combat shotgun. It could hold seven solid slugs, enough to take out everyone on stage.

The first blast of bright orange sparks happened so quickly that Steven Postiche had a hole in his chest before his smile could turn to horror. One of the evangelists now wore the blood of Postiche across his face, and a second later, he followed Postiche into the afterlife. The white and blue smoke from the end of the barrel rose to heaven like the two souls of the evangelists, if that was where they were truly going. Screams echoed horrifically through the building. A third blast rang out and a police officer fell to the ground. Bedlam ensued and people tore for the nearest exits. Another evangelist leaped over Postiche's blood-saturated body, but the assassin opened a hole in the man's back the size of a grapefruit, dropping him two steps away from his dead companion. The assassin fired a slug into a fourth evangelist's stomach, doubling him over and sending him crashing into the stage furniture. He pumped the empty shell into the air end-over-end.

Chaos and fear surrounded him, but he seemed not to notice. "I'm on a mission from God!"

A police officer fired two rounds into the man's body, but he was unfazed. Mary realized he must be wearing body armor. The assassin turned and shot the officer, then sent another evangelist to his death with a precise shot to the back of the head. "Another dead false prophet!" he shouted. With smooth and meticulous movements, he reloaded the shotgun with seven more shells. "I'm God's soldier, delivering His message!" He swung to his right and sent a another police officer to the floor with a shot to the upper part of his chest, but not before the officer fired his weapon, piercing the assassin's thigh with a bullet. But like a perfectly trained soldier, the pain he must have felt seemed to make his focus clearer.

From the very first blast, Mary had been fighting her way toward the stage against the current of panicking worshipers. Above the crowd's heads she could see thick blue smoke rising to the ceiling. She kept her eyes moving between the big screens and her destination in front of her, seeing everything as it was seen from the cameras, still trained on the stage and the supposed blind man. Good thing not all the camera personnel abandoned their equipment. She counted eight shotgun blasts and a half a dozen handgun shots. She desperately searched the stage while shoving through waves of petrified people.

Please be alive, Allen," she thought. *Please be alive!* There he was. He must be in shock. *Get the hell out of there, Allen!* she screamed in her head. She heard another shot; her heart stopped and her mind flashed an unpleasant image. She didn't want to confirm it by looking at the screen but forced herself. She fought her way through the crowd and stumbled over a dead police officer. She was close.

The assassin pumped another empty shell into the air. He turned to Allen, who remained seated in his chair thirty feet away. At the sight of Allen sitting calmly, the assassin's expression twisted in confusion, than his face turned dark. He lifted the barrel of the shotgun, but Allen stood and walked toward him as if to make it easier to kill him. Allen's face was serene and peaceful, and the cameras showed the assassin visibly perplexed, but in a calming way.

Mary grabbed the dead police officer's gun and leaped to her feet, now pushing hard through the chaotic crowd, eyes still moving between the screens and the scene directly in front of her.

The assassin shook his head and seemed to break the hypnotic spell of Allen's stare. "I am a messenger of God," he said, taking aim. He pulled the trigger, but the shotgun didn't fire. He looked at the weapon as if it betrayed him. His eyes widened with disbelief when he perceived Allen smiling down at him from the stage.

Twenty feet from the assassin, Mary broke through the crowd. She saw Allen standing on the stage looking down at the killer. Smiling. *What the hell is he doing?*

Allen's smile disappeared. "I am a messenger of God," he said sternly.

The assassin stared raptly at Allen; then his head exploded into a red and white cloud of matter before his body finally came to rest on the carpeted floor.

Mary slowly lowered the dead police officer's gun, still smoking in her hand.

Chapter 21

Annapolis, MD

K elsy sat at a computer in the back of the public library, her small, secluded cubical cluttered with printouts and diskettes from the package her mother had given her. She peered at the computer screen, disgruntled and confused. The monitor displayed hundreds of tiny dots and dashes sequenced uniformly in straight lines. The dots and dashes were organized and patterned in a way that suggested significance. She pushed some papers around on the desk to search for one in particular, periodically glancing over her shoulder. She located a paper she had printed out from one of the disks, but she was unable to read the information because the words were spelled with letters from forty or fifty different languages.

Large hands came down on Kelsy's shoulders and she nearly jumped out of her skin.

"Take it easy, Kell. It's me," Sam said.

"I didn't hear you walk up." Her heart rate slowly returned to normal.

Sam pulled a chair up. "Sorry, I didn't mean to startle you."

"I've been a little on edge lately."

He nodded toward the printouts and computer screen. "Is that from the disks?"

"Yeah."

"It's Morse code," he said.

"Can you read it?"

"It's been awhile," he said, pulling out his reading glasses. "Let's see." He wrote on a piece of paper, intermittently glancing at the screen.

She watched anxiously, reading her uncle's translation of the information to paper. "Is the entire screen just names and job titles?"

"Looks like it," he answered. He ran his finger along the screen until he reached the bottom. "Yup, all names and what they do."

"There's a lot of scientists and archaeologists."

"Yeah, and a lot of American military and government officials, too."

"What do you mean?"

"See here," he said pointing to a column on the right of the screen. "These are serial numbers. Serial numbers used by government agencies and the Pentagon. These numbers are just like fingerprints."

"What's the list for?"

"It doesn't say."

Kelsy moved some papers around on the desk and slid one of the printouts in front of Sam. "What do you make of this?"

He brought the printout closer his face. He tilted his head, puzzled by the data. "I recognize some of the letters. Like these are Greek letters, and these over here are Arabic," he said pointing. "And I see a lot of Hebrew in there, too."

"Can you read any of it?"

"No," he said putting it down. "There's never more than one of the same type of letter in one word and some of the letters I don't recognize at all."

"What do you think it all is?"

"I don't know," Sam said, removing his glasses. "But whatever it is, it seems to be worth killing for and someone desperately doesn't want anyone to see it."

She looked down at the printouts; page after page of similar scrambled wording. "We're going to need some help."

"Are these the only copies?" he asked.

"I made two copies," she answered. "One, I sent to Mary."

"Where's the other?"

"My apartment."

*   *   *

Washington, D.C.

Jordan and Shelly sat in the back of the restaurant having drinks and waiting for their dinners to arrive. Shelly fidgeted with a card on the table with the word "reserved" printed across the face in large block letters. Most of the patrons had gone for the night, but Louie, the owner always stayed open late for Shelly and Jordan and the other public figures of the city.

"Beautiful flowers," she commented on the flower arrangement on their table.

"Yes, they are," Jordan said. "They're called passion flowers." The flowers were bright red and the petals burst outward from the center like a starfish. The tiny, finger-like center protruded from the middle of the flower with a pinkish-white brilliance. "See the distinctive corona resting in the center of the flower?"

"Yes, it's stunning."

"It's said it symbolizes the passion of Christ and the crown of thorns."

"Well, aren't we the knowledgeable one?" she asked with a grin.

"Are you impressed?"

"Always."

"The Learning Channel," he confessed with a wink.

"And they say there's nothing good on TV anymore for the kids."

"Did you hear about the massacre in Florida?" he asked.

"I saw some of it on the news. It was horrible. Did any of the evangelists survive?"

"I believe Allen Pyrit did."

"I know him; he's from this area. I bet he's counting his blessings tonight."

"I'm sure he is."

A heavy-set man walked toward their table without resistance from the Secret Service agents posted around the room.

"Well, if it isn't the couple of the year," Walter said grinning a toothy smile.

"Hi, Walter." She greeted him warmly. "Would you like a glass of wine?"

"No thank you." He took a seat and leaned back, exposing his round belly that appeared to be in the beginning stage of the third trimester.

"It's past your bedtime isn't it, Walter?" Jordan joked.

She was surprised. "I didn't know the two of you were acquaintances."

"We go way back," Walter revealed. "How are you holding up?" he asked her, appearing concerned.

"Fine."

"You seem to be doing well under the circumstances."

"What are you talking about, Walter?" she asked, clueless to whatever he was talking about.

"The investigation." Walter answered as if she should know.

"What investigation?"

Walter leaned in. "You've been accused of bribery and misusage of campaign funds. The allegations are all over the TV."

"What the hell are they talking about?" Jordan asked.

"The news broke about thirty minutes ago," Walter explained. "The House Judiciary Committee has adopted a resolution and is seeking the authority from the House of Representatives to conduct an official inquiry."

"The Committee can't press formal charges without a majority vote from the House," she said.

"I've heard they're already working on it," Walter said. "I also heard they want articles of impeachment filed."

"I didn't do anything wrong!"

"I'm really sorry, Shelly. I thought you knew."

She threw her napkin on the table and stared down at her empty plate, suddenly losing her appetite. "I have to go."

Jordan put his arm around her and they walked through the callous stares and suspicious whispers of those patrons still left. Everyone seemed to already know. Secret Service Agents closely led and trailed the couple through the restaurant.

"Bought your way into the White House!" some drunk yelled from the bar.

His inebriated friends laughed. "Let's see her buy her way out of jail!"

The insults burned like wasp stings on Shelly's vulnerable soul. She struggled to keep control of her emotions. She stepped out onto the sidewalk to a crowd of reporters and cameras. The flash bulbs flashed and the microphones stretched for her attention. She gasped for air, attempting to control her erratic breathing. She quickly regained her composure and hardened her face, not allowing anyone to witness her moment of weakness. A second group of Secret Service agents separated the media from her.

A limousine sounded its horn.

"Shelly," Jordan said, gently taking hold of her elbow. "I believe they're here to talk to you." His eyes guided her attention toward the long, black car.

She made her way to the limo and the door opened for her. She ducked into the backseat. Two men were seated across from her. One was the Attorney General, John Wright, and next to him was Tom Donald, Senior Advisor.

Wright handed her a tissue pack. "How are you doing?"

"I've had better days," she said blotting her eyes with the tissue.

"Unfortunately, I have more bad news."

She grinned sarcastically. "Great."

He handed her a half-inch thick document. "The House wants you to resign."

"I didn't do anything wrong."

"It doesn't appear that way," Tom said.

She stared at the document as if it were a foreign object that shouldn't be in her possession. "Damn it! What the hell is going on, John? Why are they moving so fast? Why do they want me out so damn bad? It's obvious it's a frame up."

Both men stared sympathetically at her, but something told her they were great actors.

"If I don't resign?"

"They'll drag you through the mud," Tom said.

Angry now, she laughed cynically. "Big damn deal. I'm already neck deep."

"They will drag Derrick down with you," John added.

Derrick had warned her when she first became his running mate, that the two of them would be under a microscope. A black president and a woman vice president would not be treated equally, and if a reason to tear them down arose, inevitably the powers within would act. The 'good ol' boys' of Congress would saddle up and ride again. But would they go as far as to set her up . . . frame her?

She stared out of the limousine window at the capitol in the distance, thinking how much she cared for Derrick and his presidency. She would never hurt him or his presidential career. She vowed from the beginning that she would do whatever it took not to harm his position. He had been criticized harshly for selecting a woman vice president. The critics had claimed she would be a glaring weakness in his administration. "If I resign?" she asked, continuing to gaze at the Capitol. "Will they back off Derrick?"

"It's in the document," John informed her. "Derrick is clear of all involvement."

She stepped out of the limousine feeling like she needed a shower. Jordan adjusted his tie while exiting the restaurant. The two met at her limo, both entering without a word.

*   *   *

Standing on the sidewalk, two of Walter's Secret Service agents laughed and exchanged animated comments. He put down the window of his limo. "What's going on?" he asked as if he were one of the boys.

The agents glanced at one another. "Well," one of them explained, "it appears that a couple of drunk idiots at the bar made some insulting comments to the vice president and . . ." The agent hesitated for a second and smiled.

"And?"

"And Jordan Iblis went back in there and kicked the living crap out of them."

The agents smiled. Walter was shocked, but he couldn't help but grin.

"He beat the tar out of those guys," the other agent said.

Walter was having a difficult time comprehending the idea of Jordan fist fighting in a bar, but at the same time, Jordan appeared to be a man you would never want to go up against. "Amazing," he mumbled.

Chapter 22

The White House

"It's so good to see you again, Greg," Derrick said, hugging him.

Greg returned the welcoming embrace. "It's good to see you again, my friend."

They sat on the couch and Greg studied his friend carefully. He had watched the latest world political developments vigilantly, and over the past several weeks he saw Derrick's peace talk efforts destroyed and the hostage situation grow worse by the day. Now, he had to watch his friend and Shelly Deanster be accused of criminal activities.

"How are you doing?' Greg asked, really wanting to know.

"I'm holding on. Sometimes with just a fingernail."

Derrick's stress was obvious to him. "It hasn't been easy for you."

"Easy isn't a word used around here too often." Derrick took a sip of tea. "Is everything okay, Greg? What brings you to this part of town?"

"Sean Carbon's prediction."

Derrick laughed. "The Prophecy of Death," he mocked, as if he were speaking about a bad horror movie. "That's the least of my problems."

He stared unblinking, not sharing Derrick's nonchalant outlook on the issue.

"Or is it?" Derrick stared back.

"I believe it shouldn't be taken lightly."

Derrick stood. "I already have people on it. What else is there to do?"

"First," he said," we must make March as safe as possible for you. The prophecy says the leader in question will fall in the month when darkness equals light. The spring equinox, when day and night are equal in time."

"Isn't there a fall equinox?"

Greg grinned. "Let's get through spring first."

They scrutinized Derrick's schedule. They reviewed every day and hour of his agenda for the month of March.

"You know," Derrick said laughing, "the Secret Service guys would kill me themselves if they found out I let you see this."

"I'm sorry to put you in this position."

"That's okay. If I can't trust you, who can I trust?"

"This will be the key to Carbon's prediction," Greg said, pointing to March 15th. "The day the President of Egypt is scheduled to arrive.

"Ides of March," Derrick mumbled.

"It wasn't a good day for Julius Caesar; it may not be a good day for you."

"I'm not Caesar, and Carbon isn't Spurinna," Derrick said. "Plus, the prophecy says there will be two rulers visiting the eagle's nest. How can two Egyptian rulers visit Washington?"

"It appears impossible on the surface."

"Why are you so worried about this prediction, Greg? Did you have a premonition?"

"I feel we need to be cautious." He saw that his tone and expression made Derrick uncomfortable.

"What's going on, Greg? Don't start holding back on me now. We've been through too much craziness together."

Craziness was right. To say Derrick's election to the presidency was a miraculous occurrence would be the understatement of the century. Presidents had been elected or placed in office by many different means. Some had made deals with the mafia and had dead people vote for them, or the government in power decided to overturn the people's choice, and sometimes one president was removed for another by assassination or threat of impeachment. Sometimes there were the landslide victories and in other circumstances there was the need to hand count every single vote in a state to determine a victor. And then, there was Derrick's election to office.

When Derrick was running for the presidency he stood before the nation and made the most extraordinary and bold statement ever uttered from a human, let alone a candidate. Derrick's proclamation came straight out of the Old Testament ages when prophets predicted plagues and other supernatural events.

Derrick had proclaimed God had chosen him to be President of the United States of America. He said he had been chosen to reform the country and lead the world to peace. To prove he was chosen by God there would be a sign; this sign would not be a mere burning bush. No. Derrick claimed nothing in the universe would be born, nor would anything die for a period of three days coinciding with Easter weekend. When he said nothing would be born or would die, he meant nothing. Not one human on the planet, not one blade of grass.

And it had happened! At least, most of the world believed it had happened, and more importantly, just enough voters. There had been claims of births and deaths during that period of time, but not without strong skepticism. Discovering documented evidence of a birth or a death during those three days was nearly impossible. Of course, many argued at the time of the election that the country was tired of career politicians, big government and the corruption and immoral behavior associated with Washington. The presidency and the government had become a lucrative business and the people were searching for someone real, someone to believe in, and someone who was going repair the spiritual fabric of the country; someone like Derrick Moore.

The country was looking for a trustworthy and spiritual leader and Derrick fit the bill, or rather, the ballot. As for Derrick's incredible claim, maybe people wanted to believe it bad enough to imagine it was true. People continued to argue about it to this day.

"Remember Luke DeMynn?" Greg asked.

Derrick stared silently at him. While God was busy campaigning for Derrick's election, the opposition was hard at work attempting to destroy it. The opposition arrived in the form of Luke DeMynn, a powerful businessman who supported Derrick's opponent, a Mafia figure named Charles Malefic. To this day Derrick's campaign manager and staff weren't sure who he was, or why he was determined to destroy him, but they were certainly happy when he disappeared.

Greg, however, believed Luke DeMynn was the incarnation of Satan.

"I thought it was over," Derrick murmured.

He knew Derrick didn't want to endure another spiritual war; Greg felt the last battle would pale in comparison to what was coming, but he kept those thoughts to himself. How could he tell Derrick that they may be on the steps of Armageddon, the final and deciding conflict between good and evil.

There was a knock on the door. "Sir," an aide interrupted. "You should see this."

"What is it?"

The aide turned on CNN.

"What the hell?" Derrick asked. "That's Jerusalem."

"The Western Wall," Greg added. "The wailing wall."

The news footage showed a massive pile of books, maybe a hundred thousand in number, stacked a hundred and fifty feet high engulfed in a raging blaze. The flames extended upward like burning claws scratching at heaven's door. On television it appeared as if a mountain were set on fire.

"What in the world are they burning?" Derrick asked.

Greg was filled with trepidation. "Bibles," he whispered. There were three great forces of evil being drawn to one another by a sinister energy, and soon they would form the Demonic Trinity, and bring forth the apocalypse; and then, all hell would break loose.

*   *   *

Orlando, Florida:

Allen carefully collected Mary's case photographs and notes from her lap. She had fallen asleep during the one-hour delay on the tarmac. Understandably so; she had sat in a smoky room with the local law authorities for eight hours, filling out paperwork and answering questions concerning her involvement with the shooting death of the assassin. She also watched, for what seemed to be a million times, the footage of the incident; the last thirteen seconds of a mad man's life. Eventually, she was released and no charges were filed. But of course, the nut case's family would probably sue her. Also, by tomorrow, every media outlet in the country-hell, in the world—would run footage ever minute of the day. It wasn't everyday you get to see a messenger from God get his head blown-off by an ex-FBI agent.

The airplane slowly taxied along the Orlando International Airport runway positioning for take-off. Mary's head tilted and nearly wakened her, but Allen quickly adjusted her pillow, allowing her to remain comfortable and asleep. It was better if she slept through the take-off. Much better. The airplane leveled out at a cruising altitude of twenty-five thousand feet; the seat belt sign went off, and the flight attendant started to push the drink cart down the aisle.

Allen glanced through the pictures of the infidelity case Mary was working on, which she warmly regarded as, "The Mr. Pig" case. The photos were of three men, one being the suspect himself, Mr. Pig. He smiled; she had him calling the husband Mr. Pig. Her notes stated there wasn't another woman, but there may be another man. The husband was possibly living a double life, yet she had no hard evidence. He placed the case pictures and notes neatly into the file.

*   *   *

Mary was dreaming. She was a young FBI agent and it was thirty-six hours after her partner had been shot and killed. She stood in the dim office of the assistant director. The blinds were positioned in a way that allowed a stingy amount of midday sun into the room. Seated off to the side, barely visible in the shadows, were two men wearing the customary gray suits that seemed to be standard-issue apparel in the government. They preferred to be present, but not seen.

Assistant Director Amps took his place behind his desk and asked her to take a seat. "Thank you for coming, Agent Jopuez," he said with a phony pleasantness.

She sat directly across from his desk, crossing her legs and placing her hands in her lap. Her body language implied she didn't have a choice but to come.

"The Bureau is happy with your work," Amps said, opening a file.

"Is that why I was called to your office?" she asked, glancing at the two men hidden in the shadows.

Amps put his glasses on. "Partly."

"Is there a problem with my report, sir?"

"The truth of the matter is," he said, looking up from file, "we would like you to drop your current investigation."

His statement gave her a jolt, but she maintained her composure. "We?"

"The Bureau would like you to drop your investigation, Agent Jopuez." Amps' tone became direct and suggestive.

She got the impression that it was already a done deal.

"We prefer to handle our own dirty laundry," Amps continued.

"The man in your report," a voice from the shadows quietly said," is a very high profile individual within the bureau. Your investigation and report would lead to public exposure. We need to keep his identity confidential."

The second figure spoke from the shadows, his voice was deep and strong. She pegged him for a military man. "We don't want the other side to know we've captured him. We plan to use him to expose his contacts."

"It's important that Joe Public isn't aware of this incident," Amps urged.

"That would give the agency a black eye," one of the voices from the shadows added. "It wouldn't look good if the media discovered one of our own double-crossed us. We've already had our share of problems; we don't need anymore."

The military voice tried to patronize her. "If recognition is your concern, your efforts won't go unrewarded."

"My concern is justice," she said staring into the shadows coldly.

"Then, there's nothing to worry about. He will be dealt with accordingly for his crimes against the government and for the murder of your partner."

"We would simply like to deal with this matter within the agency," Amps explained. "We'd like to keep a bad incident from becoming worse."

She stood. "Is that all?" she asked sardonically.

"Yes," Amps said, also standing.

She turned and walked toward the door.

"We would like all the evidence and files from the investigation," one of the men said from the shadows.

She continued her exit from the office, never turning around.

"What's going on?" she asked, and realized she had awakened from a dream. The flight attendant had bumped the seat with the drink cart.

"Do you want something to drink?" Allen asked.

The dream had left her nauseated. She stared out the window of the plane. "Coffee."

He passed the coffee to her. "You have to let it go."

She realized he knew she had been dreaming again about the bureau and her dead partner. "He should be rotting in jail," she said, locking eyes with him. "People died because of that—." She stopped and turned away.

"He won't get away with it, Mary. One day he'll have to answer for what he did."

"They let him go. He was selling government secrets; he killed my partner and they let him go." There was a deep sense of rancor in her.

"I thought he escaped."

"They made a deal. He sold the other side out and they let him go." The conversation made her rigid and irate.

One of the flight attendants recognized Allen. "I'm so happy you weren't hurt, Mr. Pyrit."

"Thank you."

The flight attendant moved along the aisle, occasionally glancing back at Allen with admiration.

"If you're going to travel with me, you need to stop shaving and start wearing a hat and glasses," Mary said, making it sound more like an order than a suggestion. "You need to blend in and stop being famous; there are more nuts out there."

Nearly thirty years of friendship had made Allen numb and accustomed to Mary's ingenuous personality. He didn't respond, but he agreed with her; he must become less recognizable in public if he planned to roam the country without professional security. Then again, he had the best protection sitting right next to him. A best friend who was a highly skilled ex-FBI agent, who had proven without a doubt, she was capable of protecting him.

"Why didn't you run?" she asked. "Why didn't you try to get away?"

He had had a dream a few nights before the assassinations, and in the dream he saw six unblemished lambs standing on a stone altar. From the sky a winged beast descended with a mighty scream, announcing God's hand was upon them and a messenger would deliver a judgment by fire and thunder. A message and judgment of blood. But one lamb would be spared and would be a witness to the judgment. Allen conjectured he was the unblemished lamb who would live and be the witness. It never crossed his mind that he might be wrong. He felt he couldn't tell Mary he didn't attempt to escape the madman with the shotgun because of a dream. She would call him a damn fool and probably shoot him herself. "Because I knew you were going to stop him," he finally answered.

"If that's true, you're a damn fool. You stood there like a deer caught in headlights."

A minute of silence passed between them. "I wasn't afraid."

"You weren't?" she asked, unconvinced.

"I've never been afraid to die."

"To remain that calm and not experience fear when facing certain death isn't humanly possible. You were scared."

"Were you afraid?"

"No. I was too busy trying to save your butt."

He smiled. "I knew you would."

She glanced out the window. "I'm glad one of us did. Rodney Hart—do you think he's going to live?" she asked.

Hart was one of the evangelists who, along with Allen, didn't die on the stage, but suffered a gunshot wound to the stomach. He shook his head. Only one unblemished lamb would live.

Mary turned to look out again. "Didn't you find it strange that those two speaking in tongues were the only one who understood each other?" He stopped reading *Moby Dick* and stared at her, wondering where that question came from, considering she insisted they never discuss religion or anything concerning his profession.

"They were acting like two 'good old boys' telling each other jokes," she said disapprovingly. "They turned a spiritual gathering into a mockery."

"How do you know I didn't understand them?"

"Did you?"

"No, I didn't," he said, marking his place in the book before closing it.

Mary returned a magazine to the pouch behind the seat in front of her. "Don't you find it somewhat uncomfortable when 'holy laughter' breaks out in church? People start barking like animals?"

He hoped the shock on his face wasn't obvious. *Remarkable,* he thought. This woman never ceased to amaze him.

"Is it Biblical?" she continued.

He collected his thoughts. "So," he cracked a smile, "does this mean the gag order has been lifted on religious conversations between us?"

She popped a peanut into her mouth. "We can discuss it only when we're twenty thousand feet in the air," she said with a thin smile.

He leaned in toward her. "I've never been compelled to speak in tongues or laugh uncontrollably in church."

"But, is it Biblical?"

He shook his head. "There's nothing in the Bible to support 'holy laughter.' Speaking in tongues is Biblical, but there are guidelines that must be followed."

"Are the guidelines being followed?"

He leaned back into his chair and shook his head.

"Why are you a part of it?" she asked. "And why are you allowing it in your church?"

"I believe it's a movement of God, and maybe I'm just not getting it." The insecurity in his voice emerged.

"I'll tell you what a movement of God is," she said callously. "What happened yesterday was a movement of God."

"Good Lord, Mary." Images of yesterday's massacre flash through his mind. "Many people will view it as the work of a madman and the devil, not God. Four religious leaders assassinated, and the fifth soon to join them are being called martyrs and ordained as saints on every television screen on the planet every minute of the day . . . not because God struck them down, but because they were struck down for God."

They had seen the early morning news reports. He, himself was now being worshiped by millions of followers as some anointed deity because he had survived the assassinations.

"You have a gift, Al. You open people's eyes. You make believers out of nonbelievers. You make people *want* to believe. You make them feel good and confident about what they already believe. All that stuff surrounding you only gets in the way. You need to get back to your roots. The way it was in the beginning when you were a preacher, not a TV star."

"People expect theatrics," he said under his breath. "There are deadlines, investors, advertising agreements . . ."

"It sounds like you're running a business."

He rubbed his eyes. Deep in his heart he felt he had compromised his beliefs in some ways, but only to bring more people to God.

"When did God become a business?" she pressed.

"When did you start caring about any of this?" he asked quietly, almost wishing she would go back to not talking about religion again.

"I don't care about any of it," she said in a voice so low, Allen barely heard her. "I care about you."

He smiled. "I wish I had a tape recorder."

"I can't remain silent about it any longer. It's become a threat to your life now. I think you should consider getting out of the limelight for a while."

"You know I can't do that."

"You need to take a good look in the mirror and figure out who you are and where you're heading, and figure out what's really important to you. You're a preacher, not the ringleader of a circus. And you don't need to be a damn target for some religious fanatic."

He looked down at Melville's novel in his lap. The cover of the book had a great white whale breaking the surface of the ocean. The whale was demolishing boats and propelling men into the air while being speared by long, vicious harpoons.

"I used to listen to you on the radio from time to time," she confessed.

"You don't anymore?"

She shook her head. "Your message changed. You changed."

Her comments reminded Allen of the interview with *Time* magazine. "I had an interview with a reporter from *Time*. He told me the Easter healings last year were fake. The people in question were paid to fake their illnesses and their recoveries."

"Were they?"

He was taken back by the question. "I didn't know anything about it."

"How did the reporter find out?"

"He checked it out after someone tipped him off. He wouldn't say who. I believe he's telling the truth."

"What's going to happen?"

"I convinced him to wait on the story." He took a drink of his coffee. "I don't understand; why would they fake it?" He sounded betrayed.

"They were paid off. Money is the great compromiser."

"I don't get it. Why bother?"

"Sensationalism sells. Your ratings were probably down." Her eyes filled with a disgruntled stare. "I bet that manager of yours had something to do with it."

"Robert?"

"He's in it for the money, Al."

He pondered the thought of Robert conceiving the Easter deception. "He defiantly encouraged the development of the worldwide Easter revival with Sean Carbon and GCE. And he's in charge of the floor."

Mary glanced out her window again at the endless blue sky. "The God business is good money."

"It brought a great many people to the church."

"Under false pretenses. It's getting out of control. That preacher in Pensacola was telling people not to pray and the other one said if you're not laughing or rolling around on the floor your faith is weak. If you're sick or poor it's because your faith isn't strong enough. I even heard them say you weren't a true believer if you didn't respond in certain ways."

He looked down at the book cover again, at the great white whale being hunted.

"They ask for money in the name of Christ and spend it on themselves." she added, sounding irritated.

They remained silent as the flight attendant passed.

"You need to talk to Robert," Mary said.

"Why?"

"I don't trust him. Something stinks. And it's in your church." She fluffed her pillow, leaned back and closed her eyes. The conversation was over. The plane must have dropped below twenty thousand feet.

He thought about what Mary said, but not for long. The troubles in the church would work out, eventually. His thoughts drifted to the search for his biological parents, but the thought that troubled him the most was the dead woman in Florida, Sarah Rosenberg.

Chapter 23

K elsy gathered her personal belongings from her little cubical work area and placed them in a backpack. The bureau had suspended her with pay until internal affairs had fully investigated the shooting incident concerning the two mystery men in the van. She didn't mention the package or the unauthorized search she performed on a civilian's background that no doubt was the reason for the violent crime. She maintained a naïve and baffled pretense throughout the questioning. She remained silent with the facts and didn't volunteer any spurious theories on why the incident took place.

The moment she saw the blood leaving her mother's head was the moment she became less of a FBI agent and more of a vigilante. The old Kelsy would have spilled her guts, told the whole truth and nothing but the truth. But that person was gone. She lied and withheld information from the FBI, but not because she feared punishment. No. She wanted to be the one who got the shooter. She wanted to be the one who brought down the man with the Windex eyes.

She opened a drawer and retrieved an unmarked file. This was the file people were apparently dying over. Last night, while she was at the hospital, her apartment was burglarized again. This time they got one of the extra file copies.

Her computer bleeped and a tiny envelope icon flashed across the screen. She clicked on the icon and her e-mail opened.

"I'm sorry about your mother and friends," the e-mail read. "I can help you get the people responsible." An image of her mother flashed through her head and she instinctively glanced toward Bob's old desk, briefly remembering her nerdy friend.

"We need to meet." the e-mail continued, followed by instructions to a rendezvous spot. The e-mail was from the mysterious man who called himself James.

She deleted the message.

*   *   *

Mary entered her apartment and noticed that her computer was on. She never left it on. She also noticed her work desk had been tampered with. She pulled out a 9mm from the kitchen drawer, checked the clip, clicked the safety off and started to search the apartment. It appeared the apartment had been broken into, but nothing seemed to be missing. After she was satisfied she was alone, she walked to her answering machine and hit the blinking red button.

"Mary, it's Kelsy." Her voice sounded anxious. "I need to see you as soon as possible."

The machine went to the next message.

"Mary, I'm at the hospital." Kelsy's voice resounded with the roughness of someone who hadn't slept in days. "They shot my mother."

Mary was heading for the door when another message stopped her. It was Kelsy again. "She's in a coma," her voice cracked. The answering machine began rewinding. Mary was out the door and on her cell phone.

*   *   *

The church was empty and dark, with the exception of dim security lights in the hallways. A rectangle of light poured into one of the corridors from the office where Allen searched through a file cabinet for anything relating to last year's Easter healings. He'd promised Mary he'd stay put in the hotel room until she returned, but he just couldn't sit back and do nothing. The accusations of the false healings were eating away at him. He needed to find the truth.

He noticed a shadow on the wall in the hallway. He pulled a one iron out of a golf bag resting in the corner of the room, but he changed his mind and returned the club and grabbed a seven iron instead. He never could hit with a one iron. He cautiously approached the door with the golf club cocked over his shoulder, ready to strike. The figure entered the office, and Allen drew back the club.

"Stop!" the man yelled, "It's me!"

It was Robert Ward, Allen's public relations man.

"You shouldn't sneak around in the dark," Allen warned.

Robert lowered his hands. "What are you doing here?"

"Playing through," he said. "What's it look like?"

"Where have you been?" Robert asked. "I've been worried. Are you all right? The news reports were horrifying. You didn't call."

"I'm fine."

"That whole Florida thing is exactly why you have to listen to me. Incidents like that are why I keep insisting on bodyguards at all times," Robert griped.

"There were over one hundred security personnel on the premises. If someone wants to kill me there's no way to stop it from occurring. What is meant to be will be. I prefer not to put other lives in danger because of me." A fleeting thought of the innocent people who had already died or had been harmed because of the search into his past came to mind.

"That's what bodyguards are for; that's what they're paid to do."

"My bodyguard is God."

Robert rolled his eyes. "Please, Allen, be reasonable."

"There were six of us on that stage, Robert. Five are dead. I'm alive. For some reason, God wanted me to survive."

"You were lucky, Allen! The psychopath ran out of bullets! By the way, what are you doing in my office?" Robert asked.

"There's talk about the ministry being involved with false doctrine and fake healings," he said, flipping through the file cabinet.

"Who said that?"

"Have you heard anything?"

"No," Robert said looking down at the files. "What are you looking for?"

"Names."

"Whose? Why?" Robert began returning the files to the cabinet.

"I was told there was a group of people, two women in particular who attended the church last Easter weekend claiming to be cancer patients. They were miraculously healed."

"And?"

"I was told they never had cancer," he said staring hard into Robert's eyes.

Robert looked incredulous. "Who told you that?"

Allen grabbed some documents. "It's not important who." He jotted names and addresses on a piece of paper and prepared to leave the office.

"Where are you going?"

"I'll call you."

"When?" Robert yelled before Allen disappeared around the corner. The sound came to him of Robert slamming the file cabinet shut.

*   *   *

Mary eased into the hospital room where Kelsy lay, slumped over, her head resting on her mother's bed. The equipment hummed and beeped rhythmically in the sterile, white room. The sight of cold machinery, a dozen tubes, and hoses running in and out of Kelsy's mother sent a chill throughout her body. She gently put her hand on Kelsy's shoulder. She woke with a sudden jerk, her glare fixed on Mary. It was the look of someone coming out of a nightmare, only to realize they were still in one.

"Kelsy, it's me."

Kelsy's facial features relaxed and a tired smile struggled to replace the fear. Her eyes reflected a deep pain and her face had become pale.

Mary casually glanced down and observed Kelsy had her gun drawn, close to her body in an attempt to conceal it, and it was pointed at her. She was prepared, but for what, or for who? "Are you all right?" she asked, returning her attention to Kelsy's weary eyes.

"They shot her," she said softly.

"Who?"

"I don't know. Whoever it is that wants the information. Whoever it is that doesn't want us poking around in Allen's past."

"What information?"

"Mom received a package with disks," she said glancing at her mother. "I think William sent it."

"Your friend from the Pentagon? The one who died shortly after Bob?"

Kelsy nodded.

"The elderly woman I was supposed to meet in Florida was murdered minutes before I arrived at her house," Mary said, suggesting it was related somehow to the other deaths.

"Was that a coincidence, too?"

She deserved Kelsy's little cynical jab for not believing her conspiracy theory. "No, you were right. Someone doesn't want us to know something, and they're willing to kill to keep that something a secret."

Kelsy pulled a piece of paper from under her mother's mattress and handed it to her. "This is a list of names from one of the disks. Uncle Sam has some of the other disks. He's looking for someone to help him decipher the information."

Sam had been a mentor to Mary and Kelsy. He prepared them for the bureau and he was always there for them. A year had passed since Mary had seen or spoken to him. She missed him dearly. This wasn't the way she wanted to get back together.

She skimmed the list before she folded it and put it in her pocket. "You might want to lie low for awhile."

Kelsy lifted her head into the light. Mary saw something in her face she had never seen before. Pure hatred. She turned her gaze to her mother. "I don't think I can do that." The rancor and vengeance in her voice was unmistakable.

This wasn't the same person Mary knew before the Florida trip. The passive, pleasant, good-natured person had transformed. Kelsy had gone into a daze, staring stone-like at her mother, but Mary could see something boiling within her, something raging, something very ugly.

*   *   *

Two pairs of concealed eyes watched Allen hurry out of a side exit of the church and head for the front of the building. The sun had set a half hour before and a low lying fog had moved in, washing out the exterior security lights, making visibility poor. A group of shrubs and trees had been permitted to grow wild alongside the walkway, adequate cover for an ambush. And that was precisely what awaited Allen. Hidden within the black and gray shadows of the foliage and undergrowth was a snake, not of the reptile variety, but a man who was only known as the Viper. He had no name, no social security number and no record of any possessions. He did not exist. He was an agent in an organization that couldn't be found in the yellow pages, the history books, or any government directory. He was part of a network ambiguously known as the Shadow Government.

The Viper clutched a syringe in his gloved hand filled with a clear liquid. A concoction designed to stop a man dead in his tracks, quickly followed by an excruciating death. He found a gun too simple and impersonal. He enjoyed the thought of the expression on the forensic scientist's face working the body when they discovered his little surprise; a calling card of sorts. One of the components in the poisonous mixture he used on his victims came from the duckbill platypus of eastern Australia. The platypus had a sharp, hollow, spur on the inside of both hind leg ankles, which were connected to a venom gland that produced a very deadly toxin. It made him smile complacently knowing they would find this unique substance. What a stir it would cause. It would be the talk of the office. And then, they would slowly learn with great astonishment there had been fourteen other unsolved murders with the identical distinctive toxin.

Allen's pace increased with every step, now only ten feet away from where the Viper was lurking. He carefully raised the syringe, preparing for the strike. His target was the back of the neck. Allen paused for a moment and glanced over his shoulder, as if he thought he was being followed. There was nothing behind him but white fog.

The Viper couldn't believe his luck. His prey stopped directly in front of him. He stepped out from behind the tree, the syringe leading the way. Unexpectedly, a gust of wind rushed down through the trees, so strong and forceful that it blew Allen's baseball cap off his head and the papers out of his hand. Two beams of light appeared at the end of the sidewalk. A taxicab pulled up to the corner and sounded its horn. Allen jogged the rest of the way with his hat and papers in hand.

Near the base of the tree where the Viper had waited for Allen, lay the syringe, still full. The Viper had been dragged into the blackest part of the shadows by a leather-gloved hand pushed firmly over his mouth and a powerful arm constricted around his neck. James, who himself was employed by another agency that also didn't exist had subdued the would-be assassin.

He placed his mouth close to the Viper's ear. "My name is," he whispered, "The King Cobra."

The Viper's eyes widened as if that meant something imperative; something fatal.

"Do you know what a King Cobra feeds on?" James asked. An eerie moment of silence passed. "Other snakes," he hissed, followed by the sound of snapping vertebra.

Chapter 24

The White House

"With all due respect, sir," the senior advisor pleaded. "We cannot reschedule an entire month."

"He's right, sir," the aide concurred.

"If the American people discover we altered our agenda because of Sean Carbon's 'Prophecy of Death' prediction," the senior advisor continued, "we'd be a laughingstock."

"Our polls are down, sir."

Derrick was already aware of this. He knew he'd lost favor with the people over the past few months. What was once a love affair had slowly grown cold. Three years ago America needed someone like him to bring respectability and hope back to the country, and he did just that, but now the critics had grown louder than the supporters. He remembered an old adage a preacher back home liked to say to the infrequent visitors of the church. "The church is always full in times of trouble." Three years ago it was a time of trouble and Derrick was the church.

Derrick's critics had always believed he employed more religion than politics in his policies, and that opinion was becoming popular with the media. The same critics deemed the White House the White Chapel and Derrick the Pennsylvania Avenue Preacher. His method of running the country was a refreshing change and was received with open arms, but it now it appeared he'd worn out his welcome.

"We can't afford another Black Christmas, Mr. President," the advisor cautioned.

Derrick thought back to that. Two years earlier in December, the United Nations had invited the leaders of fifty-six countries to

Jerusalem for a celebration of peace and to sign a good-faith treaty. But Derrick had not attended. He had been persuaded by Greg to stay home. After translating an ancient manuscript, Greg believed a great earthquake would strike Jerusalem killing thousands, including Derrick.

The earthquake never occurred and the media had a field day with the story. They wrote callously that he wouldn't make a political decision without consulting a psychic hotline or having his palm read. There were comic strips of him sitting in front of a crystal ball seeking advice; every late-night show did endless satires of him. During the ensuing fifteen months, he slowly and painfully won back the respect of the American people and the world.

Greg's credibility had also been damaged. To his credit, he'd been right about things of this nature a number of times before. He had warned Derrick of potential dangers lurking in his future. They were the type of dangers the spiritually cognizant would understand, the type of dangers Greg called spiritual battles in the physical realm; turning points in the war between good and evil. He was alive because of Greg, but Greg never received the recognition he deserved because the danger was spiritual in nature, and when those type of things were spoken of, they were received with hard skepticism and disbelief. Detractors said the unseen or the unexplainable events Greg spoke about were simply religious marketing to keep God alive. Unexplainable didn't necessarily mean ghosts and goblins, the critics argued.

Derrick found himself caught in the middle of a struggle between his head and his soul, between politics and religion. His head told him he was the President of the United States of America and he must do his job, period. His soul, on the other hand, was on high alert for something on the spiritual horizon, something that would touch the entire world, something that would change him, forever.

The senior advisor and the aide glanced at one other, and he thought he knew what they were thinking. It had been obvious for some time. They believed Greg was a religious fanatic who would do more harm than good to his decisions, and would only cloud his judgment with religious nonsense.

A military official entered the oval office with a printout.

He scanned the sheet. "*A push* isn't a loss."

"Sir?" the advisor asked.

"The hostage situation hasn't changed," he explained. "Everything is still quiet."

"That's a good sign," the aide said.

Yes, it was a good sign, but no one was celebrating. Today's news was like stopping the bleeding of a gunshot. Now the real work would begin.

*   *   *

Down the hall from the oval office, Shelly Deanster was meeting with her attorney, finalizing her resignation. The committee investigating her current situation had leaked a story implying her health was failing. She'd had a bout with ovarian cancer three and a half years ago and now the committee found it suitable to have her cancer recur, giving her adequate grounds to resign from her position. She had yet to tell Derrick of her plans to resign.

*   *   *

Annapolis, MD

Kelsy maneuvered into the right lane and headed for the City Dock. She hated driving in Annapolis, but the people stuck behind her probably hated it even more so. An eighty-year-old woman driving at midnight without headlights was more aggressive than she was. When it came to parking in historic Annapolis, timing was everything: The planets and stars had to be properly lined up and hell had to be hosting the winter Olympics for that to happen.

She eventually headed toward a garage and parked. She waded out into the masses. The historic town was buzzing with people;

nothing like a warm day in March to bring them out in droves. She stood at the corner waiting for a chance to cross the street.

The red bricks of Main Street reminded her of an ex-boyfriend who had attended the Naval Academy. He had been arrested for attempting to steal one of the red bricks out of the street for her; a romantic gesture, but stupid all the same. Although he really wasn't arrested. The Anne Arundel county police officer had him sit in the back seat of the cruiser for twenty minutes before he eventually let him go with a warning. The memory brought a smile to her face.

She entered Riordan's and took a seat at one of the small, round tables with the high barstool-style chairs. It was near the picture window and allowed her to watch the passers-by. She ordered a diet soda with a salad and waited.

"Hey, Kell," Sam said, taking a seat across from her.

"I didn't see you walk in."

"I was already here. I was in the bathroom," he said as the waitress handed him his Scotch on the rocks and an order of crab balls.

"How long have you been here?"

"About an hour."

"Parking spaces are getting harder to come by," she said, frustrated.

He popped a crab ball into his mouth. "I'm staying on a friend's boat until Carl brings mine up from Florida."

"At the dock?"

"Yeah," he answered taking a sip.

"It's a little early for that, isn't it?"

He grinned. "I'm on European time. Where's Mary?"

"She's on her way." She picked at her salad. "Did you decipher the disk?"

"No, but I found someone who'll be able to help us."

"Who?"

"His name is . . ." He reached into his pocket and pulled out a wrinkled piece of paper. "Professor Gregory Orfordis. He's a theologian."

"A theologian?"

"He also specializes in linguistics."

"How did you find him?"

"Through a friend."

"Can we trust him?"

"I trust my friend."

Kelsy looked out the window for Mary.

"We have to drive to D.C." Sam said.

Kelsy saw Mary pull up in front of Riordan's and double-park her car. She turned on the hazards and popped open the hood, giving the impression of a car in distress. She walked into the restaurant.

"Great idea," Mary said sarcastically. "Let's meet in Annapolis on the weekend on a sunny day at noon."

"Quit your whining," Sam said, standing to hug her.

"Uncle Sam!" Suddenly, Mary sounded more like a little girl. She extended her arms wide with a big smile.

She buried her face into his broad chest. She looked thirteen in his massive embrace. His large frame and arms engulfed her. She pulled back and tugged on his beard. "Getting a little gray, aren't we?"

Sam glanced at her backside. "Putting on a little weight, aren't we?"

She reached up and rubbed his completely shaved bald head. "All right, Mr. Clean, I give."

He grabbed her and hugged her again. "I missed you, you little smart ass."

"I missed you, too." She looked up at him. "I'm sorry about Aunt Kat," she whispered.

"She'll be fine," he said under his breath. "And we'll be fine when we get who's responsible."

"Let's go."

"So much for the pleasantries," Mary joked. The three of them stepped out onto the sidewalk. "Where are we going?"

The breeze coming off the Chesapeake Bay had increased, and so had the crowd of people pouring into town.

"We have to go to D.C.," Kelsy answered.

"Great!" Mary rolled her eyes. "The parking is much better down there."

Sam put his arm around Mary and smiled down at her. "And you get to drive."

They piled into her car and Mary merged onto route 50 west and whipped into the fast lane, nearly running another car off the road in the process.

Sam grabbed the dashboard. "Nice move."

In the backseat, Kelsy dropped the file in attempt to find something to hold on to. She gave Mary a dirty look. "What are you doing?"

Mary grinned in the rear view mirror at her.

She hated the way Mary drove. Not too many people would find Mary's driving comfortable, unless they were a blind stunt man with a death wish.

"Relax, Kell," Sam said calmly. "The person in the backseat rarely dies."

Mary crossed three lanes of traffic to pass a group of cars. She quickly switched lanes again returning to the fast lane. Sam located his seat belt and fastened it and Mary gave him a condescending smile.

"It's the law," Sam said.

Mary laughed.

"I like your coffee cup collection," Kelsy said noticing the twenty or more 7-11 styrofoam cups on the floor of the car.

"Thanks. As you can see, the twenty ounce cups are in mint condition."

"What if Toto was a pit bull?" Sam blurted out of the blue.

Mary gave him an odd look. "What?"

"It was a bumper sticker on the car you just passed."

Mary laughed. "What if Toto was a pit bull?"

"I'll tell you what," Sam joked. "That would change the storyline a little."

"Cujo in Oz," Mary grinned. "Miss Gulch would be dead meat before the movie got started."

"That reminds me," Sam said. "Something about that movie always bothered me. Where do you think the red brick road leads to?"

"What are you talking about?" Mary asked.

"In the movie the yellow brick swirls outward from the center of Munchkinland. There's a red brick road too. Where do you think that one leads to?"

"Annapolis," Kelsy answered.

"Only you would notice something like that," Mary said. She whipped in and out of traffic.

Kelsy shook her head and rolled her eyes. "You can *not* drive."

"Oh yeah, and you're a great driver, Grandma Kell" she mocked.

"I've never had a speeding ticket in my life."

"That's because you either show the cop your FBI badge or bat your big blue eyes at them."

"First of all," Kelsy shot back, "I would never do that. Secondly, I don't get pulled over."

"Sure."

"Plus, I've also never had an accident in my life, unlike someone I know."

"No, you just cause them," Mary teased.

Sam grinned. "Some things never change."

"You'd think you would've gotten used to my driving after all these years," Mary said.

Kelsy snickered. "How do you get used to near-death experiences?"

"Are we there yet?" Sam said, like a little kid. "I have to pee."

"Keep it up," Mary said. "There won't be any Happy Meals for you."

One of Kelsy's favorite songs came on the radio. She started to sing along with the words.

"Who sings this song?" Mary asked.

"Anita Baker."

"Why don't you let her sing it?" Mary cracked.

Kelsy let out a fake laugh and flicked her in the back of head. Mary threw an empty cup at her.

"All right kids," Sam said, "knock it off."

"She started it," Mary laughed.

After a moment of peace between them, Sam opened a folder. "Did you get any information from the woman in Florida?"

Mary glanced at him. "She wouldn't talk over the phone. She got real nervous when I brought up Allen's name."

"Her name shows up on the disk a few times. She's definitely involved."

"Was," Kelsy said sharply. Her old self had slipped away again and the Kelsy who was filled with anger, hate, and revenge had appeared. She knew her feelings would play emotional ping-pong till she learned to deal with them.

"So, we all agree there's a cover up?" Sam asked.

"I can't see it being anything else," Mary said. "Cover ups and conspiracies always leave a trail of dead bodies."

"We need to keep following the bodies," Kelsy said.

If there was any skepticism before, there was no indication of it now. The car hummed with silence the rest of the way.

Mary pulled up to a church. "Is this the right place?"

Sam glanced at a piece of paper and checked the address. "This is it."

"There's a parking space over there," Kelsy said pointing across the street.

Mary stomped on the gas pedal, causing the tires to squeal and smoke. She turned the steering wheel hard and made a sharp U-turn, then slammed on the brakes. Cars passed with blaring horns and dirty looks and a few colorful words. Mary smiled sarcastically at them as they passed. "Have a nice day." She threw the transmission into reverse and quickly backed into the parking space.

Sam paled. "I bet you passed the driver's test the first time you took it."

"Yup."

Upset, Kelsy glared at Mary.

"What?" Mary asked.

"Are you out of your mind?"

"Did I scare you?"

Kelsy got out of the car, happy to be alive. She saw Sam and Mary make eye contact.

"Don't think I don't know you're making fun of me," she said, half joking. The old Kelsy was back. Mary and Sam started laughing out loud.

"It's all right, Kell," Sam said. "I'll tell you what . . . I'll drive home."

"You're no better than she is. I'll take a cab."

"I'll let you drive," Mary said holding out the keys.

Kelsy snatched the keys out of her hand. "Thank you."

"Should we go through the front doors?" Sam asked.

Mary shrugged her shoulders. "I don't know."

They stood gawking at the enormous and beautiful stone gray church with its oversized stained glass windows and large wooden doors at the entrance. The bell tower seemed to reach to the heavens.

"I got this Wizard of Oz feeling," Sam said.

"Let's see if the wizard is home." Mary added.

"Which one of you is Dorothy?" a voice asked from behind them.

They turned to find a young black man. He was wearing the traditional black clothes and a white collar of a priest.

"We have a meeting with Professor Gregory Orfordis," Sam said, looking like he was caught telling a dirty joke in church.

The priest smiled. "I'll take you to him if you'd like."

"Thank you," Mary said.

The young priest led them through the large wooden doors and down a brilliant white and cream marble floored corridor. On the left wall there were stained glass windows portraying Biblical events. When the sunlight filtered through them they exploded brilliantly in a vivid display of color. Lifelike statues of saints carved of ivory colored marble lined the right side of the corridor.

They exited the side of the church and reached a staircase leading up to what appeared to be an adjoining apartment or office. The priest knocked. "Professor Orfordis."

"Come in!" a voice yelled.

The priest stepped aside. "You may go in," he said opening the door for them. "Welcome to Emerald City," he added with a wink.

They entered the office, which was sectioned off into two halves by file cabinets. One side was a mess, looking more like a storage area than an office. The other side of the room was neat and orderly. A gold plated plaque that read, "Don't allow religion or science to keep you from God, rested on the messy desk.

"What can I do for you today, young Father Jones?" Greg said from behind a stack of boxes.

"Professor. I'm Sam Dent. I called."

Greg's gray, balding head appeared over the boxes. His complexion was flushed. "You sound exactly like Father Jones," he said, pushing a box aside.

"I called yesterday. I made an appointment."

"Oh, yes, of course," he said, coming around the boxes. "Excuse the mess." He threw boxes off the chairs. "Please sit."

Sam introduced them. "This is Mary Jopuez and Kelsy Anderson."

"Very nice to meet you," the professor said.

Kelsy and Mary sat while Sam stood. Mary glanced at the neat and orderly side of the room. Greg continued to move things about the room when he noticed Mary observing the other side. "I share the room with a colleague. Obviously, one a little tidier than I," he added, smiling.

"Neatness is overrated," Mary said.

Greg dropped a box full of papers. "I agree." He walked across the room and took his place behind his desk. "You said you have something for me to decipher." He wiped the perspiration from his forehead.

"That's right." Sam handed him the file.

Greg searched his desk. Mary stood and lifted a piece of paper, revealing his glasses.

"Thank you, young lady." He slid his glasses on, opened the file and read for a moment. He scanned through some of the other papers. Sam's hand written notes were also in the file. "From your own notes I see you already know this is Morse Code and these are names and occupations," he said, still flipping through the file.

"Yes, we figured out some of the names making up the list," Kelsy said.

Greg read something in the file that made his eyebrows arch. "What is it?" Mary asked.

"It appears our government stole an ancient artifact from a Middle East museum some years ago." He appeared very interested with this fact. "In Tel Aviv to be more precise."

"Tel Aviv?" Kelsy asked.

"This part speaks about a covert mission," Greg said, running his finger across the printout. "They burglarized the Museum of Antiquities. I'm not entirely sure what is said here. I need time to decode the other letters, but what I'm able to translate offhand is that the United States government sent a team of SEALS to retrieve an artifact." He took his glasses off. "I remember reading about an artifact that was stolen from an Israeli museum in the early sixties. It caused great tension between a number of countries."

"My father was in the CIA," Sam said. "I remember him talking about it to other agents. There was a lot of finger pointing."

"I believe a prime minister's son was killed during the burglary," Greg recalled.

"My father thought there was going to be military confrontation because of the stolen artifact," Sam added. "Of course, the public was never made aware of the potential dangers."

"Of course," Mary said satirically.

"I remember the Russians and the Americans were blaming one another," Greg said. "And the Israeli government was blaming both of them."

"What happened?" Kelsy asked.

"The rumors were that an Arabian cult was responsible, but no criminal charges were brought," Greg explained. "No organization claimed responsibility for the crime and there were never any arrests."

"And the artifact, was it found?" Mary asked.

Sam leaned against a filing cabinet. "No."

"What was it?" Kelsy asked.

"That's one of the remarkable things about this story. No one has ever said," Greg answered. "It was discovered in a tomb outside of Jerusalem by French and American archaeological teams. The tomb was believed to be the true resting place of Jesus Christ after the crucifixion. Many are convinced the artifact had something to do with the burial."

"Maybe it was his bones," Sam suggested.

Kelsy looked up at him. "Whose bones?"

Sam swept them all with his glance. "Jesus'"

"That's impossible," Greg said. "Jesus was resurrected."

"Oh that's right," Sam said, retreating. "I forgot."

Kelsy stared at him as if she'd discovered something new and disturbing about her uncle.

Mary laughed and wiggled a finger at Sam like a parent to a naughty boy.

"Feel free to voice your opinions Mr. Dent," Greg invited.

"Some other time, professor," Sam said with a glance at the girls.

"What do you think the artifact was?" Mary asked, saving Sam from a theological debate with Greg.

"Possibly a shroud or a scroll, a manuscript of some kind."

Sam gave Mary an appreciative wink.

"Why would anyone want to steal it?" Kelsy asked. "It would be nearly impossible to sell it and they could never display it openly."

"I don't believe they intended it for a display case or for financial gain." There was a haunting undertone in Greg's reply. "over the years, a legend was affixed to the artifact. It has reached mythical status."

Mary, Kelsy, and Sam were intrigued by Greg's sudden somberness. "The legend goes, who ever possesses the artifact will reign over the earthly domain, and be the king of kings. It's believed to have unspeakable power. The power of God."

Mary stood. "So, this file says our government stole an artifact from an Israeli museum and killed a prime minister's son in the process. That way the good ol' U.S. of A. could have world domination."

"Sounds like *Raiders of the Lost Ark*," Sam joked.

"Assuming the file is genuine, it's obvious they stole the artifact," Mary said.

Kelsy nodded. "Right. If the information is authentic, then that gives us our motive for the murders."

"Murders?" Greg asked.

"We believe people are dying because of these files," Sam finally said. "Whatever is in these files, the repercussions must be immeasurable."

"Worth killing for," Kelsy added.

"You don't have to get involved, professor," Sam said. "You have the option to turn down the job. It's going to put your life in the line of fire."

"We would understand if you refuse to assist us," Kelsy said.

"I'll begin tonight," Greg said without hesitation.

"How did you come across the information?"

"A friend discovered he was adopted," Mary answered.

"We stumbled across the data while digging around in his past," Kelsy said. A hint of sadness emerged with the thought of her dead friends.

"When you searched this friend's past, this data came up?" Greg asked.

"That's right."

He stared at the file. "Stolen artifacts and covert missions," he said more to himself than to anyone else. "Are there any obvious connections between your friend and the file? Does he have a military or government background?"

"No," Mary answered.

"I work in the FBI," Kelsy said. "I searched his name and his file opened a network of other confidential files."

"Well, it appears your friend's foster parents or biological parents were involved somehow, and your friend was the key link to the data. I'm willing to guess you have ruled out any chance of this being a coincidence or some unfortunate accident."

Sam, Kelsy, and Mary nodded, ruling out that option.

"If it's a conspiracy," Greg said, "I'm sure I'll find evidence of it in here." He tapped the file with his finger.

"Professor, what's that symbol?" Kelsy asked of a drawing on the chalkboard.

"It's the sign of the Demonic Trinity."

"I've never heard of that."

"It's from ancient writings found in the foothills of Qumran, near the Dead Sea, written by a group known as the Essenes."

Sam walked over and took a closer look. The symbol was one large circle with three smaller circles within.

Greg stood and used a pointer. "There are three sixes connected to one another that creates this circular symbol. Each six represents one of the individuals in the Demonic Trinity."

"Six, six, six, the number of the beast," Mary said.

"Revelation 13:18," Greg added.

Sam scrutinized the symbol."What's a Demonic Trinity?"

"When the Antichrist, the False Prophet, and Satan become one."

"What does that mean?" he asked.

Greg smiled. "Bad news."

"Has this happened already?" Kelsy asked.

"I believe it will occur in the near future." Greg's demeanor suggested that could be tomorrow.

Mary and Sam glanced at one another; both of their 'weirdo-alert-antennas' went up.

"It looks like you're really into it," Sam commented.

"It's a hobby." Greg sat down behind his desk. "Like studying different languages. Mr. Dent, I noticed your hand. Did you hurt it?"

"I don't really know," Sam said glancing down at his reddish hand.

"It looks like a rash," Kelsy said.

"You should have someone take a look at it." He held up the file. "I'll have this done for you at the end of the week."

"Thank you, professor," Sam said, heading out the door.

Kelsy and Mary exchanged parting pleasantries with Greg before leaving.

"Where did you find him?" Mary asked, insinuating Greg was a tad on the odd side.

"Ten ninety-six" Sam said, pertaining to the 10-code used by police departments. A 10-96 stood for "mental subject."

"Quiet, he might hear you," Kelsy whispered.

"What's the symbol for screw loose," Sam grinned.

Mary flicked him with her finger in the back of the head. "You need to respect your elders."

"Do you believe that religious, demonic nonsense?" Sam laughed. "This guy rides the short bus."

"You better be careful, before God strikes you in that big, fat, bald head of yours," Mary said with a snicker.

Sam reached for her, but she ran down the corridor of the church. He chased after her. Their laughter echoed through the church.

"I can't believe they're doing this," Kelsy mumbled. She attempted to keep up without running.

*   *   *

Washington, D.C.

Allen stepped out of the elevator and made his way to the lounge of the Hilton. He ordered an iced tea.

His public relations manager, Robert took a seat next to him. "I'll have a martini."

"It's a little early for that, don't you think?"

Robert glanced at his watch. "It's 12:01, Allen. That makes it officially afternoon," he said, stirring his drink. "So, tell me what you found out about the fake healings."

"It appears the healings were staged."

Robert finished his drink and quickly ordered another. "This is bad."

"You knew nothing of this?"

"No," Robert said defensively. "I didn't."

"Then, who could do this, who could conceal it from the both of us?"

"We have over a hundred people on staff and twenty of them are responsible in the guess department."

"Find out who's responsible, Robert."

"What do you hope to accomplish by doing this?"

"Millions of people look to me for guidance and for the truth," he said. "I don't need lies and cheap tricks associated with me."

"All right, Allen." Robert pushed away from the bar and threw money down. "I'll get on it."

"I want a statement prepared."

Robert shook his head. "Are you going to go public with this?"

"Yes, but only to *Time*."

"Why?"

"It's better if we expose ourselves."

Robert and Allen walked out of the hotel together.

"I need a ride," Allen said.

"Hop in." Robert opened the door to the limo.

Ten minutes later the limousine pulled up to the hospital.

"Thanks for the ride," Allen said, jumping out.

"You shouldn't be running around alone," Robert yelled out of the window.

"I'm a big boy."

"I'll wait," Robert yelled.

"I'll call Mary," he yelled back before disappearing through the hospital entrance.

Allen stood beside Kelsy's mother's bed in prayer for ten minutes. He thought or he believed that if he came to the hospital that he could heal her mother. So did Kelsy. It appears he was wrong. What would he say to Kelsy? It wasn't God's will for him to heal her. It wasn't meant to be. Allen knew there was a reason for everything. Kelsy's mother's coma had a propose, but God only knew; and He wasn't talking.

Chapter 25

Washington, D.C.

Sean Carbon sat at a small, rectangular table, accompanied by his lawyer. One Secret Service agent stood guard at the door; a second was positioned against the far wall.

A man in a dark blue suit paced the floor. "Guardian Angel Program," the man asked. "What is it?"

"An Internet advice column," Carbon responded in a cool business-like manner.

"And the 'Crystal Ball Program?'"

Carbon's attorney leaned in. "You don't have to answer anything."

The man in the dark suit leaned in toward the lawyer. "Oh, I think he does. You see, Mr. Thousand Dollar Suit, if he doesn't answer my questions to my satisfaction I'm going to lock the both of you up under the laws of terrorism and national security. Yes, you will eventually get out of jail, but not before I put you in with some big, hairy monsters who may think you're cute."

He knew that the Crystal Ball Program was a chat room where Carbon made personal commentaries on the world's affairs. The chat room had a member's only status. The members were believed to be the world's clairvoyant, psychic, and telepathic, who made predictions on future historical events. They were said to have correctly predicted the deaths of Princess Diana and JFK Jr., as well as President Clinton's scandalous affair. Rumors said that the members and the Crystal Ball prophets wagered large sums of money on the next famous individual to die. It was notoriously known as the "Dead List." Some said it was more like a hit list. But no one had ever seen it.

"That program has been eliminated," Carbon finally answered. "Soon after the failure of the Y2K prediction."

"Well, Mr. Carbon," the dark-suited man said, "our sources say the Crystal Ball program is now under a new name, 'The Phantom of Nasadomnes.'"

Carbon's eyes remained cool. "That is my personal chat room where I air out my opinions on current affairs and future events."

"It isn't the Crystal Ball Program?"

"No."

"So, the Phantom of Nasadomnes is your personal chat room where you can express your views and thoughts about the future?"

"Yes."

"Like the Prophecy of Death?"

"Yes."

"Is the Prophecy of Death a threat to the President of the United States of America?"

"No." Carbon answered. "The prediction was a publicity stunt."

"Thank you for your time, Mr. Carbon. You're free to go."

He watched as Carbon walked out the door and snickered. Carbon may have millions of dollars, but he had just tasted real power. The power of the government; the type of power that could snatch your freedom at will.

*   *   *

Kelsy entered her apartment and noticed a folded map on the floor. She drew her weapon and scanned the room. This time she automatically clicked the safety off. She was getting accustomed to carrying a weapon, and becoming very comfortable handling one. There were no obvious signs of a break-in. She checked the apartment one room at a time and when she was convinced she was alone, she relaxed.

She pushed the map with a broomstick making sure it wasn't a bomb. She lifted the map with tweezers as if she were picking up a dead mouse by the tail. After examining both sides of the map she unfolded it carefully. The thought of anthrax entered her mind.

She nearly jumped out of her skin when the phone rang. It scared her so much she threw the map clear across the room.

"Hello," she said, aggravated.

"Did you get the map?" James asked.

"What the hell were you doing in my apartment?"

"Dropping off the map."

"Stay out of my home."

"Sorry." His sincerity was evident.

There was uncomfortable silence on the line from both ends.

"Just don't do it again," she finally said, but her voice softened.

"Sure."

She went to the refrigerator. "So, what's the map for?" she asked while searching for a beer. She was positive there was one more left.

"I located a warehouse with more information that can help you. It's your choice, of course."

"I'll think about it," she said, still digging through the fridge. "Aren't you worried the line's bugged?"

"It's not."

"You would know."

"About that warehouse. There may be something about the people responsible for your mother's shooting."

The line went quiet again.

"I have to go."

"Sure," he said, not pushing the matter further. "One more thing."

"What?"

"I owe you a beer," he said before hanging up.

She noticed an empty beer bottle on the kitchen counter. "He drank my last beer."

*   *   *

"As you can see behind me," the reporter said into the camera, "people from all over the world are throwing their Bibles into the raging fire here in Jerusalem."

The camera zoomed to a wide-angle shot. The burning books had grown to a mountainous size. The foundation of the bonfire alone covered two acres.

"We've been told by a local source," the reporter continued, "that the burning protest is a demonstration against a group called the Christian-Jewish Witnesses. CJW has been here in the Holy Land for three and a half years preaching doomsday sermons and strongly criticizing the New Faith Order. From what we were able to gather, the CJW believes the New Faith Order is corrupting the world's religions, and has degenerated the faith of the Holy City. The CJW claims the Holy Land has become Sodom and Egypt, the symbols of immorality and materialism, and God's judgment will soon fall upon them. What you see behind me is the backlash of the CJW movement."

After five seconds of a close-up of the blazing books, the camera refocused on the reporter. "And this isn't the only location where this type of demonstration has occurred. We have reports from all over the world. There are thousands of Bible-burning protests. Also, there have been countless deaths related to the protest. In Spain, fifteen are dead after an attempt was made to stop a burning protest and yesterday a man shot down six people who were trying to burn their Bibles."

"All in the name of God." Art had a difficult time concealing the distaste in his voice.

Greg turned the volume down on the TV. "You must remember, Mr. Hanson, the wolf in sheep's clothing isn't just a catchy phrase."

"What do you mean?"

"I'm saying evil isn't always monsters with big teeth and claws. All that glitters isn't gold. Sometimes evil is cloaked in a robe hidden within the church."

"I'm sorry," Art said, "but it just seems religion is behind most of the problems in the world."

"No, Mr. Hanson," Greg corrected. "Human nature is." He walked around his desk and sat. "They simply use God for their own personal agendas. This has been prophesied."

"You mean it was supposed to happen?"

"It's a sign. A way God tells His believers what's coming."

"A Bible bonfire is a sign from God?"

He grinned. "Not exactly. The book of Revelation says there will be two witnesses professing the word of God for three and a half years before they are killed and their bodies are left in the streets of Jerusalem for the nations of the world to look upon. The Christian-Jewish Witness group preached in the Holy Land for exactly 1,260 days, which is three and a half years."

"Exactly?"

"Exactly."

"I didn't see any bodies on the news. Where are the two witnesses?"

"I believe the two witnesses murdered and left in the streets are the burning Bibles themselves."

"I don't get it."

"I believe the Old Testament and the New Testament are the two witnesses."

"So, what happens next?"

Greg flipped to a section in his Bible and read. "But after the three and a half days a breath of life from God entered them, and they stood on their feet, and terror struck those who saw them. Then they heard a loud voice from heaven saying to them, 'Come up here.' And they went up to heaven in a cloud . . .'"

"Sorry, professor, you lost me," Art said shrugging his shoulders. "It doesn't make any sense to me."

"That will occur next," Greg said. "I'm not certain how this will unfold myself, so we're just going to have to wait and see. And after these things take place there will be an earthquake."

"I know where I'm not vacationing."

Greg couldn't help it. Art's offhand comments made him smile. He put away his Bible.

"You might want to take care of that," Art said glancing at Greg's Bible. "It might be a collector's item the way things are going." He tossed a file on the desk. "Here's some more stuff on Jordan Iblis."

"Have you had that checked?" Greg asked, noticing the rash still on Art's hand.

"Not yet."

"I see Jordan met with the same people," Greg commented as he read the file. "Did he meet with anyone new?"

"No."

He closed the file. "I'll finish reading this later. You should get that looked at," he suggested again.

"Sure, professor," Art said, already half way up the stairs.

He opened his Bible again and turned to a section in Revelation. "Then a third angel followed them, saying with a loud voice, 'If anyone worships the beast and his image, and receives his mark on his forehead or on his hand . . .'" He thought about the rash on Sam Dent's hand and the identical one on his friend Art's hand. Was it a coincidence that they were both non-believers?

Chapter 26

Parked beneath a large oak tree, Kelsy sat in a dark blue Ford Taurus thinking how ironic it was that her FBI training was being employed to burglarize a warehouse and commit larceny. She looked at the windowless, five-story gray cinderblock building. What the hell was she doing here? She was fifty miles outside Washington in a remote, wooded area in Calvert County. There were no markings on the building, no signs suggesting what might be inside, and no address. All of these subtle facts didn't surprise her, considering she'd had to take a dirt road for two miles to get to the location, a road James had to draw because it didn't appear on the map.

Stupid. The word kept popping up in her head. She was sitting in her car in the middle of nowhere because some guy gave her a map and told her she might find information there. Some guy she didn't know or trust, who may be out to get her, who may be setting her up. She looked around at the thick woods, then at the road, which was the only way in and more importantly, out. Stupid.

She meticulously calculated a plan in her head. Evade contact with people; the least number of witnesses, the better. Avoid conversations and security cameras. If seen, act as if you belong on the premises. Move fast, be careful, and keep it simple. She looked in the rear-view mirror, adjusted her fake prescription glasses and checked her black wig, making certain her blond hair was concealed. If she was caught on camera or spotted by someone, the description wouldn't fit her own. She touched her ankle where an extra weapon was affixed. Insurance. *What the hell am I doing?* she asked herself, staring into the rear-view mirror. *This is insane.*

She was moments away from breaking into a building for who knows what? The building, the trees, everything became a blur while thoughts ran through her head. This was a crossroad, a bridge, a life-changing decision; before her lay a moral line. Thoughts of anger, friends, laws, revenge, jail, morality, God, and her mother swirled around like a tornado. She felt cornered, trapped by a suffocating and driving force. She was caught in emotional blackmail.

James had promised her efforts would be rewarded, there would be answers for her friends, and ultimately the information on her mother's shooters; that thought alone was the vindication that fueled her desperate actions. And James was certainly aware of that fact. She gripped the door handle, regardless of the training she had successfully endured. There was no way to stop the negative scenarios from creeping into her head.

Stop! her mind yelled, attempting to break the tension. She gathered her thoughts and seized control of her nerves before finally jerking open the door. Another thought dawned on her. The car she'd rented was under her real name. Stupid.

She walked to the security fence. No sign of security guards or cameras. She cut a straight line in the fence and pulled back a section that allowed her to squeeze through. She returned the cut section so that from a distance the fence appeared unharmed. She reached two large gray metal doors, and still no indication of security anywhere. She picked the lock with surprising ease. Sam would be proud of her; he'd taught her how to jimmy a lock when she was a child. He had her and Mary compete in lock-picking races. It was one of the rare things Kelsy could beat Mary in.

It's not too late, a voice in her head said. *You can turn back.* She had no idea what was waiting for her on the other side of the doors. Employees working, security guards, attack dogs, or . . . or what? The penitentiary. She could feel the gray hairs pop out of her scalp.

She took a deep breath, then slowly turned the knob and eased the door open. She stepped into the darkness. No alarms, no people, no dogs, nothing but blackness and silence. She checked the door and the surrounding frame with her flashlight, for a security panel. Nothing. She let out a sigh and started to breathe again before she caused any major brain damage from the lack of oxygen. Whatever was in here didn't seem to be worth having a high quality security system. When she pointed her flashlight before her, the beam of light revealed an enormous warehouse-like structure the size of several football fields and approximately four stories high. Hundreds of rows were marked with large red letters and small black numbers.

There must have been a million wooden crates and cardboard boxes stored on large metal shelves throughout the entire building. She unfolded the map and shined the light on James' notes in the corner. *GGG 1318*, she read.

She walked along the front of the towering storage shelves and passed the single and double lettered rows. When she finally reached the triple letter section, she hurried to the triple G row. One set of numbers on the right read, '0-2000'; the set on the left read, '2001-4000.' She walked down the right side where she believed 1318 should be located and stopped in front of section 1300, where she realized that the numbers 1300 to 1399 were vertical.

She retrieved one of the many sliding ladders connected to rails on the platforms. She slid the ladder along the track into position and climbed up fifteen feet to the section marked 1310. She stepped off the ladder onto the platform that had a narrow walkway leading twenty feet inward. Her flashlight revealed crates, cardboard boxes, and an area with file cabinets. One of the cabinets was marked 1318.

She opened the top drawer of the cabinet and found thirty files, one of them being the Rosenberg file. She read the file to herself. *Sarah L. Rosenberg. Born December 25, 1940. Died April 15, 1964.* She found the death certificate. It said she died immediately after giving birth. Kelsy knew that was not true because she had died recently in Florida. Unless Mary had the wrong Rosenberg. She continued to read but there was no mention of the child.

She took pictures of the information with a small camera, then moved on to another folder which appeared to be a medical report on the Rosenberg woman. The file was a documentation of test results. She took more photographs, but also decided to take this file. The next one was sealed and had 'Confidential' written on the cover. She ripped open the folder and found photographs and a small 16mm movie reel. The photographs depicted a surgery in progress. The photos could be interpreted to be a woman in labor or an abortion procedure. Two photographs revealed a clear picture of the woman's face. Mary should be able to determine if the woman in the photos was the same as the woman who had been murdered in Florida.

The unmistakable sound of a large metal door opening startled her. Her heart caught in her throat and another batch of gray hairs popped out of her head. She grabbed an armful of the files and inched to the edge of the platform, listening for more movement. There was nothing but uncomfortable silence. Without warning, the entire warehouse erupted with phosphorescent light. She ducked back into the narrow walkway and pulled her weapon. 'James had set her up. He would know exactly where to find her. He had tricked her to come out to a remote area so he could take her out. If it wasn't James, whoever it was would never find her in this warehouse. But that thought was quickly dismissed when she heard the sound of what could only be dogs. Big dogs with big teeth, and they were getting closer.

To her astonishment, one of the Doberman pinschers had climbed the ladder. The second had positioned himself at the bottom, patrolling the floor. Eighty pounds of muscle and teeth had reached the 1300 section, then howled in pain before falling to the concrete floor dying instantly. Kelsy had sprayed the animal's eyes with a potent repellent. She heard a man racing to the top of the ladder, but she was already climbing down the other side. He opened fire on her as she reached the floor and ran. She dove into one of the narrow walkways while bullets bounced off the concrete behind her. She could hear the other Doberman approaching.

She poked her head out from the walkway and bullets ricochet around her. The man started climbing down the ladder. She decided to make a run for it. As she jumped out into the open, she fired at the man, who was now in the middle of the ladder. He returned fire but not before he took one of Kelsy's bullets in the kneecap.

He fell hard, landing on his lower back and hip. He grunted as his gun spun away and his blood spilled across the cool concrete.

She turned and ran hard for the exit with the files tucked beneath her arm like an All-American halfback. The Doberman had turned the corner and was at full speed, closing the gap in seconds. The pointy white fangs of the beast shined viciously in the bright lights. She was fifty feet from the door. The dog was closing fast on her; only twenty-feet separated her from the snarling jaws. She could hear the dog's nails scraping the concrete floor and its heavy panting. She grabbed the knob just as the dog leaped, mouth gaping and growling ferociously. The slam of the door was followed by the hard thump of eighty-pounds of anger crashing into metal.

For a moment she held the door closed as if the dog might be able to open it by turning the knob. She could hear it sniffing and growling at the bottom of the door, apparently unfazed by the collision. She turned to see if anyone was waiting for her. To her relief, no one was there. She ran back to her car and slid behind the steeling wheel. She threw her fake prescription glasses onto the passenger seat next to the files and mumbled something about gray hairs before pulling off.

*   *   *

"Damn, she got out," the FBI agent said, watching through binoculars and impressed with Kelsy's escape. He wondered what happened to the Shadow Government agent and his four-legged friends that went in after her.

"Let's get the files," his partner said.

The agent watched her pull away from their position deep in the woods. "No, we're just supposed to keep an eye on her for now." He smiled. "She looked good with black hair."

Chapter 27

Allen and Mary checked-in, went through security, and walked to their departure gate. To Allen's surprise, no one had recognized him. He personally didn't think the beard and hat would work, but it had. No one had given him a second glance. He had forgotten what it felt like to be anonymous, normal, to simply walk in public without the ovations and the curious confrontations. He liked it, and he could easily get used to it.

"Why did you leave the hotel room?" Mary asked.

"What?"

"Why did you go to the church?"

He looked at her suspiciously after stuffing his carry-on baggage in the compartment overhead. "How did you know I went to the church?"

She looked out her window. "Who were you talking to in the lounge?"

"Robert," he answered, unaffected by her cool cop demeanor. He smiled. "Let me guess, you had someone watch over me?"

"That's right. A fellow P.I. I knew you wouldn't stay put, and someone out there might still think there's unfinished business from Pensacola. Did you confront Robert?"

"Not yet."

"What's going on with the church? Anything with the fake healings?"

"Maybe. That's why I went. To get some papers."

"What's the Bible burning thing I read about yesterday?"

"It seems an organization called the Christian-Jewish Witnesses has a problem with the New Faith Order. From what I understand, the CJW has been preaching against the New Faith Order and people have taken offense and began burning Bibles. I had nothing to do with it."

"Why don't you stop them?"

"I tried. I went on the Internet, radio, and released an official statement to the media opposing the actions. You never told me why we're flying to California."

"We have to check out this guy on the list."

"The list Kelsy came across."

"Yeah."

A feeling of discomfort eased into his mind. He thought about Kelsy's mother in a coma and her friends who had died since this whole thing started. "How's Kelsy doing?" he asked, trying to ignore the disturbing thoughts.

"Fine."

"How's her mother?"

"Her condition hasn't changed."

"Have the shooters been caught?"

"No," she answered, still staring out the window. An uneasiness had settled in.

She stood and headed for the restroom. In her seat was a small paperback book. Allen read the cover. *Conquering Fears.* One particular section had been marked. Aviophobia, the fear of flying. He smiled to himself, knowing how much her fear, anxiety and vulnerability was killing her. She hated not having control over her emotions.

She returned to her seat looking slightly less pale than before.

"Is it helping?" he asked.

"What?"

"The book."

"Sure. I only puked once this time."

"What does the book suggest for aviophobia?"

"Sky diving."

He looked at her, uncertain if she was joking.

"It encourages you to fly as much as possible."

"Did you see all the different phobias?" he asked. "There are some really disturbed people running around. To think that someone out there is afraid of colors, or peanut butter sticking to the roof of their mouth is frightening."

The airplane had started to taxi down the runway and Mary gripped the armrests of the seat.

"Look at this," he said leaning toward her. He put the book in a position so the two of them could read it together. "Osmophobia," he read out loud.

Mary read the definition. "Fear of body odors." She turned and sniffed at him. "I'm afraid of you."

"That's because of my ablutophobia."

She scrolled down the page. "The fear of bathing," she laughed after reading. She had released her death grip on the armrests while they were talking about the phobias. The plane reached a smooth altitude. She reclined the seat and put a pillow behind her head. She threw a couple of pills into her mouth and swallowed them without the aid of a drink, then closed her eyes.

He unfolded a blanket and spread it over her.

"Thanks," she said, never opening her eyes.

He gazed at her for a moment. The sunlight filtering through the window washed a golden glow over her face, and the auburn streaks in her rich brown hair shined brilliantly. *She's beautiful*, he thought. He had always thought she was good-looking, but for some obscure reason, he saw through the tomboy facade and the childhood buddy relationship and saw the beautiful woman that Mary truly was.

He started to view her differently, and it made him uncomfortable.

*   *   *

California

The young lady returned to the rental car counter. "We're sorry for the mix up with your reservations."

"May I have a car now?" Mary asked, feeling the urge to pull her over the counter and remove the fake smile from her face. The jet lag hadn't helped her personality.

"We're attempting to find you a car now," the girl said, reading from the computer screen.

"Try real hard." Her hands inched closer to the woman.

She glanced out at the parking lot and saw a red Mustang convertible. "I want that one."

"I'm sorry, but that vehicle is reserved for—"

"Hey," Mary interrupted. "I believe you should get your supervisor before something really bad happens to you." When she reached a certain level of frustration, she sounded like Linda Blair in *The Exorcist*. A voice from the depths of hell would best describe her tone at the moment.

The young woman promptly hurried off to retrieve her superior.

After a five-minute discussion with the young lady's boss, Mary could have had any car in the lot. For free.

Mary revved up the V8. The Mustang's motor rumbled like a mechanical symphony. Allen quickly reached for his seat belt.

"How do we get to the Getty Center from here?" she asked an employee standing on the sidewalk.

"Take the 110 north to the 10 west, and then get on the 405 north," he explained. "Follow the signs from there. There's a map in the glove compartment."

"Thanks," Mary said. She threw the stick into first, popped the clutch, and punched the gas pedal. The rear tires left a trail of burning gray smoke in the parking lot.

They cruised down the freeway with the top down while she attempted to tuck lose strands of her hair under her Washington Redskins baseball cap. Allen reached over and held the steering wheel while she quickly fixed her hair, then she took over the steering again.

Allen turned on the radio and found a pop station. Sheryl Crow's, "Soak Up the Sun" was playing. Mary reached down and turned it up. Allen leaned back and closed his eyes with a smile.

Forty minutes later, she turned into a parking lot and pulled up to a man that had enough camera equipment on his body to open a photography store.

"How do I get to the Getty Center?" she asked, glancing up the hill.

"You have to park over there and take the shuttle up," the tourist answered with a strong New York accent.

She thanked him and pulled off.

She paid the parking fee and took the five-minute ride to the Center. It was atop a promontory on the southern edge of the Santa Monica Mountains in Southern California. The center was surrounded by tens of thousands of California oaks, eucalyptus, citrus and jacaranda trees, making the three-quarter mile shuttle ride up a beautiful sight. Once on the platform, the first thing Allen noticed was the unique stonework bordering the balcony of the Harold M. Williams Auditorium.

"That's beautiful."

An attractive female employee of the center stood next to him. "It's Italian travertine."

"Really."

""It's a combination of marble and granite," she added.

"Are those real fossils in the stone?"

"Yes, they are. They were discovered during the cutting process."

"Where can we find Alfred Buckler?" Mary interrupted, in her not so graceful style.

The woman smiled at her. "Go through the café and restaurant area, then follow the signs to the Research Institute. Someone at the front desk will be able to help you from there."

Mary started walking away.

"Thank you," Allen said, then turned to catch up to her.

They made their way past a number of glorious gardens and fountains throughout the complex.

"I've heard they have a great collection of French 17th and 18th century decorative arts, and an impressive body of 19th and 20th century American and European photographs," he said suggestively.

"Really," she said, uninterested.

"I've read that they have Rembrandt's 'Abduction of Europa' and van Gogh's 'Irises.'"

"Really," she said again. His obvious desire to see these works of art were falling on deaf ears. They didn't have time to play tourist.

"And, they have James Ensor's, 'Christ's Entry Into Brussels,' and Fra Bartolommeo's 'Rest on the Flight Into Egypt.'"

"That's great," she said, walking up to a fragile-looking man standing behind a counter. "Is Alfred Buckler here?"

"He went on a research, slash, vacation trip," the man said cheerfully.

The five-foot-nothing brittle stature of a man wore a white collared shirt with tiny purple dots, a purple jacket and a skinny black tie. She was convinced that his outfit, his tiny loop earring, and his thin gold bracelet out weighed him by a pound or two. His black hair was cut tightly with the exception of the top, which was curly with streaks of blond.

She glanced at his name tag. Some good old-fashioned flattery may get the information she needed a little quicker. "I love your hair, Joel."

Allen smirked and gave her a look that said, "you're so fake."

Joel stroked his hair and blushed. "Thank you. I just had it done."

She gave Allen a look, suggesting he too, should compliment Joel on his hair.

"It's lovely," Allen remarked.

"Where can I find Buckler?" she asked politely.

"Greece."

"I was told on the phone he would be here today."

"He decided to leave for Greece early."

"I love Greek food," Allen said.

Joel smiled broadly at Allen. "I find Mediterranean cuisine simply scrumptious." She and Allen looked at one another, waiting to see who would laugh first.

"I was in Mykonos last year," Joel said. "The meals were simply . . . ,"

"Scrumptious," she and Allen said, finishing his sentence.

"Yes."

"Is there any way to contact Buckler?" she asked.

"I can send him a message," Joel proposed.

"No, I need to speak to him personally," Mary said with an urgent stare. "It's important."

"You're the second person today that needed to see him," Joel said as he started to tap on the keyboard of the computer. The screen showed Buckler's agenda. "I can reach him at seven in the morning, tomorrow."

"Good Lord," Allen blurted out. "Is he going to all those places?"

"Yes," Joel said turning the screen away from Allen.

"Someone else was looking for Buckler?" Mary asked.

"Yes." Joel's face became disturbed. "And he was very rude," he added in his dainty manner.

Mary had become impatient and a tad irritated. "Can I get a printout of Buckler's agenda?"

"I'm not permitted to do that."

She turned around, considering what to do next.

"What now?" Allen whispered.

Mary spun back around and grabbed Joel with one hand by the front of his collar. She flashed her wallet with an FBI badge. "Listen, I need to see Buckler."

Allen turned and walked away from the desk.

"Refusing to aid a federal agent is a federal offense."

Joel's face cringed as if it were preparing for a slap.

"I need the information."

Joel typed on the keyboard nervously. "You people are so rude."

"What do you mean, you people?"

"You gun-wearing, badge-flashing, macho government people."

"Who?"

"I don't know. He just stuck his badge in my face and demanded the agenda. Like you," Joel said, upset.

"Did you see the badge?"

"Of course. He shoved it in my face." He handed the printout to her. "It said National Security Agency. That's all I know. Now, can you please leave me alone?" He appeared to be on the verge of fainting.

"Thank you, Joel," she grinned. "I really do like your hair."

She and Allen hurried down the hall. "What was that?" he whispered.

"Flashback. Sorry," she said folding the printout and putting it in her pocket.

"That reminds me. What are you doing with a badge?"

"Long story."

Allen smiled a sheepish grin. "Our friend Joel certainly doesn't have androphobia."

She stared inquisitively.

"Fear of men." They made their way through the Getty Center back to the platform and boarded the shuttle. "What's next?"

"We need to get to Buckler before they do."

"Who?"

"I don't know." She didn't believe the man was from the NSA. "Are we going to Greece?"

"That's where Buckler is."

"Op-ha! I love Greek food. I find it simply . . . ,"

"Scrumptious," they said in sync.

Chapter 28

Washington, D.C.

A warm golden glow of candlelight surrounded Greg and his desk. Outside of the circular radiance of flickering light was a dark coolness of space, where objects were unrecognizable. He removed his glasses and leaned back into his chair. He rubbed the bridge of his nose and recalled the information he had analyzed the past three hours. He stared blankly into the darkness and thought about the bizarre data. The printouts Kelsy had given him conveyed one recurring theory; a joint conspiracy between the government and the military.

A military unit of some sort backed by the government had stolen an ancient artifact. The documents alone easily proved the government's involvement in the incident. But why steal it in the first place? Why risk so much? Could it be simply because of a mythical tale of divine power? Could the people in government have truly believed that by possessing the artifact they would reign over the world with some mystical force, with divine power? He shook his head in disbelief of such a ridiculous thought. But why couldn't he dismiss the possibility of this motive? He tired of the thought and relegated the document to a drawer.

A tan folder on the edge of the desk with the name "Jordan Iblis" caught his eye. His intuition told him there was something about Jordan Iblis to fear. He had a similar feeling about a man named Luke DeMynn, who, in Greg's opinion was the incarnation of the most evil-Satan. Somehow, DeMynn had returned in the form of Iblis. If he was wrong about Iblis, he could only hope Shelly could forgive him.

"Professor?" a voice asked from the darkness.

"Yes," he answered, unfazed by Art Hanson's sudden appearance.

Art made his way down the rickety wooden steps, which he proudly had mastered. He slowly cut through the darkness toward the light. "Doesn't it creep you out sitting down here in the dark by yourself?"

"I'm never alone, Mr. Hanson."

"Oh right," he responded. "You believe God is always with you." He handed Greg a folder. "Our boy Jordan has been a very busy man. He met with the scientist from New Mexico twice, the V.P. look-alike once, Speaker of the House, Walter Web three times, and he visited a fuel distribution company six times, twice at three o'clock in the morning. He seems very interested with the delivery trucks. All his movements are documented with photos, plane tickets, rental car reservations, limo services, hotel registrations, and restaurant payments. He's a smart man; all of his trips and meetings were masked as UN business."

"Great job, Mr. Hanson."

"He's definitely up to something," Art said, "hell if I know what it is."

He sounded as if he were fishing for information. Greg stared at him for a long moment. "Would you like to hear what I think he's up to?"

"Sure."

"Jordan Iblis is planning a coup d'etat and he's preparing to place himself in a position of power so he can put forth his agenda."

Art sat. "He's already in a pretty powerful position as is, don't you think?"

"That's true, he does maintain a great deal of power at the UN. He was the chief proponent for the one currency system in Europe. He practically accomplished it himself. He continues to propose the same for the entire world."

"That's what I mean," Art said. "He has power. It sounds like a lot of it."

"It's not enough," Greg explained. "Not only does he want a single economic system, but he also wants a single body of government controlling all international affairs, the UN to be more precise. He also has proposed a document suggesting no religions be recognized other than a unified system under the guidelines instituted by the UN. He states the vast separation in religious beliefs has led to the major conflicts in the world. All nations must submit to the UN's premise of beliefs or they will not be allowed to trade on the economic market, plus nations not conforming will feel the effects of other embargoes."

"What kind of beliefs would the UN try to force on a nation?"

"A godless one," Greg answered. "Jordan argues there's no place for religion in the business world. Money is god, financial and material accumulation is the answer to a successful society and the key to happiness and prosperity. If a nation wants to be a part of the world economic system they first must agree to put aside their religious beliefs and government policies that conflict with any other member within the new system of order created by the UN."

"Nations will have the option to join. No one will force them, right?"

"The economic pressure and the resources needed to survive would cause nations to accede to the UN's demands."

"Is that a bad thing? Getting everyone together, making all nations rich, and getting everyone believing in the same thing?"

"It is if he's the one who everyone begins to worship."

Art grinned. "Wait a minute. Jordan Iblis wants to be God?"

"That would be correct," Greg responded with a grin of his own.

He watched the wheels in Art's head turn.

"Who do you think Iblis is?"

"Satan."

"Come on Professor O. There's no doubt Iblis is up to something, probably no good, but a fallen angel, the Devil trying to rule the world? Even if I did believe in God, I don't think I can swallow any of this. If he's Satan, why the elaborate plan? There must be an easier way."

"He must use others to do his work. He needs to convert the free will of others to his. The one currency system is simply a stepping-stone to a bigger plan. If he convinces the world a single economic system and a one-government structure works, surely an economic-based religion will follow."

"I realize how crazy this sounds to you because of your personal beliefs," Greg said, "but I implore you to please have patience with me until the end."

Art grinned with some guilt. "I'm going to stick it out, professor, no matter how crazy it gets. The truth of the matter is, I just can't walk away. It's like driving past a car accident; you have to look."

*   *   *

Allen waited in Mary's car while she made arrangements for Greece with the travel agent. On the side of a bus was a billboard advertising Allen's evangelical program. The billboard had a photograph of Allen standing at a pulpit preaching a sermon with shining, bold, silver letters printed beneath his picture that read, "Follow me, I know the way." Someone had spray painted "1 John 4:3" across the billboard with red paint. The light turned green and the bus pulled away, but he continued to stare at the spot where the bus once stood.

He was familiar with that biblical passage, but for some odd reason he was unable to recall it, which he found alarming because of his photographic memory. It was the sixth time in the past month his memory had failed him pertaining to scripture. He hadn't forgotten anything that many times in his entire life. "I must be getting old," he mumbled, making light of the episode.

He started to search for his Bible when he came across a file containing hand-written notes and photographs of people. The photographs were mostly of a large man wearing dark glasses with gray hair and a matching beard, who had come to be duly known as Mr. Pig. Occasionally, Mr. Pig was photographed with another man who resembled someone from the Middle East. Mary's handwritten notes indicated there wasn't another woman, but she mentioned evidence for a relationship between Mr. Pig and the two other men in the photographs. The type of relationship wasn't specified. He placed the notes and photos of the infidelity case back into the file. Mary had been working the Mr. Pig case for weeks, but she hadn't been able to come to any conclusions. He knew she would have closed this case by now if it weren't for him and his latest circumstances. She had been neglecting her case because of him. He felt a tinge of guilt as she walked across the street with airline tickets in her hand.

*   *   *

Kelsy trudged down the cool, white, antiseptic hall of the hospital with a handful of fresh flowers dangling by her side. She watched a short, heavy-set man with curly gray hair exit her mother's room. He paused a moment in the hall to slip on his jacket. That was when he noticed Kelsy approaching. He turned and hurried in the opposite direction, apparently attempting to avoid her.

She jogged down the hall. "Hey," she yelled closing in on the stranger. "Excuse me! What were you doing in my mother's room?"

The man continued to walk away, ignoring her questions.

"Stop right there!" she yelled, this time her tone was sharp and angry. "FBI!"

The stranger's pace quickened.

Doctors and nurses watched curiously.

She was in a full sprint and it only took seconds before she was on the stranger. She grabbed him by the collar of his shirt and jacket and shoved him face-first against the wall with her gun pressed into his lower back. "Who the hell are you? What were you doing in that room?"

"I'm a friend of your mother's," he said, his words muffled from having his face pressed against the wall.

Sam hurried down the hall. "What's wrong, Kell?"

"Check on Mom," she yelled back. One of the nurses at the desk was on the telephone calling security. Sam disappeared into the hospital room.

"Please, let me explain," the stranger implored.

"Turn around with your hands away from your body."

The man slowly turned with his hands in the air. His face was pale with fright. "I'm a friend of your mother's, Kelsy," he explained, rattled by the sight of the gun pointed at him.

"She's fine," Sam said, returning. "Hey, Charlie." He gave Kelsy's prisoner a cheerful smile. "How've you been?"

Kelsy's stare shifted toward her uncle. "Do you know him?"

"Sure. Charlie Hunt."

"Why were you running from me?" she asked.

"May I?" Charlie asked glancing at his hands.

Kelsy put her gun away and Charlie lowered his hands.

"Everything is fine," Sam declared to the security guards approaching from both directions of the hallway.

"What's the problem?" one of the security guards asked. He was more curious than anything else.

"It's a misunderstanding," Sam answered.

The security personnel started back to their posts as they radioed the false alarm to the rest of the building.

"We met at a charity function a year ago, and we've been friends ever since," Charlie said with a fond smile. "I care for her a great deal."

"Charlie's your mom's boyfriend," Sam added.

"What? Boyfriend? She didn't tell me anything about a boyfriend."

Charlie looked down at the floor. "She didn't tell you about me out of respect for your father's memory and knowing how it would make you feel about her."

Kelsy stared, dumbstruck.

"Kell, are you all right?" Sam asked.

"Yeah, I'm fine. It was nice to meet you Charlie," she said walking away and disappearing into her mother's hospital room.

"Are you all right, Kell?" Sam asked, catching up with her.

She sat beside the bed holding her mother's hand. "It just scared the hell out of me."

"I know." He placed a comforting hand on her shoulder. "I got your message. What's going on?"

"I got some more information connected to the other files."

"Where did you get it?"

"Long story."

"What kind of information?"

"Remember the names from the list?"

"Yeah."

Kelsy stood. "Some of those names are on a file I discovered, a file that explains a confidential government experiment. Some type of surgery was performed on a woman named Rosenberg. The same woman Mary went to Florida to speak to, but she was murdered shortly before Mary arrived at her house."

"We've gone from magical artifacts and covert military missions," Sam said, sounding contemptuous, "to secretive surgeries on American citizens, all because we want to find some guy's biological parents."

Kelsy saw past the sarcasm and heard the frustration in his voice. "There are a lot of pieces missing."

"It's pretty simple to me," he said. "We accidentally discover material that incriminates the government and the military with murder and burglary. They steal this artifact and kill a someone's son in the process. Why? Who the hell knows? And now they're trying to cover their tracks. I don't know what Allen Pyrit has to do with it and I really don't care. I don't care about artifacts with mystical powers. I don't care about secret surgeries and covert military operations. I just want to know who shot my sister."

Kelsy could feel and understand his need to avenge his sister. It was the first time she had seen him drop his jolly and playfully sarcastic character and expose the raw hatred and vindictive feelings she herself had been harboring. They found solace in each other's common goal; to make the people responsible, pay.

Chapter 29

The White House

Derrick organized the paperwork on his desk before shoving it into his briefcase. He rubbed the worn brown leather of the case and thought of his young daughter who had given it to him on Father's Day. The image of her proud smile warmed his heart. Around him, White House aides rushed about the office preparing to depart for the airport. Secret Service agents stood dutifully fixed at the perimeters of the room and waited for the orders to mobilize.

"Please be careful on this trip." There was almost a pleading in Shelly's voice.

"More than usual?" Derrick gave her a passing grin before checking a list on his desk.

"Yes."

Derrick sensed her angst.

"The President of Egypt is arriving in Washington this weekend," she said, insinuating it was more than just another political figure visiting the nation's capital.

His expression hardened slightly. "I cannot alter my duties because of a prediction on the Internet." His face softened again. "Plus, the prediction said that there would be two Egyptian leaders visiting the eagle's nest."

I know, it's just . . . the trip, the timing of it all. I don't know, the security in Mexico has me nervous."

"The Mexican government and their security are more than adequate for the conference," he assured her. "They have everything under control. We're taking all of our people, too."

"It doesn't feel like a coincidence," Shelly said. "The Egyptian president arriving, the spring equinox, a full moon, it all feels . . ."

He smiled and finished her sentence. "Prophesied."

She looked at him gravely, obviously not sharing his unperturbed attitude toward the subject.

He placed the remaining papers in his briefcase. "I can't stop being the president every time something like this happens." He gave her a wink. "The full moon is next week; I checked."

"But Greg . . ."

He cut her off. "I can't take a chance on Greg." It pained him to say it. "He's been wrong before. It's not that I don't trust him, it's just that I can't afford another political humiliation."

Shelly walked to the French doors and looked out at the White House grounds as if it were the last time.

"I'm scheduled to meet with President Rims of Egypt three days from now," he said. "We'll all get together and have a big laugh about this. How are you doing?" he asked, not as the president, but as her friend. He had the extraordinary ability to make people feel as if they were the most important issue at the moment.

She kept her back turned. "The House and the Legislation Council want to meet again this afternoon."

"I was told I have no pardon power in his situation," he said unable to conceal his irritation. Of course, he knew this for some time, but felt he had to say it out aloud.

"I know."

He glanced at the *Washington Post* on the oak coffee table. The headline read, "Vice President Misuses Campaign Funds," and in small print in the lower corner it read, "Deanster Cleared of Bribery." "I was told you were cleared of all bribery allegations," he commented, finding something positive in the conversation.

"That's a good sign," she said softly.

He knew Shelly had signed the resignation documents yesterday. It would become official in seventy-two hours. The dismissal of the bribery charges was a goodwill gesture from the Impeachment Council. Accusations could disappear as mysteriously as they appeared, he discovered. By resigning, she had also guaranteed he would not be associated with the scandal. Shelly and her attorney, plus her advisors would retain copies of the agreement, insuring the integrity of the document. They felt confident Shelly would be found innocent of the allegations in a civilian court system, but the question was, would her reputation survive the damage? "Derrick, there's something I have to tell you."

There was a knock on the door and an advisor poked his head into the Oval Office. "We're running behind, Sir."

Derrick waved the advisor off. "What is it, Shelly?" He locked his briefcase.

"I resigned last night," she confessed, attempting to maintain eye contact.

"I know." His pain and sadness were obvious. "I wanted you to tell me when you felt the time was right."

"I'm sorry," she said. "I've let you down. My predicament was beginning to threaten you and everything you've accomplished."

He was determined. "I'm not going to let them get away with this."

"It's done, Derrick."

There was another knock on the door. "Sir," the advisor said, apprehension etched on his face.

"Yes, yes," Derrick snapped. "I'm coming."

"You should be going." She started for the door.

He placed a supportive hand on her shoulder. "This isn't over, Shelly."

She somehow found the strength to smile. "All right, Derrick."

"When I return, we will deal with this." By the determined look in his eyes, there was no doubt he meant it. He hurried out of the office to the awaiting helicopter.

Chapter 30

Kelsy and Sam followed the young Father Jones across the church's garden grounds.

"Where did you get the new information?" Sam asked.

Kelsy focused on an old oak tree in the distance, not sure how to answer her uncle. She didn't want to tell him about the warehouse, the Dobermans, and the man who tried to shoot her. She had a strong suspicion he wouldn't take it well.

"Kell, did you hear me?"

Her eyes studied the broken shapes of sun and shade blanketing the newly blooming spring flowers throughout the grounds. "Do you promise not to get mad?"

"No," he answered.

Their footsteps seemed loud to her in between sentences. Her stomach turned with an anxiety. "James told me where to get it," she said, forcing the words out.

"Christ, Kell," Sam exclaimed, stopping on the cobblestone walkway. "What are you trying to do, get yourself killed? You don't know who the hell this guy is."

"I know." She lowered her eyes to the walkway. She knew it was stupid and dangerous. James could have been the very one who had set her up, but she had convinced herself he didn't. She had also come to trust James. She didn't know why; it was a feeling she had about him, but she would never tell her uncle that.

The hard tension behind Sam's cool stare softened. "Please, Kelsy, next time, call me so I can come along."

"Shall we?" Father Jones asked. "The professor is waiting."

The three of them continued through the beautifully landscaped garden. She watched two cardinals chase one another through the limbs of the trees. Spring was here and love was in the air.

"You could've gotten hurt," Sam added."Something bad could've happened to you."

"Like being shot at while two eighty pound Doberman Pinchers chase you through a secluded warehouse," she said, avoiding eye contact.

Father Jones glanced over his shoulder at her and gave her a look that basically said, "holy crap."

Sam stopped again. "Listen to me," he said, putting his large hands on her shoulders and staring down into her eyes. "The thought of something happening to you . . ." he hesitated and swallowed. "I can't have something happen to you. Do you understand? I wouldn't be able to handle it."

The thought of her mother in a coma loomed over the both of them, suddenly making the shade of the oak cooler. "Okay," she whispered. "Next time I plan on doing something stupid," a tiny grin appeared on her lips, "I'll take you with me and we can be stupid together."

Sam exhaled a long breath. "Thank you." He placed his thick arm around her.

They crossed the garden and reached the professor's office without additional surprises.

"Professor Orfordis will be with you in a moment," Father Jones said leaving the two of them in the room.

Kelsy took a seat and began browsing through a book from Greg's bookshelf. The book was titled, *Behind the Battle Lines.* "Listen to this. It says there's a war between good and evil going on around us all the time."

Sam glanced around the room and his mouth curled into a thin smile. "A very quiet war." He casually surveyed the hundreds of books on the shelves against the wall.

"Some choose sides," she continued to read, "and others get a calling of sorts." She turned the page. "Unique individuals at special times in history are chosen to do battle for the army of light."

"I guess God has to have a draft, too," he joked. "Maybe that's how we got the Salvation Army."

"Do you think there's a war going on between God and Satan and we're a part of it?"

"I don't see a war, I don't hear a war, and I certainly don't feel like I'm in a war. I spent nineteen months in the jungles of Vietnam; I saw my share of what war was. Hey, look at this." He lifted a section of scroll the size of a place mat, sealed in plastic.

"You'd better be careful; it looks brittle, and valuable."

Sam carefully sat the scroll back on the desk and studied it closer. "Listen to this. 'A time in human history will come to pass, when the Demonic Trinity will form and the earthly realm will feel the grip of evil tighten.' He shook his head and smiled. "This is some crazy stuff."

"Are you reading from the scroll?"

"No, the professor's notes."

"Isn't that what he was telling us about the last time we were here?"

"Yes," Greg answered, entering the room, "It was."

"Sorry, professor," Sam apologized and moved away from his desk. "Sometimes I stick my nose where it doesn't belong. Old habits die hard."

"That's quite all right," Greg said with an amiable smile. "If it were for my eyes only, it wouldn't be lying about in plain sight." Greg's tone and body language were warm and relaxed, and put Kelsy and Sam at ease.

"Will this really happen?" Kelsy asked. "Do you believe a Demonic Trinity is forming?"

Greg answered without hesitation. "Yes."

Sam leaned against the wall with a skeptical smirk.

"Do any of those scrolls say when?" she asked, interested in the subject. With every visit, she'd become more fascinated with Greg and the spiritual warfare subject he studied. She felt a connection with him, as if she were meant to meet him. Strangely, she felt the same type connection with another she had encountered of late—James.

Greg stacked papers on the corner of his desk. "The scrolls I possess give signs and warnings."

"Like a blood moon or a great earthquake," she said, almost excited.

"Maybe a swarm of locust and frogs." Sam's tone was spiked with mockery.

Greg stopped organizing his papers and looked across at them. "One of the signs is occurring at this very moment in Jerusalem."

"The Bible-burning protest," Kelsy said.

"Right." Greg explained how the Old and New Testaments represented the two witnesses who were murdered in chapter eleven of Revelation, and the burning protest was a symbolic sign of that prophesied event. He also explained how God would raise the two witnesses after three and a half days, and within the hour an earthquake would follow.

"How do you raise burning books?" Sam joked.

"I don't know, but we won't need to wait long for the answer. Today is the third day." Something in his words was different now; there was a tone of anticipation. "By this time tomorrow, it will be done."

"So," Sam grinned, "tomorrow the Bible-burning party is over?"

Greg nodded, but seemed preoccupied, as if another thought seemed to have entered his head like an unwelcome guest.

"Are you all right, Professor Orfordis?" Kelsy asked, noticing the change in his mood.

"I'm fine," he answered, but he didn't sound convincing.

She saw some of his notes on the bookshelf and was dying to ask him about them, but she didn't want him to think she was snooping through his papers, although she was. "Professor, I have a question." She paused, but finally asked, "Is Sean Carbon the false prophet?"

"What would give you that idea?"

"I saw your notes on the shelf," she confessed, somewhat embarrassed.

He waited for a moment before confirming with a nod.

Sam laughed. "The psychic guy?"

"Sure, why not?" she asked now standing. "He started the 'Prophecy of Death' prediction. Something about a great leader being assassinated. Using his Internet business, GCE, he promotes and spreads all over the world an alternative Bible that has removed any mention of Jesus' physical resurrection. I think that qualifies as a false prophet."

"You guys think he's one of the three in this Demonic Trinity thing?" Sam inquired. "No offense, but the both of you need to be fitted for an extra-long-sleeved jacket. Don't mistake one man's greed and inventive capitalism for some evil plot. Carbon's a hustler; he feeds off people's insecurities. Some people need a crutch and he provides one."

"Do you think people who believe in God or who are religious need a crutch?" Greg asked.

"That's always been my experience."

"Einstein, Lincoln, Washington, Edison, Newton, Mozart, do you believe these gentlemen needed a crutch?" Greg asked, smiling.

Sam grinned. He'd walked right into that one. "I see what you're saying, professor, and I respect it, but I just can't put my belief in something I can't see, touch, or smell."

"So, Mr. Dent, it's safe to assume you don't believe in spiritual things."

"If you mean that I don't believe in angels and goblins fighting over souls, then yes, I'm a nonbeliever." Judging by Sam's posture and tone, he didn't lack confidence in his beliefs. "I don't believe in supernatural forces plotting against one another."

Kelsy hoped desperately she was wrong about her uncle, but his last statement confirmed what she already knew, but didn't want to believe; he didn't believe in God.

An uncomfortable look passed between her and Sam.

"What do you believe?" she asked, attempting to conceal her disappointment with curiosity.

"I think when something happens that can't be explained right away, it becomes the work of the supernatural or spirits. Look at history, for instance. Thunder and lightning and other solar and celestial phenomena were thought to be the work of gods, but now we know that's not true. People were burned at the stake for being witches and doing the devil's work, when in reality they were being eccentric and most importantly, non-Puritan. I think people want to believe in something, anything. I personally don't care how the universe started and what happens after we're dead. I live in the present. I'll tell you one thing I do believe." He shifted his large frame like a prosecuting attorney preparing a case against a defendant. "People like to think humanity is special, that humans are above all living things, that we're the center of the universe, but I think we're just another animal; a little smarter than most, but nevertheless another animal, trying to survive.

We try to pretend we're not, but our actions suggest otherwise. We're territorial like animals, we like our space. We like to have our yards with fences and well-defined boundaries. From Columbus declaring wherever he landed his own, to Armstrong sticking an American flag on the surface of the moon, it's all about territorial, animalistic behavior. Ninety percent of the laws are made to protect our things. Our natural mindset is to think, 'mine.' We have to be taught to share and get along. It's evident from little Johnny wanting his own room to one country wanting its neighbor's territory. Hell, we've being fighting and murdering one another over land since the beginning of time. We like to run in packs and gangs. We get into our little circles and pick on the weak. It starts in preschool and continues into adulthood.

Look at the most basic and raw animal instinct there is—sex. We're separated only because we do it more for pleasure than reproductive reasons. In the early stages of humanity males wanted to have sex as often and with as many partners as possible to spread their seed for a better chance to continue the bloodline. That's why it's so important for a man to have a son, so his bloodline and namesake continues. But the male has evolved to the point where he wants sex without the responsibility of offspring and commitment."

"What about love and family?" Kelsy asked.

"I believe love is a concept created out of need," Sam answered. "The need of wanting something more important and meaningful than the animalistic lust that somehow in history became wrong, or evil. When a man or a woman look at and desire a young attractive person, they're doing what comes naturally. We're selecting a mate for the best chance of survival for their offspring. It's no different in the animal kingdom. Animals don't reproduce with the weak and unhealthy. When a man sees a beautiful female with a good figure his first instinct is to have sex with her. It's natural, it's built into his DNA blueprint, he's been designed to procreate as often as possible, but a controlling society and religious beliefs are trying to rewire humanity and convince us we're not animals, that we must commit to one mate and raise offspring for life, which is unnatural. The high rate of infidelity and divorce proves it.

We're not built that way. Some animals are; some have the same mate for life, like the swan and some of the wolf breed, but I don't think humanity is one of them. Women have also evolved in their search for a mate. Not only will a female be attracted to a young and strong male, they're also attracted to wealthy and powerful males, who fulfill another animal instinct—finding a provider for her and her offspring's needs. But humanity has evolved to the point of feeling guilty for wanting to do what comes naturally. We feel the pressure to be married, and only then may we engage in sex and bear children. We, as a species, have been struggling with our natural animal desires for centuries, and will continue to do so as long as we believe we're not animals."

After the shock of her uncle's remarks wore off, she said, "So, you believe in Darwinism and evolution."

"No," Sam answered. "Darwin's theory of evolution doesn't hold anymore; there are too many unanswered questions and missing links. As for evolution in general, I believe in micro-evolution, not macro."

"What's the difference?" she asked.

Greg answered. "Micro-evolution is changes within a species. A bird's beak changes form to adapt to new surroundings, but still remains the same species. As for macro-evolution, the changes are more dramatic. There are major leaps where an animal transforms into an entirely different species—for example, monkey to man."

"I'm a firm believer in thermodynamics," Sam added. "The First Law of Thermodynamics to be more precise. Scientifically, energy cannot be created nor destroyed, which puts a damper on the Big Bang theory and evolution. Evolutionists and Darwin have no explanation for the beginning of life. You just can't say it was always there or it appeared out of nowhere, because that's unscientific or miraculous." He smiled at Greg. "That's no different than just saying a unseen entity simply spoke it into existence. Puff, let there be everything."

"I don't understand," Kelsy said. "You believe in some forms of evolution and not others and you don't believe in God, What exactly do you believe?"

"I don't have an explanation for how everything started, and I don't know what happens after we're dead, I simply believe we are a species of animal that thinks. I don't believe in the spiritual or that we have a soul with a destination."

"I'm not going to attempt to change your mind, Sam," Greg said. "But I would like you to think about something."

Sam agreed with an indulging smile.

"I have observed in life a common fact," Greg said. "There are opposites that create a balance to the universe. Such as male and female, day and night, hot and cold, up and down, life and death."

"Yin and yang," Sam remarked.

Greg nodded. "The opposites maintain equilibrium and harmony in the universe."

"I've explored Taoism and Confucianism in the past," Sam said. "It has an interesting message."

"Then, you would know the opposite of physical is spiritual," Greg insisted. "One cannot exist without the other."

"I do believe in antithetical ideologies. I agree with the concept, but I don't subscribe to the religious connection."

"Please," Greg said, "humor an old man and define the opposite of physical."

"I believe the opposite of physical is thought. It's within us, but it can also be a separate identity from the body. A meditation of sorts, but those thoughts can become physical again. We can make our thoughts reality and that's what makes us different, putting us above the rest of the animals in the evolutionary ladder.

There's a lot of question marks in life, professor, but I just choose not to fill in the blanks with God."

Greg and Sam exchanged a few more of their beliefs, remaining complimentary to one another's point of views before moving on to the information Greg had been deciphering. But Greg made Sam promise to continue the conversation at a later time.

He pulled out a piece of paper. "Here, I made copies of the deciphered printout." He handed two copies to Sam and Kelsy.

"Professor, was there anything about a woman and a surgery?" Kelsy asked.

"Yes, there was. Something about an experimental surgery involving the woman's uterus." Greg flipped to the data. "Look at page six; the report also says that the surgery was a success."

"What kind of operation was it?" Sam asked, turning to the page on his copy of the printout.

"Some type of implant," Kelsy said, reading off her copy.

"What kind of implant?"

Greg turned a page and pointed to a section on the sheet. "I found throughout the data the mention of synthetic drugs like Clomid, Pergonal, Humegon, and so on, which today are mainly used to stimulate ovulation and follicle development to retrieve eggs from the fallopian tubes. There was also mention of fertilization and transfer techniques."

Kelsy looked up from her copy. "It looks like they were experimenting with test tube babies or *in vivo* fertilization."

"Wait a minute," Sam said, "Isn't this data from the sixties? Test tube babies and IVF didn't come along until years later."

"I checked into it," Greg explained, "and the first test tube baby known to the public was in the summer of 1978 in England. We didn't do it until March 1982. But I'm sure testing and experimenting was occurring years before the public became aware. It's no different than microwave ovens and cordless phones. The government had them years before they were introduced to the mainstream. It wouldn't surprise me if they were experimenting with *in vitro* fertilization decades before it became common practice."

"We've got documents on the government stealing an artifact and killing someone important in the process and now we've got them performing secret surgeries," Sam said. "We've got proof they were experimenting with embryos, but is that worth murdering people to keep it quiet?"

"Was there any mention of sperm?" Kelsy asked.

Sam gave her an odd look.

"No," Greg answered. "I found that peculiar; hundreds of documented files and no mention of sperm or a male donor. The blood tests and several other medical tests never suggest the need of sperm."

"Does that mean something?" Sam asked.

"Genetic engineering," Kelsy answered. "They were using DNA."

"In the sixties?" Sam questioned.

"I think they were attempting to clone someone," Kelsy said. "That's worth murdering over, that's worth keeping quiet."

"No way," Sam said. "Not back then."

"They've been experimenting with genetics for years," Greg explained. "Fruits and vegetables have been modified and altered since I was a child. Do you believe seedless watermelons and thornless roses are natural? Animals weren't excluded. Bigger cattle and fish that grow to adult size in half the time are products of genetic tampering. What do you think the next step would be?"

"Humans," Kelsy answered.

Greg nodded. "After genetic engineering ran its course, the obvious next step is cloning."

Sam paused for a moment. "If the government were experimenting with human cloning, that would be a good motive for murder. It just seems impossible. Cloning in the sixties. I don't know," he said, taking a seat.

"Oh my God," Kelsy mumbled.

Sam and Greg stared at Kelsy's widened eyes.

"Allen," she said, as if she'd been enlightened. "He's a genetically engineered human being. He's a clone."

"That would make sense," Sam said. "It all started with him."

They stared at one another, realizing they had moved closer to unraveling the conspiracy. Kelsy pulled out a file and another disk from her jacket. "Maybe this will fill in the rest of the pieces," she said handing the material to Greg.

He opened the file, finding more of the same coded and cryptic information. "I'll begin right away," he said putting on his glasses and clearing space on his desk.

Kelsy and Sam thanked him for all his help again, then walked in silence toward the car.

"I can't believe that you don't believe in God," Kelsy said, fastening her seat belt. "You were always involved with church functions and charity causes."

"You don't have to believe in God to care about those things and want to help people," he said. "There are a lot of good people out there who act more Christian than Christians."

"Yeah, but . . . ," she attempted to find the words.

Sam grinned. "Are you worried about my soul, Kell?"

"Yes," she responded, feeling he too, should be.

"If I had a soul," he said, forcing a tired smile. "I left it in Vietnam." His eyes couldn't conceal the old pain in his words.

Chapter 31

Air Force One

The Boeing 747-200 cruised across the night sky. The nearly full moon illuminated the bold inscription on the side of the aircraft that read, THE UNITED STATES OF AMERICA. The tail of the plane was embellished with the American flag and the presidential seal.

One of the president's aides stepped out of the stateroom with a printout. He walked down a long, blue-gray carpeted hall toward a lounge area, passing a number of staterooms and offices, where Derrick sat in one of the four first-class-style leather seats facing one another over a coffee table. The aide handed the printout to Derrick and departed.

A genuine smile appeared across Derrick's face as he read. The printout was peppered with loving sentiments from his wife and child. He realized it had been a long time since he smiled like that, but then again, there hadn't been much to smile about lately.

The aircraft buzzed with the daily goings on of politics. The staff was moving about the craft, attending to their business. The stewards were busy preparing drinks and appetizers. The conference room was bustling with aides in preparation for a briefing. The upper deck of the aircraft was the most sophisticated and advanced mobile communications center on earth, known as the Mission Communications Center, where three air force specialists operated the wall-to-wall top of the line, state of the art electronic and satellite equipment.

The steward handed the president his double Scotch on the rocks. "You deserve this one, Sir."

"Thank you." He smiled, thinking he deserved the entire bottle.

"Can I get you anything else, Mr. President?"

"No, thank you."

The steward turned and disappeared down the corridor.

Derrick took a long draw from the glass. The Scotch tasted good, too good. He was developing a drinking habit, and he was quite aware of it. He promised himself he would stop drinking, soon. He found himself alone for the first time on the trip. He took another pull from his drink and closed his eyes and listened to the hum of the four GE-F103 turbofan engines of Air Force One. He thought about his family and how much he missed them, but like so often, those thoughts were rudely interrupted by thoughts of hostages, nuclear weapons, Shelly's resignation, peace talks, and the predictions of death. He looked out of the bulletproof window at a curtain of stars and silvery clouds. He watched an F-15 Eagle glide effortlessly across a tranquil sky, one of two jet fighters escorting Air Force One. A monstrous man-made mechanism of war, it was a thing of necessity and solace.

The deputy National Security adviser climbed down the winding stairs from the Mission Communications Center with the latest printout. Secret Service agents strolled through the aircraft and occasionally stopped to engage in general conversation with one another or a passing steward. The agents tended to relax slightly on Air Force One and became more sociable. The aircraft engendered a feeling of invincibility, of being in an impregnable flying fortress.

The tranquil flight was suddenly disrupted, and the most important airplane in the world started to shake violently.

The fierce turbulence sent one Secret Service agent into a door frame, knocking him unconscious. Two stewards were forced to the floor from the jolt.

"Sit down and put on your seat belts!" Derrick yelled.

After scrambling to the nearest seats, personnel and crew members fastened themselves securely.

The plane leveled out slightly, but strong vibrations continued to send objects rolling and banging throughout the aircraft. The president's telephone buzzed.

Derrick snatched the receiver. "Yes?"

"Everything should be fine in a moment, Sir," the pilot, Colonel Merrain assured him. "We hit some wind sheer, but I believe we have it under control now."

Derrick relayed the news to the staff, hoping to ease the tension. He perceived nervousness among the staff and crew before the flight, but now he sensed fear. They too, knew about the Prophecy of Death; they also knew the Egyptian President was in Washington and the moon was nearly full. He looked about the cabin and observed the obvious tension on some of the faces of the staff, but not all were convinced Sean Carbon's prediction was worth the anxiety, and some just thought he was full of it. For a fleeting moment, he felt contrition creep into his mind for not postponing the trip to Mexico. If tragedy were to strike, no one would blame him for carrying on with business; on the contrary, he would be applauded for his valor. Only volunteers had been selected for the trip to Mexico, but he found no comfort in that thought.

*   *   *

Mary read from a sheet of paper. "Buckler's going to be in London for two days, then the Acropolis for a day before flying out to the islands." She stared out of the plane window at the control tower of Baltimore-Washington International airport. "We should be able to catch up to him at the Acropolis Museum."

A wide grin spread across Allen's face. "Good. I've always wanted to see the Parthenon."

She hoped Buckler lived long enough for her to question him. She kept thinking about the Getty Center in California. Someone got there before her and was asking about him. Whoever it was, they were a step ahead of her and that could be the difference between life and death for Buckler. A feeling of urgency turned in her gut.

She took a deep breath and watched a plane taxi down the tarmac. She had a feeling Buckler was an important factor in all of this and had the answers they needed. For instance, how was Allen connected to the conspiracy? She could feel the plane preparing to depart. The phobia book said to fly as often as possible. Facing one's fears head on was the best therapy. The thirteen-hour flight should provide an abundance of therapy.

The plane rolled along the strip and the engines hummed with increasing power. "What time are we due to arrive in Frankfort?" Allen asked.

"About eleven A.M., their time," she answered. She gripped the armrest.

"What time is the connecting flight?"

"Ninety minutes after we get there."

"Do we have directions from the airport to the Acropolis?"

"We're taking a cab."

"What time will Buckler be there?"

Mary reached into her pocket and pulled out the piece of paper. She started to read, but stopped suddenly. "Here," she said tossing the printout on his lap. "You have a photographic memory. Take a picture."

Allen smiled and studied the itinerary. "Why aren't any of his hotels on here?"

"It's his business schedule. It's obvious he prefers to keep his personal affairs personal. Any more questions?"

"No," he answered with an amused grin. He pulled *Moby Dick* from his carry on bag. "This book has been giving me some crazy dreams."

She glanced at the book. "What are you talking about?"

"I keep dreaming about a large ship crossing the ocean, smashing through towering waves and a furious wind under a dark and ominous sky, the captain determined to reach it's destination, refusing to stop, obsessed with the thought of destroying the white whale. But every time I see the face of the crazed captain at the wheel, it's me. I'm always Captain Ahab. Isn't that weird?"

She shook her head. "Only you would dream something like that."

"If it's a good book and you relate with the characters, sometimes you put yourself in their position."

"Trust me, Al," she said, eyeing him, "It's weird."

"I can't wait to finish it and see how it ends."

"You'll love it." She grabbed her pillow and blanket. "It has a happy ending."

The airplane had reached a smooth altitude and so had she.

*   *   *

Kelsy entered her apartment and walked directly to the kitchen. She opened the refrigerator and stood in the cool light staring at the single beer on the shelf. It reminded her of James. He hadn't been here, because the last beer was still here. She grabbed the bottle and hit the answering machine on her way to the dark living room where she sank into the couch.

"Kelsy, it's Mary. Allen and I are in Greece. Be back soon."

Kelsy gave the answering machine an odd glance. "Greece?" she asked out loud.

From the chair across the room, a voice quietly said, "They're on the right trail."

Within an instant, Kelsy had her weapon drawn and pointed in the direction of the voice. "Who's there?"

"You don't recognize my voice. I'm hurt."

"James," she said, perturbed, but secretively relieved. "My friend," she added sarcastically.

"That's right."

Her hand slid toward the lamp on the end table. She tilted her head to obtain a better view, but it was too dark in the corner of the room to separate the obscured outlines. "What do you mean they're on the right trail?"

"They're following Alfred Buckler. He has some of the answers."

His voice sounded muffled by something, perhaps a mask. "What's wrong with your voice?"

"Why?"

"You sound strange," she said snapping on the light suddenly and taking aim at . . . at . . . at nothing. No one was there. She stood and walked over to the chair. Positioned between two pillows was a transmitting and receiving device. "Cute," she mumbled.

"Do you like it? Government issued."

She walked to her window and searched the buildings in the distance. She pulled binoculars out of her desk and surveyed the rooftops lining the horizon. She spotted a man wearing a trench coat with binoculars of his own staring back at her.

"Hello," he said in a cordial manner.

"I told you to stay out of my home."

"I didn't have a choice. They're listening, but this little toy is the latest in keeping the nosy out."

He continued to explain the mechanical aspects of the device, but Kelsy wasn't paying attention to his technical babble. She examined him through the binoculars, attempting to procure a physical description, but she was unable to because of the baseball cap he was wearing and the lack of light around him. She estimated him to be six foot tall and athletically built. She threw the binoculars on the desk.

"That's no way to treat fine equipment."

"You almost got me killed at that warehouse."

"I'm sorry about that. I don't know how they found out."

"Why not just tell me everything? Why this game?"

"I'm telling you what I know as I get it myself."

"I don't believe you," she said staring into the night. "And I don't trust you." Which wasn't entirely true.

"That's good," he said.

"What do you want, James?" she asked, feeling tired. "I need to get some sleep."

"I want you to remember a name. Zachary L. Smits."

"Why?"

"I'll tell you later, but it's important. Remember the name. Don't write it down anywhere."

"Sure," she said, rubbing her eyes. "Zachary L. Smits." She turned toward the transmitter. "I'm going to bed now."

"We need each other," James said.

She looked at the transmitter. There was something in his voice that enthralled her. His smooth and deep resonant tone solaced and soothed her defenses, easing her mind. She did trust him.

"We can help each other. I'll help you find the answers for your friends." A moment of silence passed. "And we'll find the people responsible for your mother's shooting," he added empathetically.

"What's in it for you?" she asked.

"I want the same people."

"Why?"

"Because they're dangerous and must be stopped."

"You can't stop people like that," she said abruptly, now thinking about her mother. "People like that don't go to prison."

"That's not always true, but you're right," James agreed. "There are too many corrupted links in the system."

"So, how do you expect to stop them?"

"We . . . we retire them."

"You mean you kill them," she snapped. "Isn't that what you mean?

A cold and unsettlingly silence lingered between them before James finally answered, "Yes."

"You're no different than them," she whispered. She lifted the transmitter and turned it off. The only sound in the room was the hum of kitchen appliances. She walked to the window and scanned the building's rooftop through the binoculars, but no one was there.

*   *   *

"I'm Skip Robertson, live in front of the U.S. Capitol," the reporter said with the glowing dome of the building over his shoulder. "There will not be an impeachment trial, nor will there be further charges brought by the Judiciary Committee or the House of Representatives."

The television screen flashed to a different channel.

"Vice President Shelly Deanster resigned late last night," another reporter said.

The screen flashed again.

A panel of journalists appeared on the screen. "Judgment in cases of impeachment shall not extend further than removal from office and disqualification to hold an office of honor," the analyst explained. "But, the vice president will be liable and subject to indictment, trial, judgment, and punishment, according to law."

The bartender changed the channel again.

"President Moore was unavailable for comment concerning the resignation of the vice president," a reporter stated. "He is attending the Mexico Unified Conference."

The bartender tossed the remote control off to the side with frustration. "Damn resignation crap."

Walter Web, and Jordan Iblis sat comfortably in soft black leather chairs in the lounge of the Washington Hilton and watched the bartender give up his search for something other than the latest news concerning the resignation.

"It's over," Walter said somberly.

"What's wrong?" Jordan asked, sipping his fifty-year-old brandy. "You sound depressed."

"Aren't you? She's your girlfriend."

Jordan crossed his legs, unconcerned. "Shelly will bounce back."

"She appeared pretty devastated."

"She'll be fine."

"You know her best."

Jordan snapped his fingers toward a young man. "Two more, please," he ordered.

"Why did the UN call you back to North Africa so urgently last week?"

Jordan looked around the room and checked his surroundings for anyone within earshot. He stared gravely and revealed with a whisper, "We believe the hostages are dead."

"Christ," Walter exclaimed. "All of them?"

Jordan nodded.

Walter sank into his chair. "Are you sure?"

"Not one hundred percent," he answered. "But we'll confirm the data within the next couple of days."

Walter's face became angry. "We should blow those parasites off the planet."

His fervent remark brought a wicked smile to Jordan's face.

Chapter 32

Athens, Greece

Mary and Allen maneuvered through the smoky, sweaty and crowded airport.

"It's hot," Allen said, wiping his forehead.

Mary nodded toward two men wearing military uniforms and carrying automatic weapons. "I bet those guys are hotter than we are."

He stopped at a stand, bought two bottled waters, and had a conversation in Greek with the tiny old woman behind the counter about the weather. He handed Mary one of the bottles. "The woman behind the counter says it's much warmer than usual for this early in the year."

"I guess we're just lucky," she said, in her usual sarcastic tone. She stared out the terminal window.

"What's wrong?"

"That guy over there," she said, indicating a man walking toward a group of taxicab drivers leaning lazily against their cars waiting for passengers. "With the gray suit. I think I see a holster under his jacket. I know him from somewhere."

He got into a taxi and Mary started trotting.

Allen began to jog, attempting to keep up with her.

Stepping out of the building, the heat hit them like a sultry slap. Allen could feel his khakis sticking to his legs from the perspiration. Mary focused on the taxi pulling off.

Allen dropped the two duffel bags to the sidewalk and waved a taxi to the curb. "What's up?"

"I think he's an operative," she said quietly. "And if so, who does he work for?"

Mary slid into the backseat and Allen followed with the bags.

The driver glanced into the rear view mirror and asked in English with a heavy Greek accent, "Where are we going?"

"Follow that taxi," Mary said pointing to the blue and white cab fifty yards away.

The driver pulled off without questioning her request.

Allen took a deep breath and inhaled the air rushing into the cab. "That's a little better."

Mary wiped the sweat from the back of her neck with a bandanna. "I've got a sick feeling that Buckler's a dead man," she whispered. She scanned the traffic ahead. The taxi they were pursuing disappeared in a sea of vehicles. "He drives like Kelsy. We lost him," she grated.

"No, we haven't. Our driver radioed the driver of the other cab and asked the destination of his passenger."

"Good," she mumbled, sounding nearly apologetic for cussing the driver.

The taxi driver glanced in the rear view mirror at Allen. "Do you understand Greek?" he asked in his own language.

"Yes."

Allen and the driver, whose name was Demetrios, discussed in Greek the weather, the best sites to visit, and where to eat in town. During the ride, the conversation turned to a more serious subject pertaining to his sour ex-wife and her unwillingness to allow Demetrios more time with their two children.

People seemed to open up to Allen and talk about their most personal matters. It had been that way for him as far back as he could remember. They naturally trusted him. He had had this conversation hundreds of times with members in his congregation. After hearing the details of the dilemma, he gave adept advice and Demetrios welcomed the counseling with gratitude.

A few minutes later the taxi pulled up to the curb. They quickly stepped out onto the sidewalk, where the hot and humid day welcomed them with a suffocating embrace. Allen and the driver, still speaking Greek to one another, exchanged a few pleasant words as he handed him the cab fare. The driver thanked him and pulled off with a smile. Allen trotted along the sidewalk and caught up to her, who had already started the walk to the Acropolis.

Mary was kicking herself for not telling the driver of the cab to radio the other driver and have him drive the man in the gray suit around the city so she and Allen could get to the Acropolis first. A blown opportunity that might get Buckler killed. "What were you talking about?"

"I was telling him dirty jokes."

"Yeah right, and I go to church every Sunday."

"I gave him some advice."

"About what?"

"A family matter." He rolled up his shelves and wiped his forehead. "I thought it was going to be cooler this time of year."

Mary had felt precarious in the taxi, not being able to understand the conversation. There were a few occasions she believed they were speaking about her. "Is that what you were talking about the whole time?" she asked, attempting not to sound insecure.

"Mostly. We talked about you, too."

She narrowed her eyes at him, expecting him to elaborate.

He grinned. "I'm kidding. We didn't talk about you."

"I don't care if you were."

Allen acted like he just remembered something. "Oh, yeah, he did ask me something about you."

She continued to walk with eyes forward.

"He asked me if you were my wife or girlfriend."

Her eyes remained on the path ahead, but he had her attention.

"I told him you were my . . ." he paused intentionally. "Baby sister."

"That's what it feels like," she snapped.

They made their way up the ancient cobblestone walkway known as the Panathenaic Way.

Allen pointed up at the ancient ruins. "Wow, look at that."

The Parthenon stood majestically on the rocky summit, commanding reverence and respect. Twenty-five hundred years of architectural brilliance framed by the pristine blue sky. Pericles, who commissioned construction in 447 BC would be pleased to know that the Acropolis had endured the ravages of war, the removal of treasures, and toxic pollution.

Mary gave the ancient marvel a disinterested glance. "Nice." She had no interest in what she called, "a bunch of old rocks piled up.'"

"It's a tribute to the early Greek culture and their architectural brilliance," he said, attempting to convince her of this fact. "When I was a young boy, I listed the great wonders of the world and resolved to visit every one. But this isn't exactly the circumstance I envisioned."

Mary knew he still carried the list in his wallet to this day.

They continued to climb the cobblestone ramp toward the entrance of the Acropolis, periodically catching a glimpse of the ancient buildings through the pine and cypress trees. They cut through tourists gathered around a guide.

"And here is the Beule Gate," the guide announced with a wave of the hand. "A gate built to protect the Acropolis from barbarian incursions. The left tower of the Beule Gate reaches over twenty meters in height, but sadly all that remains of the right tower is an outline of the base where it once stood."

Allen smiled, looking up at the entrance known as the Approach of Classical Times. "It's simply overwhelming. Think of who walked here in times past. People who walked the same steps we're now was taking. Socrates, Plato, Aristotle, Alexander the Great, Shakespeare, Napoleon, hundreds of other world figures of history. All have stood at this same entrance where we're standing now.

Entering the sanctuary of the Propylaia, Allen marveled at the white columns reaching skyward like mighty oaks. Mary, on the other hand, was too preoccupied with the search for Buckler and the man in the gray suit to care about Greek history.

Once out of the those ruins, the crowning jewel of Attic architecture and the Periclean era confronted them. Standing proudly on a slight incline was the regal Parthenon, the most eminent building of the Acropolis, if not in all of Greece.

Allen stood, fixated with amazement. "Incredible. Just incredible."

An elderly man observed Allen's veneration for the Parthenon. "Beautiful, no?" the elderly man asked in his thick French accent.

"Very beautiful." Allen replied intuitively in French, never taking his eyes off the building.

Side by side, Allen and the elderly man began to walk up the riddled and jagged rocky slope circling the Parthenon toward the Acropolis museum, but Mary moved ahead toward the museum.

Allen and the elderly man reached the museum and climbed down the stairs where Mary waited behind a group of tourist, to a partial open-air foyer, where the temperature was ten degrees cooler. On the right side of the doors was a pedestal on which sat a marble owl, the sacred bird of Athena.

Allen leaned close to the wide-eyed bird and read the inscription on the pedestal. "500 B.C.," he read.

"As old as me," the elderly man joked.

Allen patted him on the shoulder with a laugh. "You look good for your age. You don't look a day over twenty-one hundred."

The next wave sightseers moved into the museum.

Mary suddenly bolted across the marble floor after she spotted the man in the gray suit with a 9mm fitted with a silencer. He was gliding through the crowd with his gun by his side. She was pushing and bumping the tourist as she tried to cut the assassin off. The gunman was fifteen meters away and preparing to fire at Buckler. She covered twenty steps before leaping into Buckler, sending him to the floor. The single shot from the gunman was barely heard. The bullet struck a teenage Italian boy in the neck. Security guards were on the scene in seconds. Someone fired. The gunshot was incredibly loud. The gunman dodged in and out of the panicked crowd and escaped in the mass of people pouring out of the museum. Buckler had also disappeared somehow.

Mary headed for the exit. She saw Allen near the heavy wooden doors that were abruptly opened by a stampede of frightened people rushing out of the museum attempting to escape the danger within. Allen had the elderly man pushed against the wall and used his own body to create a protective barrier between the tiny, man and the chaotic mob. A river of screaming and falling people continued to push past them.

"And my wife said, that the museum was boring," the old man said.

Two armed security guards and Mary ran through the doors and up the stairs; Allen followed. Mary and Allen scanned the landscape. Security officers were running throughout the scattering tourist. There was no sign of the gunman or Buckler. Maybe he was still inside, she thought.

When Mary and Allen returned inside the museum they discovered two guards leaning over a young boy's body in a circle of people.

The boy's eyes were pools of tears and horror.

Allen took the boy's hand in his. "You're going to be fine," he said staring into his eyes.

"He doesn't understand English," the boy's tour guide said. "He's from Italy."

Allen repeated himself, but this time in Italian. The boy didn't say anything. Maybe he was afraid to move his throat because of the wound, but he didn't have to use words to respond. The transformation in his eyes was instant. The fear, the horror, and the angel of death were gone. Certitude had replaced the darkness of doubt. He was going to live, and he believed it because this man leaning over him holding his hand said he would. The paramedics arrived and started working on the boy.

Mary and Allen sprinted out of the cool, dim museum again and emerged into the daylight. The ancient grounds were nearly abandoned. She hoped Buckler had somehow escaped the man in the gray suit. After a moment, the stinging feeling of guilt hit her. It was her fault the young Italian boy was shot. If she hadn't pushed Buckler out of the way the boy would be fine right now. He took Buckler's bullet.

Mary continued to stand unblinking with a glazed stare. She didn't see the ruins or the remaining nervous tourists gathered in groups or the beautiful sunset. She saw thoughts and words bouncing around in her head; and the face of a boy. And blood.

"Miss?" A man in a plain blue suit stood beside her. "My name is Kosta. I'm with the police. May I have a word with you?" His Greek accent was hardly noticeable.

She looked at the tall, thin man with the thick mustache, which covered his entire lip. She slowly came out of her thoughts.

"The gunman," the officer asked. "You don't know him?"

"No." She looked at the officer, seeing the way the other men on the scene deferred to him. They approached, departed, and conducted themselves with respectful tones, careful wording, and eagerness to please. It was no different back home in the States when a high-ranking department official was present. But he had introduced himself without a title. He had simply used his first name, and didn't have a macho attitude or appear to be on a power trip.

"The man you pushed to the ground," Kosta asked. "Do you know him?"

"It was an accident. I was trying to get away from the gunman and knocked him down."

Allen's eyes sharpened on her, questioning her answer.

Kosta joined Mary and stared at the burning orange ball hovering over the horizon. "In that case, you wouldn't know why the gunman was trying to kill that man?"

"No, I wouldn't."

"Well," Kosta grinned beneath his mustache, "good thing you ran into him. It saved his life"

It would only complicate matters if she told him the truth, so she remained silent, watching the ruins cast long shadows across the ground.

Kosta shoved his hands into his pockets and kicked a stone. "Too bad there had to be a kid behind him," he said, turning to leave.

An image of the boy's face appeared in her mind—and the blood.

252 A.T. NICHOLAS

Kosta gave Allen a parting glance, as if he recognized him. "You look better without the beard," he said before walking away.

"Some disguise," Allen said.

Mary spent the next thirty minutes filling out paperwork for the police report. *Half-truths,* she thought, *or half-lies, depending on your conscience.*

Chapter 33

Washington, D.C.

Art Hanson walked into Sean Carbon's office chewing on the uncut end of his Punch cigar. "Thank you, for seeing me, Mr. Carbon." His voice rasped from years of smoking.

Carbon laughed. "I didn't feel I had a choice."

He stepped from behind his desk and Art realized what a contrast they must make; Carbon's athletic build next to his own five-eight chubby frame. They shook hands.

"You call and tell me that you're a private investigator and you have proof my silent partner is involved with organized crime. You made the 'things to do' list real quick." His voice was smooth and composed, which went along with his "bronze god" looks.

Art grinned. He knew that line would get him in the door. "Sorry, I hope I didn't worry you too much." He could care less if it worried him or not. Hell, he hoped it did.

"You certainly got my attention."

"Is your partner's name Jordan Iblis?" Art asked, making it sound more like a well-known fact.

Carbon's face remained relaxed and calm. "That information is highly confidential. May I ask how you obtained it?"

Art had friends at a firm that tracked all international enterprises and accounts for tax and security reasons, especially high profile ones. This firm was a very low profile branch of the government involving the NSA, the Department of the Treasury, and Homeland Security— unofficially, of course. "My sources must remain confidential." He grinned behind his cigar. "You understand."

Carbon handed him a gold, double-blade guillotine cigar cutter. "Of course."

He was surprised, but maintained a poker face. Carbon was inviting him to light his cigar. He remembered seeing at least a dozen "No Smoking" signs in the building. "This is a smoke free building."

"I own the building," Carbon reminded him.

A gentlemanly and classy gesture, Art thought, inviting a man to stink up your office. He clipped the tip of the cigar and Carbon struck a wooden match for him. "Thank you," he said, blowing a cloud of bluish-gray smoke toward the ceiling. Carbon couldn't be all bad. He slid another Punch from a three-fingered, leather pocket cigar case and offered it to Carbon.

"Don't mind if I do."

He returned from the wet bar with two crystal snifters. The golden amber color of the Remy Martin, Louis XIII cognac permeated the air with an enthralling feeling of decadence. Art palmed the glass and inhaled the breath of the petite champagne cognac, before taking a sip. "Not bad."

Carbon raised his glass and stared at the swirling golden liquid. "The grapes for this bottle were picked in the late ninety twenties. There's nothing like seventy-five year old cognac."

"Maybe a week-old cold beer on Sunday afternoon during the Skins-Cowboys game," Art countered.

Carbon laughed.

Art took another sip. *This is good,* he thought, *real good.* "How much does a bottle of this cost?"

"Somewhere in the neighborhood of thirteen hundred." Carbon answered, as if he'd said thirteen dollars.

Art took another drink and swallowed with a grin. "There goes twenty bucks of it."

The two men sat across from one another on soft leather chairs enjoying the aroma of the captivating, creamy, coffee tobacco of the cigars swirling in the office. The sweet bouquet of the cognac satisfied their nostrils with every sip. They puffed their cigars and sipped their cognac for another hour, discussing Carbon's business and Art's information on Jordan's involvement with organized crime.

Sometime during the course of the conversation, Art decided Carbon was innocent of criminal involvement and naïve to Jordan's extra activities; and a nice guy, for a billionaire. They also resolved that the Cuban cigars they were smoking were harmless, and government politics shouldn't interfere with a good smoke.

"Well, who ever your client is," Carbon said, "I appreciate the information."

"He wanted to make sure you knew who Iblis was." There was no way he was going to tell Carbon that Greg believed Jordan was the devil.

"I'm not sure what I'm going to do next, now that I know."

"I suggest you get the hell away from him soon as you can." Art grinned. "It's about to hit the fan real quick. A friendly warning," Art added, becoming serious. "My client warned me and I'm going to warn you. This guy is dangerous. He runs with the scum of the earth. I've seen him with crooked federal agents and lawyers, congressmen, and known hit men. He's got power and status from the UN." He threw a thick file with photographs and documents of Jordan's illegal endeavors onto the table. "This kind of stuff will get people killed. Watch your back." He stood to leave.

"Thanks." Carbon flicked his ashes into a black marble ashtray. "Sounds like you should watch your back too."

He smiled. "Always do."

*   *   *

Art sat in his car in the church parking lot, not believing what he heard on the radio. A sudden heavy rain had extinguished the mountainous burning Bibles in Jerusalem. Three and a half days after the first burned Bible, just like the professor had predicted. If that wasn't stunning enough, the storm rained solely over the blazing books. The story continued to get more bizarre by the minute. After the rains subsided, an unexpected whirlwind sucked up the scorched books into the heavens. He found himself wanting to get to a TV and see the news footage, which at that very moment the entire world was witnessing.

*   *   *

Six blocks away from the church, Kelsy and Sam sat at a stop sign staring confoundedly at one another after they heard the latest from Jerusalem. She punched the buttons on the radio, searching for more information. The amazing story was told again, and then again, and again. Every radio and television station was running the breaking news. A miraculous rainstorm and a tornado-like whirlwind appeared suddenly, and moments later the burning Bibles had completely vanished, right before the eyes of billions of viewers.

*   *   *

Walter sat alone in the rear of the restaurant ignoring his salad and working on his third drink. He pushed a package for Jordan aside and read a file report sent from Congress, detailing the resignation of Shelly Deanster. It also had Derrick Moore's list of names to replace her. There was an investigation article demanding from the president, a further inquiry concerning the allegations against Shelly.

Jordan entered the restaurant with two personal bodyguards trailing. The dozen or so patrons of the bar and restaurant applauded Jordan's presence. Jordan had become a local hero when he beat the tar out of the two men who had heckled Shelly. The incident had given birth to a drink that the bartender appropriately named, "Jordan's Punch," concocted with Bacardi 151, dark rum, pineapple juice, and Hawaiian Punch. Jordan and the United Nations were being sued by the two men, but witnesses of the incident were hard to come by, and it would take years before anything could result from the incident.

Walter grinned and shook his head. "Have a seat, Rocky."

Jordan smirked. "You're not drinking a Jordan Punch."

"Too strong for me. You've become a celebrity in this town."

A waitress arrived with a fresh drink for Walter and a martini for Jordan.

"Thank you," Jordan said, handing the young lady a twenty dollar bill. "This is for you. It's a long walk from the bar."

She smiled politely, the way all waitresses smile to humor flirty men.

"What's with the package?" Jordan asked.

"I don't know," Walter shrugged. "Some old guy dropped it by my office and told me to give it to you. He said his name was Professor Orfordis."

"I hope it's not a bomb," Jordan joked, pulling the brown paper wrapping off.

"The security boys already checked it out."

The gift brought an amused smile to Jordan's face. "Yum," he said, removing one of the cigars and ran it beneath his nose. "I know what we're having for dessert."

Walter studied the band around the cigar. "St. George. I've never heard of this brand.

"It's a pretty good smoke," Jordan declared, but it was not the quality of smoke that was important, it was the message. Professor Greg Orfordis was given notice. On the band around the cigar was a detailed depiction of Saint George slaying a dragon.

"Who's this professor?"

"An old war buddy," Jordan answered, grinning with admiration for the old man. He was certainly a worthy adversary.

Walter closed the file he was reading.

"What were you reading?" Jordan asked.

Walter threw the file on the table. "The last details of Shelly's resignation."

Jordan frowned, but there was something phony about his grief.

"And President Moore's list of replacements for her."

"Really." Jordan's eyes sharpened with interest. "Anyone I know?"

Walter nodded and slid the file across the table.

Jordan skimmed the document. "More conservatives and bleeding hearts," he said with a smirk. "I see Moore is going to challenge the charges against Shelly."

"The contest papers are filed and being reviewed as we speak," Walter said. "Someone in Congress said Moore has proof she was framed." Walter never did like Shelly or the president, but he did feel some sympathy for the way Congress treated her. A woman vice president never did settle well throughout the House, and there were rumors that some powerful people within the system were waiting for a reason to get rid of her. She was removed so quickly, it raised eyebrows in Washington, and that wasn't easy to do. As for being framed, that theory was beginning to get some attention because of the women's group demonstrations and protests.

Jordan smiled and slid the file back across the table. "I hope he can prove her innocence," he said, but didn't sound convincing. He also slid another file across the table.

"What's this?"

"Something that will interest you."

Walter opened the folder and read the contents. He glanced up at Jordan with disbelief.

"This material is highly confidential."

"Why are you showing this to me?"

"I trust you, Walter."

He continued to read. The file contained sensitive information involving the hostage situation in Libya. He reached a collection of photographs. "Where did you get these pictures?"

"Infrared satellite imagery has reached new levels of eavesdropping, hasn't it?" Jordan leaned forward and whispered. "We also have a listening device on the inside feeding us information. We believe they started killing the hostages."

He felt sick to his stomach. "I can't believe it, how many are left?"

"I don't know. They're being murdered in cold blood. Plans are in the works for an assault," he whispered.

Walter's eyes widened, not believing what he was hearing. "What about the biological and chemical warheads?"

Jordan flipped two photographs over. "Do you see the photographs?" he asked pointing directly at one spot.

Walter pushed aside the bloody thoughts of the host examine the pictures. He'd been in the military for years before he became a politician, but the technology had changed so much, he knew little concerning military infrared satellite photographs, and certainly wouldn't be able to interpret them. Regardless of his lack of knowledge, he stared at the array of colors and shapes for a moment.

"Those photos are evidence the warheads are inoperative," Jordan said taking a long draw from his drink.

"They're bluffing?"

Jordan acknowledged with a slight nod. His face hardened and his eyes became intense. "And we're about to call them on it."

"Who?" he asked. "Who's going to do it?"

"The good ole' U.S. of A," he said almost laughing. "Derrick deployed a strike force two weeks ago to assist NATO Troops in North Africa."

"Moore knows about the assault?"

"He's being briefed on Air Force One." Jordan got a confident glimmer in his eyes. "Once he's aware of the current situation with the hostages, I'm sure the strike force will receive the green light."

"I hope you're right about those warheads," he said, under his breath. "Because if they're active . . . ." The thought sat lodged in his throat. He felt himself pale as the possibility settled in his gut of biological warheads being detonated. He knew Jordan must have considered the hundreds of thousands of deaths and the chaos a catastrophe of this nature would cause. And it appeared to have no effect on him in the slightest.

*　　*　　*

Art stepped out of his '69 black Cadillac, unlit cigar tucked in the corner of his mouth. He looked at the blue sky peeking through the breaking clouds and took a deep breath. Spring showers always prompted memories from his childhood in western Maryland. He crossed the wet parking lot toward the main entrance of the church, when he noticed two suspicious-looking men standing near the sidewalk. The closer he got the more they look like well-dressed thugs. He figured they must be some of Jordan's flunkies. He tucked the large folder under his armpit and shoved his hands into the pockets of his trench coat.

The two men blocked his path. "What's in the folder?" the skinny man asked.

He stared at the skinny man, who weighed maybe a hundred forty pounds soaking wet. The little man reminded him of Dracula. He had black, greased back hair with a widow's peak, a pointy chin and a wide forehead. "Who are you? The Postmaster General?"

The second man grinned. "No, he's the Surgeon General and he thinks your attitude is hazardous to your health."

His attention slid to the second man, but he was always cognizant of the hands of both thugs. "I got the patch," he said, switching the cigar from one corner of his mouth to the other. "But it doesn't seem to be working."

The grin disappeared from the second man's face when he stepped forward. He wasn't much taller than Art, but he was thick with muscles, the kind of muscles that a suit couldn't conceal. Mr. Muscles looked foreign, maybe Mediterranean. Full dark hair, permanent tanned skin and chiseled features, but he seemed to have lost his razor for a week.

"We want the folder," Mr. Muscles demanded.

Dracula stepped in. "Since the patch didn't work, maybe you just need some encouragement." He pulled his coat aside and exposed the grip of a pistol.

Art allowed the folder to fall from beneath his armpit. Both thugs instinctively followed the folder down to the pavement. A bad and painful mistake. His right hand slipped out of his trench coat pocket armed with a small, black object slightly larger than a lighter. Before either thug realized he had pepper-spray in his hand, they were blinded with the painful, burning liquid. They yelled in anguish and pawed at their faces for relief.

He sent a crippling kick into Mr. Muscles kneecap, snapping bone. Dracula had drawn his weapon in a blind effort to defend himself. He jerked his gun aimlessly from side to side searching for a target. Art made his move, sending the skinny punk into the air with a crashing blow to the bridge of the nose with the palm of his hand, but Dracula fired off two shots before he hit the pavement, unconscious. Blood gushed down his cheeks onto the wet sidewalk.

Art retrieved the blood-stained folder and took the two guns belonging to the thugs. He continued across the church parking lot leaving one man clutching his knee agonizing in pain while the other visited la-la-land.

*   *   *

Fifteen minutes later, Kelsy and Sam pulled into the church parking lot.

"What's going on over there?" Kelsy asked.

"Got me."

A little man was attempting to help another man, who was six inches taller and nearly twice his weight, into the car.

"Is that guy's face covered in blood?" she asked.

"Looks like it." Sam stepped out of the car. "You guys all right? Need any help?"

Mr. Muscles cried painfully after bumping his knee against something in the the car. Dracula gave Sam a dirty look as he made his way to the driver's side.

"I guess not," Sam shrugged.

The two men sped away.

When Kelsy and Sam reached the garden, they saw the professor and another man talking.

"Hi, Professor Orfordis," Kelsy said, always happy to see him.

"Good day, Kelsy," Greg greeted her joyfully. "Hello Mr. Dent."

"Professor," Sam said with a shake of Greg's hand. "Nice to see you again."

"Is it?" Greg asked grinning.

"Sure."

"Kelsy Anderson, Sam Dent, This is Art Hanson."

They exchanged greetings and handshakes.

"I want to congratulate you on the prediction," Sam said. "You were right, the Bible bonfire thing ended in three and a half days, just like you said it would."

"It wasn't me," Greg corrected. "The Bible prophesied what would occur."

"Do the people there know an earthquake is next?" Art asked, actually believing it might happen.

"I pray they do," Greg answered.

"I forgot about the earthquake," Sam said.

Greg looked at him. "Do you believe an earthquake will follow?"

Sam knew the question wasn't about an earthquake. It was about believing in something other than the tangible or physical. It meant believing in something spiritual. "I don't know."

Greg noticed droplets of blood dotting the walkway beside Art's shoes. "You're bleeding."

"Yeah," Art said, lighting his cigar. "The skinny one got a lucky shot off before he went night-night."

Kelsy and Sam looked at the blood, then at Art.

"Were you responsible for Laurel and Hardy out in the parking lot?" Sam asked.

"Yeah," he answered. "I didn't think they were so funny."

Sam laughed. "You're a tough audience."

"Are you going to be all right?" Kelsy asked. "Can we do anything?"

"I'll be fine," Art said.

Greg forced Art to go to the hospital. The four of them got into Kelsy's car. "Do you have more information for me?" Greg asked Sam. "Or did you come by for an update?"

Sam hesitated.

"It's all right, Mr. Dent," Greg insisted. "I trust Mr. Hanson."

Kelsy, Sam, and Greg exchanged glances. She shrugged. "If you trust him, then so do I."

Sam pulled out a sheet of paper. "We found where most of the financial backing came from for the archaeological expedition and the secret surgeries. It's a pharmaceutical company started back in the fifties that now is known as BioloTek International. In the first forty years, the name Luke DeMynn appeared most often. The last three years the name, Jordan Iblis suddenly appeared on a regular basis. Why do I know that name?"

"He's the Secretary General of the United Nations." Art smiled from behind his cigar. "He's also Sean Carbon's silent partner in Golden Calf Enterprises, the ex-vice president's boyfriend, and the owner of three major fuel distribution companies." Art gave Greg a grin. "Oh, I almost forgot, and he's Satan."

Sam folded his arms and stared skeptically. "Right."

"What does he mean by that?" Kelsy asked, looking at Greg in the rear-view-mirror.

A moment of silence passed before Art spoke up. "Don't get shy now, professor."

"I believe Jordan Iblis is the incarnation of Satan," Greg answered.

"And he's one hell of a business man," Art added.

"As the Demonic Trinity Turns," Sam joked, amused by the professor's obsession with spiritual warfare.

Kelsy was riveted by the new information.

Art could tell by Sam's reaction, that he, like himself, didn't believe in the professor's religious nonsense, but the young lady, on the other hand, believed every word, hook, line, and sinker.

"What do you think?" Sam asked Art. "Is Iblis the devil?"

Art grinned and switched the cigar from one corner of his mouth to the other. "I don't know too much about devils and things. But I do know bad people." He turned serious. "Jordan Iblis is as bad as they come."

"We have evidence that proves Iblis framed Shelly Deanster," Greg explained. "We also connected him with an underground organization within the government."

"Something called the Shadow Government," Art added.

"The same people we're dealing with," Kelsy said, coming to a complete stop at a flashing yellow signal.

"It's a good thing I'm not bleeding to death," Art joked because of Kelsy's driving.

Sam laughed and Kelsy endured another blow to her driving skills, or lack of, as Mary would say.

Art had been wondering for ten minutes what the relationship between the professor and the big man and young lady was about. At first he thought they were two more investigators the professor hired, but it didn't appear to be the case. "Are you guys investigating Jordan Iblis too?" he finally asked.

No one jumped to answer him.

"Hey, you don't have to tell me anything."

Greg started at the beginning with the archaeological discovery in the sixties and how the Israeli government forcefully claimed the artifact; and how a SEAL team executed a covert mission and committed a burglary, stealing the artifact back from a museum and murdering a Foreign Minister's son in the process. He told Art about the mysterious surgeries in sub-floors of government buildings and the experimental testing on embryos. He explained how the sudden, current murders and the past events were connected by a single conspiracy perpetrated by the Shadow Government. Finally, he told him about Allen Pyrit, who appeared to be the source of the entire story because he might be the successful clone of the government's unethical experiments with human genetics.

Art had become accustomed to the professor's eccentric beliefs and stories, but the bizarre tale he just heard reached a new level of craziness. And for some reason, he believed every word of it. Misery loves company, they say. So did insanity, he thought.

While waiting at an intersection, a bus pulled beside Kelsy's car. Greg noticed the advertisement plastered across the side of the bus. It was another announcement of an exhibit at one of the many museums in Washington, D.C. Staring eye to eye with Greg was a large photograph of Tutankhamen, also known as King Tut. The king of Egypt from the 18th dynasty glared mockingly at him. And then, it hit him, a wave of nausea spreading through his body like a disease. The Prophecy of Death. Sean Carbon and GCE's prediction. 'When two Egyptian rulers visit the eagle's nest, and in the month when darkness equals light, a world leader, a man of God will fall.' The president of Egypt arrived in town today and the King Tutankhamen exhibit opened this morning. "Two Egyptian rulers visiting the eagle's nest," Greg mumbled. How could he miss the connection? Suddenly, it got worse. Today, he remembered, was the spring equinox, the twenty-four hour period when day and night are equal in time. 'In the month when darkness equals light,' the prophecy stated. "May I use someone's phone?" he asked abruptly.

"What's wrong, professor?" Art asked, noticing he looked shook up.

Sam handed his phone to Greg.

"The Prophecy of Death is being fulfilled," he answered.

"What?" everyone in the car asked.

Greg quickly explained as he punched in a number on the phone.

"Who are you calling?" Sam asked.

"The President."

Chapter 34

Air Force One

Colonel Robert Haynes and his copilot, Lieutenant Colonel Gram Norton frantically scanned the display equipment, searching for the malfunction. The computer screens and control panels were shrieking and blinking like an over-decorated Christmas tree. Warning signals came from everywhere; systems failure alerts screeched throughout the cockpit. Major Thomas Tips, the navigator, scrambled to locate the nearest airport, requesting an emergency landing.

"She isn't going to stay up much longer," Haynes warned.

"I got one!" Tips yelled. "Ciudad Judrez." He pointed at the illuminated wall map with small clusters of blinking icons. The largest of the icons was Air Force One.

Haynes would have preferred to land in El Paso, but under the circumstances, a Mexican airport would have to do. An unscheduled landing on foreign soil was going to give some folks in Washington a heart attack, he thought with a grin.

The pilots of the two F-15 jet fighters watched helplessly as the crippled aircraft struggled uncontrollably in the night sky. They feared they would be the witnesses of one of the nation's greatest tragedies. They continued to glide dutifully beside Air Force One and her important cargo, escorting the wounded bird to her final destination, wherever that may be.

A skinny twenty-something aide with wire-framed glasses entered the cockpit. "The president refuses to entertain any escape plans," he said attempting to maintain his balance.

Haynes snapped his head around and ordered the aide back to his seat. "You can send them to college, but you can't teach them common sense," he said to no one in particular.

The three pilots didn't need to be told what they already knew. Derrick Moore wouldn't leave the aircraft and his staff under any circumstances. He had guts and honor, and that was why many people who worked under him respected him and considered him a great president.

"Number four engine is on fire!" Norton yelled, pointing out the window.

Haynes calmly pulled the bright red fire handle overhead. A discharge of extinguishing halon gas moved into the burning engine, suffocating the flames. The number four engine whirled to a halt, while a stream of gray smoke trailed. Haynes adjusted the left rudder to compensate for the lost engine, and then slowly trimmed out.

Norton programmed the coordinates for Ciudad Judrez Airport. He informed the Situation Room in the White House of their status whenever communication was possible. He radioed ahead to the airport, checking again the status of the rescue units at the emergency landing site.

"What's the airspeed and the altitude?" Haynes asked.

Norton shot out the information and it was all negative.

Haynes studied the instrument panel again. His face was etched with determination. "What the hell's going on? The whole damn aircraft is falling apart."

There was a total of fifty-nine years of flight experience in the cockpit of Air Force One, and all three men were veterans of war with thousands of combat hours in either Vietnam or Desert Storm; but this mysterious malfunction had left them perplexed.

"The controls are tight." Norton said. "We're losing fuel from somewhere, too."

An electronic alarm sounded, followed by a metallic voice. "STALL. STALL. STALL." The flashing red letters accompanied the alert.

Haynes dropped the nose of the aircraft, attempting to avoid stall conditions. "The damn controls feel sluggish now," he said, laboring to regain control.

Air Force One dove; the engines shrieked. Screams from the cabin filtered into the cockpit. Their bodies gravitated forward.

Slowly, Haynes leveled the aircraft out of the dive. The engines quieted to a lower hum.

The aircraft began to climb uncontrollably. "STALL. STALL," the audio voice warned. Haynes struggled with the controls and released the stick, which should automatically activate the autopilot, but there was no response. The plane continued to climb. Unsecured objects crashed throughout the cabin.

They could feel their bodies grow heavy from the G-force as they were pressed into the seats. Their stomachs raised, followed by nausea at the peak of the climb. A sensation of weightlessness ensued at the pitch oscillation of the aircraft. Then sickening sensation faded.

Haynes leveled the aircraft out; immediately the shrieks of the stall alarm ended. The loose objects settled to the floor and the engines returned to a steady roar.

"Slats and flaps?" Haynes asked with an exhausted glance.

Norton and Tips gave him an affirmative nod.

He ran through a physical and mental checklist for the hundredth time, and the results were a negative and depressing conclusion. The one thing he found reassuring was that the aircraft was built to withstand a nuclear blast; he hoped it could withstand a very rough landing.

Derrick, the aides, the secretaries, and the Secret Service agents remained belted in their seats and unharmed. One of the aides held a bag to her mouth, spurting vomit. Derrick's thoughts were with his family. The other three aides struggled to remain calm, but their fear was too great to conceal. The two secretaries were pale and looked on the verge of becoming ill. The distress in the Secret Service agents' eyes was surrounded by stone-faced expressions. Derrick prayed silently.

The White House

In the Situation Room, a group of anxious people sat around a large, oval, oak table. Walter Web sat at the head of the table on the telephone to the Special Rescue Unit and the National Security

Team. On his left and right were the Attorney General Robert Collins, the chairman of the Joint Chiefs of Staff General Roger T. Blake, and the Secretary of Defense, Anthony Ackinson. The room hummed with teletype machines, radar equipment, and several other communications systems. A half dozen aides were rushing in and out of the room with information and updates.

Two men entered the room, and all eyes fixed on them. The room became silent for a brief moment, acknowledging the two men's presence before returning to its busy state. The Assistant Director of the CIA, Edwin Gortervich, and the Secretary of State, Frank Shapino, walked directly to the end of the conference table and joined General Blake and Secretary of Defense Ackinson. The four men discussed the 'football' among themselves. The 'football' was an attaché case that had the doomsday nuclear codes, plus a little extra information they had purchased from a vacationing Cuban citizen in Mexico. After a grievous five minutes of conversation, Secretary of State Shapino stood. "Has anyone spoken to the president or special agent Cyprus?"

"No, not yet," Walter responded immediately.

The four men appeared to have gotten headaches simultaneously. It was imperative they speak to President Moore, and it was just as crucial they contacted Cyprus. He was handcuffed to the attaché case.

"Where's the Special Rescue Unit?" the Secretary of Defense asked.

"En route."

"Are our people at the emergency landing site?"

"They're twenty-two minutes away," a communications officer answered.

"Christ," Shapino mumbled. "How in the hell does something like this happen?"

"Has the Mexican government been contacted?" the CIA Assistant Director asked.

"Yes," someone answered from across the room.

Again, the four men began conversing among themselves, preparing strategies for the many possible outcomes. The CIA and

NSA secretly didn't care about the passengers of Air Force One. If the aircraft did crash, they hoped the attaché case would disintegrate in a blaze.

The communications officer raised his hand to quiet everyone. "I've got a transmission." He started writing the information down as quickly as he could. When he finished writing, his eyes stared up soberly. "Air Force One is going down."

*   *   *

Air Force One

"Land now or crash later," Colonel Haynes said almost jokingly. "We land now," Norton and Tips said.

Haynes began dumping the remaining fuel. Norton radioed to Mission Communications Center located on the second floor of Air Force One to proceed with operation "Fumble." The communications officer briefed special agent Cyprus on the latest developments. Cyprus immediately tapped in a code on a device resembling a small cell phone.

Derrick's beeper squawked from his belt-line. He reached down and read the message. The screen displayed the aircraft's status, followed by a request for authorization to execute operation, "Fumble." He instantaneously punched the "proceed" code into the beeper.

Cyprus received the green light. He unlocked the attaché case with a key, then quickly worked the combination lock, then finally entered a code. He started feeding papers through a shredder. Nuclear missile information, the Single Integrated Operations Plans, missile launch codes, and nuclear war strategies hit the floor, piling up like paper confetti.

Air Force One descended. Haynes' knuckles were white from struggling with the throttles and controls. *We're not going to make it,* he thought. He didn't want to be remembered as the pilot who crashed Air Force One and killed the President. The aircraft unexpectedly clipped treetops. Haynes and Norton held the altitude steady to clear the trees, but it was too late. Visibility became zero. The ground was a sea of black. The aircraft's wheels smashed through tree branches. The equipment in the cockpit flashed warnings and blank screens; Tips was unable to verify altitude. The aircraft shuddered violently. Everyone held on tightly, while loose objects ricocheted throughout the cabin and the aisles. Air Force One felt as if it were going to come apart at any moment.

"What the hell is going on?" Tips yelled.

The turbulence shook pieces of equipment loose in the cockpit, striking Norton in the head, knocking him unconscious. The crew of Air Force One was unaware of the 9,422 feet of mountain directly ahead of them. The aircraft struck a level section of the mountain terrain, snapping the front wheel off in a shallow ravine, causing the nose of the aircraft to drive into the rocks. The metal frame scraped across the rocky surface, leaving a trail of dust and sparks in its wake.

In the cabin, the staff members were yelling and screaming. One of the aides vomited uncontrollably. Derrick held on tightly to the armrests. Two of the Secret Service agents were gritting their teeth with eyes shut tightly; the three others maintained intrepid stares.

The aircraft started to lose speed from the impact of solid rock against the frame, when suddenly the right wheel beneath the wing collapsed, sending the aircraft into a spin. The right wing splintered and propelled through the air. Air Force One slid aimlessly through a clearing. One of the aides didn't properly fasten her seat belt and was thrown from her seat onto the floor, hitting against the walls of the cabin and seats, breaking her arm. The aircraft continued to skid, decreasing in speed and leaving parts in its trail. Derrick reached for the woman. He unfastened himself and dove toward the aide. Two Secret Service agents followed, struggling to maintain their balance. Derrick grabbed the aide; the two agents clutched onto the president and the woman. They somehow belted the aide safely into a seat.

Crawling, the agents escorted the president to a seat. One of the agents hooked his arm around an armrest and assisted the president into a seat while the second agent assisted from directly behind. Air Force One struck a row of large trees, snapping the fuselage clean in two. Derrick was catapulted out of the aircraft toward a thick shrubbery area near a steep ridge. One of the agents was thrown against the ceiling; the impact broke his neck. The second agent was lodged between seats. The plane did a cartwheel motion once more before coming to a stop in a small group of low-lying trees. A fire ignited in the aft of the aircraft. Norton and Tips were alive, but unconscious in their seats in the cockpit. Haynes was also in his seat, staring out of the undamaged bulletproof glass.

"The glass held up," he said to himself, grinning painfully. He thought about his wife, his children, and his grandchildren as he bled to death internally. Without warning, the rear section of Air Force One exploded into a ball of fire. The orange glow expanded skyward with a black cloud leading the way. One fourth of the Communications Center on the second floor was burning with the aft cabin and tail section of the aircraft. The front of the fuselage had two aides dangling from their belted seats and a Secret Service Agent mangled, unrecognizable beside the main cracked exterior frame. A number of bodies had been hurled throughout the wooded area still belted in their seats.

Air Force One had gone down in a rough mountainous wooded area in a remote section of Mexico's Sierra Madre Occidental.

The Situation Room

The room was dead silent. The teletype machines had stopped, the communication systems were quiet, and Air Force One had disappeared from the large radar screen. They waited for the beacon, the tracing device fitted in the aircraft to activate.

Chapter 35

Athens, Greece

Allen and Mary walked into an extraordinary and spacious hotel. The entire west side of the lobby was constructed of windows, and sliding glass doors allowed a panoramic view of the Aegean Sea; the purest blue as far as the eye could see. The doors opened to a large balcony suited to entertain over two hundred guests. The warm, late-afternoon breeze blew in from the coastline, moving white, transparent drapes like ghosts in the moonlight. The bone white marble floor reflected the setting sun's golden rays onto the pallid stone decor and large tropical plants in the lobby. Beautiful stonework of mythological gods and goddesses stood watchfully throughout the hotel and the brilliant hand-painted pottery spoke of ancient tales.

"Do you have a room available?" Allen asked the desk clerk in Greek.

Mary walked across the lobby to an area furnished with a dozen inviting couches facing the Aegean and its salty breath. She sagged down on the over-stuffed cushions and closed her eyes. The breeze swirled across her body soothingly, and the late afternoon sun touched her face gently.

"Mary," Allen said softly, leaning close to her.

Her eyes remained closed.

He leaned a little closer. He studied her face for a moment and pushed a strand of hair away from her eyes. The breeze lifted the scent of her hair and skin up to him. He inhaled deeply and exhaled with contentment. "Mary," he whispered.

"What?" she said wakening, disoriented.

"Come on, I got the room."

He helped her to her feet. The gold-plated elevator doors closed behind them. He saw her struggling to stay awake in the reflection of the elevator doors. She needed sleep desperately. He realized he could use a little rest himself, after noticing the dark circles under his eyes. He could use a haircut and a shave, too. But that would have to wait until this ordeal was over.

He slid the card into the door lock, the light went from red to green and a click sound followed. The room was warm and stuffy and smelled of a fresh cleaning.

"You go ahead and take a nap, and I'll make arrangements for Rhodes," he said, turning on the light. "I'll make some calls and see if I can locate Buckler's whereabouts. Maybe I'll get lucky."

Mary glanced at him with weary "Good idea."

"We'll get some dinner later," he said, throwing the bags on one of the double beds.

Mary threw herself on the other bed face down and immediately fell asleep. He pulled off her shoes and placed a blanket over her. He adjusted the thermostat on the wall before leaving the room and took the elevator to the roof, where it came to a jerky stop, followed by a ding sound. The doors parted and the odor of chlorine from a pool rushed into the elevator. He loved the fresh clean smell of a pool; it reminded him of his childhood. At the pool-side bar he ordered a glass of red wine. The bar itself was in a gazebo, but he sat at a small table near a waist-high stone wall and railing that kept guests from tumbling ten floors down. He watched the sun begin its hypnotic decline into the Aegean. Across the street the palm trees and the masts of the boats docked in the harbor became silhouettes. The warm wind pushed inland off the sparkling water and carried the fresh scent of the sea to the rooftop.

Allen shook his head in astonishment. He couldn't believe he was sitting on the roof of a hotel in the middle of Athens drinking a glass of wine, watching the sunset. The reality of it amazed him. He'd traveled three thousand miles over the Atlantic Ocean, chasing a man across Greece, who may or may not have information concerning his past.

Two questions dominated his thoughts: Why were people dying because of him? Who was responsible for the killing? His thoughts ping-ponged in his head, attempting to make sense of it all. The inner struggle invariably ended with the true driving motive within him, and it revealed itself in the same haunting question. "Who am I?" Once that question was answered, everything else would become clear. But how many more people must die before he discovered the answer? He found himself wishing his father had never told him he was adopted. He wished he'd never started searching into his past.

He drank his wine and closed his eyes, seeking rest from the vexing questions. For a peaceful moment his mind drifted, free of thoughts, but it wasn't long before thoughts crept back into his mind. But it wasn't a question or really a thought. It was more of an image; an image of Mary. "What's going on?" he asked, irritated with himself. He stared at his wine glass. Why did he find Mary physically attractive and feel something more than friendship for her suddenly? The thought hung there like an essay question he didn't study for. He hoped Mary hadn't sensed the change in him. Maybe he should tell her how he felt, but that thought was consumed by ambiguous emotions. He closed his eyes again and concentrated on the warm breeze and the sound of traffic far below. His mind started to drift, slowly slipping somewhere between a daydream and a light sleep. Visions of his childhood moved in like an early morning fog.

"It's too high, Allen!" Little Joey Brown yelled from the ground.

"Come on, chicken!" Mary yelled from the tree house.

"You can do it!" twelve-year-old Allen said optimistically.

"Come on, Joey!" Frank yelled.

Nine-year-old Joey started to climb the wooden planks nailed to the tree.

"Don't look down," Allen warned.

Twenty feet up, Joey stopped and shouted, "I can't do it!" He peered up at the other children with a frightened glance.

"Keep going, Joey." Frank attempted to encourage him. "A few more feet." More like ten or fifteen more.

"I can't do it!" His eyes closed tight and his hands had become colorless from the grip of fear he had on the planks.

"Joey, look at me," Allen said.

Joey opened his eyes and looked up at Allen.

Allen smiled and reached out his hand. "Look at my hand Joey, as you climb."

After an agonizing minute, Joey started to climb again. He stared at Allen's hand, occasionally glancing at Allen's confident eyes urging him on.

"You're almost there, Joey," Allen said.

"You're doing it," Frank cheered him on.

"I knew you could do it," Mary added from over Allen's shoulder.

Joey reached for Allen's hand, but suddenly his foot slipped off one of the wooden planks. His out-stretched hand fell away from Allen's grip and his upper body moved away from the tree. Mary gawked with horror and Frank's mouth opened but no sound came out. Joey and Allen's eyes locked as the distance between them increased. Hearts raced and breath seized in what felt like slow motion. Allen reached out and grabbed Joey's wrist, holding him suspended thirty feet above the ground. Joey weighed nearly seventy pounds, making Allen's feat no small miracle. Joey dangled below Allen, staring up with eyes blurred with tears and fright.

"Please, Allen," Joey pleaded, his voice trembling with fear. "Help me."

"I got you, Joey," Allen said, leaning back into the tree house, simultaneously pulling him up with the aid of Mary and Frank.

"Oh, my God," Mary said ecstatically. "You're so lucky."

"How did you do that?" Frank asked with eyes bugged out.

"How do you feel, Joey?" Allen asked calmly from a kneeling position.

Joey threw his arms around Allen, nearly choking him.

"I told you, you could do it," Allen said grinning.

"Boy, that was exciting," Frank exhaled.

"We still have to climb down," Mary said.

A car horn from the street below woke Allen. He sipped his wine with the dream still fresh in his mind. A month earlier he'd received a letter from little Joey Brown, who now lived in California with his wife, two boys and baby girl. Joey was a pediatrician and operated a health clinic for people who were unable to afford medical treatment. The letter was accompanied with a photograph of Joey and his family in a tree house. On the back the inscription read, "Thank you—Miss you and all the guys—Love Joey and the new gang." Allen laughed out loud when he thought about the photo of Joey and his family in their tree house. The tree house was only two feet off the ground.

He finished his wine and returned to the hotel room. Mary was taking a shower. The bathroom door was slightly ajar allowing steam to pour upward to the ceiling. He sat down on the edge of the bed and stared into the dresser mirror. He was exhausted and it showed. He decided to take a short nap before dinner. He stood to turn of the light and that was when he saw Mary's naked silhouette through the sliding glass shower doors. The physical attraction for her emerged again. He scolded himself for looking. His friendship with Mary had been the one of the most important parts of his life, and that relationship he had always held in high esteem. But now a new element had entered, and he couldn't help but view it as a threat. His feelings for her could only lead to disaster and misery. This new love and overpowering lust was nothing he had ever experienced before. He needed to sleep and forget. He turned off the light and lay down on the bed craving rest, but the thought of Mary's nude body infiltrated his mind, causing him aggravation and discomfort. He prayed for strength and self-control. Fortunately, his exhaustion finally subdued his thoughts and he fell asleep.

Mary stepped out of the shower and noticed the lights were off in the room. She cautiously poked her head out of the bathroom door and called out for Allen, but there was no response. She heard the drapes flapping from the breeze entering through the open window. Her wet shoulders gleamed in the moonlight filtering through the large sliding doors of the balcony. She saw Allen sleeping. He woke and jerked up into a sitting position on the edge of the bed. With the towel around her, Mary walked toward him. He started to stand but she stopped him by putting her hands on his shoulders. She allowed the towel to fall to the floor as she held his stare with her alluring eyes. He could feel his body surrender to his desire. He watched a droplet of water travel along the curvature of her neck, then down the cleavage of her breasts and over her abdomen, finally disappearing into her navel. His hands succumbed to temptation. He gently placed his craving hands on her waist and pulled her close to him. He kissed her stomach and worked his way up, but suddenly, the telephone rang.

His eyes focused on the ceiling. The telephone rang again. He blinked his eyes, and waited for something or someone to tell him what was going on. After the sixth ring he sat up and answered in a mumbling voice.

"Wake up call, Mr. Pyrit," the front desk clerk said.

"Wake up call?" he asked, half asleep.

"The young lady asked me to give you a wake up call."

He held the telephone not saying anything, gathering his thoughts.

"Sir?"

"Thank you," he said, and hung up. He rubbed the sleep out of his eyes and glanced around the room. There was a note on the dresser from Mary that said to meet her at the restaurant downstairs in the hotel. He walked into the bathroom. 'What the hell is going on?' he asked himself in the mirror. His church was on the verge of a scandal, he discovered he was adopted, people were dying because he was searching into his past and now he thought he was either infatuated with his best friend or he was in love with her. He turned on the faucet and cupped his hands beneath the running water until they overflowed. He leaned down and splashed the cold water onto his face. The dream of Mary flooded his mind, regardless of his attempt to avert the thought. He turned on the shower. He stepped in and grimaced under the cascade of ice-cold water.

*   *   *

Mary had visited three hotels in Athens while Allen was asleep. Before the flight to Greece she'd reserved rooms for herself at three small, inconspicuous hotels, then mailed three separate packages to the three hotels by three various mail carriers. All addressed to her, but under an alias. Dealing with criminals over the years, she learned a few things. Like how to ship weapons. The first hotel hadn't received the package, but the second hotel had a small, brown package, the size of a child's shoebox waiting for her at the front desk. She presented her counterfeit identification, the Customs Declaration Dispatch Note, shipping forms, and the shipper invoice tracking number. The desk clerk glanced at the documentation. He didn't ask her to remove her sunglasses or her baseball cap, and she didn't volunteer. She signed for the package and left. She opened it in the backseat of the taxicab. Within the bubble wrap and the packing material was a Browning compact 9mm pistol and a thirteen-round magazine clip. She had mailed herself three unregistered weapons, which had come into her possession in her FBI days. Souvenirs. Like the first, the third hotel didn't have a package waiting. She had heard it was common practice for guns to get stolen from warehouses and storage facilities of shipping companies. She also knew international Customs arbitrarily and frequently opened packages to confiscate illegally shipped material, such as her guns. It appeared the other two packages had found such fate.

*   *   *

"How was your nap?" Mary asked.

"Fine." Allen pulled a chair out and sat at the dinner table across from her. "How was yours?"

"Good."

He felt guilty for having an erotic dream about Mary, but then again, he also felt foolish for feeling guilty. He could see this new emotion was going to be bad news. He rubbed his forehead self-consciously, as if the words, "I love you" were written there for the whole world to see. "Did you go shopping?" he asked, observing her new outfit.

She was wearing russet colored cargo shorts with slash pockets and an olive green baggy pullover sleeveless shirt suitable for concealing a weapon.

"I needed something more appropriate for the climate."

"Looks good," he said.

"I got you something, too." She dipped a piece of warm, freshly made bread into a white, creamy dip. "Here, try this."

"What is it?"

"It's called, tzatziki," she pronounced the word mechanically and rehearsed.

"Tzah-zee-kee," Allen repeated, leaning in to get a good whiff of the dip. "Wow." His face transfigured, resembling someone who just sniffed smelling salts. "What's in it?"

"It's yogurt with cucumber, garlic, olive oil, and a touch of mint."

"A little heavy on the garlic, isn't it?"

"That's why you have to have some. I've had a bowl of it already."

"I know." He waved his hand across his nose.

"Very funny."

Allen took a cautious bite and made a pleased sound. "This is . . ." He hesitated pretending to search for the words. "Simply scrumptious!" he finally announced.

Mary laughed, and he knew she remembered Joel at the Getty Center. He dipped the rest of the soft bread into the bowl.

"Hey, no double dipping," she said, playfully slapping his hand.

He laughed. "Are you worried about my germs?"

The waiter approached the table with a plate of dolmades. He sat the green-leafed appetizers down on the table.

"I went ahead and ordered some appetizers," Mary said.

"What are they?" he asked, examining one of the egg roll shaped appetizers.

"Their called dolmades," she said, pronouncing the word perfectly. "They're rolled grape leaves stuffed with rice, onions, pine nuts and flavored with herbs."

"Sounds good." He took a bite. "This is . . ."

"Simply scrumptious!" they said in unison, laughing.

The waiter stared at the two laughing Americans, baffled by their sense of humor. "Are you ready to order?" he asked, after allowing them their moment of amusement.

Allen ordered souvlakia using his fluent Greek. The waiter asked if he preferred pork, lamb, or beef. He settled on pork that would be grilled on a skewer and marinated in olive oil and lemon juice.

"I think I'll have the mousaka," she ordered, closing the menu.

Allen smiled. "Very good pronunciation. You're beginning to sound like the locals."

"Thank you," she replied with a cocky attitude.

The waiter smiled and gave Mary a wink while he gathered the menus.

Allen took a sip of water. "You're picking up on the language pretty quick." He reached for another dolmades.

"The waiter worked with me before you got here," she confessed.

"That was nice of him." He hoped he didn't sound jealous.

"He's a nice guy."

"He sort of looks like the guy you're dating."

"Was dating," she quickly corrected.

A primitive emotion from somewhere deep in his male chromosome awakened. He was pleased with the news, but he felt awkward for being pleased. "What happened?"

She didn't say anything for a moment, avoiding eye contact. "It just wasn't going anywhere."

"Sorry," he said empathizing with her. He felt like her best friend again, as opposed to a predator with an opportunity. "Was it something in particular?"

"It didn't feel right," she added quietly with a glance downward.

"I know what you mean." He could identify too well with her experience.

Mary waited with a probing stare. His relationships had always been secret, 21 even from her; he seldom mentioned the women in his life. He glanced across the room at a couple holding hands, obviously in love with one another. "I've been involved three times in my life and it never felt right."

Mary seemed stunned that he had confided in her. "What ever happened to Beth?" she asked, somehow remembering the name of his dinner date from some gala in Georgetown a couple of weeks ago.

He turned his attention back to her. "We stopped seeing each other two weeks ago." He remembered her face, meaningless, evoking no emotion.

"Why?"

He took a sip of ice water. "She broke up with me."

"Why?" she asked again.

He hesitated and eventually smiled. "I wouldn't sleep with her."

Mary laughed. "No, really. What happened?"

His smile was slowly replaced by a candid stare.

"Are you serious?"

He shrugged his shoulders. "That was her reason."

"There had to be something else, or someone else," she added with a suspicious glare. "Another guy." She sounded convinced of it.

"She said she couldn't stay with someone who wouldn't get intimate with her."

Mary's expression became perplexed. "How long did the two of you date?"

He tapped a spoon on the table. "Nearly a year."

"And you didn't sleep with her?"

He looked around the restaurant, concerned his personal matters were being overheard. "Do you think we could keep this conversation at this table?"

"I would have broken up with you, too," she jested with a smirk.

"I'm old fashioned, I guess."

"What's wrong with you?" she asked laughing. "What were you waiting for?" She shot him an odd look. "How long do you wait before you sleep with someone?"

"Time has nothing to do with it. When it feels right then . . . Maybe I'll just wait until I get married."

She narrowed her eyes in an inquisitive stare.

Here it comes he thought.

"Wait a minute. You haven't slept with anyone before?"

He blushed slightly and the corners of his mouth curled to a demure grin.

"You're a virgin?" she asked, straightening up in her chair.

He scanned the restaurant again for eavesdroppers.

"Unbelievable."

"Is it?" he asked.

"Sure. You got through high school and college without having sex. You were a good-looking jock. The girls hung all over you. The hundreds of parties we went to, not to mention the fraternity parties, and you never . . ." She shook her head with bewilderment. "It's amazing to me you didn't take advantage of it or experiment or do it once out sheer curiosity." She gave him a suspicious look. "What's wrong with you?"

He laughed.

"I think you're messing with me," she said, throwing a balled-up napkin at him. "You never talk to me about this stuff. You're joking, right?"

"I never got comfortable enough with anyone," he explained, bordering on defensiveness.

Mary was almost gawking at him. "You better not be lying to me."

He interlocked his hands on the table. "I would never lie to you about anything; certainly not something like this."

She seemed to relax. "So, you're going to wait until you get married?"

He could tell she was on the verge of laughter."Maybe, maybe not. I don't think about it too much. I've waited this long, why not?"

Mary shook her head. The disbelief still lingered in her eyes. "And I thought I knew you. Some best friend you turned out to be," she joked. "Keeping secrets from me."

He smiled. "It won't happen again."

Chapter 36

Washington, D.C.

Kelsy unlocked her apartment door and threw her umbrella into a tall copper canister. The sound of thunder rumbled in the distance, now just a harmless reminder of a once driving force. The storm had taken the neighborhood's electricity out and left thousands without power. She scanned the dark room with her 9mm by her side. She always walked into her apartment with her weapon in hand now. It had become a habit; so had visits to the shooting range. She went into the kitchen and pulled out three large candles and a flashlight from the drawer. She placed the candles throughout her apartment. The flickering candlelight illuminated the room with a golden spread of light. The tapping raindrops on the windows had come to a stop. After she turned on a small portable radio, she dropped into an over-stuffed armchair. Her cell phone rang.

"How are you doing, Kelsy?" a warm voice asked quietly.

"I'm fine." She must be really lonely, because she was happy to hear his voice. She liked his voice. "How are you, James?"

"I'm well, thank you."

"Did you hear about the Air Force One?" she asked.

"Yes," he answered.

"Was it them?"

"I don't know," he answered.

There was something in James' voice she couldn't make out. A deep sadness or anger, maybe both. But it sounded raw and intense.

"Do you enjoy Mozart?" he asked, breaking the silence.

"Yes, I do." She was surprised he could hear the music. Mozart's *Laudate Dominum* was being performed. "You have good ears."

"That's a first. I usually get complimented on my smile. What's your favorite piece?"

"*The Marriage of Figaro*," she answered without hesitation.

"I like *The Magic Flute*. When I was in London a couple of years ago I saw the London Philharmonic Orchestra perform and that specific piece impressed me."

"Were you on vacation?"

The question flooded his mind with memories of his past. He remembered his wife and himself formally dressed, enjoying the brilliant music of Mozart under a star-filled sky. He remembered life was perfect then, but that was a long time ago; that life was dead now. Wiped out one rainy night on a mountain road. Everything he loved was taken from him right before his eyes. He suppressed the memories, returning them to the coffin in his mind.

"Hello. Are you there?" she asked, breaking the silence.

"Sorry."

"Are you all right?"

He slammed the coffin lid. "I'm fine."

"The information I have about the—Is the line clean?"

"Yes."

"We have enough evidence on the genetic engineering and the experimental cloning with human embryos performed by the government, to cause serious ramifications," she said cautiously.

"It won't do the foreign relationships and peace talks any good. I'm sure treaties, policies, and economic relationships would be affected."

She agreed. "Especially, since the U.S. was the country most against human cloning."

"Now what?"

"I have a name," James said. "But we need to talk on another line.

"I thought the line was clean."

"I just want to be sure. This is important."

"Why don't you talk to this person yourself?" she asked.

"I can't get close to him."

"Why?"

There was silence on the line for a moment. "They're waiting for me to make a move," he finally said.

She got the urge to ask him all the "what and who" questions again, but the only words that came out were, "Who are you?"

"Ask your uncle," he answered. "I have a feeling he knows."

"My uncle?"

"I'll contact you later and we'll meet."

The line went dead and she thought about what her life had become. Since the shooting of her mother, she broke the law a dozen different ways and had become consumed with vengeance that would ultimately lead to murder. And she seemed unable to stop the downward spiral her life had taken. A numbness of pain eased throughout her body. Her mother was the last thing she thought about before she eventually dozed off into blackness.

A figure of a man stepped out of a back room of Kelsy's apartment. He had a dead hit man draped over his shoulder. He slid his cell phone into the pocket of his trench coat, extinguished the candles and softly placed a throw blanket over Kelsy before he quietly slipped out of the apartment. "Goodnight, Kelsy," James whispered.

Chapter 37

The Situation Room, The White House

"I want the whole damn area secured!" Frank Shapino, the Secretary of State yelled into the telephone. "No one gets within ten miles of the crash but our people." The veins on the side of his bald head were throbbing.

"The fire fighters and rescue teams have to get to the scene," Attorney General Collins reminded him. "Our people are still an hour away."

Shapino stared, emotionless.

"Damn it, Shapino!" Collins exclaimed. "We're talking about the President of the United States."

"The Special Rescue Unit is on the site," the Assistant Director of the CIA, Gortervich said.

"You know damn well the SRU isn't there for survivors," Collins argued. "You have to let the local authorities and rescue teams up there."

Shapino's voice was cool. "My job is to protect the country."

Gortervich grinned at Collins. "Come on, Bob," he started, with a syrupy patronizing tone. "You know the president would agree. The country comes first. There's too much sensitive material on Air Force One. This is a national security issue."

Walter Web, the Speaker of the House hung up the phone and crossed the room, stone-faced. "I'm in command, Shapino." His voice was unwavering and loud enough for everyone in the room to hear. "Tell your people to allow everyone through," he ordered.

"Who the hell put you in charge?" General Blake questioned.

"Why are you here in the first place, Walter?" Shapino asked. "This is national security issue."

The Secretary of Defense Ackinson and Gortervich stood, joining Shapino and the General's confrontation with Walter.

White House aides and staff members nearly froze with discomfort. Walter allowed the room to hum for a moment in silence before he 'schooled' them. "The Presidential Succession Act of 1947," he said authoritatively.

The twenty-fifth Amendment to the Constitution allows the president to appoint a new vice president should the office become vacant through death or resignation. If the office of the presidency is vacant for any reason, the vice president shall assume the position. Under the extreme circumstance that both officials are incapable of performing the duties of the presidency, an order of succession found in the Presidential Succession Act of 1947 commences.

Everyone in the room knew exactly what the Presidential Succession Act was, but some of them were attempting to ignore that little fact.

Walter allowed a 'checkmate grin' to form across his lips.

Shapino reluctantly lifted the telephone. "This is Shapino. Let all personnel through. You heard me." He returned the phone to the table.

Gortervich threw his pen on the table in frustration and sat.

"Are you assuming the president is dead?" Ackinson asked.

"We're assuming the president is incapable or unable to discharge the powers and duties of office." Walter returned to the other side of the room, and thought, *these bozos don't have a clue how the government works outside of their little cloak and dagger world.*

Ackinson returned to his seat, daunted. Shapino, Gortervich, Ackinson, and General Blake stewed in their collective powerless juices at the moment. How they despised red tape and accountability.

An aide entered the Situation Room and handed Walter a file with the Congressional Seal on the cover. He read the documents. Congress had drafted a declaration which immediately yielded the powers and the duties of the presidency to the Speaker of the House. Walter was acting president. He had the full support from both Houses. *They didn't waste any time,* he thought. He explained the latest developments to the people in the room with an unceremonious attitude, but his voice had a punctuated tone, stating he was in charge. The kid from a tiny mining town in the foothills of Pennsylvania was now running the show; the thought brought a hidden smirk to his face. A former Lieutenant General and congressman pulled the ultimate leapfrog, and it was salt in the wound, insult to injury for some of the boys in the room. He needed to watch his back. If they had muscled the vice president out, they could do the same to him. Another aide entered with a file containing the latest satellite and weather data, which he passed on to everyone in the room.

"Sir," one of the communications officers said. "We have a visual."

All eyes watched the wide projection screen. The white static on the screen cleared and an overhead view appeared from a U.S. Army rescue helicopter.

"Sweet Mother of God," Walter mumbled.

The mountain terrain and the field were engulfed with raging fires. Glimpses of the aircraft appeared through flames and black smoke. The front section of the fuselage and cockpit was undamaged by fire, but was surrounded by burning fuel. Fifty yards away, the rescue units were preparing to enter the burning terrain and wreckage with fire-resistant gear.

Shapino and Ackinson whispered to one another. They felt confident the attaché case was destroyed in the fiery crash, along with their anxieties. They certainly believed the odds were in their favor by the looks of the crash site.

Walter sat in one of the leather chairs and closed his eyes. The images had left him disheartened. An aide handed him a sheet of paper. Walter immediately stood. "Shapino. Gortervich. We got clearance from the Mexican government," he said, urgently.

Shapino grabbed the phone and barked a long list of orders. Gortervich was also on the phone doing the same. The Mexican government had allowed the United States to secure and investigate the airport from where Air Force One departed. As an act of good faith and a gesture of goodwill, they immediately secured the airport after receiving the stunning news. Their eagerness to assist in the matter was due to the strong relationship Derrick had established with the Mexican government.

Shapino tucked his cell phone away. "We're rolling," he said avidly.

*   *   *

Television screens across the country concurrently flashed the familiar words, "BREAKING NEWS," followed by a newscaster's grave expression. "We interrupt our regular programming for a special report. It has been confirmed that Air Force One has crashed. Leaving Mexico City, Air Force One experienced a malfunction; a distress signal was sent, followed by an emergency landing. The aircraft separated into two sections and exploded into flames." The newscaster paused. "President Moore and a staff of eighteen were on the plane." His voice cracked. The president has not been recovered."

People in businesses and households from coast to coast stared at their television screens in shock. Millions of people in their vehicles found themselves staring at the radio in disbelief. A state of abeyance loomed over America. An older generation recalled the familiar feeling from November 22, 1963, when President John F. Kennedy was assassinated. Others were reminded of September 11th. Daily lives and activities crashed into a wall of incomprehension. An uncertainty fell over the country, suspended in a haze of grief. People looked to one another for answers, only to find confused, fragmented facts.

The newscaster continued with the special report. "Rescue teams from both Mexico and the United States are at the crash site. All rescue measures are being utilized."

A map of Mexico appeared behind the news desk with a small red dot simulating the crash site.

"A Special Op Team left Washington for Mexico immediately after the distress signal was sent. The team specializes in mountain terrain rescues." The newscaster read off facts of the mountainous region and the possible difficulties the rescue teams would encounter. He read a list of names of the passengers on board Air Force One and their occupations, but was interrupted by the latest developments from Mexico. His face transformed from tediousness to excitement. "Emergency helicopters have made visual contact with one of the passengers at the crash site," he said, unable to conceal his optimism.

The newscaster disappeared in a flash of static, then the screen was replaced by a slow transposing image; finally a distinguishable picture appeared. A news helicopter was filming a military helicopter on the scene. The word "Live" appeared in the bottom right corner of the screen. A team of U.S. Army Rangers and Green Berets from Fort Benning, Georgia hovered above burning crash site in a CH-46 helicopter. Fifty feet below was a thick, swirling black smoke and fiery orange heat that was slowly, but incessantly, devouring the landscape.

A black and gray cloud of smoke obscured the camera's view, but suddenly, a dramatic scene unfolded before millions of viewer's eyes. Emerging from the sea of burning chaos was a person waving his or her arms desperately to the rescue helicopter. Raging fires surrounded the survivor, accompanied by choking black smoke, unbearable heat, and spontaneous explosions. In between desperate waves to the rescue helicopter, the figure covered up from the burning debris floating wildly. A steel cable rescue line with a harnessed Special Op Ranger dropped down to the passenger into the hellish condition. The reporter in the news helicopter was reporting the rescue attempt in a play-by-play fashion. Viewers across the country watched intensely, praying and hoping for a miracle.

The Ranger secured the woman, Amy Dow into the second harness and latched her to himself. He fitted her face with a mask, which was being fed compressed air from a tank on his back. The Ranger pressed a button on his wrist sending a strobe light signal to the crew above, who quickly started the motored winch aboard the helicopter. The rescue line moved upward with the Ranger and Amy in toe. Viewers held their collective breaths as the two figures twisted upward away from the inferno's grip. A swirling black curtain of smoke blinded the camera's view again. The television audience waited on edge for a clear view, but before the camera regained sight of the two souls dangling over the blaze, an explosion and a glowing orange flash filled the screen. Then, there was nothing. No visual, no sound, simply an eerie blackness. A sinking feeling spanned the country. The television program returned to the news room, where the newscaster quietly uttered, "We have lost visual."

*   *   *

The reporter from the news helicopter was lying on his back due to the explosion's shock wave. The cameraman had somehow remained on his feet. In the backdrop the fire raged and the CH-46 helicopter had disappeared in a cloud of black rolling smoke.

"We are unable to see the rescue helicopter. The fire is spreading uncontrollably because of leaking fuel," the reporter said into the shaky camera, unaware he had been cut off from the news program. "The heat is incredible." He glanced over his shoulder. "We have learned the ground firefighters and rescue units have recovered two bodies." A cloud of smoke rolled through the open doors of the news helicopter. "We don't know if they were alive or not," he said, fighting through choking coughs. "Neither of the bodies was identified as the president." Before the reporter could continue, a loud voice blasted over an intercom.

"You are in restricted air space! Evacuate the area immediately! You are in a restricted area!" the voice announced with military authority.

The reporter pointed his cameraman toward the military helicopter.

"You are in restricted air space! Evacuate the area!" the voice warned.

The pilot of the news helicopter remained hovering in position. He looked at the reporter with a nervous stare, waiting for the withdrawal orders. The cameraman continued to film. The reporter spoke into the microphone.

The door located on the side of the military helicopter slid open. A soldier with a M-16 emerged, his intent was apparent. He fired his weapon above the news helicopter's blades. "This is your final warning!" the voice blasted. "Evacuate the area or we will force you down."

The news reporter and the cameraman screamed at their pilot, who promptly left the area with the military helicopter closely behind.

*   *   *

Washington, D.C.

Carbon turned off the television after watching the special report on the Air Force One crash. Disgusted, he threw the remote control across the room. A sick feeling pushed against his skull, then slid down his chest like claws across a chalkboard, and finally settled in his gut like a bad meal. He thought about the Prophecy of Death, and then about President Derrick Moore in that mangled, burning wreck of what was once Air Force One. He thought about Jordan Iblis and what Jordan had said to him one night. Jordan had proposed the idea to post the Prophecy of Death on the Internet to boost sales and stir up free publicity. A bizarre thought emerged. Could Jordan Iblis have assassinated the President of the United States and intended for him to take the fall? Art Hanson told him Jordan was connected to organized crime. Did Jordan leave some kind of fake incriminating evidence leading to him?

A young woman entered. "Mr. Carbon," she said timidly. "There are two gentleman here to see you."

Carbon's expression remained unwavering. *Right on cue,* he thought. "Send them in."

Two men in black suits entered the office, their credentials aimed before them like weapons. Both men were tall and solid with stone faces. "I'm Agent Rice and this is Agent Brown. We're from the National Security Agency. We would like to speak to you."

Carbon grinned. "I thought you guys didn't exist," he said dryly.

Their identifications disappeared back into their jacket pockets. "Only when we have to."

Carbon walked to the wet bar, which was constructed of the finest crystal and cherry oak. "Drink?" he asked without looking at them.

They declined the offer.

"Mind if I do?" he asked halfway through his drink. "What can I do for the NSA?"

"We would like to ask you a few questions," Agent Brown said.

"Am I going to need a lawyer?"

"We don't think so," Agent Rice answered.

"Does this visit pertain to the prediction of a great leader dying?"

"Yes, sir."

"The prediction was a gimmick, to get free exposure for the company." Carbon turned to fix another drink. "You guys can't believe I had anything to do with the plane crash." His tone was slightly defensive.

"No, sir."

This did surprise Carbon and his hard expression softened. "I don't understand."

"We would like to ask you about a man named Jordan Iblis."

*   *   *

Greg sat in his apartment crying. He watched the news flashes and updates concerning the Air Force One crash on CNN. "Why, Lord? Why Derrick?" he asked. His heart was breaking with every passing moment.

Chapter 38

Athens, Greece

Mary and Allen exited the hotel and stepped out into the warm, bright morning sunshine. They discovered late last night that all flights departing from Greece were canceled. Bomb threats were believed to be the cause of the delays. All flight schedules would proceed after the threat had been resolved.

They spent several hours last night searching and telephoning hotels, motels, bed and breakfasts, and villas in Athens for a guest named Alfred Buckler—the results were sore feet and frustration.

Demetrios, the taxicab driver, was leaning against the side of the taxi smoking a cigarette and reading a newspaper he had neatly folded into a square.

Allen threw the carry-on bags into the cab. "Good morning, Demetrios."

He flicked his cigarette to the ground and greeted them with a cheerful embrace. "How did my friends sleep?"

"Good," Allen said, stretching and yawning.

Mary put on her sunglasses and groaned.

"We have some time to kill," Allen said. "What do you want to do?"

"I don't care," Mary moaned.

"She's not a morning person," he told Demetrios. "Matter of fact, she's not an afternoon or night person either."

"Ha, ha," she responded, rolling her eyes.

Demetrios handed Allen the newspaper. "Did you see this?"

Allen read the headline, "Air Force One Crashes. President Moore Missing,"

Mary shook her head. "Does it say why or how?"

"No," Demetrios answered.

Allen handed the paper back. "That's unbelievable."

Demetrios stepped on the cigarette, tucked his paper under his arm and announced, "Lets go."

"Where are we going, Demetrios?" Allen asked.

"A surprise," he said waving them into the cab. "We go."

"I'm sure it has something to do with old rocks piled up," Mary mumbled. "And some of the rocks," she added with sarcastic excitement, "will be toppled over and spread randomly across the barren ground."

Demetrios whipped his taxi out into traffic and made what appeared to be a suicidal U-turn into oncoming traffic.

Mary saw the tension on Allen's face and grinned. "What's wrong?"

"Demetrios' driving reminds me of someone I know."

Mary smiled. "Kelsy would love the driving here."

He laughed. "We would have to sedate her every time we wanted to go anywhere."

Demetrios swerved in and out of traffic, speeding past other cars with moves that would impress any NASCAR fan. Soon the congestion of the city was behind them and the Saronic Gulf came into view. Hundreds of sailboats swayed gently along the shore among the market places and interesting cafés. The drive along the coast was magnificent. The shoreline unfolded before them like a sparkling emerald and blue glass field. Every winding turn along the cliffs revealed another breathtaking site. The aroma of fresh fruits and seafood being prepared for market entered the taxi with each passing of a tiny port town.

Demetrios directed their attention to a rocky bend quickly approaching. Their vehicle took the turn and the jagged mountainside gave way to an awesome sight. A large cliff with a temple high above on a rocky summit appeared across the shimmering sea. The white marble of the temple ruins bathed beneath the sun's light. The enormous, square blocks of marble randomly dotted the sloping landscape. Some of the massive stones were the dimensions of a small automobile.

Mary looked up from her list of hotels she had been calling on her cell phone. "Oh, surprise," she smirked, "More rocks, and of course, they're on top of a big hill."

"What is this place?" Allen asked, impressed with the beauty of the site.

"Sounion."

"Which god was this one built for?" Mary asked apathetically.

"Poseidon, the mighty god of the sea," Demetrios answered.

He took the only road leading to the temple grounds. The rocky bluff of Cape Sounion unfolded majestically before them, splitting the azure waters of the Aegean Sea. Mary, Allen, and Demetrios pushed through the tourists, passing a souvenir shop to reach an open-air café. The dining area consisted of fifty tables or more, some beneath a blue and white canopy.

Demetrios recognized four men at one of the tables. Before joining them he told Allen where he would be and would be happy to wait for them.

He handed Demetrios enough money for a drink."Have one on me." He accepted with a smile, gave Allen a friendly pat on the shoulder and left to join the others.

Mary and Allen walked toward a small booth, where they paid to enter the temple grounds. Mary hung up her phone after another unsuccessful search for Buckler's whereabouts. "Where's Jeff Gordon going?" Mary asked.

"He's going to join some friends at the café."

They walked along a rugged cobblestone roadway up to the temple.

"The Temple of Poseidon stands at the highest point on the headland. It was built in the Archaic period, but was demolished by the Persians in 480 B.C.," a young man explained to his companion, attempting to make the fact sound casual.

"Really," the young woman said, looking up at the temple.

Allen was impressed with the young historian.

Mary shook her head. She wasn't enthused and she looked it.

Allen motioned with his hand to Mary, and moved closer to the couple. He leaned in to listen.

"The new temple was built in the Classical period, in the mid-fifth century," the young man stated.

The couple walked around the temple and neared the edge of the cliff. Allen closely followed, urging Mary to keep up. The young man continued to rattle off facts about the ancient temple, unaware of the historical pleasure he was providing Allen. The young man turned to Allen and asked him to take a photograph of himself and his new bride. Allen took the young man's camera.

"Just aim and press the silver button on the top," the young man instructed.

Allen struggled with the camera for a moment, and then looked through the lens. "Say cheese," he said pushing the button, but nothing happened. He stared at the camera.

"May I?" Mary asked, rolling her eyes. "Say feta." She took the picture and handed the camera back to its owner.

The young man thanked them and walked toward the edge of the cliff. Allen followed, dragging Mary along.

Mary leaned toward Allen's ear to divulge a secret. "Do you know what?" she whispered. "When I took their picture, I cut their heads off."

"No you did not," he whispered back.

She smiled mischievously.

The young couple along with Allen and Mary stood only inches from the edge of the cliff. They stared down at the white breaking waves crashing against the jagged rocks hundreds of meters below. The salty air rushed upward and across the face of the rocks, bringing the scent of the sea to the top of the summit. They looked outward at the horizon at the small, uninhabited islands of brown rock breaking out of the cool, blue sea.

"Isn't there a Greek myth connected to this spot?" Allen prodded the young man.

The young man glanced at him eagerly. "Yes, there is."

Mary's head slumped in anticipation of a long, boring story. She wanted to push Allen and the guy off the cliff.

"The legend goes back to the time when King Minos of Crete demanded from the Athenians an annual tribute of seven young men and seven maidens to satisfy the appetite of the Minotaur, the fearsome half-man, half-bull monster of Knossos," the young man explained. "Aegeus was King of Athens at that time, and one year his own son, Theseus, asked to be included in the death squad. Before he left he promised his father that if he succeeded in killing the Minotaur and escaped, he would replace the ship's black sails with white ones for the return journey to Athens. Theseus slew the dreaded monster, but in the excitement and revelry of the voyage home, he forgot to change the sails. King Aegeus, meanwhile, was keeping an anxious vigil at Sounion to catch the first sight of the returning vessels. When he saw their black sails on the horizon," the young man said pointing out at the beautiful horizon, "he was so overcome with grief that he leapt from the cliff's edge into the sea."

The four of them looked down again at the jagged rocks far below.

The young man continued. "His name is immortalized in this most Greek of all the seas, and has been called the Aegean ever since."

"How sad," the young wife said.

Mary looked out at the horizon. "What happened to the son?"

The young bride waited for her husband to ramble off the answer, but the young man merely stood with a blank expression.

"He united the states of the territory under a constitutional government in Athens," Allen explained. "He later went on to fight the Amazons, and he also was one of the Argonauts, the band of heroes who set sail in the Argo to find the Golden Fleece."

The young newlyweds were impressed with Allen's knowledge.

Allen gave Mary an inconspicuous wink.

The young man asked Mary to take another photograph of himself and his wife.

"I'll do it." Allen grabbed the camera and gave Mary a rigid look.

After thirty minutes on the summit, Allen and Mary found a table at the open-air café and had a drink. Mary pulled out her phone and list of hotels and tried to find Buckler.

Demetrios sat down with them. "This Buckler you told me about yesterday. Are you still looking for him?"

"Yes," Allen said.

"The old man in the picture, yes?"

"This man," Allen said, showing him the photograph of Buckler again.

"I asked all my friends to keep an eye out for him." Demetrios smiled. "I have hundreds of friends and they drive taxis."

"Great," Mary said, "We have the Greek taxi force networking for us."

Demetrios grinned. "We found him."

"Where?" they both asked.

"He's going to Rhodes," Demetrios answered. "He was at Piraeus, the port of Athens, waiting for a ferry, but now the airports will run again at four o'clock, so my friend said he's going to the airport."

"We need to go," Mary said, jumping to her feet.

Demetrios made it back to the city in record time. Waiting at a stoplight, Allen looked out the window of the taxi. "Do you ever wonder what those numbers and letters stand for on the tires?" he asked staring at the tire on the car stopped beside their cab.

"Ratio of height to width, diameter of wheel in inches, load index speed rating, width of tire in millimeters," Mary answered. She was trying to decide whether she should call the local authorities and have Buckler detained at the airport.

Allen gawked at her as if she just performed an amazing trick like a street magician.

Demetrios glanced in the rear-view mirror with eyebrows arched, evidently fascinated with her knowledge of automobile tires.

"Temperature grades and tread wear traction, tire ply composition and the type of material used," she added with a passing glance. "The small numbers and lettering are U.S. Department of Transportation safety standard code numbers."

The traffic light turned green and Demetrios raced for the airport, but not before looking into the mirror again, and smiling, amused by Mary.

"How do you know that?" Allen asked.

"I own stock in Goodyear."

He shook his head, not surprised by her answer. "Sure you do." He could detect her sarcastic demeanor in its smallest doses.

Before Mary's parents had enough money to move out of the slums of Mexico City, they lived near a tire factory, where her father worked a third job at night. She was only five at the time, but she would never forget the smell of tires and everything about them, including the markings on the side. But that part of her life she kept to herself.

A moment later Demetrios whipped his cab into the airport unloading area. Mary and Allen jumped out, attempting to catch the first flight to Rhodes. Demetrios hugged them both, then directed a smiling comment to Mary.

She returned the smile and waved, not understanding a word Demetrios said to her. Allen thanked him for everything before he and Mary ran down the corridor to the ticket counter.

Demetrios lit a cigarette and leaned against his cab. He pulled out his cell phone. "I just dropped them off," he said into the phone. "Are you sure you don't want me to follow them to Rhodes?" He nodded as he listened. "Okay then. Andeeo." He put the phone away and engaged in conversation with his fellow taxi drivers.

*   *   *

Thousands of miles away in Washington, D.C., James sat on a balcony eating his breakfast in view of the Washington Monument. "Good job, Demetrios," he said in Greek to himself.

*   *   *

"What did Demetrios say back there?" Mary asked.

"He said, 'good bye, smart, pretty lady.'"

They discovered they had already missed the first flight to Rhodes, but they were able to purchase tickets for the next flight, which would be leaving in twenty minutes. They made their way to the gate, scanning the crowd for Buckler; maybe he missed the first flight too. They didn't see him. The transport bus arrived.

They joined the crowd of passengers and boarded the bus, and after a short drive across the shoulder of the runway the bus came to a halt near a small, fifty passenger aircraft.

Mary stepped off the bus and looked at the unimpressive plane apprehensively. "Is this what we're flying in?"

Allen smiled. "Look at it as the advanced course for your fear of flying therapy. This is your final exam."

She scanned the passengers' faces again before sitting next to the window. Allen threw their carry-on baggage in the compartment above their heads. He looked down at Mary, who was staring anxiously out of the window. She wasn't anticipating this. He grinned discreetly, admiring her determination to cure herself of aviophobia.

"This is a small plane," she stated, giving the short wingspan a glance.

"It's a charter plane."

"Yeah, well, it's a small charter plane."

The last of the passengers boarded the aircraft. The crew finished with the final preparations for the flight and went over the procedures for take-off.

"I'm going to the restroom," Allen said. He strolled down the aisle and engaged in conversation with a flight attendant about the possible activities on the island of Rhodes. She suggested a number of places to visit and politely asked him to return to his seat. Allen thanked her and obliged her request, but not before scrutinizing the faces on the plane.

"No Buckler." he reported to Mary.

Mary continued to ponder a handful of questions in her head. Did Buckler get on the first flight? Did someone get to him? Could he have doubled back and taken a ferry or hydrofoil to Rhodes? Why was he still going to Rhodes? If she knew he was going there, so would the person who tried to kill him. He must know they were out to get him by now. At least he was still alive. Unless Demetrios and his fellow cab drivers were mistaken and had identified the wrong guy. A feeling of incompetence slipped into her mind. She should've had him by now. She was an ex-FBI agent and a private investigator; she was supposed to be good at what she did. She just hoped she wasn't too late.

The airplane started to taxi down the runway, passing the flashing lights.

"Have you ever heard of the, Colossus of Rhodes?" Allen asked, breaking the silence.

"No."

The aircraft continued to taxi.

"It was a statue, erected in homage to the sun god, Helios. It's alleged to have been a hundred and twelve feet tall," he explained, showing her a picture of the Colossus.

The picture was of a bronze statue of a man with a crown on his head straddling a harbor and holding a torch of fire. The muscular figure was clothed with a cloth draped around his waist and a bow and arrow slung over his shoulder.

"It's said that ships would enter and exit the harbor beneath his straddling legs," he said, pointing to the waterway beneath the Colossus' legs.

Mary looked at the picture of the enormous man-made wonder. "I know what you're doing."

"What?"

"You don't have to babble on like this, trying to distract me while we're taking off."

Allen grinned. "Was it that obvious?"

"I appreciate it, but I'm fine." She knew what he was up to from the first flight to Florida. "It did help, but now it's annoying," she said, like her old, nasty self.

"It was counted among the ancient Seven Wonders of the World," Allen continued about the Colossus. "But it fell in pieces during an earthquake only sixty five years after its completion."

The flight to Rhodes was uneventful, fortunately for Mary. They rushed into the hotel lobby where Buckler was scheduled for a business meeting.

"There's no way he's here," Mary said. "Coming here would be stupid, not to mention suicidal."

"We would like to see Alfred Buckler," Allen said to the woman behind the desk.

"I'm sorry," the woman responded. "Mr. Buckler just called and canceled his appointment."

"Did he say where he was going?" Mary asked. Maybe they would get lucky and get some information.

"No, he didn't."

So much for being lucky, Mary thought.

"But he did ask for directions."

"Where to?" Mary asked, sounding a little desperate.

The woman handed her a pamphlet to a secluded tourist site called, The Valley of the Butterflies.

"Thank you," Allen said and they rushed out of the hotel.

"Where the hell are the cabs?" she asked, frustrated.

Allen disappeared around the corner of the hotel, where a young man was renting motorbikes. He handed him two-hundred dollars and quickly explained the situation to the young man, who seemed eager to help. Allen jumped on one of the motorcycles and skidded to a stop in front of the hotel entrance. "Get on," he said grinning.

"Do you remember how to drive one of these things?" She climbed on and wrapped her arms around his waist.

He flew down the driveway and merged into traffic with skill and ease. They came to a long straightaway, exactly what he wanted to see. He popped the front wheel off the street and rode on the back wheel for thirty meters. Many of his childhood afternoons were spent on the back of a dirt bike on the wooded trails of his parents' property. He pretended for years to be a daredevil in a famous traveling circus. It felt good to be back on a bike, but not as good as having Mary's arms tightly around his waist. Both felt natural.

They raced along the road of Plateia Eleftherias, passing the Government House and Mandraki Harbor, where the two bronze deer statues of a doe and a stag stood proudly on their high pedestals, guarding the harbor entrance. This was where the Colossus was believed to have once stood. They passed Aquarium Beach, then quickly reached the northern tip of Rhodes City at Cape Zonari. They made good time on the long and less traveled roads, passing through the tiny town of Kalamonas. They continued along the country road not seeing a soul for a good twenty minutes. He pointed at a sign that read, "Petaloudes,'" the Greek word for "butterflies;" soon after another sign read, "Valley of the Butterflies." *Five more kilometers to go,* he thought, pushing the bike harder. They followed the signs along a curvy mountain road cut from the rocky terrain.

He glanced in the side mirror and noticed a speeding vehicle approaching from behind. He checked his speedometer and it read eighty. The car must be doing at least ninety kilometers per hour. His intuition told him to get the hell out of the way. At the very last moment he swerved hard to the left and down shifted, allowing the car to pass. The two tons of blur nearly hit them. Mary's arms tightened around his waist, startled by the sudden roar of a car passing. The driver of the car seemed to have every intention to run them down.

"He's going after Buckler," Mary yelled over the motorcycle's whine.

Allen shifted gears and popped the clutch, lifting the front wheel off the ground, and accelerated to eighty kilometers per hour. He took the twisting and guardrail-less roads at dangerous speeds. One mistake now would be certain death. The car disappeared and reappeared a quarter kilometer ahead on the bends of the mountain. Allen was quickly closing the gap between himself and the car. Sixty seconds later he was twenty meters away. His eyes widened with surprise because of the sudden appearance of Mary's gun beside his head.

"Where did you get that?" he screamed, trying to concentrate on the road and not the gun in front of his face.

Mary extended her arm, preparing to fire.

"What if he's not who we think he is?"

She hesitated, but the driver of the car extended his arm out of the window with a weapon of his own, and he didn't hesitate. Allen heard one of the bullets zip past his head. He swung the bike to the blind side of the car. Mary fired, shattering the back windshield. The driver slammed on the brakes, attempting to have

Allen slam into the back of the car. The car skidded across the pavement and partly disappeared in a cloud of gray smoke from the heated tires. Allen veered right, avoiding a direct collision, but his left leg grazed the back fender of the car, sending a jolt of pain through his knee. He broke out of the cloud of smoke at a high speed and found himself confronted with two options; try to stop before reaching the cliff at the bend in the road or accelerate and attempt to jump the gap of ten meters at an incline on the corner. He didn't remember making a decision. The only thing he thought about was Mary and her safety.

Mary on the other hand was peering over her shoulder at the driver of the car, looking for a clear shot through the smoke, but before she could fire she realized the bike was airborne and two hundred meters above a mountain gorge lined with jagged stone and pine trees. She didn't remember dropping her gun, but she must have, because she didn't have it when they landed on the other side. Matter of fact, she was astonished she didn't break Allen's ribs from her clasp around his waist.

The landing was perfect, to Allen's amazement. He was good on a bike, but not that good. He gave the good Lord a quick "thank you" for the divine assistance.

The trouble came in the form of loose gravel and dirt on the shoulder of the road. He gained control of the motorcycle after the landing but the front wheel dug into the ground and sent the bike onto its side. Fortunately, they both landed on top of the bike and rode out the twenty-meter slide, suffering minor bruises, cuts, and burns. Meanwhile, the car sped past and continued along the road.

Nearly a full minute later they were able to restart the bike and resume the chase. They finally reached a shaded parking lot, where a small restaurant overlooked a valley below. Mary pointed to the car they had been chasing, abandoned now. She lifted the hood and removed the distributor cap and tossed it into the bushes.

They rushed over to a booth, where Allen purchased two tickets. They followed the cobblestone path downward. Thick tree cover high above, darkened the valley with cool shadows, lowering the temperature significantly. One could lose the sense of daylight in the mile-long gorge if it weren't for the occasional ray of sunlight breaking through the treetops and streaking the valley floor. Cool, flowing springs wove through the vibrant, green vale of foliage and unusual trees, accompanied by cobblestone walkways, punctuated with the occasional wooden bridge. The peaceful silence harmonized with the running brooks and cascading waterfalls, but the true beauty was found in the inhabitants of the valley. Acres of the valley floor were blanketed with hundreds of thousands of brown butterflies, which were really Jersey Tiger moths. These moths were attracted to the scent of oriental amber, sweet gum trees, and the golden resin of the storax trees, which exuded a vanilla scented gum. The moths were the size of an American quarter with a triangular configuration. They displayed a brown to auburn color pattern with tiger-like stripes and dark spots while at rest, but their wings flashed scarlet when in flight. But that was an infrequent sight because there were dozens of signs requesting people to be quiet, so not to disturb the resting moths.

A tourist group casually strolled the walkway, slowing Allen and Mary down. The path was also crowded with smaller groups of sightseers and random couples.

"Allen," she said quietly grabbing his arm.

He looked in the direction she was staring. "He's got Buckler," he whispered.

The Shadow Government operative, Diamondback, led Buckler along the path toward the mountaintop, fifty meters ahead. Mary and Allen cut through the crowd. Diamondback continued to shove Buckler along the path and over a wooden bridge. He forced him up a set of steps carved from the mountain. From the top of the steps, Diamondback spotted Allen and Mary approaching.

"He saw us!" Mary started to sprint, forgetting she had lost her gun.

Allen stayed right behind her. They maneuvered through the tourists, but not without receiving dirty and inquisitive looks.

Diamondback whistled and clapped his hands as loud as he could. The disrupting sound echoed through the valley, causing the moths to flutter and reposition chaotically throughout the valley. The moth's wings flashed a beautiful crimson hue in the spotty sunlight of the trees. Allen and Mary were forced to stop the pursuit because the multitude of flying moths became blinding. Tourists ducked and moved about disorganized; a number of young ladies screamed when moths settled on their bodies, little children covered their faces, and other tourists were happily entertained with the exquisite incident. The moths eventually settled down.

Diamondback and Buckler had disappeared. Allen and Mary climbed the steps and ran to the end of the path, which led to a dirt road nearly atop the mountain. Allen stopped to catch his breath. His knee was hurting badly from hitting the side of the car, but he kept the pain hidden. Mary pressed forward after he insisted she continue without him.

The road led to an open field that appeared to sit on top of the world. The view was extraordinary. The panoramic scene unfolded for miles in every direction, revealing a number of other mountains in the near distance. The drifting clouds appeared to be within reach. Off to the side at the crest of the mountaintop stood the Moni Panagias Kalopetras monastery. The faded white stonework of the walls and the crimson tile of the roof appeared ran down and neglected. The knee-high grasses dominated the landscape surrounding the old church. The north side of the field was lined with rows of olive trees.

Mary stood quietly waiting for a sound, but the only thing she heard was the wind rustling through the leaves of the olive trees. There was an eerie silence on the deserted mountaintop. The skin on her arm crawled with goose bumps and a chill ran down her spine. Out of habit she reached for her gun, but when it wasn't there she quickly remembered what happened to it. She got another chill thinking about the crazy stunt Allen pulled.

Mary carefully walked around the monastery, but suddenly stopped when she heard something inside. She reached again for a gun that wasn't there. She cussed to herself. She turned a corner and took a peek into a small building attached to the church. It was a storage shack of some kind. A muffled gunshot was fired and pieces of stone flew around her head. She didn't know what kind of pistol Diamondback had, but she quickly discovered his gun was fitted with a sound suppressor. She hoped Buckler was still alive.

She climbed a wooden ladder to a wrap-around balcony, glanced over the railing, but didn't see anyone. She heard feet shuffling over gravel on the other side of the church, where she discovered Diamondback with a gun pressed against the back of Buckler's head. Movement from the field caught her eye. It was Allen, and he was hurrying directly into the path of the assailant. Diamondback looked around the corner and saw Allen coming. He pulled the gun away from Buckler's head and waited for Allen. Mary anxiously attempted to get Allen's attention from the balcony. Diamondback continued to wait for Allen to get within thirty meters, a comfortable kill shot for him.

"Turn back!" Buckler yelled.

Diamondback violently struck Buckler across the back of the head with the gun. Buckler fell to his knees, then limply to his side. Allen sprinted for cover as Diamondback stepped out from around the building and took aim. There was no way Allen would reach safety in time. Suddenly, from five meters above, a figure dropped hard on the Shadow Government operative. Both let out an agonizing scream of pain. Diamondback hit the ground face first, letting the gun fall to the side. Mary's fall was broken by his stout body. She rolled off him and knelt, holding her wrist. Diamondback attempted to struggle to a crawling position. Mary staggered over and kicked him in the ribs, sending him on his back gasping for air. She noticed his leg was bleeding below the knee. She could tell it was broken. She kicked him in the wound out of animosity. He yelled in pain and rolled over, grunting and suffering. She stumbled away, then dropped to her knees where his gun lay. Her eyes were drawn to Buckler's groaning. The sudden blast of a gun jerked her attention back in the direction of the gunman. Diamondback was holding a small weapon he had taken from an ankle holster, but Allen had his arm pinned down with his foot. Allen seized the gun and checked him for more weapons.

"Are you all right?" he asked, rushing over to her. His nerves and adrenaline were about to burst out of his skin.

"My kind of vacation." She groaned painfully getting to her feet. "Let's check on Buckler."

"What about him?" he asked of the gunman.

"He's not going anywhere. His leg is broken." She turned and punched Allen.

Allen grabbed his arm. "Hey, what's that for?" He was more surprised than hurt.

"For that Evel Knievel stunt," she said rubbing her wrist. "I lost a good gun because of you."

It appeared the bike ride shook her up a little. After years of enduring her radical driving, Allen finally got some payback. Sweet revenge. He smiled. "Did my driving scare you?"

"Child's play," she smirked unaffected, but Allen's jump did scare the hell out of her. But she would never admit it.

They walked back around the corner of the monastery. "I think he's going to be all right," Allen said, checking the bloody wound on the back of Buckler's head. "He's going to have a mean headache."

Police sirens could be heard approaching from somewhere down the road.

Mr. GQ emerged from behind the monastery. "Is he dead?" he asked.

Allen pointed the gun at him.

"It's all right, Al," she said. "I know him."

"How you've been, Mary?" Mr. GQ asked in a way that insinuated they had a history.

"I've had worse days," she said as if he had something to do with those days. "What are you doing here, Brad?"

Allen sensed an emotional bond between Mary and Brad.

Brad glanced at Buckler. "Looking for him."

"Really." She stared at him suspiciously. "Who are you looking for?"

"Alfred Buckler."

"What do you want with him?"

Allen felt like a third wheel. A feeling of jealousy crawled into his mind, an unusual emotion for him.

"We just want to ask him some questions." Brad grinned, but maintained a professional tone.

Mary smelled the stench of duplicity like a backed-up septic tank. "They must be some damn important questions, chasing him all the way over here."

"I'm assigned at the embassy in Rome, so it wasn't a big deal." He grinned again. "Legate."

Legate stood for legal attaché, a technical expert on the diplomatic staff of an embassy or ambassador.

"Moving down in the world, I see," she said, unimpressed.

"Oh, how I miss your charming ways."

"So, what do you want with Buckler?"

Brad shrugged his shoulders. "We thought he could answer a few questions, help clear up some things concerning something back in the States. You know, formalities."

That septic tank was over flowing. Her eyes narrowed at him. "We used to have a saying in the Bureau. There's a fine line between fertilizer and B.S."

"Which reminds me." He gave her his best investigative stare. "What do you want with him?"

"We're old friends from his teaching days at College Park," she said without blinking an eye. "I recognized him heading up the path, and by the time I caught up to him, he was in a confrontation with the goon." She grinned. "You know me, being a good Samaritan, I helped him." She could lay the fertilizer pretty thick herself.

Brad looked her over for a moment. "You're right," he finally said. "There is a fine line."

The local police arrived. Mary, Allen, Buckler, and Brad's next six hours were filled with paperwork, lawyers, embassy representatives, and a great deal of explaining.

Chapter 39

Washington, D.C.

Kelsy woke from a restless night on the couch. It was still dark, but she was unable to fall back to sleep. She stayed up late watching the endless coverage of the Air Force One crash. She took a shower and got dressed. The sun was threatening to rise when she slid into her car and headed for Annapolis. She tried to call Mary again and tell her about the cloning information, but there was no answer. She parked her car at the Annapolis City Dock and fed the meter before heading over to Sam's forty-two foot yacht, appropriately named after the Greek mythological god of wine and music, Dionysus. She leaped onto the aft cabin's swim platform and entered through the sliding glass doors to the open, split-level salon. The boat gently rocked on the morning tide.

She was surprised to find it in such a neat and orderly state, a rare sight knowing Sam's standards. She noticed two empty wine glasses on the cherry wood convertible dinette table, and a champagne bottle turned upside down in an ice bucket. He was entertaining last night. She grinned; that explained the tidiness of the yacht. He always cleaned up the boat for a date. She panicked. Was the woman still here? Her eyes darted around the room searching for evidence of his party friend's presence. She shouldn't have barged over; she was already embarrassed, simply with the thought of an awkward encounter. She looked in the master stateroom, but could only distinguish a single large lump of blankets. She inched closer, and then exhaled with relief; Sam was alone.

Whoever the woman was, she'd left a note on the counter. Kelsy couldn't help it; she had to read it. She was nosy.

The note read, "Thank you for a funky time, call me up whenever you want to grind. Nikki."

Kelsy shook her head disapprovingly. "Classy," she mumbled sarcastically. She made a pot of coffee and fixed herself a cup before sitting at a counter that doubled as a wet bar and computer station. She grabbed a file from one of the cabinets and loaded a disk into the drive. Sam transferred the paper documents and photographs to diskettes and CDs. She opened the Rosenberg file and loaded the medical file from the warehouse. She skimmed through the medical jargon, but suddenly stopped at a section virtually blank. This specific section should document the male components of the experimental surgery. The donor, sperm count, blood type, and six other health classifications were also blank. At the bottom of the document was a hand written note that stated a concern with the blood type, but no mention of the reason for the concern. Apparently, they preferred to keep this section regarding the male specifics of the experiments classified, or they deemed it unimportant.

She stared at the glowing monochrome screen of the computer, mulling over the information. Allen was the successful clone experiment, she thought. Okay, big deal, he may have been the first, but he certainly wouldn't be the last. It had already happened with animals in other countries. Were they trying to hide the way they did it and all the gruesome failed experiments? From the data collected thus far, it was obvious the government had deceived innocent people who believed they were dealing with a family medical clinic, trying to help couples who couldn't have children naturally. Also, from what the data claimed, there were hundreds of failed attempts, and with every failed experiment the words "terminate and eradicate" followed. Translation: abortion and murder. Was that it? Would they murder people today to keep the failed experiments a secret? That couldn't be the only thing. There must be more. She was convinced there was much more. Matter of fact, she believed the entire thing hinged on an artifact stolen from a museum in the Middle East over forty years ago. That was the missing piece. If she could connect the artifact and the experiments to one another, then she felt the truth would reveal itself.

"What are you doing?" Sam asked, lumbering out of the stateroom half-asleep. He tugged the belt around his waist on his black robe.

Kelsy looked over her shoulder with a smile. "Good morning. There's fresh coffee in the galley"

"I smell it." He stretched and yawned. His massive three hundred pound frame expanded, consuming space around him. "What's up?" He sat on the cream-colored leather couch after pouring himself a cup of coffee.

"I couldn't sleep."

"I thought I overslept."

"I'm early."

"How long have you been here?"

"About thirty minutes."

He stood and studied the computer screen. He squinted his eyes and made a painful sound. "It's too early for that." He sat across from her on a stool and rubbed his head.

"Too much drink?" she whispered.

"Too old." He grinned.

She shook her head with a laugh, knowing he would be at it again tonight. "Here, she left a note."

He read it to himself, and a faint, tired grin crossed his lips. "She loves Prince," he said, throwing the note away.

"I gathered. Is her name really Nikki?"

"Nosy," he said.

"It runs in the family." She got a refill of coffee. "I'm sure she looked like a Barbie."

"It's not my fault," he protested. "The psychiatrist said it derived from my childhood. I played with Barbie dolls when I was little and never got over it."

"Ha, ha," Kelsy mocked. "You're hopeless."

"I just can't find the right woman," he said, attempting to be sincere.

"Oh really," she smirked. "What happened to Debbie?"

"We just weren't compatible. She put the toilet paper roll facing the wall," he said as if it were a sin.

"What?"

"You know. When you put a new roll of toilet paper on, you have it roll away from the wall or toward the wall. She put it on facing the wall. And I hate that."

She laughed. "You got issues."

"I'm looking for that one woman who . . ." Sam stopped to ponder. "I'm looking for a nymphomaniac who owns a liquor store."

Kelsy threw a piece of paper at him. "You'll never change."

Sam laughed. "You know me, honey. It's wine, song, and interns."

Kelsy simply shook her head.

"Hey, little fella," he said to a pill bug crawling across the counter top. "How did you get in here?"

"I hate insects." Kelsy quivered with the thought.

"This little guy isn't an insect." He fiddled with the pill bug, sometimes called a potato bug, with his index finger. The bug itself was light gray, oval shape, humpbacked, with seven pair of legs, and appeared to be covered with segmented armor. "He's part of the crustacean group."

"Like shrimp, and crayfish."

"Yup."

Kelsy leaned down to examine the bug. She gave Sam a look that implied she was questioning his expertise on creepy crawlers.

"I was once a PCT," he said. "I know these things."

"A what?"

"A PCT. A pest control technician."

Kelsy gave him that look again.

He stood and retrieved a ring of keys. He unlocked a hatch on the lush, white, carpeted floor and removed a large footlocker. He lifted a backpack compressed air sprayer out of the locker, the type of application and liquid dispersal equipment an exterminator possessed.

"You were an exterminator?" she asked, amused by the thought.

"Excuse me," he said snobbishly. "A PCT."

She laughed. "Remember the movie, *Arachnophobia* with John Goodman?" She started laughing again. "I bet you looked just like him."

He turned the handle on the compressed air sprayer and removed the pump rod and plunger cup, exposing an audio transmitter. Then, he detached the inner supply tube that housed an electrical device the size of a prescription bottle. "This piece has high-tech recording capabilities, specifically for recording conversations," he explained. He continued with each mechanism's design and function. A second recording device was connected to a fiber optic camera positioned in the nozzle and the extension valve. The wiring led through the hose and strainer and could be activated by the spray control valve. The taping mechanism records in color onto a compact disk the size of a Ritz cracker. The hose adapter contained a powerful satellite antenna for transmitting to or from the compressor tank. He opened a small holding case with tinted miniature vials marked with warning labels cautioning, "hazardous biological liquids." He unscrewed the cap and poured out onto his large palm a dozen tiny black listening devices, commonly known in the spy business as "bugs." His mouth curved wickedly. "As you can see, bugs are my business."

When Kelsy was a teenager, she remembered asking her mother what Sam did for a living, after seeing his weapon under his jacket during a visit. Her mother said she didn't know exactly, only that he worked for the government. No one in the family had any notion what he did for a living. Sam never spoke about which branch of the government he worked for, and he certainly didn't talk about the type of work he did. It was after his retirement when he informed the family it was the CIA. She looked around at the elaborate yacht. "Exterminators make good money."

Sam laughed. He returned the compressor to the footlocker along with the hooded coveralls, gloves, boots, and goggles.

She pictured him dressed in that getup. "An exterminator." She laughed again thinking of John Goodman.

"It's a great way to get the job done." He returned the footlocker to the storage compartment and locked the hatch. "We used to walk into an embassy or wherever the job was, and show a document saying something about crab and body lice or oriental rat fleas carrying bubonic plague and murine typhus." He grinned. "You never saw ambassadors, head representatives, and diplomats move their butts out the door so fast."

"I would be right behind them."

"I'm hungry," he said glancing out of one of the portholes. "Let's go over to Garvey's."

"They're not open."

He jiggled the set of keys. "It is for me." Sam got dressed.

They stepped out of the boat's cabin into the fresh morning air. Sam took a deep breath as he watched a pretty brunette jog past. "I love fitness."

"I thought you liked blondes," Kelsy commented.

"Brunette, blonde," he shrugged. "It's like picking between the Beatles and the Stones, or between the Four Tops and Temptations. Can't go wrong, it's all good."

As they walked over to the restaurant, Sam told her about the time he wired the Russian embassy. How he came to the embassy doors outfitted in his white hooded coveralls, goggles, armed with the sprayer, and with documents from the Health Department, loaded with warnings of infectious diseased insects from the Federal Insecticide, Fungicide, and Rodenticide Act and the Environmental Protection Agency.

She laughed again, visualizing him in his exterminator costume.

"The Russian embassy security guards would try to observe me while I worked," he explained. "But I would use an aerosol generator to spray an artificial toxin into the air that smelled so bad that the security guards would have to leave the room before vomiting," he said laughing. "The stubborn guards had respirators, but not nearly as dependable as the CIA's, so when I sprayed with anaphylactic and antigen an allergic reaction and illness would occur. They quickly exited for the bathrooms. In most cases I didn't have any problems. It doesn't seem to matter what country you're from, people in general have some kind of fear of bugs. Plus, any reason is a good reason to get out of working."

Kelsy listened and laughed. She was amused by his stories.

Sam had a new sensation, a new emotion evolving within him. He had divulged things about himself and his life to Kelsy that he had never told anyone outside the agency. *It's good,'* he thought. He liked it.

Once in Garvey's, they passed the main bar and turned left into the raw bar section of the restaurant. The natural light filtering through the skylights and the live trees planted in the floor gave the room a comfortable feel. The ceiling fans ran on a cast iron trolley system. Sam went directly behind the raw bar and started the steamer.

"What do you want? Shrimp? Mussels? Clams? Oysters?" he asked digging around in the icebox.

"For breakfast?"

"Seafood is, any time of the day food," he said with a grin. He popped up with a bucket of mussels. He slid four dozen into the steamer, and tapped in three minutes on the timer.

"Is there any shrimp?"

He fetched a couple of pounds.

"Old Bay?"

Sam looked around the bar, searching for the seafood seasoning. He brought a container of the orange seasoning out from beneath the bar. He shook the spicy powder over the shrimp.

"More," she said.

He continued shaking the seasoning over the shrimp and gave her a questioning stare.

"More," she said again, grinning.

"Do you want some shrimp with your Old Bay?" He shook his head fearfully. "What are trying to do, kill me?"

"If you're going to make steamed crabs or shrimp, you gotta coat them with a ton of Old Bay. I believe it's a Maryland law."

Sam laughed. "Speaking of laws." He stepped out from behind the raw bar and moved behind the bar with the alcohol. He mixed himself a Bloody Mary. "You want one?"

"I'll take a diet Coke."

"Is Mary still in Greece?"

Kelsy nodded yes, taking a sip from her soda.

"Has she found Buckler?"

"I don't know." She read one of the files she brought with her from the yacht. "What's this?" she asked, pointing to a list of names.

Sam took a quick glance before answering. "I put together a list of people who died since you started digging into Allen's past, trying to find a connection."

Kelsy studied the names; her two friends were on the list. Her stomach turned and her throat tightened with the thought of their demise. The guilt followed.

"Outside of your two friends, all the names are connected in one way or another," Sam said.

"They had something to do with the archaeological dig, or the burglary at the museum," he explained.

"What about the surgery?"

"There's another list in the back of the file."

She flipped through the folder. There was a list of nine names with a short description beneath each one. "What's the red 'D' for?"

"Deceased."

"What about the 'V?'"

"Vanished. All the information concerning these people stops existing after the year 1962. Did you notice what the names with a 'V' have in common?"

She looked the names over and the brief paragraphs of information affixed to each name. She took note of the relating terms such as, terminologist, cytologist, enzymologist, and other associated words like chromosomes, nucleic acids, protein synthesis, and molecular biology. She looked up with the answer already in her eyes. "They're all genetic engineers."

"Very good," he said, placing steamed shrimp next to the mussels on her plate. He handed her a small fork and arranged tiny plastic cups of butter, Old Bay, and cocktail sauce. He pulled a mussel off the shell with a fork and dipped it into a bowl of melted butter. He put the mussel on a saltine cracker and added cocktail sauce with a pinch of Old Bay, and then shoved the entire thing into his mouth. He grinned with his mouth full, clearly pleased with the taste. He noticed Kelsy's expression had changed. "What's wrong?"

"I know this name."

"Which one?"

"Zack Smits."

"Who is he?"

"I don't know," she said quietly. "James said I needed to see him."

"He disappeared in 63."

"He must know where he disappeared to."

"I want you to be careful with this James guy," he insisted again.

"That reminds me," Kelsy said. "He said if I want to know who he is or what he is, to ask you."

He shifted his body slightly, and his mood. He wiped the red cocktail sauce off his hands with a napkin. "He's what we call in the agency a Dead Agent." He turned and pulled a bottle of Irish whiskey off the rail and poured a shot. "He's most likely an agent who vanished from the face of the earth only to resurface as a dead agent."

"Who are they? What are they?"

"Remember the Shadow Government?"

She nodded her head.

Sam's face turned emotionless. "The Shadow Government is made up of agents from all the agencies. New, old, and retired are approached. Some are recruited and slowly phased out of the everyday government, others remain in the main stream, but are loyal to the S.G. No one leaves or turns on them."

"How do you know this?"

"I was approached." He shot the whiskey down.

"What happened?"

"When I first joined the CIA a man questioned me in a so called 'special' meeting."

"What did he ask you?"

He poured another drink. "I've never told anyone this," he said quietly. "They wanted to know if I was willing to put aside my

morals, ethics, religious beliefs, and humanity for the country."
He paused. "Among other things." The shot glass came down
empty onto the bar. "I didn't realize what it was all about at the
time. I thought it was just another stupid test. They were always
testing us. It wasn't until a few years later when I heard the rumors
about the Shadow Government, and that's when I put it together."

"So, James and the dead agents are Shadow Government?"

"No," he answered. "It's true, the dead agents are also ex-agents
of various agencies, along with military men and renegade law
enforcement people just like the S.G., but they're an entirely
separate organization."

"Another unofficial organized agency," she said derisively.

"They're known as White Cell." He maintained an expressionless
stare. "From what I understand, a man named David Gill started
White Cell in 1963, after he discovered the Shadow Government
assassinated President Kennedy. Gill was appointed leader of the
first SEAL team in 1962 by Kennedy, who he worshiped. After
discovering the assassination plot of Kennedy, he disappeared with
his entire SEAL unit."

"Is it true?" she asked, stunned. "Did the S.G. murder Kennedy?"

Sam nodded yes.

"Oh my God," she mumbled. When the shock finally wore off
she asked, "So, is White Cell a counter agency to the Shadow
Government? Are they the good guys?"

"Some people think so."

"Do they manipulate world affairs, orchestrate coups d'etat,
and control puppet presidents like the S.G.? Do they remove federal
officials at will?" She stared at him somberly. "With any means
possible?"

"They remove S.G. operatives."

She had heard the countless rumors about the Shadow Government
throughout the years, and now, she knew it was all true. Strangely,
she found some comfort in knowing something about James. Her
intuition told her James was one of the good guys. Now the question
was, what constituted a good guy?

Chapter 40

Mexico, The Sierra Madre Occidental

In the center of the desolated landscape lay immense sections of mangled, twisted metal of the once proud aircraft, Air Force One. Millions of viewers around the world witnessed the horrors of the fallen plane on television. The terrain was burnt to a chalky black ash, the soil was saturated with toxic fuel, and the surrounding trees stood bare like eerie black poles. The blaze continued to burn, but for the first time in ten hours, it was under control.

The roar of a low cruising C-130 aircraft with a large tank attached to its underbelly flew overhead. The trap doors of the tank parted, freeing the fire retardant to drop to the crash site. The slime-like reddish orange substance blanketed two square acres of scorched ground, allowing firefighters to advance farther into the burning, smoky maze.

Working the perimeters of the crash site were Hummers with water cannons. Other Hummers had been converted to ambulances, which had already transported four victims to a a crude landing pad that had been constructed for emergency helicopters.

Twelve men suited with unmarked shiny silver fire resistant hooded coveralls began penetrating the outer boundaries of the crash site, entering the network of scalding wreckage. The group was only known as Search Team A, and took their orders from only a few men in Washington, D.C. Their primary agenda wasn't the president himself, but an attaché case. The goal was to locate and retrieve it, or discover proof of the case's destruction. Other items on the scavenger hunt included the cockpit voice recorder, digital flight data recorder, and quick access recorder, better known as "black boxes."One of the Search Team entered a section of fuselage. His flashlight beam led him to a clutter of chairs, where there appeared to be a briefcase of some sort trapped within the debris. His heart rate increased from the excitement; he believed he found the attaché case carrying the nuclear codes and other covert data. His breathing quickened with every step closer to the case. He carefully avoided the piles of scorched aircraft interior.

He stumbled across a moaning body, a woman pinned to the ground by a thick sheet of metal. She cried for help, her voice weak. He looked coldly through his clear mask for a moment, but only as he stepped over her. She cried for help again. He ignored her while he leaned down and examined the briefcase. It was firmly snagged between two large pieces of metal frame. The woman's cry of agony filtered from beneath the piece of metal. The agent continued to pry the briefcase, attempting to free it from the wedged position. He had no intention to help the woman five feet from him. The gusting winds on the mountain had changed directions and a choking cloud of smoke had entered the fuselage. He grew impatient and started to tug on the case heedlessly. Finally, one last tug jerked the briefcase from the grip of the mangled metal. He stood to leave, but the tugging on the briefcase had loosened a large section of metal above his head that snapped suddenly and collapsed violently, trapping him to the floor. He would bleed to death in ten long and painful minutes from internal injuries. The weight of his body and the fallen metal had, ironically, shifted the metal sheet on the woman in a way that allowed her to pull herself free and into a small clearing outside of the fuselage.

*   *   *

Washington, D.C.

Two dozen news trucks with twenty-five foot antennas protruding toward the morning sky, lined Pennsylvania Avenue. The steady chatter of numerous reporters choked the airways throughout the world, all reporting the same staggering story of the crash of Air Force One. The endless reporting continued with background history of crew members, the possible rescue of survivors, photographs of the crash site, live images, specialists from all walks of life on the subject, and premature reports of the president's death. People from all over the world were engrossed with the tragedy. Across from the White House in Lafayette Square, two thousand people had gathered overnight to burn candles in vigil. At the base of the black iron fence surrounding the White House were thousands of flowers, notes, and prayerful messages, most directed to the First Family.

On the second floor of the White House, far from the hectic network of people, two figures sat in the dark room in a rocking chair. Sondra Moore embraced her sleeping child in her lap and sang a gospel song. Her thoughts and prayers were with her husband. Thousands of people searched frantically for the President of the United States, the experts had already buried him, the media had widowed her, and the search and rescue operation had become a recovery mission. But Sondra Moore knew, deep in her heart and soul, that her husband was alive.

*   *   *

Kelsy left the hospital after visiting her mother, who still remained in a coma and in critical condition. She felt the fibers of her faith unraveling with every passing day. Today, the doctors suggested euthanasia.

Kelsy knelt in prayer at one of the pews of the church. She opened her teary eyes and looked at the life-size replica of Jesus Christ that hung on the cross. She stared into the eyes of Jesus with a weary and desperate gaze. "What should I do?" she asked, expecting an answer. The thought of losing her mother terrified her. Her stare intensified. "Do something!" she demanded. "Heal her or take her!" She stood and exited through the large wooden doors and walked down the corridor toward the garden. She saw the professor pulling weeds.

"Hello, Kelsy," Greg said, standing to greet her.

"How are you doing, professor?"

"Getting older." He put his hands on his hips and stretched his back. "I have more information for you."

"I'm sorry about your friend," she said of the president. She still couldn't comprehend the profound connection between the Prophecy of Death and the Air Force One tragedy.

"Thank you," Greg said.

"Is there anything on the disk about a man named Zack Smits?" she asked, leaning against a large oak. She felt a slight chill in its shadow.

Greg walked to the stone bench and searched through his printouts. "Sounds familiar." After a minute, he located the information. "Here it is."

"How's he connected to all this?"

"He was a military security officer. His name appears often on military personnel records. He was responsible for clearance orders and release forms; he was also assigned to security duty at the Pentagon in the early sixties."

"I'm flying out to see him."

"Hopefully he has some answers." Greg opened a folder. "The name Pike is mentioned once, and Francis McCarr. I was unable to identify them." He continued to speak about some of the details in the files.

Kelsy heard him, but she wasn't listening. Her mind drifted back to the hospital, back to her mother.

"What's wrong, Kelsy?"

"It's my mother." Her eyes glassed over and her head sunk to her chest. "They want to take her off the respirator."

Greg stood and put a consoling hand on her shoulder. "Listen, Kelsy." His voice was solacing, but firm. "Don't give up on her."

She looked up with a painful, searching stare.

"I know you have doubt. The negative thoughts are human, but you must continue to have faith in God and in your mother."

It was exactly what she needed to hear. After another thirty minutes with Greg she felt her faith revitalized.

*   *   *

Art stepped out of his car with a grin and a folder. He had documentation connecting Jordan to the fuel distribution company responsible for the deliveries to the Mexican airport from where Air Force One departed. He had photos of Jordan and the fuel company's main administrator, the truck driver, and two Mexican security officers from the airport. He believed Jordan obtained a chemical agent from the scientist at the New Mexico chemical facility and then delivered it to the fuel distribution company. The truck carrying the fuel for Air Force One was contaminated before delivery. Ultimately, the contaminated fuel brought down the President of the United States. There were lose ends, but there was enough proof to start a serious investigation. He walked along the sidewalk with his cigar, heading for Greg's church.

Two forty-something women crinkled their noses at him. "What an awful smell," one snobbish woman said to the other.

"It's disgusting."

These same two women were saturated with enough perfume that a skunk would complain.

He smiled warmly. "At least I don't smell like a chemistry experiment gone terribly wrong." He blew a big, blue puff of smoke into the air, turned his nose up and walked away.

He entered the garden grounds and smiled. The incident with the two women reminded him something Sean Carbon said about cigar smokers and non-cigar smokers; "one man's odor is another man's aroma."

"Professor O," he yelled, crossing the grounds.

"Hello, Mr. Hanson."

He removed the cigar from his mouth. "Hey Kelsy. I never did thank you for the ride to the hospital."

"How are you going?"

"It was just a scratch," he said. "Have you heard? There was an earthquake in Jerusalem. First the two witnesses, now the earthquake. You scare me professor."

"It isn't me."

"I know, the Bible," Art corrected himself. A sly grin developed behind his cigar. "Is there anything in there about tomorrow's lotto numbers?"

Chapter 41

Greece

The hospital lobby was in a chaotic state. American embassy representatives, lawyers, federal agents, local authorities, doctors, nurses, and a couple of government officials were standing around in groups. They were all discussing the same thing, the incident at the Valley of the Butterflies. Why were gunshots fired? Who are you? What were you doing up there? Who was the man with the broken leg? Was there anyone else involved? Who did the guns belong to? Questions were being asked in rapid-fire fashion, but the answers came in vague or suspicious form, to the unsatisfied pleasure of the local authorities and the Greek government officials.

Allen walked into the hospital room. "How do you feel?"

"I'll live," Mary said, seated on the examining table.

"Here." He threw a pair of jeans and new shirt to her and turned to Buckler. "How's your head?"

Buckler rubbed the side of his head. "Much better if you wouldn't yell."

Allen grinned, knowing if he whispered it would still seem like yelling to him.

Buckler walked over to the mirror. "Good Lord. I look like a mummy," he said, examining the bandages around his head.

"You took a pretty good hit to the head, Buck," Mary said. "You're lucky you can still use the bathroom on your own."

He staggered slightly.

"Here, have a seat," Allen said walking him across the room to a chair. "You need to take it easy for a while."

"Would someone like to tell me what's going on?" Buckler asked, feeling the ill effects of the blow to the head.

Mary slid off the examining table. "We need to ask you some questions."

"Who are you people?"

"We're looking for some answers that you may be able to help us with," Allen answered.

"About what?"

"We'll talk about it later," Mary said. "You need to relax."

"Mary Jopuez," a man's voice announced from the doorway. "Ex-FBI, current private investigator. How are you doing?" He entered the room smiling beneath his thick mustache. "Remember me? Your old friend from the Acropolis, Kosta."

Mary remembered the detective, and she remembered lying to him, too.

"It's a good thing," Kosta joked, "that you're a clumsy person. Every time you run into Alfred Buckler it seems to save his life."

"I was never the most graceful person," Mary said.

Kosta looked at Buckler. "You're a lucky man."

"Right." He rubbed his head. "Lucky."

"Well, I just wanted to see how you were feeling," Kosta said. "Next time you're in town, drop in and say hello. You can trust some of us." He returned to the bureaucrats in the hall.

Allen walked over to the doorway and looked down the hall. The exchange of words was getting louder and the hand gestures were flying with every explanation. Brad was speaking to the authorities and he appeared to be getting some positive results. "Do you think we'll get out of here soon?" he asked Mary.

"If I know Brad, he's already made a deal," she said gathering her new clothes. She was contriving a plan of her own. She needed to get Buckler to the States and find out what he knew.

"How long did you work together?" Allen asked.

"Who said we worked together?"

"I thought the two of you . . . ,"

"We dated," she said before disappearing into the bathroom.

"Oooooh, an ex-boyfriend," Buckler said smiling.

"Very ex," she said from the bathroom.

Allen's mind turned with questions he would never ask out loud.

Buckler grinned. "The jealous monster raises its ugly head."

Allen's demeanor and expression remained cool as ice, but his eyes were scorching darts, and he aimed them at Buckler.

"What?" Mary asked.

"Nothing," Allen answered.

Buckler winked at Allen. "You're jealous," he whispered.

"No, I'm not," he whispered back.

Buckler grinned again. "How long did Brad and you date?" he asked.

"None of your business," she responded bluntly.

"The two of you appear to have been close," Buckler said grinning at Allen. "Reeeeeeally close."

Mary ignored him.

Buckler continued, finding humor in the subject. "It just looked to me like the two of you could pick up right where you left off."

Allen threw a rolled-up elastic Ace bandage at Buckler, striking him in the head. He shrieked from the sharp pain.

"What happened?" Mary asked, coming out of the bathroom.

"Nothing," Allen said. "He bumped his head on something."

"Does my personal business interest you?" she asked.

Buckler attempted to look innocent. "I think the two of you make a nice couple, that's all."

Mary gave Buckler nasty look. "You have a better chance than he does." She returned to the bathroom.

Buckler started to say something again, but decided against it when he noticed Allen had armed himself with another rolled-up bandage.

"Al, come here for a second."

Before Allen entered the bathroom he showed Buckler the rolled-up bandage as a warning. He walked in and saw Mary unbuttoning her shirt. "What are you doing?" he asked, turning away.

"My shoulder is hurting, my thumb has a hair-line fracture and my wrist is sprained. Do you think you can help me out a little?" she asked derisively. "You're the one who bought a button-up shirt."

"All right, don't get uptight." He grabbed the new shirt and walked around to the back of her. He thought her injuries must be serious. She'd prefer to have a tooth pulled than to ask for help. "Did the doctor give you anything for the pain?"

"Yes."

"Maybe he can give you something for your attitude."

"You need some new material."

It wasn't the pain that had Mary agitated. The loss of any independence, even the most insignificant thing like buttoning a shirt, didn't sit well with her. Being dependent on anyone for anything was inadmissible. Bad relationships could do that to a person.

Allen stood for a moment holding the shirt.

"Anytime."

He gently removed the shirt from her shoulders. Her bra was bright white in contrast to her tanned skin. He stared at the smooth curvature of her lower back. He followed her spine until it disappeared into her jeans.

"Helloooo," she said. "It's starting to get a little chilly in here."

He quickly and carefully slid the bandaged arm through the shirtsleeve, concentrating only on the arm. He did the same with the other arm.

Mary turned around. "Button it for me, please," she said, attempting to be nice.

His face slowly reddened. It wasn't what he could see of Mary that discomforted him. It was his thoughts. He started to button the shirt from the bottom, focusing on the buttons very hard, but when he reached the last few buttons, his eyes glanced for a split second at her cleavage. He buttoned the last two in a quick and mechanical manner.

"Anything else?" he asked like a disgruntled servant.

"I need you to zip and button my jeans."

His heart jumped a beat, and his mind formulated an erotic thought.

"Are you all right, Al?"

"Yup, just fine," he said. He reached beneath her shirt and zipped the zipper and buttoned the jeans as quickly as possible. "I need something to drink. Do you want something?" he asked hurrying out of the bathroom.

"No thanks," she answered with an odd expression. *What's wrong with him?* she wondered.

"How about you, Buckler?"

If Buckler answered, Allen wouldn't have heard him, because he was already half way down the hall.

* * *

The airplane waited on the runway. Mary was seated near the aisle, Allen had the window seat and Buckler was in the center. Brad was behind them, but Buckler didn't know he was there. Not many questions were answered at the hospital concerning the shoot out at the Valley of the Butterflies. The Greek authorities suggested they all leave the country, immediately. Diamondback ended up in the custody of Brad's people.

"You were the head archaeologist on an excavation in Israel in 1961?" Mary asked Buckler.

"That's right."

She returned her attention to the file.

"Why am I being detained?" Buckler asked for the hundredth time. "I didn't do anything wrong."

No one answered him for the hundredth time.

"This is against the law," he protested.

Allen looked at him. "It seems there's a lot of that going around."

The "fasten seat belt" sign illuminated and the airplane taxied down the runway. The 747 slowly lifted from the earth, left the ancient land of Greece behind and jetted for the new world across the Atlantic. The airplane leveled off and a flight attendant started down the aisle with a drink cart. She looked at Mary's bandaged hand and wrist, and then at Buckler's bandaged head. "Oh my," she exclaimed. "What happened to the two of you?"

"Checkers," Mary answered.

"They beat me up," Buckler said with a nod toward Mary and Allen. "She hurt her hand doing it." There was no jesting in his tone.

"It's the medication," Allen explained.

Buckler ran his hand over his wrapped head. "These bandages feel too tight."

"The drugs must be wearing off," Mary said.

The flight attendant distributed the drinks and continued along the aisle, but not without a parting curious expression at the odd trio.

Buckler stared at Mary. "Are you FBI?"

"I told you I wasn't," she answered.

"Why would they let me go with you?"

"They who?" she asked, reading the file.

"The FBI."

"Did they question you?" she asked, still looking through the file.

"Yes."

"Did they charge you with anything?"

"No."

"So, why hold on to you?"

"Because someone is trying to kill me," he said caustically. He rubbed the back of his head, which was throbbing from the pistol whip he endured from Diamondback. "It's obvious someone is trying to kill me. Shouldn't I be in witness protection or something?"

"You're safe for now," she said, scanning the file.

"Maybe," Allen said, "they're using you as bait."

That thought didn't sit well with Buckler.

"I told you," Mary said, "you'll be fine."

"No offense, but an ex-FBI agent turned private investigator is not exactly what I had in mind."

Allen had his head slumped over on a pillow. "She saved your butt back there at the monastery," he said, never opening his eyes.

"Don't forget the Acropolis," a voice said from the seat directly behind Buckler's. "If she weren't there, you would be a dead man."

Buckler turned his stiff neck around painfully, and saw Brad's smiling face in between the seats. He peered at him angrily, but he was also relieved to see him, feeling less like bait. "Thanks," he mumbled to Mary.

"I was starting to feel unappreciated," she responded sarcastically. She continued writing notes in the file.

"Do you feel better now that you know there's a real FBI agent with you?" Allen joked.

"Yeah."

"Hey, don't look at me," Brad said. "I'm just catching a ride back to the States. You're not my responsibility." He leaned in close to Buckler. "But if I were you, I'd stick real close to Mary. She wants you alive."

"Why is someone trying to kill you?" Mary asked.

"I don't know," Buckler groaned from the sharp pain in his head. "Why aren't you a Fed anymore?"

Mary didn't respond.

"Couldn't handle it, or did you just get fired?"

Mary continued to ignore him.

"I can tell you," Brad said from in between the two seats.

Mary's eyes remained on the file, but her gut tightened thinking about the night her partner was murdered.

"Go ahead, I'm listening," Buckler said, interested.

Brad leaned in close to the seat inches from Buckler's ear. "When she was in the Bureau," he whispered, "she killed a smart aleck archaeologist."

Mary's face softened slightly, Allen grinned to himself, and Buckler faked a laugh. He took a peek at Mary's file.

"What are you looking at?"

She closed the file and stared at him.

"What? Is it top secret stuff?" he asked with a deriding tone.

She continued to stare at him, not sure where to hit him.

"Why are you holding me against my will? What do I have to do with you?"

Allen let out a sigh, realizing he was going to pester her until he was told something. "I discovered I was adopted," he said bluntly. "When we searched for my biological parents, a sudden epidemic of murders started."

"A lot of your friends got bumped off," Mary said. "But you knew that, didn't you?"

Buckler got a sick feeling in his stomach.

"That's why he was running," Brad added.

Mary had filled Brad in about Allen and their current situation. That was one of the reasons Brad decided to help her get Buckler back to States.

"Why Greece?" Mary asked. "And why would you tell everyone you were going there?"

"I'll tell you why," Brad volunteered. "First, he thought no one would believe he was going where said he was going. And if they did, he thought he would be long gone from Greece before someone caught on, leaving them searching the hundreds of islands for him. As for why he was there in the first place, money. He has bank accounts there. He was going on the run. His wife works at the Acropolis Museum with the artifact restorations department, and so he went there to explain the situation before he disappeared. Maybe plan a rendezvous for later. He went to Rhodes for the evidence. Evidence he planted at the church many years ago for safekeeping and leverage. Just in case the boys in the black suits decided to clean house. And it looks like they did."

"What about his wife?" Allen asked. "Would that put his wife in danger?"

"She doesn't have the same last name," Brad answered. "Plus, they're not legally married. They were married on the island of Santorini by an unlicensed preacher thirty-five years ago. There's no record of the marriage. So, he thought there was no way to connect him with her."

Buckler's expression turned puzzled. "All those people, my friends," he said to Allen, "are dead because you started looking for your real parents?"

"That's right," Allen answered.

"Who are you?" he asked, confounded with the notion.

"Allen Pyrit."

"The religious guy," Buckler said. "I knew I recognized you. The longer hair and beard threw me off." The confused look returned. "I don't get it. Why would someone want to kill me or anyone because of you?"

"We were hoping you could tell us," Brad said.

"I don't know anything about him."

"What evidence were you getting?" Mary asked.

"I wasn't getting evidence," Buckler insisted. "I was trying to lose the gunman."

"Right," Brad said, grinning. "I have my people up there right now searching the church and every inch of that mountaintop."

Mary was sure Buckler was playing dumb, but there may be an outside chance he was an innocent participant in the entire ordeal. Regardless, she didn't trust him. "What do you know about an artifact at the dig site in '61?"

"I was in charge of the team that found the artifact. Well, not the artifact, but the sarcophagus containing the artifact. After we discovered it, the Israeli government took it away. A few years later there was a burglary and the artifact was never seen again."

"That's all you know?"

"I did hear a rumor about the artifact." He leaned in as if he were going to tell her a secret. "I heard the artifact had mysterious and great powers. Powers that could make a nation invincible."

Mary shook her head skeptically and rolled her eyes.

"What was the artifact?" Allen asked.

"I don't know," Buckler answered.

"What about experiments?" she asked, changing the subject. "Do you know anything about experimental surgeries?"

"I told you, I wasn't involved with anything outside of the archaeological research department," Buckler said defensively.

Mary glanced at a list in the file. "Who are Stainwick and Smits?"

"Stainwick is the one you need to talk to," Buckler said. "He ran the operation in Israel. The rumor was he was some sort of secret agent or spy. There was talk about a Shadow Government, a government within the government."

Mary had heard her share of rumors about the Shadow Government. The man who murdered her partner was an S.G. agent. A passing expression of distaste appeared on her face. There were a number of reasons she continued to pursue this conspiracy theory. One reason being, they were too deeply involved to stop and the conspirators simply wouldn't go away and allow them to live with the information they had. But down deep in her soul there was a dark impetus that fueled the search—her personal vendetta against the Shadow Government and the man who murdered her partner.

"I don't know anyone named Smits," Buckler said. "Is that why you're holding me? Are you trying to tie me in with the Shadow Government?"

"Just look at it this way," Brad said. "You're physical evidence."

Buckler laughed. "Are you kidding? You guys are trying to build a case against the S.G." He shook his head. "We're all dead."

Chapter 42

Baltimore, MD

T he airport terminals were congested with vacationers and business travelers. Airplanes arrived and departed with an incessant roar of noise. Thousands of people hurried and shuffled their way to their flights to somewhere. Many arrived to greet friends and family, but most appeared worn down from another mundane business trip.

Kelsy sat on a stool and had a drink in one of the bars at the Baltimore-Washington International Airport. She was waiting for instructions. James told her he would call her with flight information.

"Another?" the bartender asked.

"No, thank you." She continued to nurse her diet soda.

The bartender answered the telephone. "Are you Kelsy Anderson?" he asked.

"Yes."

The bartender handed the telephone to her. "It's for you."

"This is Kelsy Anderson," she said, nearly whispering.

"Hi, Kelsy," James said.

"It's about time."

Before James could respond, the sound of a child crying filled the receiver. Kelsy thought it was the same child across the terminal at a row of public telephones.

"I called as soon as I could."

She stood and attempted to improve her view of the phones down the terminal.

"There's a man named Henderson at the ticket counter," James explained. "He'll have everything you need."

"I'm assuming you made arrangements for me in Arizona."
She stretched the telephone wire as far as it could reach, nearly
leaving the bar area.

"Yes, everything is taken care of."

The jet engine roared by the window and drowned out the rest
of James' sentence. She was convinced it was the same 747 landing
in her line of sight of the airfield. She scanned the pay phones again.
There was a tall man wearing a black suit at one of the phones. Next
to him was a heavyset white man, also using the public phones. A
woman with a crying child sat directly behind them, and a black
man on his cell phone watched the planes on the airstrip. The tall
man and the heavyset man had their backs turned to her.

"Hold on for a second," she said, placing the phone on the
bar. She maneuvered toward the pay phones, cutting through the
crowd of passengers departing from a flight. She remembered James
appeared tall and athletically built when she viewed him through
the binoculars. She ignored the heavyset man and locked onto the
tall man. She headed straight for him and once there she tapped
his shoulder. He turned and looked down from his six foot four
height inquiringly.

"James?" she asked with a staid expression.

The tall man stared down at her and smiled politely. "Excuse
me?"

"I'm sorry, I thought you were someone else."

"I wish I were James," he said flirtatiously.

She apologized again and began to return to the bar, but
stopped and decided to approach the black man on the cell phone.
"James," she said, tapping his shoulder.

The man turned and stared at her with his warm brown eyes.
He spoke in a smooth natural language that Kelsy recognized as
Spanish.

She didn't remember any of the Spanish she took in school, so
she didn't attempt to be cute and respond. "Sorry," she mumbled,
turning away.

The black man returned to his conversation on the phone.

The bartender greeted Kelsy with a dirty look.

"Hello," she said, picking up the phone.

"What happened? Where did you go?"

"To check on something," she said, feeling stupid. "I want to know something."

"What is it?"

"Are you a dead agent in White Cell?"

"Yes," he answered without hesitation or trepidation.

She didn't expect him to answer so quickly and candidly; matter of fact she really didn't expect a direct or honest answer at all.

"Hello," James said. "Anyone there?"

"Yeah, I'm here." She regrouped. "Are you trying to take down the Shadow Government?"

"Yes," he answered. "And right now is the best time to do it."

"Why?"

"The S.G. is in the middle of a civil war," he explained. "Someone is attempting to take over. I believe the new S.G. group is trying to get the information you've discovered and use it against the old S.G. regime."

If there ever was a good time to attack the S.G., it was when they were divided, she thought.

"That's why I help you," James said earnestly. "Helping you helps me, and you helping me will help you get want you really want. Your mother's shooters."

Kelsy threw a five-dollar bill on the bar. "The guy's name is Henderson?"

"Right."

"When do I leave?"

"In about forty five minutes."

"That's nice."

"I'll see you around," James said. "Watch your back."

"Thanks."

"You're welcome," he said in Spanish before hanging up.

She looked back at the pay phones. The tall man was still there and two teenage girls were now using the other phone. The woman with the child was preparing to leave. The man on the cell phone who spoke Spanish to her had disappeared into the crowd.

She grinned, realizing she had been face to face with James. The strange thing was she couldn't remember what he looked like with the exception of the warm brown eyes she looked into for a brief moment.

*   *   *

Arizona

Kelsy stepped off the airplane and the afternoon Arizona heat filled her lungs. It was hot, but not uncomfortable. The sky was clear and a striking vivid blue. A sharp contrast to the thick, humid, hazy, and unhealthy summer days of Washington, D.C. She gathered her newly bought overnight bag and clothes from the rental car. Her hotel was a small, two-floor building adorned in peach and white with a black iron balcony that wrapped around the entire second floor. There was no fancy landscaping, no entertainment complex or built-in pool. Not much to look at, but like the saying went, you get what you pay for, and it certainly applied here. Tiny brown lizards ran amok throughout the hotel grounds, warmly regarded by the locals as Arizona cockroaches. It was a small town a few miles outside of the airport that mostly catered to travelers who didn't plan to be here the next day.

Fatigue had dulled her senses; she hadn't observed the dark blue van parked across the street. She checked into her small room, desperately needing a nap. She placed her bag and laptop on a small round desk, hoping no tiny guests hitched a ride. Beside the child-like table, the room consisted of a single bed and a small lamp table. The peach, black and white color scheme matched the exterior of the hotel.

The dark blue van waited at a small strip mall, attempting to blend in with the other vehicles. The three men in the van were dressed in black coveralls, armed with 9mm pistols and listening devices in their ears. One of the three pointed a satellite dish the circumference of a Frisbee at Kelsy's room. From a hundred yards away, the dish could eavesdrop on telephone conversations, Internet chats, intercept e-mail and fax transmissions, and run-of-the-mill conversations. The bits of sound waves and digital information flowing in and out of her room were intercepted, then shot to a three billion dollar satellite in space. Then they were relayed to a mega-computer somewhere in Washington that digested and interpreted the data before transferring the deciphered information to a wall of high-tech electronic equipment in the van. All this was accomplished in twelve seconds. These wonderful toys were supplied by the taxpayers of the good ol' U.S. of A. Not bad for an agency that didn't exist. Seated in the rear of the van, one of the S.G. agents was fitted with headphones, prepared to listen to any potential verbal conversations. He also watched a computer screen for transmissions via the Internet.

The telephone in Kelsy's room rang.

The sound of her phone ringing registered in the van. The S.G. agents perked up.

"Hello," she answered while attempting to get undressed.

"How was your flight?" James asked.

He always sounded sincere when he spoke to her. Either he was a great actor, or he actually cared about her welfare. "Long," she said, throwing her pants on the floor. "Where's Stims?"

Stims was Smits spelled backward. James had instructed her to use the name Stims for security reasons. It was a simple defense strategy against electronic ears and inquisitive neighbors. Plus, it confused the hell out of them for a little while.

"He's at a retiree complex called Sunny Valley."

"Sunny Valley," she confirmed, unsnapping her bra from beneath her t-shirt. It joined the pants on the floor. "I'll talk to you later, James. I need some sleep."

"Kelsy," he said stopping her from hanging up.

"What?" She collapsed on the bed.

"Watch your back."

"I know. Good-bye," she said in Spanish before hanging up.

He smiled and remembered her beautiful blue eyes staring into his own at the airport.

The dark blue van sped off down the street with the recorded telephone conversation in its computer database. The S.G. agent in the rear handed the passenger in the front seat a computer printout of a map furnished with directions to Sunny Valley. "Stims," one of the agents said quietly. He said the name in a manner that insinuated he was speaking of the deceased.

There was a soft knock at Kelsy's door. She pulled her gun from beneath her pillow and leapt to her feet. She peered through the security hole in the door. Standing timidly in front of the door was a young man, no older than eighteen years of age. She remembered him from the registration desk. He had an envelope in his hand. Kelsy looked out the window, checking for anyone else on the balcony before opening the door.

"Yes, what is it?" she asked, hiding the gun behind the door.

"Ms. Kelsy Anderson?"

"Yes."

He his eyes traveled over her braless t-shirt and exposed legs. "Yes," she said regaining his attention.

"I have a note for you, Ms. Anderson." He handed the envelope to her with a quick glance at her t-shirt.

"Thank you. Wait here for a second." She closed the door and retrieved five dollars from her pants. "Thank you," she said. handing the bill to him.

He smiled gratefully while backing away and looked over her body once more.

She closed the door and grinned. She was flattered a young man found her attractive. For some reason she thought about James. The name "James" was on the envelope. She opened it and pulled out a single sheet of paper. Written lightly with pencil was a message from James that read that Stims could be found at South Haven, not Sunny Valley. If anyone had been listening to their conversation, they would be on their way to Sunny Valley, which was eighty miles in the opposite direction, he explained. Now she understood why he was so casual with the Sunny Valley information. She originally thought he had been careless over the phone. The note also said she had nearly three hours before they realized what had happened and she should be on her way to South Haven.

"So much for my nap," she mumbled. She memorized the address of South Haven and then burned the note in an ashtray and flushed the ashes down the toilet. She pulled the curtains slightly back and peeked outside. She looked at a map pinned on the wall and asked the young man at the registration desk for directions to a shopping center five miles before South Haven. If someone were to ask him for her destination he would send the inquirer to the decoy location. She also asked the young man about the note. He explained the note was sent overnight delivery. She charted her route and drove to South Haven; her back still ached from the plane ride.

*   *   *

Across from the hotel, a taxi pulled out of the parking lot and followed Kelsy. The driver of the cab was also a Shadow Government agent by the name of Adder, but he was from the splintered band of S.G. who was attempting the takeover. He was a tall, thin man with black stringy hair and a bony face. Behind his sunglasses were two dark brown eyes, sunken deep in their sockets beneath thick eyebrows. He had endured twenty-one years at the FBI, gawking at a monitor chasing computer hackers. His boredom and grievances with the Bureau were overheard by the right ears one day, and then shortly after, a surreptitious offering was made for a career change. Now, here he was two years later, playing 007. He was convinced he was protecting the country from evil entities, such as traitors and terrorists. That was the reasoning and justification for his work and his existence. His present assignment was to follow Kelsy to the target, which was Smits, and kill him. Kelsy's death was optional. Adder had thought this option over while waiting for her to leave the hotel. He decided, if possible, he would avoid killing her. It would be a shame to remove something as beautiful as Kelsy from an already fast-growing-ugly world.

A thud came from the back seat of the cab, followed by muffled and shifting movement. Again, the sound came from the back seat. Adder ignored the commotion. The source of the noise was the real driver of the taxicab, who was bounded with nylon rope on the floor of the vehicle. His eyes and mouth were duct taped shut. The sedative that Adder injected him with was wearing off. More moaning and struggling ensued from the back of the taxi.

"All right," Adder finally said. "I'll give you a little more." He said it as if he were speaking to a child who was badgering for more candy. He slid a syringe filled with a yellowish concoction out of his jacket and slipped the protective cover from the needle. He took one quick glance over the seat, followed by a prick in the driver's neck. "Night, night." He started to think about Kelsy's shoulder length red hair and blue eyes again. If she were in his department of the Bureau a couple of years ago, he would had never left the agency. He liked red heads very much. He smiled to himself thinking about the other S.G. idiots that fell for the phony information over the phone. He thought of them speeding along the highway heading in the wrong direction. "Premature evacuation." He laughed out loud.

Kelsy pulled into a convenience store and the taxicab followed, substantiating her suspicions. She'd noticed the taxi immediately after leaving the hotel. A minute passed before she decided to speed off. The taxi followed her, confirming the driver's intentions. She turned onto a flat desert two-way highway, increasing her pace. The taxi maintained a five-car separation.

Adder knew he had been made, but he would let her make the next move. He liked games, particularly life and death ones.

Kelsy couldn't go to South Haven with a tail. Her mind was turning with options. Should she try to lose him? Should she confront him? Maybe return to the hotel? She could call the police. She was going to have to make a decision soon; the next exit was South Haven.

Adder's cell phone rang in his jacket. It was his partner who had been investigating resident directories for three hours and had discovered two Stims in the region. Adder frowned before he returned the phone to his jacket. He was given new orders. Kill the FBI agent.

Kelsy decided to call the police and say, she was being followed by a suspicious taxi driver. If she was wrong about the driver, though she was a hundred percent sure she wasn't, she would happily apologize for the misunderstanding. At the precise moment she started to dial the police, the taxi pulled beside her on the driver-side of the car. The man in the taxi stared at her and appeared apologetic. She watched the driver with quick periodic glances. She sat the phone down between her legs and gripped her weapon.

"She's beautiful," Adder said to himself. She was more beautiful up close than he imagined. He continued to cruise beside her vehicle. Everything slowed down in his mind's vision. Her red hair gracefully flowed around her soft, pink face, and her bright, blue eyes watched him with a brisk liveliness. He smiled at her warmly and then he removed his sunglasses, attempting to appear alluring.

Kelsy smiled back uncomfortably. Her heart pounded; her abdominal muscles contracted. She slipped her gun out of the holster and clicked the safety off. She kept the car steady by placing her knee against the steering wheel while she felt for the digits on her cell phone with her thumb. She counted and searched for the digit numerals nine and one without taking her attention off the taxi or the road ahead.

"It's a damn shame," Adder said with a frown. His face grew grim.

Kelsy's eyes widened when she recognized the steel blue metal object raised into view. It was a full-size submachine gun with a sound suppressor. She slammed both feet on the brake pedal. She saw white flashes leaving the taxicab, and heard bullets piercing metal on the front fender and hood of her car. She skidded to a halt. The taxicab sped ahead, but the brake lights came on.

"Good move, beautiful lady," Adder said grinning. He placed the submachine gun on the passenger seat and started a three-point-turn. "Let the games begin," he announced. His expression turned suddenly to amused shock. The five seconds that Kelsy was out of his sight was a costly mistake for him. *She's going to ram me,* was the last thought he had before the thunderous crash of metal and glass erupted and devoured his world.

Kelsy's car smashed directly into the passenger side of the taxi. The two vehicles were one, forming a T-shape. The air bag had impeded her line of sight. She immediately unfastened her seat belt and leaned down, using the dashboard as a barrier while attempting to collapse the air bag. Her mind screamed, *Hurry up! Hurry up!*

Adder had a stinging, throbbing pain in his neck and shoulder, where glass had entered his body. He felt a sticky, warm blood flowing down his face from a deep gash in his forehead. He reached for the submachine gun that had fallen to the floorboard of the cab, but the seat belt restricted him. "Thank God for seat belts," he grimaced in pain. He unfastened himself and leaned down for his weapon. He lay against the seat for a moment, attempting to clear the white, blinking spots floating in his head. Damn. He'd let his guard down because of a pretty face. He couldn't help but smile with admiration. Her brake stunt was a good move, but the ramming maneuver was a thing of beauty. He could love this woman.

Where the hell is the traffic? Kelsy wondered. Not one car had driven past. She slowly sat up in her seat with her weapon at the ready. She was shocked by the violent damage the collision had caused. The steam from the broken radiator was obstructing her view, but from what she could make out, she demolished the passenger side of the taxicab. There was no sign of the driver. Maybe he was dead. Maybe he got out. Maybe he was sneaking up on her right now. Her eyes darted around, searching for any movement. Then, she saw it, slightly above the door of the taxi. An arm emerged with a submachine gun, like a cobra raising its hooded head preparing to strike.

Adder continued to lie on his side firing his weapon blindly, listening to the metal and glass fracture and pop over his suppressed fire. He stopped and listened carefully for any groaning or dying. Maybe he got lucky.

Kelsy threw the car into reverse and slammed the accelerator pedal to the floor. Now, sitting upright with her gun aimed at the taxi, she made a getaway.

Adder sat up to witness the retreat only to be greeted with a barrage of bullets ricocheting throughout the frame of the taxi. Smashing glass and shredded fabric from the interior fell around him like confetti at midnight on New Year's Eve. The dull thumping sound of hurling lead piercing through clothing, flesh, and bone cut the chaotic tumult. He clenched his teeth as a burning sensation ran up and down his arm. His silk, olive green shirt blackened from the collarbone down. The blood spread quickly. *That hurt,* he thought, falling to his side. He heard tires squeal and the high-pitched howl of a motor. He peeked over the dashboard to behold a charging car. She was going to ram him again. He turned the key in the ignition, but there was no response from the motor.

Kelsy gripped the steering wheel with a death lock and her eyes selected the passenger door as the target once again. Adder could hear the roar of the engine closing in on him. He could feel the pain he was about to suffer again. Kelsy braced herself for the collision. Adder turned the key again in one last-ditch effort. The motor clicked, clicked, clicked, and then hummed for a split second before turning over. A miracle! The roar of the taxi's engine provided a glimmer of hope. The interior of the cab filled with the odor of gasoline. A spark would turn the taxi into a ball of fire. Kelsy was within striking distance. He punched the gas pedal, managing to avoid another crushing blow by inches. Kelsy's vehicle rushed by the taxi as the back draft shook the cab. She continued without looking back. The taxicab rolled to a halt. Adder stuffed a compressed wad of cotton the size of a quarter and a half-inch in girth into his wound. *The chase scene begins,* he thought with a painful grin.

Kelsy's vehicle was leaking radiator fluid badly, threatening to give up the race at any moment. She checked her rear-view mirror and discovered the fast-approaching, battered taxicab. She swore that the driver of the cab was grinning. Her hand tightened on her gun, which reminded her that she was on her last magazine clip.

Adder started his incursion and positioned for a clean shot. "There she is," he said quietly, as if he'd just beheld an angel from heaven. *There's that beautiful hair,.* She glanced over her shoulder. *Those divine blue eyes looking at me. Yes that's right, look at me.* He slowly lifted his submachine gun.

Kelsy readied her 9mm, waiting for an opportunity for a kill shot. Patience, stay cool. Wait for the shot.

Adder's soft expression saddened. He was nearly beside her car. He frowned. "Sorry, beautiful." He took aim at her head.

A sudden crash sent a violent jolting sensation throughout the taxicab, jerking Adder's submachine gun upward. His weapon filled the roof of the cab with bullet holes. His startled eyes looked in the rear-view mirror to identify the source of the impact. "What the hell?" he exclaimed. There was a large gray Mercury making its way around to his side of the taxi.

Kelsy was quickly distancing herself from both vehicles. She didn't intend to hang around for introductions.

Adder turned his weapon on the Mercury, putting six holes in the hood and windshield before running out of bullets. He threw the submachine gun down and retrieved his 357 Magnum. As he brought the gun and his attention back around to the Mercury, he discovered he was staring down the twin barrels of a sawed-off shotgun. He froze, unable to bring his gun up into a firing position. He forced himself to think of Kelsy's face. Then, a loud blast of two barrels firing twelve gauge slugs echoed over the desert landscape.

Kelsy glanced over her shoulder after hearing the shotgun blast. She saw a cloud of black and gray smoke. The gray Mercury parted the smoke in pursuit of her car. Her bullet-riddled vehicle started to lose speed and the motor sounded sick. The Mercury had reached her and slowly pulled beside her smoking car. She had her weapon aimed and ready to fire, unaware of how many bullets she had left in the clip. Her trigger finger relaxed and she sighed with relief.

"Nice car," Sam yelled.

*   *   *

Kelsy and Sam turned left onto a road that led to a large, black, iron gate supported by white marble columns. Perched atop the columns were twin black marble male lions watching like majestic guardians. To the right, encompassed by an array of exquisite flowers, stood a black and white marble entrance wall proudly announcing the name of the community in scintillated gold writing—"South Haven." The gate silently and smoothly parted, allowing Sam and Kelsy access to the neighborhood. They looked around for the person responsible for their admission, but found no one. Concealed and unbeknownst to them, their vehicle triggered a motion scanner hidden within one of the lion's eyes, which transmitted a signal to the motor in the gate columns. Its function operated similarly to systems found at super-market entrances and exits. Kelsy and Sam traveled through the opulent neighborhood, overwhelmed by the luxurious homes sprawled across the well-manicured lawns with desert theme landscaped gardens. Woven throughout the million dollar homes was an extravagant country club golf course resort, complete with all the superfluous things wealthy people required. They glanced at one another confirming what they're both thinking. *Big money.* Their gray Mercury looked conspicuously out of place in the uppity community of Mercedes Benzes, Porsches, Cadillacs, Jaguars, and Ferraris.

Kelsy shook her head. "Doesn't anyone own a Ford or Honda in this neighborhood?"

Sam laughed.

"Hell, I can't afford those little golf carts they keep in their driveways," she added.

They self-consciously stepped out of the economical, inexpensive, cheap, inferior, middle-class rented gray Mercury and approached a spacious white-washed ranche-style home with a crimson shingled roof. Nearly all the homes in the community were built with a Spanish décor and decorative cactus gardens.

A security patrol vehicle quietly rolled up behind the Mercury. An armed uniformed officer stepped out of the white and tan, freshly polished cruiser.

Sam noted the insignia on the patrol car's door that read, "South Haven Security Unit." "The community has its own police force," he said, irritatingly impressed. A paradise in the middle of the desert; a tiny, rich enclave with rich people protecting their rich butts and overpriced stuff.

"Excuse me, folks," the officer said, approaching with a swagger. His well-built frame filled the uniform perfectly and strands of sandy blond hair slipped into view from beneath his hat.

Kelsy cursed herself for leaving her weapon in the car. Sam nonchalantly positioned himself in a way that allowed him to step in front of Kelsy if something threatening were to occur. They waited in the middle of the driveway, not sure what to make of the officer. Neither one of them were in a trusting mood.

"Is there something I can help you folks with?" the officer asked with a kind, country-boy-like drawl. His manner was of one who was eager to assist rather than harass.

"Is there a problem . . ." Kelsy glanced at the officer's name tag. "Officer Tobret?"

Tobret removed his hat in a gentlemanly fashion. "No, ma'am," he said politely. "We know Mr. Smits isn't home and doesn't plan to be anytime soon. We also know he isn't expecting guests." His green eyes smiled down at her.

Damn, he's good looking, she thought, staring back into his eyes.

Sam tilted his head inquisitively at the cowboy. "I have a question or two."

"Yes sir."

The young officer addressed him with a respectful tone. Sam liked that. "How do you know he's not expecting company and how did you know we were here?"

"There are two ways to enter South Haven, a north and south gate." Tobret explained. "We have security cameras scanning every vehicle leaving or entering the community. The description of the car and the tag is run through a computer immediately. The computer has a list of every vehicle in the community and a sub-list for past visitors. When your car entered South Haven the computer couldn't find you on the resident or past visitor list." He smiled. "And you weren't on the guest list, so the computer alerted us of your presence."

Sam shook his head. "Big brother is watching."

Tobret smiled. "We're the gate keepers. At least that's what the residents like to call us."

Paranoid rich people, Sam thought.

Kelsy flashed her FBI badge. "Could you tell us where Smits is? We need to speak to him."

A trace of worry entered his green eyes. "Mr. Smits was taken to the hospital this morning."

The worry in Tobret's eyes moved to Kelsy's. "What happened?" she asked.

"I'm not sure." Tobret answered. "An ambulance took him away early this morning. No one has heard anything. Mr. Smits is a very private man; he keeps to himself."

"Where's the hospital?"

Tobret wrote down the directions. Kelsy and Sam thanked him and hurried to the Mercury. Sam sped out of the community.

Kelsy stared out of her window at the passing dry landscape. "I hope someone didn't try to kill him, too," she said quietly, thinking of Smits. A worse thought came to mind. What if the S.G. impersonated paramedics and drove off with Smits in a fake ambulance?

*   *   *

Kelsy walked directly up to the information desk in the lobby of the hospital. She was winded from the run across the parking lot. "I would like to see Zack Smits," she said politely.

"Smits. S-m-i-t-s." The receptionist tapped on the keyboard and studied the computer screen. "Zachary L. Smits."

"That's right."

The receptionist grabbed a chart and flipped the pages authoritatively. "I'm sorry, he's resting," she reported. "He's recovering from emergency surgery."

"What kind of surgery?"

The receptionist was beginning to dislike Kelsy's sudden attitude change. "Are you family?"

Sam peeked at the computer screen and took a quick, but informative glance at the registration chart.

"I would like to see Smits. It's important," Kelsy explained.

"I'm sorry he, just got out of surgery. No visitors." She smiled. "Doctor's orders."

Kelsy pulled out her FBI identification, accompanied with an aggravated glare. "It's very important."

Sam had walked down the hall toward the elevators.

"I'll have to call the doctor," the receptionist said, lifting the telephone.

Sam waved Kelsy over to the elevators. She rushed toward the closing doors.

"Please wait here," the receptionist said with a phony courteousness. "If you wait one minute, I'll have Doctor Carol come—" Her voice was cut off as the elevator doors pinched together.

"Where are you going?" Kelsy asked.

"One thirteen," he answered with a shifty grin.

They entered the dimly lit room. Kelsy's mind flashed back to her mother; a quick tinge of pain followed, but she pushed it away. The man lying in the bed was easily in his mid-to-upper sixties with thin, gray, crew-cut hair. He had a white bandage wrapped around his neck. The entire drive from South Haven, Kelsy was convinced that "they" had gotten to him.

"He looks okay to me," Sam commented, studying the monitors. He pulled Smits' chart off the door and read it over. "Listen to this. He had an allergic reaction to his new medication. Apparently, his throat became swollen and they needed to perform an emergency tracheotomy," he read.

Kelsy felt a sense of relief, but she was still suspicious. The S.G. could have tampered with his medication.

Sam returned the chart. "Well, it looks like he's going to live, but I don't think he's going to be talking anytime soon."

Kelsy's cell phone rang. It was Mary, but the connection was bad.

Doctor Carol entered the room with a young-arrogant-fresh-out-of-medical school posture. His contemptuous baby face and narcissistic demeanor revealed his inexperience like a pimple on an adolescent. "Who are you people?"

"Family," Sam responded.

"Hello," Kelsy continued to say into phone. "I can barely hear you." She plugged one of her ears with a finger. "Mary, are you there?"

"Excuse me," Doctor Carol said tapping Kelsy's shoulder. "I need the two of you to leave."

Kelsy introduced her FBI badge to the young doctor's face. "I'm in Arizona," she said into the phone, ignoring him. "I need to . . ." The telephone went dead. "Damn it!"

"Why are you here, Agent Anderson?" Doctor Carol asked.

"Mr. Smits is an FBI witness. That is all you need to know," she said in a dry tone. She started to call Mary back.

Sam put his arm around the young Doctor Carol's shoulders. "Come on outside with me, doc. I'll explain the whole thing to you," he said leading the doctor to the door. "It's quite a funny story."

Chapter 43

The Sierra Madre Occidental, Mexico

A man lay motionless a thousand feet below a canyon ridge in the cool shadows, half a mile downriver from the crash site. His suit was shredded, muddy, and stained with so much blood that its color and design was unrecognizable. His face was scratched from branches and stones, his cheekbone and lower jaw were fractured, his right eye swelled shut, and his lip was split in two places. He had a severe concussion, a gash on his forehead that would need numerous stitches, and a countless number of other wounds on his body that would require sutures. His wrist, hand, collarbone and four ribs were broken, but the worst of the damage was the internal injuries.

A young Tarahumara Indian girl with a clay jug appeared out of the low-lying fog of the wooded terrain. Her footsteps were silent on the rocks of the riverbank. She knelt to scoop the fresh water flowing past when she saw the image that stopped her heart. She froze like a deer hearing a noise while drinking from a stream. A light breeze lifted the fog, revealing the body of Derrick Moore lying half out of the river. She vanished into the thick woods, leaving the clay jug and the body of Derrick on the river's edge.

*   *   *

White House

The Speaker of the House, Walter Web, sat behind the desk in the Oval Office, wondering, *How in the hell did I become President of the United States of America?* Forty-eight hours ago he was practically unknown, having dinner in a small Mexican restaurant. Now he was on the cover of fifteen magazines; his face was spread across every news program on the planet. Walter had become bigger news than the plane crash. There was one consistent theme running through every commentary—Who is Walter Web?

That question and a hundred others were being answered with every passing hour. First thing this morning, a story about his poor and humble childhood was aired—how he was raised in Pennsylvania, where at an early age he leaned the value of hard work and bravery from his coal-mining father. His father's motto was, "You go to church for God, you go to war for your country, and you go to hell and back for your children."

Walter had gone to college with the money his parents and relatives raised for him, but in his last semester of college the Vietnam War had begun and he enlisted the same day he graduated. Eight years later he returned as a Lieutenant General and highly decorated. A year later he was representing Pennsylvania in the Senate. He served twelve years in Congress before he eventually was chosen by his peers in the House of Representatives to be the Speaker of the House.

His mind spun in a whirlwind of thoughts, but a tan folder on the corner of his desk became the focus of his undivided attention. The contents of the file was Shelly Deanster's removal from office. He'd discovered it in Derrick's desk. He stared at the presidential insignia on the cover of the folder. He gripped it in his hands in the same manner a student embraced a final exam. He exhaled before opening the folder. As he read the file, questions popped up like crabgrass in a garden poorly kept, and a few of those questions nagged at him. For something that was common practice in Washington, why was her removal from office pursued so aggressively? Why was she removed so quickly? The formal charges and the majority vote rushed through the House of Representatives at warp speed, and the support of the Chief Justice of the Supreme Court was also swift to convict.

Walter couldn't help but think about Richard Nixon's Vice President, Spiro Agnew, who in the early 1970's was investigated by the U.S. attorney for income tax evasion and for allegedly receiving payoffs from engineers seeking contracts in Baltimore. He pleaded *nolo contendere*, "no contest," and quickly resigned due to pressures from Congress. And amazingly, President Nixon shortly followed with his resignation, also subject to Congressional pressure. When Congress wanted you out, it appeared that red tape and bureaucracy magically disappeared.

Maybe Shelly was guilty, maybe it was simply because she was a woman. She hadn't been warmly received by her peers. Most congressmen believed she wasn't qualified. She was certainly not the preferred choice by many in the political realm. There was an unspoken disapproval within political circles during the election year, but the ticket was overwhelmingly applauded by a large percentage of the country. The minorities favored the choice, and clearly, the woman's vote was assured; no one dared to oppose it publicly. Although Walter couldn't help feeling suspicious, the ordeal had an odd vibe. She was charged with bribery and the misuse of contributions and campaign funds.

The Civil Service Commission determined Shelly was solely involved in the practice of trading government jobs and preferences for political and financial support during the time in question. He nearly laughed out loud at the thought; Shelly was the only official making promises and unprincipled deals in Washington. "Yeah right," he said sarcastically. But the Commission never clearly proved her guilt.

He reviewed the third implication in the folder, a minor infraction that took place three years ago, which he found puzzling. Shelly was accused of violating the five-year law that prohibits a former government official from lobbying and influence—peddling directly from a past employer. Shelly had been employed by the Environmental Protection Agency, where she was an executive official for two and a half years. After leaving the position she maintained relationships with friends who remained at the agency. But now those relationships were under scrutiny because of funds donated to Derrick Moore's presidential campaign from the EPA.

He flipped the pages and came to the most damaging accusation and hardest to repudiate, the hidden bank account in Grand Cayman that had a balance of five-hundred-thousand dollars. Shelly insisted the money wasn't hers and strongly contended she had no knowledge of the account. Yes, the money was there, and yes, the money was in her name, but there was no evidence of her depositing the money or any other transaction linking her to the account. Although, there was a five-hundred-thousand-dollar campaign surplus of contributions and funds she was responsible for that she couldn't substantiate with documented proof the money's present whereabouts. He found this information suspicious, but certainly not solid evidence against her. To make matters worse, the bank in the Caymans was taciturn toward the situation. They made the Swiss banks look like gossiping old women, so no hard evidence or documentation from the Cayman side was obtained. This left Walter shaking his head with disbelief that she was removed so easily. It appeared she was framed. He looked over the rest of the papers of the president's appeal on Shelly's behalf, and the request for a closer inquiry into the accusations. "Sorry Shelly," he said, dropping the file in the wastebasket.

There was a soft knock at the door. A young woman entered with eyes full of grief. Her face was a reminder why Walter was the acting president. She was one of the many White House staff members still in shock over the recent developments. "Excuse me, Mr. Speaker . . ." She hesitated and became slightly uncomfortable. "Mr. President," she said correcting herself. "The data that you requested just arrived from the Pentagon and CIA. The Department of Defense said they're sending a man over to speak with you." She handed him the folders, avoiding eye contact, and without another word she walked away.

He put aside the folder from the Pentagon and apprehensively looked at the sealed file with the CIA insignia on the cover. He remembered an earlier conversation with Jordan, who showed him disturbing photographs of the hostage situation last week. He was anticipating more of the same from this file. A passing thought of President Moore and the plane crash crossed his mind, which reminded him of the young secretary and the expression on her face, the pain, the disbelief, the horrifying reality of it all etched painfully in her features. She was a perfect delineation of the country's state of mind and condition.

He pushed the thought out of his mind, broke the seal on the file and flipped through the contents, slowly uncovering a discrepancy between the information before him and the data Jordan disclosed a week ago. The CIA file plainly stated the warheads were "hot," meaning they were armed, and all the hostages were still alive—an enormous disparity between the UN and Jordan's data.

He took a troubled breath and felt his plan for a military rescue of the remaining hostages had been infested with indecisiveness. He'd moved a small troop of soldiers into North Africa last night, feeling confident the mission was justified and safe, with the assumption the hostages were being murdered and the warheads were supposedly disarmed. Now, there was uncertainty with the data, and he had troops waiting for his command.

Indecision was like a fatal cancer to a mission and a military man like him; it spread quickly and lethally. He cursed himself for not waiting for the CIA report before moving the troops into the North Africa. He'd convinced Congress and the Pentagon yesterday that he was sending the troops as disaster support in the event that the hostage situation went bad, but he'd had a strong suspicion the boys in the Pentagon got wind of his true intentions. He was confident the Pentagon folder was a condemnation of the troop movement and rescue attempt. After opening the folder, it was clear he was correct; the Department of Defense profusely condemned his efforts and was attempting to impede any other military action of his doing.

The Pentagon and the Congress stated he had abused his position as Commander in Chief of the armed forces by deploying troops overseas for a hostile rescue mission, and by doing so had endangered millions of people's lives, and put a strain on international relations. He shook his head. "Politicians and their politics," he said to himself. He never did like politicians and the contemptuous bureaucracy. But he understood the game they played; he too, had become one of them. He was aware of his legal right as Commander in Chief of the armed forces to deploy troops anywhere at anytime he saw fit, but he also acknowledged he was a little impetuous in his endeavors, and maybe he should have taken a more diplomatic approach to the situation. He guessed lying about the mission didn't help. His cabinet advisors warned him there would be a negative response throughout the government to his impudence if they discovered his plan. It was most likely was one of his pencil neck aides who ratted him out.

His actions and zealousness to mobilize troops in North Africa and launch a military rescue mission was more than a reckless patriotic crusade. There was a much deeper motive there, an infirmity. Like all good men, there was invariably a flaw in the armor, and those blemishes came in many forms, one being addiction. He was no stranger to addiction—he had the mother of all addictions, *power.* Power was no different than heroin or alcohol. Freud called this neurosis the "God complex." Most addictions put you on the highway to hell; power was the HOV lane.

Walter's first taste of power was in Vietnam when he was put in charge of thousands of troops, where he manipulated and sacrificed them like pawns in a chess game for his own amusement. He never forgot the rush of having thousands of lives at his command, and the feeling that he could end any of those lives at any moment he chose. After the war, the craving grew and politics was the next step to quench the obsession for power. He spent his years in Congress as a representative lobbying for the Speaker of the House position, which he considered an influential stepping-stone to his ultimate goal, the White House. From the Speaker of the House position he began to make the prominent connections that would aid him in obtaining a nomination for the presidency.

But to his surprise, he wouldn't need a nomination or years of sucking-up to his peers; his goal had become a reality overnight. He was the President of the United States. The power junkie scored his biggest fix.

Chapter 44

Baltimore, MD

"I want to go with Agent Brad," Buckler whined. Mary shoved Buckler into the taxi next to Allen. She slid in, forcing Buckler to sit in the middle. The three of them traveled in silence along the Baltimore-Washington Parkway, adjusting to the seven-hour time change.

"Where are we going?" Buckler asked.

Allen was half asleep and Mary ignored him, her mind too occupied with potential problems awaiting them.

Buckler became uncomfortable with the silence. "Where are you taking me?"

After he asked for the third time, Mary finally mumbled. "I have some questions you're going to help answer."

"I told you everything I know," Buckler said, continuing to whine. "Give me a break, I'm just an archaeologist."

"Oh, really," she said shooting him a dirty look. She unfolded a computer printout and handed it to him. "Look familiar?"

Buckler read the printout line by line. He handed it back to her. He appeared to have had the wind knocked out of him. "Where the hell did you get that?"

Mary returned the printout to her pocket. The information on the printout documented Buckler's many professional accomplishments, public and not so public. And most of those accomplishments had nothing to do with archaeology.

"What's going on?" Allen asked.

"Alfred 'I'm Just An Archaeologist' Buckler isn't being straight with us."

Allen's eyebrows raised. "He lied to us?" he asked, pretending to be shocked.

"Buckler's also a biologist," she revealed.

"Wait, allow me to guess." Allen mimicked a man pondering a difficult question. "Genetics."

"Give that man a prize," she said, impersonating a carnival booth attendant.

"It doesn't matter, I still don't know anything," Buckler said defensively.

"I think you know everything about those experiments."

"No one knows everything," he said.

"No one?"

Buckler stared down at his hands uncomfortably; either his head hurt from the wound he suffered or a bad memory had surfaced from the darkest parts of his mind.

"Listen," Mary said. "One way or another I'm going to find out what you know."

The taxi fell silent again.

Mary was thinking about the phone conversation with Kelsy from an hour ago. Kelsy filled her in on the latest developments, mostly about the cloning. Mary told Allen he was most likely a clone. He took it well. He wanted to know the 'why and who', which there were no answers to yet. "We know about the cloning," Mary said. "We know about the failures, too. I want to know about the artifact."

Buckler rubbed the bridge of his nose, avoiding eye contact. "I have no idea about the artifact. We didn't ask questions. It was a scary time for the other scientists and myself. We didn't think we were going to get out of there alive."

"You never saw the artifact?"

"No. My team and I were kept in different parts of the building, and most of the time they kept all of us separated."

"I don't believe you."

"I don't understand," Buckler said. "Why are you doing this? It's suicidal."

"Someone has to pay."

"Pay for what?"

"They killed my friends, and my best friend's mother is in a coma. Someone has to pay." She also believed the people behind the conspiracy were the same people responsible for the death of her partner.

"You're crazy. It's impossible . . . it's too big. How in the hell do you think you're going to bring them down? With that document? With me? It's not enough."

Mary stared out of her side of the taxi, ignoring him.

Allen looked hard at Buckler. "You and the S.G. attempted to be God. Now all of you will be held accountable."

*   *   *

The cheerful security guard smiled. "Hello, Miss Mary."

"Hey, Joe."

He handed her the mail. "You missed the excitement."

"What excitement?"

"We had a bomb threat."

This bit of news worried her, but she concealed it. "When?"

"Last night. We had to evacuate the whole damn building while the bomb squad searched every floor. People running around like they're crazy, bomb squads and dogs going up and down the building." Joe smiled. "But it was a false alarm."

"Oh sure, I'll be safe here," Buckler mumbled.

Joe patted Allen on the shoulder. "Hey, Al, I like the beard. How's the God business?"

"Dangerous," Allen said smiling.

"I'm glad you're okay. I read about those crazies and the assassinations in the papers. They almost got you too. Scary stuff. Good thing Mary was there."

"She's my hero."

Joe glanced at Buckler. "Who's your friend?"

"Alfred Buckler. He's helping us out with a few things," Allen answered.

Buckler looked at Allen. "Someone tried to kill you, too?"

"Yeah," Allen answered. "But it wasn't the same guys who tried to kill you. He didn't like my preaching."

"Everyone's a critic," Buckler scoffed.

Joe looked at them intensely. "Is anything I can do Al?"

"Keep your eyes open, Joe," Allen said.

They disappeared into the elevator, leaving Joe to his Wizards game on his ten-inch television behind the desk.

The elevator ride was a quiet one. Mary walked into her apartment followed by Allen and Buckler. Her apartment had been ransacked. Most of her furniture had been cut open and the stuffing ripped out. All the desk drawers had been pulled and dumped out and her computer was on the floor, dismembered. The hard-drive was missing. Everything in the apartment had been rummaged through. She thought she heard a noise in one of the back rooms. She placed her finger to her lips, signaling the men to keep silent. Allen and Buckler looked at one another, not sure what to make of her request. She went to the refrigerator and opened the freezer, retrieving a meat loaf microwave dinner. She pulled a 9mm out of the frozen box and proceeded to check the apartment.

"She probably has extra bullets in the chicken fried steak," Buckler whispered.

Mary returned from the back rooms and pulled out the vacuum cleaner and unsnapped a device from the bottom. It looked like a small metal detector. She walked throughout the room waving the device, watching the beeps on the small display screen.

"What's she looking for?" Buckler whispered to Allen.

"Bombs."

Worry filled Buckler's eyes.

Allen smiled. "Bugs."

Mary located two listening devices that she promptly covered with metallic tape, keeping the device activated, but incapable of picking up sound, but still conveying the conception of an empty apartment.

Buckler stepped over the cluttered mess on the floor. He wasn't sure what to make of Mary. She either was a paranoid, disturbed young lady or a highly trained professional. "I like the way you decorate your apartment. It has that post-frat-party ambiance."

"Did you have anything here?" Allen asked.

"Printouts and disks, but they were copies."

"This isn't comforting." Buckler glanced around the room. "Bomb threats, burglaries, bugs, and I'm supposed to feel safe?"

"Relax, Buckler," she said. "It's just the beginning."

"You weren't doing too well on your own out there," Allen reminded him.

"Looks like we're going to be filling out police reports all night," Buckler said, sitting down on a shredded cushion, causing white stuffing to blow into the air.

"I don't think so," Mary said looking around her apartment, considering her options to stay or move to another location.

"You're not going to call the police?"

"Tomorrow." She found the telephone and her answering machine, but the tape was missing. She searched the floor.

"What are we looking for?" Allen asked.

"The tape."

"You know," Buckler said. "They have a telephone that has call waiting, caller I.D., and answering service all in one."

She found the tape and returned it to the machine, then pushed the button to rewind it.

Buckler shook his head. "Primitive," he mumbled.

The machine beeped. "Hey Mary, it's Kelsy. I'll be back from Arizona soon. I'll call you later." The machine beeped again. The voice was soft and pleasant. "Hello, Ms. Jopuez, it's Amy Jones. I was wondering if there has been any progress with my case. Please call me. Good-bye." The machine played a number of business calls and some solicitors. "Mary, it's Kelsy, I have news, I'll call you later." The machine stopped and rewound.

Allen started to clean up, but Mary stopped him. "It's late, don't worry about it," she said. "Let's get some sleep."

"Good idea." Buckler grabbed some pillows and collapsed like a sack of potatoes.

Allen headed for the guest room, and Mary disappeared into her bedroom. She gathered the clothes off the floor and threw them into the closet, then put a few other items in order before she opened the doors that led to a small balcony off her room. She pulled the thin white drapes aside, then the heavy royal blue curtains back. There was a suspicious car in the street below. She called Allen into the bedroom. "Someone is out there," she said, peeking through the curtains.

Allen turned off the light and walked up behind her. He leaned against her and looked over her shoulder. Leaning against her felt good, but he tried not to think about it. "Where?"

"The car under the tree."

Her apartment was on the fourth floor, making it easy to scan the street, but only half the car was visible because of the hanging branches.

"How do you know there's someone in the car?"

"Watch."

They stared at the car below, waiting. In the meantime, his senses were overloading, the smell of her hair, perfume, and body lotions driving him crazy. A puff of smoke came out of the driver's side window.

"What do we do?"

Mary pulled out her cell phone. "Brad, it's Mary. Do you have anyone out in front of my place?"

Brad told her he had two agents on the way. She told him about the car beneath the tree.

Brad's two guys arrived minutes later and parked behind the suspicious car. The agents got out and approached the car, but before they reached the driver, the motor turned over and the car raced away. The agents returned to their car and reported to Brad. They were told to sit and watch.

"That takes care of that," Allen said, closing the curtains. "You're still in the FBI, aren't you?"

"After Ed's killer walked away," she explained. "I spent the next two years trying to prove the S.G. was responsible, but I got nowhere. So, I quit and became a private investigator. But I never stopped searching for Ed's killer. Years later I got a call from Assistant Director Amps."

"The same man who helped Ed's murderer go free?"

"That's right. He wanted me to come back to the Bureau, but it had to be unofficial. I would continue the investigation and he would assist from the inside."

"Why the change of heart?"

"The S.G. was blackmailing him with false bribery evidence. And then, there was the affair he had, which was real. But one night he got good and drunk and confessed to his wife about his extra-marital activities. To make a long story short, Amp's wife also had had an affair, so both of them came clean and had a marital rebirth. Now, with the infidelity thing gone, and the confidence to disprove the fake bribery accusations against him, he felt it was time to call me and straighten out another regret looming in his past. He told me he had a lot people on his side, and together we could catch the man who murdered my partner and put a real hurting on the S.G. while we're at it."

"Brad and Amps are working together?"

"Yeah, but I didn't find out about Brad until I called Amps after the Valley of the Butterflies shooting."

"It's a relief to know we're not alone in this," Allen said. He wasn't sure why, but he felt hurt she didn't tell him about her little secret. "I'm going to check on Buckler before I go to bed. Good-night."

"Good-night." Mary went into the bathroom and prepared for bed.

Allen returned to the guest room and turned on a small radio. He took his shirt off exposing a tight black tank top. He had the physique of someone who took care of himself. He looked out the window at the stars and attempted to organize his thoughts. Looking at the clear night sky always helped him think.

Mary entered the guest room wearing a long t-shirt that read, "What's Your Problem?" "Hey, Al, I'm sorry I didn't tell you about it."

Allen grinned and thought her t-shirt was appropriate for her personality. "It's all right." He felt better that she apologized.

"But you did keep that little virgin thing from me."

"We'll call it even."

"Good station," she said of the music playing on the radio.

"Remember, we danced to this song last New Year's Eve."

"Yeah. It was the last time I danced," she said, standing beside him.

"Me, too."

Allen noticed the curves of her figure beneath her T-shirt, she was beautiful and striking in every way a woman could be. He turned to her and took hold of her hand. "Dance with me," he whispered.

She put her arms around his neck and shoulders without hesitation. Her lack of resistance surprised him. His hands slid around her waist and they started to slow dance with the smoothness and grace of two people comfortable with one another. The song playing on the radio was about a man and woman fearing their friendship would be ruined if they were to get involved romantically; the couple in the song decided to take the risk.

Mary's eyes held Allen's gaze. "Do you like this song?"

"I love this song," he answered, close to her ear.

Mary put her head against his chest. "I do, too," she said quietly.

"I wish this song would last forever."

"Me, too."

"Forever?" he asked. His mind was swimming. Were they talking about more than just the song and a dance?

"Forever," she answered.

Was this another one of his cruel dreams?

The song ended and Mary slowly began to separate from his embrace.

It was too good to last, he thought.

She gently took hold of his face and kissed him. Allen's emotions were sent speeding. His hands caressed her lower back naturally, as they kissed passionately.

He pulled back. "Get dressed," he said, putting on his shirt.

"What?"

"Get dressed."

"Why?"

"Call Joe, and tell him to get us a cab."

Allen went down the hall. "Wake up, Buckler!"

"What? What's going on?" Buckler said sitting up, fearing for his life.

Allen grabbed him and his shoes. "Come on."

"Where are we going?" Mary asked still putting clothes on.

Allen grabbed the cell phone. "Let's go," he said escorting them out the door.

"What in the world is going on?" Buckler said half asleep and shook up by the sudden move. "What's wrong with him?"

"I don't know," she said walking past the security desk.

"Is everything all right, Miss Mary?" Joe asked.

"Everything is fine, Joe. I think," she added to herself.

The three of them got into the taxicab.

"Where are we going at two o'clock in the morning?" Mary asked.

"What's going on?" Buckler asked.

"We're going to a wedding," Allen said, giving Mary a grin.

"What?" Buckler blurted out.

Mary shook her head. "You're crazy."

"Who the hell gets married at two in the morning?" Buckler complained.

"Me," Allen and Mary said simultaneously.

The two FBI agents continued to follow the taxi. "Sorry, sir, to call you this late," the agent said to Brad on the phone. "But I thought maybe you would want to know we're on the move."

"On the move," Brad said, trying to focus on the alarm clock. "It's two o'clock in the morning."

"Yes, sir."

"Where the hell are they going?" He hung up and called Mary's cell phone. "Where are you going?" he asked before she could say anything.

"Church," she answered, smiling.

"Church?"

"Church."

"What happened, did Allen get paged?" Brad asked.

"We're getting married," she said, gleaming at Allen.

"I usually get away with a dinner and movie."

"Good-night, Brad."

"Congratulations," he said before hanging up. He called and explained the latest developments to the agents tailing the taxi.

They pulled up to the church. There was a pastor and two other people waiting on the steps.

"Thanks for making it, Vincent," Allen said to the pastor.

The tall, thin man with gray hair smiled broadly. "Are you kidding, I wouldn't miss this for the world," Vincent said with a hug.

"Pastor Vincent Tozolos, I'd like you to meet Mary Jopuez."

"I've heard many great things about you," Vincent said.

Mary gave Allen a look.

Allen laughed. "That's right, I talk about you."

The two FBI agents walked into the church. "Do you need a couple of groomsmen?"

Fifteen minutes later Allen and Mary were married. The odd group of an evangelist, private investigator, geneticist, a pastor and his wife, the church's organist, two FBI agents, and a taxi driver shared a few glasses of champagne from the church's wine cellar. Vincent told Allen that he would fill out the appropriate forms making the marriage legal in the eyes of the secular world, and Allen promised to have a more traditional wedding and reception in the near future.

Allen instructed the cab driver to take them to his parents' house. Buckler passed out in one of the many guest rooms.

Mary and Allen started their honeymoon.

*   *   *

"Good morning, newlyweds," Buckler said cheerfully, draped with an apron that read, "World's Greatest Cook." "Breakfast will be ready in a minute. I'm sure you're hungry. The coffee is fresh. Did you kids sleep well?"

Allen and Mary grinned, trying to conceal their embarrassment. "Smells good, what are you making?" Allen asked quickly, changing the subject.

"Omelets," Buckler said and then grinned. "After breakfast, I can disappear for a little while."

"Knock it off," Mary said uncomfortable with the sexual reference.

Allen had a quick, erotic flashback from last night. He tried to hide his grin. For a man who was a virgin, he performed like . . . well, not like a virgin, leaving her satisfied in every way possible. Last night was passionate, comfortable, sublime, and felt as if it were meant to be, it was fate, and they both realized it last night. "Finally, together." They both heard those sweet words singing in their heads at some point last night.

Allen handed her a cup of coffee and their eyes held each other for a moment, but a hundred words were said and just as many emotions were felt in their fleeting gaze. Allen could claim to be the happiest man on the planet and no one could refute it. Last night was the fulfillment of his dream, and this morning he witnessed the reality of it in Mary's eyes. He was married to the only woman he had ever loved, his best friend.

Allen reached into the pocket of his robe and retrieved a half-karat diamond ring. "My mother gave this to me," he said, holding it before him. "It was hers. She said I would know the perfect time to give it to the woman I love."

A single tear formed in the corner of Mary's eye.

Buckler stared quietly.

Allen reached again into his pocket, this time he brought out a wedding band. "She also said it would be you."

The single tear in her eye had streaked down her cheek.

Allen gently held her hand as he slipped the rings onto her finger. "I love you."

Mary hugged him. "I love you, too," she said into his ear.

Buckler never cared for the mushy-love stuff, but oddly, he could feel a bizarre magical electricity in the air, as if he truly just witnessed two souls becoming one before his eyes. "All right, you're embarrassing the help."

"How did you sleep?" Allen asked Buckler.

"Surprisingly well," he answered scooping an omelet out of the pan. "I heard strange noises outside, but I was so tired, I went out like a light."

"What kind of noises?" she asked.

"Like the wind, and some thumping." Buckler smiled. "But this thumping was outside."

"Knock it off," Allen and Mary both said.

She thought about last night, but this time it was about the danger they had put themselves in by coming to Allen's parents' house. The bad guys must be watching the house or at least had it bugged. The house had a more than adequate security system, one of the best, whenever Allen remembered to arm it, but still it wasn't very bright to come here. Love was blind, she thought, but did it make you stupid, too?

"You have a nice little place here. Preaching the, 'Good Word' must be a lucrative gig," Buckler said sipping from his coffee. He had already toured the mansion.

"It's my parents' house."

"That reminds me." Buckler's expression turned serious. "Is Pyrit your real last name?"

"It's my middle name, why?" Allen looked at him strangely.

"Is your last name Trent?"

"Yes."

"I pulled this off the fireplace mantel, I hope you don't mind." He pointed to the man in the photograph. "Is this your father?"

"He adopted me."

"This man in the picture is Allen S. Trentski," he said. "I worked with him. He was the top genetic engineer on the Rosenberg experiment."

Allen's expression hardened.

"What the hell are you talking about?" Mary asked.

"You didn't know?" Buckler asked.

"You're lying," Mary stepped up into his face.

Allen mumbled something unrecognizable before sitting down.

"I'm not going to lie to you guys any more," Buckler insisted. "I decided I'm going to help you. I'm coming clean."

"Allen's father worked for NASA," Mary declared.

"Yes he did," Buckler agreed. "But he also worked for a very secretive agency within the Pentagon."

"I don't believe you," she said. "Why are you so willing to divulge secrets now?"

"I'm not lying," he said sincerely. "Remember seeing the name, Stanley Tent on the file? That was one of your father's aliases. He used his middle name and dropped the 'r' or added 'ski' to his last name making it Tent or Trentski. He was also responsible for charting and observing the experiment's progress." Buckler sounded convincing.

Allen recalled a file cabinet in the cellar, where he'd discovered folders on an experiment, and daily progress reports of a subject classified, "The Orphan, which he thought was originally a NASA project concerning a satellite put into orbit. The file never mentioned names or personal data, but it was obvious now to Allen that the material was speaking about a human subject under observation.

"I believe you," Allen said. "It makes sense. If I am the clone, as we believe, it makes perfect sense. That's why he adopted me, so he could keep an eye on me."

"I think you're right."

"What about the artifact?" Mary questioned. "Are you going to tell us the truth about that?"

"I don't know anything about the artifact," Buckler said. "I would tell you if I did."

Chapter 45

Arizona

The hospital experienced a rare silent and peaceful moment in the early morning hours. Kelsy was asleep in the recliner in Smits' room. The only activity was a flirtatious conversation between a security guard and a nurse down the hall, but that discussion and the serenity of the building was abruptly broken by a shrieking fire alarm. The desk nurse spun her chair around to study a computer screen, which displayed the floor plan of the hospital. There was no indication of a fire on any of the floors. Her baffled expression prompted the security guard to retrieve his transmitter radio.

"Where's the fire?" the security guard barked into his transmitter.

"No signs of a fire," a number of voices reported over the radio.

The fire alarm continued to sound throughout the building. Nurses and doctors did their best to control the increasing panic among the patients, not to mention some of the anxiety among themselves.

"I got smoke on floor—" the voice began to dispatch over the radio, but was cut off.

"You broke off, say again." The security guard turned to the nurse. "Anything yet?"

"Nothing. The screen is showing . . ." The nurse suddenly stopped. "The floor below," she said urgently.

The guard dashed for the stairwell. Kelsy stood in Smits' doorway with her weapon by her side waiting for an explanation.

"There's smoke on one of the floors below," a nurse told her.

"Great," Kelsy mumbled. *I need coffee,* she thought. The sirens of the fire trucks were blaring below in the parking lot. She pulled the blinds up and watched the firefighters rush into the hospital.

After a chaotic ten minutes of firefighters and hospital personnel racing throughout the building the atmosphere eventually settled down. The patients had been convinced the hospital wasn't going to burn down and were offered extra sleeping pills.

A nurse poked her head into Smits' room where Kelsy sat and watched over Smits. "Everything is under control," she announced.

"What happened?"

"They're not sure. They think there was an electrical short that caused a small fire in the bathroom below," the nurse explained, before joining a doctor walking down the hall.

Kelsy got a cup of coffee from the vending machine, but there was no sugar. Slowly she felt her nerves tightening. Suddenly, the need for caffeine and sugar was dire. She walked down the hall toward the nurses' station, attempting to remain composed and not look like a junkie needing a fix. There were a half dozen nurses and doctors standing around, discussing the excitement of the night and the President's plane crash.

"May I have some sugar?" Kelsy asked one of the nurses.

"Sure," she said, disappearing into the back room.

Kelsy looked down the hall and noticed a firefighter stepping out of the stairwell. He inspected a power box in the hall. Her attention returned to the conversation among the nurses and doctors. One nurse was telling a story about a cute firefighter she saw downstairs. Kelsy glanced at the firefighter laboring on the electrical panel.

"We don't have any sugar here. I'm going to check the other station," the nurse yelled from the back room.

"Don't worry about it. I'll drink it black," Kelsy said, noticing the firefighter had disappeared.

"I have some sugar," one of the doctors offered. "I have a secret stash in my desk," he added with a smile.

Kelsy gave him a tired grin. "Thanks."

The doctor walked to an office a couple of doors away. The nurse continued to search through the cabinets. Kelsy looked down the hall; still no sign of the firefighter. An image of him appeared in her mind. Was he still wearing his oxygen mask? She couldn't remember seeing his face. The electrical panel was two doors away from Smits' room. A disturbing thought constricted her chest and her breathing. The doctor reappeared in the hall with a jar of sugar packets.

"I found some!" the nurse yelled, holding up a container of sugar.

Kelsy was in full sprint by this time, racing down the hall. She charged into the room to discover the firefighter leaning over Smits' body. "Back away from the bed!" she yelled with her weapon drawn.

The firefighter maintained his position keeping his back turned toward Kelsy.

"FBI! Back away from the bed!" she yelled again, working her way around, attempting to position herself for a better view.

The firefighter, who was fitted in full gear, remained eerily still.

A doctor headed for Smits' room. "What's going on?" she asked.

"We don't know," a nurse responded.

Kelsy could see the firefighter had a syringe in one of his latex-gloved hands. The other hand was obstructed from view by his body.

"Drop the syringe!" she demanded, stepping closer.

The firefighter lifted his head slightly to bring his cold, tinted face shield into view.

Kelsy saw her own reflection in his tinted mask. She could see herself aiming her weapon at him. "Back away with your hands in the air." She could feel his eyes staring coldly at her from beneath the tinted face shield.

"What's going on?" a doctor asked, entering the room.

Kelsy's eyes shifted to the doctor for a split second, but that was all was needed for the firefighter to bring a gun with a silencer up from his side.

"Don't do it!" she yelled.

The doctor was frozen with horror.

The firefighter took aim at her and squeezed the trigger, but not before she fired a single shot into his shoulder, causing his gun to drop to the floor. His gunshot lodged harmlessly in the wall behind her. He maintained his balance while small rivers of blood ran along the creases of his yellow coat sleeve.

"What the hell is going on?" the doctor screamed.

"Get back!" she yelled.

Hospital personnel had crowded the doorway to Smits' room.

"Drop the syringe!" Kelsy yelled again.

The firefighter stood still as a small puddle of blood gathered near his boots.

Two security guards pushed through the hospital staff and entered the room. The guard pulled his weapon once he saw Kelsy's gun. "What's going on?" he asked. His eyes darted back and forth from Kelsy and the firefighter. "Would someone like to explain what the hell is going on?"

"Drop the syringe!" she demanded stepping closer.

The firefighter's arm shot out and drove the syringe toward Smit's body. Kelsy fired and struck the firefighter's chest. The force of the bullet piercing his body sent him crashing into the hospital equipment, then hard to the floor. She bolted across the room, kicked the gun away from the motionless body, then stepped on his wrist and seized the syringe from his grip.

The two security guards stood paralyzed with the safety still on their guns. The hospital staff rushed into the room and started administering medical attention to the firefighter.

*   *   *

The local police authorities were questioning the hospital personnel. Kelsy was on the telephone with Assistant Director Amps, who had been secretively assisting her on the S.G. case after discovering they had tried to kill her mother. Kelsy was arranging a transfer to Washington for Smits, where he could to be placed in witness protection.

Investigators discovered how the assassin obtained the firefighting gear when a local fireman was found in the basement strangled to death. But he wasn't the only innocent casualty of the night—a security guard was discovered murdered, shot in the back of the head and left in the bathroom closet. These solemn events had put a strain on the relationship between the FBI and the local authorities, but some of the cops did have a few respectful remarks for Kelsy after they discovered she was the one who put the bullet in the assassin's heart.

Two local police officers remained in the hall outside of Smits' room, and security measures on the hospital grounds had been put on high alert, but she wasn't able to relax. This wasn't exactly what she'd had in mind. There were too many people involved, too many people to check out. She had asked the hospital and law enforcement personnel not to speak to the media, who had gathered in the lobby of the building, about the incident. She explained that it was a matter of national security, but she knew she had little time before something leaked out to the press.

"Doctor Carlson!" a nurse yelled stepping out of Smits' room.

The doctor rushed into Smits' room closely followed by Kelsy, who gripped her weapon, anticipating more trouble.

"Mr. Smits is awake," the nurse announced.

Kelsy maneuvered around to the foot of the bed as Doctor Carlson examined Smits. "Is he all right?"

"His signs look good," Carlson answered. "Hello, Mr. Smits, good to see you awake. We had a few complications." He checked Smits' monitors. "But you're going to be fine."

Smits squinted, adjusting to the light of the room and his face bore the discomfort from the surgery and the tubes protruding from his body. Kelsy stepped closer to the bed, eager to speak to him.

The doctor introduced her. "Mr. Smits, this is Agent Anderson from the FBI. She would like to speak to you. Are you up to it?"

Smits was puzzled by the presence of an FBI agent, but he maintained an expressionless gaze. *Always keep your emotions in check and concealed,* he thought. Old military habits die hard. He acknowledged Kelsy with a nod.

Kelsy introduced herself again and flashed her I.D. "I need to ask you a few questions."

c

Smits glanced at the photo, name, and badge before returning his attention to her eyes.

"I'm investigating the Rosenberg file. Have you heard of it?"

There was a flicker of surprise and cognizance in his steady stare, revealing he had, and it didn't escape Kelsy's observation. His eyes shifted toward Doctor Carlson and the nurse, indicating he and Kelsy should speak in private. "I'd like to talk to him alone."

"Sure, everything appears to be fine." Carlson handed Smits a pen and notepad to write on. "I'll be back a little later. Remember Mr. Smits, no speaking and don't exert yourself."

Kelsy knew that was said for her benefit. The doctor didn't want his patient interrogated. "The Rosenberg file, you've heard of it?"

Smits nodded his head, yes. His mind flashed back to nearly forty years ago when he was a military officer assigned to the Pentagon. He was in command of the security and confidentiality on the sub-level floor that didn't appear on any floor plans, blueprints or directory. He had attempted to do everything in his power to forget those years, but he knew the day would come when the past would haunt him.

Kelsy moved in close to him. "When the file surfaced, people started dying. I need to know why."

Smits contemplated his response while surveying this pretty FBI agent standing in front of him, who was hell bent on uncovering a dark secret from the past. In the past he would had eaten her alive and made her disappear for asking questions of this nature, but he couldn't help it, he liked her. She had the tone and expression of someone who wasn't leaving until she got answers. Maybe it was time to let it go; he had lived with it too long. He decided he wasn't going to the grave with his share of dirty little secrets, and with that thought, he began to write.

Smits confirmed the Shadow Government was conducting human cloning experiments. He also confirmed the murderous unsuccessful experiments.

She recalled the photographs of the dead, deformed embryos and infants along with the death certificates of young women from the files she obtained from the warehouse, where the two Dobermans tried to have her for lunch. The immoral and unethical protocol of these experiments would undoubtedly cause international mayhem, but still, she felt like there was much more than genetic engineering of human life to the story. They could simply deny or apologize for the hideous experiments, and like most illegal government affairs, it would be forgotten within the year. Human cloning being performed thirty years ago was an extraordinary thought, but the more she thought about the possibility the easier it was to believe. The government's involvement with genetic engineering on plants over the past sixty years, along with experiments on livestock was well documented; therefore, logically humans would be next, and cloning would soon follow.

"What do you know about a stolen artifact?" She believed the artifact somehow was the key to the entire conspiracy.

Smits' stared at her, but he knew precisely what she was talking about. More dirty secrets. He wrote on the notepad and explained he wasn't directly associated with the covert operation, but he'd heard rumors within the power circles that the government had broken into a museum and stolen an artifact, killing someone important in the process. Kelsy's research had told her that at the time there were peace talks and negotiations between several nations, and there was a lot of finger pointing in those months. The burglary had caused international pandemonium within many nations and religious groups, but the artifact was never recovered and the burglary was blamed on religious fanatics.

"Does the name Allen Pyrit mean anything to you?"

He shook his head no.

"Is there anything else that may help me?"

Smits wrote again, information concerning two men named William Larson and Paul Stainwick. The last sentence proclaimed the two men knew everything.

"I need you to testify against these criminals."

Smits' eyes filled with concern and hesitation.

Kelsy helped him make the right decision. "Someone attempted to murder you earlier this morning."

What difference does it make? he thought. *Dead now or later. Time to let it go.* He agreed to help her.

She discussed a few details concerning security for Smits with the head security guard and two police officers assigned to the floor. She thoroughly checked it out herself before feeling comfortable enough to go to the cafeteria for a half an hour. Waiting for the elevator doors to open, she stared at the white floor, attempting to clear the spinning thoughts from her mind just long enough to eat in peace. The elevator doors parted and a large arm reached out and grabbed her shoulder. She instinctively went for her weapon.

"I heard you had a little excitement," a grinning Sam said.

"A little." She stepped into the elevator.

"What floor?"

"First, I need something to eat."

The doors closed. "Too bad he died," Sam said of the impostor firefighter.

"Yeah, I was going for the shoulder, but he moved."

"Killers tend to do that."

They walked into the cafeteria where the doctors and nurses were being pestered by reporters. The stares and whispers began with their entrance.

She needed to get Smits out of here as soon as possible.

"Was there any identification on the dead guy?" Sam asked.

"No." She slid along the rail with a cafeteria tray. "Where were you?"

"Checking out the road warrior we left behind on the highway."

"Find anything?"

"By the time I got back there the locals were cleaning up. I snooped around the crowd and talked to a couple of reporters. Do you want to hear something weird? They found lots of guns, bullet holes and blood in the cab, but no body, with the exception of a dead, tied up and gagged taxi driver in the backseat."

"They got him out of there pretty damn quick."

"This whole thing reeks of Shadow Government." Sam hesitated, appearing to question his own statement. "But it's too sloppy, too desperate."

"Maybe they're scared." They found a table as far away from the hospital staff and reporters as possible.

"Did you question Smits?" he asked.

"He confirmed everything we know," she whispered in between sips of coffee.

"What about Mary's friend Allen Pyrit?"

"Smits never heard of him, but he did say we need to talk to William Larson and Paul Stainwick. He also agreed to testify."

"It sounds like he cooperated."

"I think he was glad to get it off his chest."

"Confession is good for the soul," he said with a grin.

Chapter 46

Washington, D.C.

Like so many times before, Art climbed down the old rickety stairs to the church cellar to meet with his client, Professor Greg Orfordis, a man who genuinely believed he was at war with the devil himself. Greg believed Jordan Iblis, the Secretary General of the UN, was Satan, and was plotting to take over the world. The professor hired him to collect evidence against Jordan, evidence that ultimately would expose his implausible plot. If Art was convinced of anything, it was that insanity was contagious, because he was beginning to believe the professor. Who else but the devil could manipulate hundreds of important people all over the world and bend them to his will? Who else could create a network of deceit on a worldwide scale? Who else could frame the vice president and have her removed so quickly? Who else could have possibly assassinated the President of the United States by bringing down Air Force One? Who else could get close to the Speaker of the House, Walter Web and corrupt his mind with a warped philosophy and convince him to attack a warehouse potentially full of biological and chemical weapons? Who else could scheme such a mad plan to the smallest detail, from the look-a-like vice president to the driver who delivered a truckload of contaminated fuel for Air Force One. Jordan had thought of everything; well, almost everything. He certainly didn't count on a little theologian and a fat private investigator who had nothing better to do than save the world.

"Hey, Professor O," Art said, throwing another file filled with dirt on Jordan Iblis on his desk. "You got me convinced this guy framed the V.P. and is somehow responsible for the Air Force One crash, and that he's got Web brainwashed and trigger happy." Art would never admit out loud that Jordan was Satan, but he had no problem entertaining the thought to himself. "But I got a problem. You say his motive is to rule and to be worshiped. But how is any of this going to accomplish that?"

"Come and sit down Mr. Hanson," Greg said with an eager smile. "Remember the printout from Jordan's chemical factory in New Mexico you gave me?"

"Sure," Art said. "I had to get that lab nerd drunk at the happy hour joint across from the chemical plant to get it."

"One of the most essential factors in Jordan's plan is to have the U.S. attack the warehouse and have the biological weapons released. The only way that would happen is by removing the two people in his way, the president and the vice president, and then replace them with his puppet, Walter Web, the Speaker of the House, who is third in line for succession to the presidency. Once the biological weapons are released and the population is exposed, the deaths would reach countless numbers. Guess who has the remedy in vaccine form."

"Jordan's chemical company."

"The UN and Jordan are heroes and the U.S. is the goat. The UN becomes the front runner for the global leadership and pushes for a New World Order using the vaccine as leverage."

"Join the New World Order and accept their conditions or no vaccine," Art said. "Old fashioned blackmail."

"That's correct."

Art felt like he owed the professor an apology for thinking he was a loony. From day one when he'd asked him to investigate Jordan Iblis, he thought Greg was a little on the goofy side, and the more he talked to him the more he believed he was right; the professor was cracked. But here he was, helping Greg save the world from the devil. And sometime during all the craziness Art started believing in God, too. Like they say, "You can't believe in one and not the other." He wasn't sure which God, or whose God yet; he was still working on that.

"How did you connect the vaccine and the biological weapons?" Art asked.

Greg pulled out a magazine article. "By accident. This article was written by a chemical engineer, who was asked to guess what type of chemicals or biological weapon may be in the warehouse and their effects on the population. He mentioned the one hazardous biological agent found in the document from Jordan's chemical plant. Also on the document was the counter-agent, and the plant was producing mass quantities of it."

"Amazing," Art mumbled, "It's brilliant. The setup is elaborate, and yet, so simple in theory." He shook his head at the sheer thought of conceiving such a plan. "What kind of mind works like that?"

"A very gifted one," Greg said. "But unfortunately, also a very evil one."

"What's the next step? When do we drop the hammer on this gifted mind?"

"I've sent copies of the evidence to the CIA, FBI, NSA, every major newspaper in the country, and to the television media."

"By tomorrow afternoon," Art said, "The witch hunt will be on."

*   *   *

Mexico, The Sierra Madre Occidental

Derrick's eyelids flickered, then opened wide, but his vision was a blur and his mind was distorted with black and gray forms. His own thoughts seem too loud, pounding his head like a scalp massage with a two-by-four. He blinked and it hurt. His lips felt raw and chapped. The slightest swallowing movement in his neck and jaw muscles caused pain and discomfort. He could taste the acidic tang of blood in his mouth and the smell of clotted blood in his nostrils, and he had the strange sensation of being totally detached from the living.

He thought he heard voices; the conversation sounded muffled by the division of a thin wall. He strained to listen, but he was swimming in an obscured and murky world far away from understanding anything. His senses were awakening. He was beginning to feel all the pain in his body. He could feel the wool blanket laying across his skin, and it felt unnaturally heavy.

His sight was slowly returning. The first clear vision was the golden-brown grass ceiling of an adobe hut. *Not a hospital,* he decided. His vision dimmed again. He had no idea where he was, and he certainly had no recollection of how he'd gotten here. Two words unexpectedly materialized in his mind—*plane crash.* An image formed in his mind's eye;, he could see himself propelling out of an aircraft and feeling the sensation of being suspended in perpetual blackness, which was painfully and violently interrupted by the sudden collision of wood, dirt and rock against his flesh and bones.

The memory ended there with a flash of white pain. He didn't remember the thicket of shrubs and small trees he smashed, rolled, and skidded through. He didn't remember the five hundred foot plunge down a muddy canted gorge to a clay and rock horse trail, from where he stumbled in a foggy daze to a river's edge. He had continued along the cool, muddy bank of the river for a half mile out of sheer determination. He refused to give in to the blackness saturating his head and the chains of pain dragging him to the ground; but he eventually surrendered to the serene notion of resting, sleeping, and dying.

That he survived the crash was nothing short of a miracle, but his good fortune didn't end there. The region's natural conditions had slowed his heart rate and blood flow down considerably. The night air was cool, the river's water was cold, and the river mud had compressed on his wounds, functioning like bandages. Without these beneficial circumstances, he undoubtedly could have bled to death.

To his astonishment, he could feel himself getting better; he still felt the consequences of the plane crash throughout his body, but he could feel himself healing and gaining strength by the minute. Along with the various remedies administered to him, there was another significant factor to his speedy recovery—the twenty-hours of undisturbed, total shut-down, coma-like sleep he experienced. Sleep was just as essential to recovery as any medication; it permitted the body to concentrate on the injuries, and later he found out that he could thank Jamaican Dogwood for the trip to la la land. It was a powerful sedative when mixed with the California poppy.

Eventually, in the passing moments of consciousness a chilling question emerged out of the swirling cloudiness of his thoughts. The question sailed across his mind like the mysterious monster of Loch Ness, gliding above the black surface of the lake, and just like anyone who may encounter such a sight, certainly would question his own eyes. Now, likewise, the question crossed the blackness of his mind, and he futilely searched for the answer. He could hear the words in his head, he could hear himself asking the question that hung there before him, mockingly. But there was no response. Suddenly, his physical wounds were trivial. He was positive he had been in a plane crash, he was pretty sure he was alive, and it appeared he would survive. He didn't know where he was, but he was confident the answer would come shortly. But none of that mattered right now. His anxiety and consternation grew heavier with every passing moment the one question wasn't answered. Again, the words emerged and asked, *Who am I?*

Two figures entered the hut, still slightly blurred to his sight, but he attempted to make eye contact. The two men were using a Mexican dialect somewhat familiar to Derrick, but the language wasn't exactly Spanish 101. The words he was able to interpret were "explosion and glowing sky." He parted his split, chapped lips to speak. "Where am I?" As soon as the words left his dry mouth, he painfully learned he had a broken jaw. He had a number of broken bones in his face; in other words, it was going to hurt like hell to talk.

*   *   *

The White House: Oval Office

Walter sat back and enjoyed a moment of total silence. His eyes were closed and the sensation of being the most powerful man on the planet pumped his blood through his body. Jordan was right. This was addictive. He grabbed a pen and signed the document before him. He was requesting Harry Stokes to be his Vice President, since Congress disapproved of his last recommendation. Stokes was a good man. He should know; Stokes served under him in Vietnam.

His rare moment of solitude ended abruptly when a group of advisors and White House staff aids rushed into the Oval Office with pressing news from North Africa. He was informed that the U.S. rescue forces were met belligerently by Balkan troops, including allies, and blood was shed. Also, he was notified Congress had taken action to stop him.

The world media was calling America's new president a truculent tyrant that must be stopped by any means before innocent hostages were murdered and there was a biological catastrophe.

President Moore had spent two long years polishing and restructuring America's image from a bullying, interfering world power to a country of resources prepared to provide aid to any country that extended a friendly hand in need. Walter destroyed twenty-four months of promising progress in under a week's time.

He'd sent the troops as a diversion. He'd never intended them to encounter violent resistance. The actual rescue mission was a team of six Navy SEAL commandos on the roof of the building where the hostages were being held, waiting for the green light. Initially, Derrick had deployed the team for reconnaissance, but Walter altered the plan slightly.

The Situation Room was full of advisors, White House staff, military personnel, and Walter, who watched the television monitor projecting news footage of protests from across the world against the United States. There was also footage of foreign military forces mobilizing their troops, preparing to confront the U.S. rescue forces. The fax machines, telegraphs, telephones and every other means of communication were loaded with incoming calls from nearly every government in the world, all demanding explanations and an immediate halt to the rescue mission. He had gone from "country-boy-done-good" to "deranged psychopath" in a matter of hours.

"Back the troops off," Walter said, almost forcing the words out.

"Sir?" an advisor asked.

"Back 'em off." He sat down in the black leather chair and rubbed his eyes. "Send the order, and make an announcement to the vultures," he added, his term of endearment for the media.

There was a sigh of relief in the room from a dozen souls.

Walter sat in his chair, appearing disheartened and despondent, but his mind was reeling with optimism. He had the ace of spades in the hole in the form of six men positioned on a roof.

Chapter 47

Kelsy rushed into her apartment to answer the telephone; Sam headed for the bathroom. She tapped the speaker. "Hello."

"How was your flight?" James asked.

"Long," she responded, disappointed that it wasn't Mary. Her head was pounding with a migraine.

"Any problems?"

She thought about the S.G. in the taxi that had tried to kill her and the man she shot who attempted to assassinate Smits in the hospital. "No, everything went as planned. Well, there was the rental car." She smiled, thinking about the expression on the man's face at the rental car agency when he saw Kelsy's car, which appeared to have been through a demolition derby and target practice for a shooting club.

"Did you have car trouble?" James asked.

"You can say that."

"You sound tired," he said.

"Headache."

"I know a great remedy for headaches."

Kelsy threw her travel bag to the floor and chased down two Advils with a glass of water. She searched the refrigerator for a beer. "Did you drink my beer again?"

"No," he answered. "Do you want to hear it?"

"What?"

"The remedy."

"Sure," she said, still searching.

"Sex."

She turned to stare at the speaker phone from the kitchen. "Sex is a remedy for headaches?"

Sam walked into the room with a "What the hell are you talking about?" expression on his face.

"The adrenaline in the body releases a rush of hormones, starting a chemical reaction," James explained. "Epinephrine, pheromones and endorphins flow through the body and brain to combat the stress in the nerve endings that are causing the pain."

"That's romantic."

"It's not roses and candlelight in theory, but in practice it beats Tylenol."

Kelsy smiled for the first time in days.

"I see you moved Smits to D.C.," James said. "I'm assuming he's under the watchful eye of the Bureau."

"You assume correctly. He gave me two names. I'll tell you later on a clean line."

"I have some information for you," he said, suddenly sounding different, more serious.

His somber tone had her staring at the phone. "All right," she said, not sure what to expect.

"The name of the man who shot your mother is Andre Frost," he finally said quietly. "I don't have a photo yet. I'm working on it."

Her heart jumped a beat; the thought of having the name of the man responsible for the shooting was invigorating, providing an optimistic conclusion to their nightmare. "Thank you," she whispered.

*   *   *

The intercom announced the presence of a visitor at the front gate.

Allen pushed the button on the house intercom. "How may I help you?"

"Hi Allen," the speaker said cheerfully, "It's Kelsy."

Allen immediately opened the gate. "Come on up."

Mary pulled the curtains slightly back and watched the car approach. After watching Kelsy and Sam step out of the car alone she returned her weapon to the holster.

Everyone was happy to see one another. They'd all had moments where they weren't sure if they were going to see one another ever again.

"Good to see you, again," Mary said to Kelsy.

"Good to see you, too." Kelsy said, grinning. "It's been an interesting couple of weeks."

"Very interesting."

"We killed some people, how about you?" Sam asked nonchalantly.

Mary shook her head and hugged him.

"So, this must be Allen." Sam reached out with his large hand. "The source of all this *interesting* activity over the last couple of weeks."

Allen's hand nearly disappeared in the Sam's grip. "I'm afraid so."

"I was bored with retirement anyway."

"I'm so sorry about your sister." It was apparent to everyone Allen still felt responsible in some way for her situation.

Kelsy lowered her eyes. "The doctors said there's still hope." Her tone was soft and wishful.

Allen held her hand. "I believe she will be fine." His words seemed undoubtedly true. "She'll pull through."

Kelsy and Sam glanced at one another, both feeling the surge of certainty in Allen's words shooting through their bodies like a current of electricity. Kelsy wasn't a stranger to Allen's charismatic personality and inspirational character. Sam on the other hand didn't know Allen from Adam, but he definitely sensed something unique about him now. Allen put something in Sam's heart that wasn't there a minute ago. Faith. Allen had somehow convinced him with a handful of words, a look, and a tone, that his sister was going to get up and walk out of that hospital.

"Wow," Sam whispered to Kelsy. "He is good."

"I told you." Allen's encouraging words filled her with more hope.

"Good thing he doesn't sell insurance," Sam joked. "He could convince me to buy an iceberg policy in the Keys."

Buckler walked out of the kitchen. Mary introduced him. "This is Alfred Buckler, the archaeologist I told you about, also, known as exhibit 'A.'"

Sam grinned. "Is he the one with the genetic engineering hobby?"

Buckler rolled his eyes. "I see your friends share your wonderful sense of humor."

"They also share my intolerance for liars."

"I haven't lied to you."

Mary gave him a look that might be accompanied with a slap.

"Lately," Buckler added quickly.

Kelsy pulled out a document. "I got permission to question Larson," she said.

Mary grabbed the forms and checked the signature at the bottom. "Is this legit?"

"Yup."

"Good," she said throwing away her fake document. "We won't need this."

"And what's this," Sam asked, holding Mary's hand up in the air. Mary smiled coyly.

"Oh, my God, that's a wedding band," Kelsy exclaimed.

"I'm no big time detective like some people," Sam grinned. "But that would lead me to believe you're married."

Kelsy hugged her. "Congratulations." Then, she hugged Allen.

"What makes you think she married me?" Allen asked.

Kelsy rolled her eyes. "Oh, please, I knew the two of you were going to get married. I knew you loved her."

"Sure you did," Allen laughed.

"I did, too," Buckler said.

"So did I," Mary added.

"What are you talking about?" Allen asked. "You didn't know anything."

"I knew you loved me," Mary assured him. "You just needed a little push."

Allen stared at her with a quizzical expression that slowly became suspicious.

"Leaving the door open when I took a shower, allowing the sheets to fall off of me in bed," she said provocatively. "Making you help me button my shirt and pants."

"You did that stuff on purpose?"

Mary smiled seductively.

"How long have you been in love with me?" Allen asked, amazed by Mary's scheme.

"From the beginning."

"Beginning?" Allen laughed. "Fifth grade."

"Yup."

Kelsy laughed. "It's about time you came around."

Chapter 48

Washington, D.C.

M ary parked across the street and promised herself this was the last time she was going on surveillance on this case. The sky darkened with rain clouds and within minutes the heavy raindrops thumped the exterior of the car. She turned on the windshield wipers and took a look through her binoculars at the parking garage where the husband was presumed to be. "I'm here, where are you, Mr. Pig?" Time passed slowly; the rhythm of the windshield wipers and the cool taping of the raindrops eased her mind as she slipped into a daydream, into her past.

Her partner was taking photographs through the warehouse window. "He's giving him the black briefcase," Ed whispered into his transmitter.

"Shut up and get some good shots of the exchange," Mary transmitted back.

"Your transmitter sounds like crap," Ed said. "You're breaking up."

"It's the damn rain," she said. "The equipment got wet."

A man with a shotgun appeared suddenly a few yards away from Ed.

A clap of thunder returned her to the present. She blinked her eyes and refocused on a black BMW pulling into the parking garage. Stepping out of the car was a figure of a man holding an umbrella and a small package wrapped with pretty birthday paper. It was Mr. Pig. "You don't need an umbrella in a garage, dummy." She felt a surge of optimism; a birthday present could mean an intimate transaction. Maybe this was the day there was actually another woman.

A second car pulled into the parking garage; the silver Mercedes parked headlights to headlights with the black BMW. A short, foreign man with Asian features, wearing a navy blue suit, stepped out of the silver car with a black leather briefcase. Mr. Pig removed his tinted glasses after he shook hands with the foreign man, and they exchanged what appeared to be pleasantries, but in no way were they friendly in a sexual manner. This was purely a business relationship.

Sorry, Ms. Jones, she thought. This was just more photographs and additional evidence against an infidelity case. This man was not having an affair and he wasn't gay, but Mary had a hunch there was something illegal happening. Now the question was, did she pursue him or just drop the whole thing and move on with her life?

What the hell are you up to Mr. Pig? Her sense of justice and curiosity was too strong to walk away. The black briefcase triggered a memory from the night her partner was killed, but she chased the thought out of her head and focused the camera on the two men. They appeared unworried about their surroundings when they exchanged the briefcase and package. She zoomed in with her camera, firing shots, first of the subjects making the exchange, then close-ups of their faces. "Happy Birthday to whoever you are," she sang.

She captured Mr. Pig's eyes looking directly at her, but there was no chance of her being spotted; she was too far away from him to be seen by the naked eye. It was the first picture of him without his tinted glasses on, and it was the photo that was going to turn her world upside down. *His eyes, something about his eyes,* she thought. A rumble of thunder rolled across the sky above her and an icy shiver crawled down her spine. It was the same man that had murdered her partner. It couldn't be, but it was. Her head was spinning. He had put on weight and his face was covered by a beard and a thick mustache. He also had changed the color of his hair to silver-gray, but the eyes were the same; eyes that she had never forgotten.

The exchange was made; the foreign man received the package and Mr. Pig acquired the black briefcase and they withdraw to their vehicles. The two cars left the parking garage, separating a block away. Mary stayed with the black BMW. She grabbed her cell phone. "Kelsy, it's Mary. I need your help."

"Sure. What do you need?"

"I found Ed's killer." There was dead silence. "Kelsy, did you hear me?"

"Yeah," she finally uttered. "What are you going to do?"

"Get hold of Amps. He'll know what to do." Mary hung up.

The phone dropped loosely by Kelsy's side. She was stunned by Mary's call.

"What?" Allen asked. "Kelsy, what's wrong?"

"It's Mary."

"What's going on?" Allen grabbed her arm. "Is Mary all right?"

"Mary said she's following the man who murdered her partner, Ed Murphy."

"Oh Christ," Sam said, grabbing his jacket.

"Come on," Allen said, heading for the door. "We have to find her."

Mary followed the black BMW to Reagan National Airport. Her cell phone rang.

"Mary, it's Kelsy. Where are you?"

"RNA."

"We're on our way. Wait for us."

The phone was already dead.

Allen sat in the back seat praying they'd make it in time. He had been dreading this day. The day his best friend, the woman he loved, would commit cold-blooded murder in the name of vengeance.

Kelsy shook her head, sensing this situation was going to quickly get bad.

Sam was on the phone trying to get friends from the CIA on the scene.

Mary's phone rang again. "Hello."

"Ms. Jopuez, it's Ms. Jones. Is there anything new on my husband?"

The phone call caught Mary off guard, but she rebounded quickly. "Yes, there is," she said dryly. "I've discovered your husband isn't cheating on you. You have nothing to worry about. Isn't that great?"

"Ms. Jopuez, are you all right? You sound upset."

"I'm fine." She continued to follow the BMW. *What the hell is this woman's connection to Ed's murderer?*

"Is there something wrong with the investigation?"

"Before I hang up on you," Mary said coldly, "would you like to tell me who you really are and why you led me to this man?"

There wasn't a sound on either end of the line for a long moment. "Isn't that what you wanted?" the woman asked now, sounding younger.

Mary was at a total loss. "Who are you? Why are you doing this?"

The woman promised to explain everything. She told Mary to meet her at a restaurant named Carroll's Creek in Annapolis at two o'clock.

Mary's thoughts were turning over in her head too fast to make sense of them, but the sight of the black BMW parking made them all vanish instantly, except for one, revenge. She called Kelsy. "He's parked." She gave her the section of the parking lot before hanging up.

Allen continued to pray for her protection; he also prayed for God to protect her from herself.

Sam checked his weapon. "We need to hurry."

"Two minutes and we're there," Kelsy announced, sliding a round into the chamber of her 9mm.

"What's this all about?" Buckler asked from the back seat.

Allen explained what happened to Mary's partner and the ordeal that followed.

"I'd hate to be that guy," Buckler mumbled. "He's a dead man."

That's what Allen and Kelsy were afraid of.

Mary pulled directly behind the car, trapping him in the parking space. Mr. Pig was too occupied with organizing his papers in his briefcase to notice Mary approaching his car with her weapon drawn. He opened the car door and stepped out, only to find himself staring down the barrel of a gun.

"I must say, you are the prettiest and best dressed thief I've had the pleasure of being robbed by," Mr. Pig said with an undaunted smile.

Mary stared into his eyes with a burning hatred. There was no doubt in her mind that this man murdered her partner, and that he was going to die today.

"My wallet is in the right inside pocket of my coat," he offered.

"I don't want your money."

"Did I cut you off or something?" he asked with a puzzled expression. "You know they have classes for road rage."

Mary pulled the hammer back on the gun. She could end the nightmares and avenge her partner here and now.

"Please, tell me what this is about," he said with a pleading innocence. "It must be a misunderstanding."

"You don't remember me?" The words left her mouth like gravel grinding together.

"No." The man's hands moved closer to his body. "Should I?"

"I suggest very strongly that you keep your hands away from your body," she warned. "Turn around and put your hands on the roof. She pulled his weapon from the holster and dropped it to the ground.

"Oh, man. That's my favorite gun."

Mary spitefully kicked the gun across the parking lot. She searched the rest of his body for weapons.

"I'm enjoying this," he said in a sexually suggestive tone. "You seem to be enjoying it also."

Mary struck him in the back of the head with her fist. "Shut up!" She pulled his wallet out of his coat.

"I like it rough." He turned around; his mind searched for ways to stall her until help arrived. He activated a device on his watch that sent a distress signal to his associates. The device used similar technologies found in the cellular communications network, but this little gizmo was primarily for tracking his location, like Lojack for the body.

She examined the identification and shook her head in disgust. "Department of Defense," she said, throwing his wallet back at him.

Mr. Pig studied his wallet, and then looked at her suspiciously. "Hey, I'm twenty dollars short."

"Who do you really work for, Conway or whatever the hell your name is?"

"You're making a big mistake, young lady." Conway's tone and expression became grim.

"The only mistake I made was allowing you to live that night at the warehouse."

"Warehouse? What the hell are you taking about?"

She felt obligated to provide him with an explanation; he should know why she was about to kill him. "You were in a warehouse in Baltimore, selling government secrets, like today, but that night you murdered a man. That man was my—"

"Oh, my god." Conway's face suddenly appeared enlightened. "You're the partner." For the first time he was concerned for his life because the driving force fueling her actions was revenge, and that made her dangerous and unpredictable. He glanced at her crucifix around her neck and attempted to change the mood of the conversation. "Thou shall not kill, love thine enemy," he said. "Turn the other cheek, and forgiveness." He heard himself and he sounded hollow, but he needed to buy more time. "These are attributes you practice, are they not?"

She wasn't fooled by his feeble diversionary tactic. On the contrary, it kindled her anger further. "I'm feeling like Old Testament at the moment." She took aim between his eyes. "An eye for an eye." Her lust for revenge burned hot in her eyes, but something continued to conflict with the wrath within her. Deep down inside she believed she wasn't the one who was to judge and punish others, and that belief subconsciously had kept him alive up to this point.

For the first time, there was genuine fear in his eyes and Mary detected it like a predator preparing to pounce on its prey. She was unsettled and sickened by the rush she got from his fear and the feeling of pleasure at the thought of killing this man.

Conway believed he was a dead man if he didn't do something quickly. He needed a miracle.

A car skidded to a stop and Sam, Kelsy, Allen, and Buckler jumped out and raced over to Mary.

"Don't do it," Kelsy beseeched. "He isn't worth it. Don't throw your life away over this piece of crap."

"Mary," Allen said. "He'll go to jail for the rest of his life this time. You don't have to kill him."

"I like your friends," Conway said quietly.

A black Ford and an unmarked windowless van sped onto the scene. Men wearing black suits, dark sunglasses, and automatic weapons poured out of the vehicles. They were Shadow Government operatives, Conway's associates, or as he would say, the calvary.

Kelsy drew her weapon and extended her badge over her head, yelling "FBI!"

Mary's gun hadn't wavered an inch from Conway's head.

Seven S.G. operatives fanned out in a circular manner. Everyone was screaming, demanding weapons to be dropped. The situation was growing increasingly tense and dangerous. Eager faces stared and trigger fingers were getting anxious and nervous. Buckler couldn't believe he was back in a situation like this again. At least, there weren't tanks this time. Mary remained calm and focused on Conway.

One of the S.G. operatives, who appeared to be in charge, slipped his gun back into its holster, then extended his hands in the air, indicating to his men not to shoot, attempting to calm a potential bloodbath. He slowly and carefully stepped beside Mary. "We'll take it from here," he said evenly.

"Not this time," she said never taking her eyes off Conway.

"This is a national security issue." He removed his sunglasses and glared coldly, attempting to intimidate her. "Put him in the car," he ordered two of his men.

Two S.G. operatives flanked Conway, acting as if they were going to arrest him.

"If they touch him," she said, "He's dead." There was no bluffing in her voice.

"You can't kill an unarmed man."

"You're wrong." Her trigger finger moved slightly.

The S.G. confronting Mary drew his weapon and placed it against her head. "This ends now."

Conway's eyes widened. He wasn't pleased with the latest strategy.

Kelsy placed her gun against the back of the head of the S.G. holding a gun on Mary, which caused the two S.G. operatives flanking Conway to pull their automatic weapons around into an offensive position. Another S.G. man put a gun to Kelsy's head. Three other S.G. operatives were targeting Allen, Buckler, and Sam.

The situation had become a potential bloody game of dominoes. There was about to be a lot of dead bodies, and Mary was going to make certain Conway was one of them.

Suddenly, a half dozen unmarked cars filled the parking lot and twenty-four FBI agents armed for war stampede the situation. "FBI. Assistant Director Amps," he announced with a badge. "Ronald Conway is ours."

"He belongs to us," the S.G. in charge argued.

Amps walked over to him. "We need to have a talk, Tom."

The S.G. stepped off to the side after a brief stare-down contest with Amps.

"Don't shoot him yet," Amps said to Mary before walking off.

The two men had a private conversation. Amps and the S.G. operative Tom Randle were acquaintances. They trained together at Quantico and had kept a distant relationship with one another over the years, although they played for different teams. It was Randle who aided Amps in the extortion situation, making the fake evidence against him disappear. Randle's fellow S.G. operatives didn't know that—if they did he'd be a dead man.

Now, the two men couldn't ignore each other's positions. They had to make a decision on Conway. Amps understood, like all struggles between good and the not-so-good, there had to be give and take, but this time, he was going to do the taking. He gave Tom an ultimatum—sacrifice Conway or the entire organization took a hit.

An FBI helicopter flew overhead, an indication to Tom the FBI was serious this time. Forty-one people stood waiting, nearly all of them with guns, pointed at each other. It was a very peculiar sight, and pedestrians were beginning to take notice.

Amps walked over to Mary. "Agent Jopuez."

She remained locked on Conway.

"Mary," Amps said softly. "Here's the deal, there are two options. You shoot him and you go to jail, or he goes to jail for the rest of his natural life."

Conway now knew he had been betrayed. The S.G. operatives quickly disappeared into their vehicles and blended into the busy city traffic. Conway was raging on the inside. He was either dead or he was going to prison for the rest of his life; he resolved he would rather be dead.

"He won't walk away this time," Amps guaranteed.

Mary eventually lowered her weapon.

Two FBI agents moved in and escorted Conway to one of the cars.

Twenty feet away, Conway, with snake-like speed and the grace of a choreographed dancer, made a move. He extracted a sidearm from one of the agents escorting him. Conway's glare became tunnel vision. The only thing he saw was Mary's face, and everything else was a distorted wash of forms. He took aim, but before he was able to squeeze off a shot, a single bullet entered the center of his forehead. His shocked expression lingered as he fell back toward the ground. His head met the parking lot pavement with a crashing blow.

Mary lowered her unfired weapon and looked to her right, where Kelsy stood holding her gun, the barrel still oozing blue smoke.

*   *   *

Mary entered the restaurant and scanned the dining area, searching for someone to identify herself as Amy Jones with a gesture of some sort. She had a feeling Jones was a, no-show. Mary wouldn't have come if it weren't for Kelsy insisting and finally convincing her it would be a mistake not to know the connection between this woman and Conway; and of course, Mary's curiosity also helped compel her to come.

A twenty-something waiter approached Mary. "Excuse, me. Are you Ms. Jopuez?"

"Yes."

"Ms. Jones is seated at the corner table." The young waiter pointed to the opposite end of the room, where a young lady wearing sunglasses was sitting alone, staring out of the large windows at the Chesapeake Bay. Her long blond hair alienated her from the crowd like yellow straw in mud.

She maneuvered through the dining area and took a seat across from Ms. Jones.

"Thank you for coming," Ms. Jones said, removing her sunglasses, revealing striking blue eyes. They projected a deep sadness, yet there was something very familiar about them.

"I'm here simply out of curiosity." Mary made her coolness obvious. Her first impression of Ms. Jones was that she was young and beautiful, twenty years old maybe, but she appeared much older, and it wasn't simply the excess of make-up, something in her life had aged her quickly.

The sun broke out from behind the clouds, throwing a bright, shimmering display of light on the surface of the bay.

Ms. Jones squinted as the room brightened. "I'm sorry that I lied to you."

"I'm sure you had your reasons, Ms. Jones." There was something about this woman that made Mary feel unjust in her anger.

"Yes, I did," she said, dabbing her eyes with a napkin. "My name isn't Amy Jones as you probably know, and the man you've been following isn't my husband. My name is Kathleen Baker."

Mary stared blankly, still puzzled.

"But you would know me as . . ." She hesitated, then dropped the bomb. "Kathleen Murphy."

Boom. Direct hit.

Mary was awestruck. Nothing could have prepared her for what she just heard.

"My father was your partner," Kathleen said.

Kathleen's words rippled through her head like shock waves. The memories followed. After her partner, Ed Murphy was murdered, she remembered being seated in the dark, cool shadows of the living room with Ed's wife, grieving for hours in silence, praying for the nightmare to end. She remembered with the arrival of morning light, Ed's two children walking down the stairs looking for him, one five year old boy, and one fifteen year old girl.

Kathleen sipped her ice water and cleared her throat. "After the funeral my mother moved on with her life. She was a strong Christian woman. She dealt with his death with grace and with a peaceful acceptance. She was incredible," she added with a whisper of admiration. "My brother doesn't remember that night and very little of our father." Her tone had a hint of envy.

Mary stared across the table into her blue eyes, eyes of icy intensity, identical to her father's. The shell shock was slowly beginning to wear off.

Kathleen's expression hardened. "I was angry. I never had a sense of closure." There was pain in every word.

Closure. The word rang in Mary's head, a word she had carried with her like a ball and chain. She listened carefully, feeling commiseration swell in her soul for this young girl.

"In my heart I knew you felt as I did," Kathleen said, coldness settling in her eyes. "I remember the look on your face that morning. That man had to be dead or locked away with the murdering animals like himself if there was going to be any peace in our lives."

"How did you find him?" Mary managed to ask. "Why didn't you come directly to me?"

She hesitated for a very long time, contemplating her answer, almost as if she weren't going to respond. When she finally did speak, it was another bomb. "I'm married to his son."

Mary waved the waiter over to the table and ordered a drink. Her first thought was that this young woman schemed some sort of sinister plot to get close to her father's killer by marrying his son, only to destroy him. She was positive her face had betrayed her, finding it difficult to conceal her amazement. It could have been simply an incredible twist of fate that she fell in love with the young man, unaware of the bizarre connection. Or maybe it was divine intervention. Regardless how it happened, Mary was certain of one thing—justice was served.

Kathleen could sense Mary's doubt, another attribute she had from her father. "I met his son Kenny in college," she began. "We fell in love and got married after he graduated. Kenny's mother died a month ago from cancer. We were packing some of her belongings into boxes and storing them in the basement when I knocked over a carton with folders. One of the folders fell to the floor and a file marked 'confidential' with an FBI seal stamped on the cover spilled its contents out into view. I've seen hundreds of papers and files of this nature in my life. My father always left his work lying around in his office, but I was very surprised to find information like this in Kenny's house.

When I started to gather the papers to return them to the folder I realized that a number of the documents were marked 'Top Secret.' They were identical to the files I've seen in my father's office. I quickly discovered they were my father's because the notes were in his handwriting. The files consisted of photographs, passports, and numerous other documents on Kenny's father. The investigation file which my father and you built against him. As the weeks passed, I searched through his storage room and his personal files every opportunity I had, and uncovered the awful truth. The same man you and my father were investigating, the same man who murdered my father was my husband's father."

Mary listened to the astonishing story. She was not convinced Kathleen was telling the truth, but it really didn't matter.

Kathleen stared deeply into Mary's eyes. "I began to plot his murder that very moment." Her voice was malicious. "I decided I was going to kill him."

"What changed your mind?"

"I became pregnant."

"And that's when I came into the picture."

She nodded, taking a sip of her ice water.

"Does your husband know?"

A slight shake of her head, insinuating he didn't. "I hope he never has to."

If she's lucky, Mary thought, *he won't.*

"Kenny doesn't like his father. He treated his mother poorly. He was very abusive to the both of them. That is, whenever he was home. Kenny always said he could count on one hand the times they spent together, and that was two fingers too many."

Mary took a sip of her drink and looked out the window at the sailboats on the bay. Today, two women avenged a partner and father's death; justice prevailed in the most unusual fashion, but in the end, it still remained justice.

"I feel I can go on with my life now," Kathleen said, her eyes glassed over. She returned her sunglasses to hide the tears that were once full of sorrow, but were now filled with hope. "Thank you, Ms. Jopuez, thank you for giving me peace." She stood to leave.

"You never asked me what happened to Kenny's father."

"I don't have to. I see it in your eyes." She turned and walked away, never looking back.

Mary stared out at the glittering sparks of sunlight dancing on the dark blue surface of the bay, like brilliant stars in a watery universe. Slowly she began to feel the guilt lightened from her back, and somewhere deep in her soul a settling feeling of closure started to cut through the cold, thick fog of pain like a resplendent sword of light. It turned out to be a beautiful day, the first one she had really noticed in a very long time. A smile crossed her lips, barely noticeable, but still a smile. Two souls on earth could now rest in peace; and one in heaven.

Chapter 49

Sierra Madre Occidental, Mexico

Only a few days ago Derrick was sleeping and eating in the finest hotels and restaurants in Mexico, but this morning he woke up in the northeastern part of the Sierra Madre Occidental, Mexico's wildest and most rugged mountain range, nearly nine hundred miles long. The magnificent mountain range unraveled in a succession of pale mesas and canyons through eight Mexican states and territories with at least half-a-dozen Indian cultures. The landscape varied from dry and rough terrain to lush and forested Mesoamerican territories. There were miles of austere desert, and mountains that peaked over eleven thousand feet. A vast contrast from his diplomatic carpeted excursion of the country three days earlier.

Surprisingly, it took little time for him to gain the strength to stand and leave the darkness of the hut, and as the blue morning sky grew warm and brighter, his confidence in his health increased. He observed the Indian settlement and the daily rituals of the inhabitants. He watched the Indian women wash clothing on stones and prepare meals in fire blackened pots, while children fed their mules flint corn and brushed their backs with pine cones. When Derrick left the hut it appeared he stepped back into the early stages of human history. These were ancient people of ancient times, unblemished by the modern world, pure as nature itself. They lived off the land and the land seemed to live for them. The fields they farmed gave freely and in turn they nurtured the fields with care and devotion.

The outside world called Derrick's hosts the Tarahumara Indians. They called themselves Raramuri, or foot runners, also known as ultra-marathoners. The settlement was located in the remote forested canyon in the Chihuahua region, the northern part of the Sierra Madre Occidental. They dressed as if they shopped at a southwestern Good Will store. They wore wool or cotton flannel and denim garments, with the exception of the children, who mostly dressed in beautiful and colorful clothing. The majority of the Indians had coal black hair, sun beaten brown skin and strong Indian features. The elderly had ghostly gray hair, leather-like skin, and deep, brown eyes that looked like pools of perpetual wisdom, which they freely shared at the asking.

It quickly became apparent he wasn't the first English speaking individual to be a guest in their humble village. The use of English was the obvious reason to believe others had lived with the natives, but the strongest evidence was when he witnessed a ceremony that exhibited very familiar religious practices. The people of the settlement were involved in a religious festival of sorts, in which they practiced a hybrid faith mixing Roman Catholicism with the worship of the sun, lakes, and stars. Derrick later discovered that a group of missionaries stayed for a year and taught them the New and Old Testament doctrine and the practices of Catholicism. It was a fascinating sight to behold, watching the ancient religion of the modern world merge and manifest itself in the ancient Indian culture.

He spent the morning speaking to two men who entered the hut to check his condition. They explained, surprisingly well in perfect English, that he had been in a plane crash and eventually was discovered at the river's bank by one of their own who was fetching water. He was brought to the village, where his wounds were dressed and cared for, using the healing herbs and botanicals of the region. They all agreed that he was very lucky to survive the crash and his injuries. They sent a young man from the village to the crash site to bring back help. He hoped to remember who he was by the time the rescue party arrived.

*   *   *

Early afternoon gradually became evening and Derrick started to fear his memory wasn't going to return. But to his amazement, his body was beginning to feel stronger as he sat under a tree in the shade, resting and watching children kick a wooden ball across the dirt road. The scene triggered a memory of a little girl playing soccer in a yard with a woman, the child and the woman seemed familiar and important to him. He stared down at the wedding band around his finger. *Yes, they must be very important*, he thought. The children stop playing and looked up at the pine tree ridgeline of the mountain. A group of men following a young Indian man was making its way down the rocky path. Some of the men were dressed in black military fatigues. They stood out compared to the others, who were obviously rescue personnel carrying medical and transmitting equipment. As the group neared, the children ran off to their homes, abandoning the game, leaving the ball in the middle of the road. Derrick stood and looked anxiously at the group of men cautiously maneuvering down the jagged slope. The notion of not knowing who he was burdened him again, but possibly these men would be able to help him remember something, anything, and with that in mind, there was a seed of optimism.

The group of men and the Indian guide reached the base of the mountain. Once they reached the level ground of the canyon, their pace increased. From Derrick's view, these men appeared anxious and worried, but he wasn't sure what to make of them. The rescue and medical persons seemed ordinary, but the men in black fatigues appeared out of place in a normal crash and rescue situation. They weren't firefighters or medical unit personnel, and they didn't look like any rescue team Derrick had ever seen before.

The two men who'd spent the day with Derrick joined him under the tree. The Indian guide pointed him out to the group of men from fifty yards away. They rushed across the rocks toward the village, heading directly toward him, like a herd of wild animals that had no intention of stopping once they've reached him. Their faces were a mixture of fear, elation, and relief. He was immediately surrounded and the Indian men were pushed to the outer edge of the human circle. It was very obvious to him that the medical, rescue, and soldier-like persons were intensely interested in his condition, which was confusing and overwhelming to him. But the situation quickly became worse when he heard the concerned question that sent his thoughts in a whirlwind.

"Are you all right, Mr. President?"

*   *   *

The White House

There was a knock at the Oval Office door. *Female,* Walter thought of the knock. He could always tell a woman's knock from a man's, simply from the sound and number of raps. Women tended to knock with a single knuckle in a soft, rapid four-count tap that sounded like tat, tat, tat, tat, that asked, "May I enter?" But men, on the other hand, preferred to use a three count bang, employing all their knuckles if possible, giving them a more aggressive and demanding hammering sound on the door that declared, "OPEN THE DOOR."

He summoned the White House staff aide to enter. A young woman stepped into the office; he was right again. He hadn't missed one yet. She reported the Situation Room had a message for him and handed a double folded sheet of paper over the desk. The first sentence of the message jerked his heartbeat out of rhythm.

His eyes peeled away from the sheet of paper. "Did you read this?"

"No, sir."

"Who gave you this?"

"General Blake."

Blake was sympathetic toward his military actions. "Do you know who the General received it from?"

The staff aid shook her head.

He dismissed her, sank into the leather chair, and read the paper again, hoping the message had miraculously changed, but it hadn't. He read the single line message again. "The President is alive."

*   *   *

Special reports interrupted television programs across the world, with a news flash stating that a passenger from Air Force One had been recovered alive. The information was unclear as to who it was, but everyone was speculating it was President Moore. Many international governments were anxious for the latest news, hoping Derrick was alive and the madness coming from the White House would end.

A newsman stood out in front of the White House with a microphone and spoke into the camera. "At this moment we still are unable to confirm the latest on the identity of the man rescued today. White House officials continue to deny the rumors of President Moore's recovery."

Chapter 50

K elsy inched along Pennsylvania Avenue. Sam had his eyes closed, attempting to get a little sleep before they reached Greg's church.

"What the hell is going on?" Sam asked, tired of the stop and go traffic.

"It looks like a demonstration of some kind," she said. "A protest, I think."

Sam brought his seat up from its reclined position, just in time to catch a glimpse of the twenty-five or more demonstrators across from the White House near Lafayette Square. "Stop the car," he suddenly demanded.

"What?" Kelsy asked, startled by his abrupt outburst. "Here?"

He had his door open before Kelsy could bring the car to a complete stop.

"What are you doing?" she asked. "Where are you going?"

He approached two kids, about twelve, playing street music. One of them was rhythmically beating a five-gallon bucket like a drum. "I'll give you twenty bucks for your bucket," he offered, the twenty-dollar bill already out.

"Sure, man," the kid said without hesitation.

The two kids and a group of tourists watched the big man cross the street toward a small corner diner with bucket in hand. He filled the bucket with water from the diner's sink.

"What are you doing?" the Greek owner asked.

"Emergency, I need the water."

The owner and a few of his customers followed him out of the diner, curious to see what the emergency was.

"What are you doing?" Kelsy asked. "Where are you going with that bucket?"

Sam remained focused. Most people would struggle simply lifting a five-gallon bucket of water, but he marched down the sidewalk with ease.

"I'm going to get a parking ticket," Kelsy complained.

He headed directly toward the group of demonstrators, who were in the process of burning an American flag. The one protester holding the flag was too preoccupied with keeping the flag burning to notice Sam approaching from across the street. The other protesters were too busy celebrating and chanting anti-government babble to notice him.

By the time the holder of the burning flag realized what had happened, he had five gallons of water on him.

The two kids whistled approvingly; the tourists erupted with a thunderous applause, the diner owner and his customers cheered wildly, and as many as twenty others applauded Sam. Kelsy stood in disbelief.

Sam ripped the burned and drenched flag out of the protester's hands and walked away.

"Hey," the protester yelled furiously. "That's my flag."

Sam turned slowly, the smoldering anger still in his eyes. "Come and get it," he said like the grim reaper.

Fifteen more demonstrators gathered behind the soaked protester, also demanding the return of the flag. The mob stepped closer to Sam, preparing to reclaim the burnt flag physically, but they stopped, as if they all had a change of heart at the same time.

The wet protester nodded his head irately at Sam. "Keep the damn thing," he said, turning to leave.

He watched the demonstrators walk away, some still yelling obscenities at him; others gave him parting dirty looks. When he turned to leave, he discovered the reason the demonstrators left without the flag. Standing behind him were the two boys, the diner owner and his customers, and over twenty other patriotic people, insisting Sam keep the flag. He received handshakes, pats on the back, and applause from the crowd.

"What was that about?" Kelsy asked, getting behind the wheel.

He sat in the car with the wet and burnt American flag in his lap. "I killed for this flag," he said, the distant pain returning to his voice. "I watched people die for this flag."

"Didn't they have the right to burn the flag?" Kelsy reminded him. "Isn't that what it's about? Freedom. That's why we live here, freedom of speech. They were protesting the government. It was an anti-government statement. That's their right as Americans."

Sam looked down at the smears of black on his hands. "If they want to protest against the government they need to smash little souvenirs of the White House or U.S. Capitol building instead of burning the flag. Because as far as I'm concerned, burning the flag is not an anti-government statement, it's an anti-American statement. The flag doesn't represent the government, it represents America, and if you burn the flag you're protesting against America."

"But isn't it an American's right to protest against America?"

"There are flights leaving the country, every hour of every day," Sam said, grinning. His muscles were starting to relax, and so was his attitude. "What better way to protest the country, than by leaving?"

*   *   *

"Professor O," Art yelled, climbing down the stairs to the cellar.

"Here, Mr. Hanson," Greg answered from behind his desk.

"We got him on the run," Art said, waving a newspaper. He read the headline aloud. "'Secretary General Jordan Iblis Connected to Criminal Activity.' 'Secretary General of UN Disappears.' It looks like we put a kink in his plan."

"It appears that way," Greg said. "But as long as Walter Web is in power, the hostage situation is a potential catastrophe waiting to happen. I will feel better when they remove *him* from the White House."

"I don't get it; they've got all the evidence connecting Web and Iblis. He should be gone."

"Hopefully, they have removed him and simply haven't made it public."

Art noticed the professor appeared a little down. "What's wrong, professor? You should be partying."

Greg turned the newspaper on his desk around. The small headline at the bottom of the paper read, "Mysterious Red Algae Appears Around The World."

"You know me, professor," Art said. "You're going to have to explain it to me."

"It's another sign."

"I knew you were going to say that."

"The article says the red algae is spreading uncontrollably throughout the Persian Gulf toward the Indian Ocean. The identical thing is also occurring in the Adriatic Sea off the coast of Italy. The red algae has become so widespread and dense it's causing commercial shipping industries costly delays, and worse, the marine life is dying at a frightening pace." Greg turned the pages in the Bible to Revelation. He pointed to a passage and read. "Then the second angel poured out his bowl on the sea, and it became blood as of a dead man; and every living creature in the sea died."

Art stared at the photographs in the newspaper. The boats and the thousands of dead marine animals appeared to be floating in blood. "Could you be wrong?"

"Perhaps," Greg said. "I've been mistaken before. This sign is oddly out of order in comparison to the Bible's arrangement of things to come, but God has put signs in motion out of order before, only to have them align later."

"What do you mean?"

"God may begin this sign, but it won't be fulfilled until the other signs before it are complete."

"Hello, Professor Orfordis," Kelsy shouted. "Are you down here?"

"Yes, in here."

"Hey, Art," Kelsy said warmly.

"Looks like you guys got Jordan on the run," Sam said. "The media crucified him. When they catch him, he's going to jail for a very long time."

"Jordan won't go to prison," Greg stated. "He'll simply disappear and resurface elsewhere."

"Oh right," Sam grinned. "You can't put the devil behind bars."

Art could understand Sam's cynical attitude toward Greg and his beliefs. He was just like him only a few weeks ago.

"With Jordan exposed," Kelsy asked, "does that mean you stopped the Demonic Trinity from forming?"

"I believe so," Greg answered. "But many details remain."

Art smiled. "We don't have to worry about Carbon anymore," he added confidently. "I heard he sold Gold Calf Enterprises and donated all the money to charity. I would've loved to see Jordan's face when heard that bit of news."

"Did you have something to do with that?" Kelsy asked Greg.

"Mr. Hanson was responsible for Sean Carbon's enlightenment."

"I was merely a messenger," Art grinned.

"What did you do?" Sam joked. "Walk up to him and say, excuse me Mr. Carbon, did you know you're the False Prophet in the Demonic Trinity, which happens to be a sinister plot to corrupt the whole world?"

Art laughed. "How did you know?"

Sam smiled. "Come on, you told him that?"

"The truth is," Art said, we sat down one afternoon with cigars and cognac and had a long talk about his silent partner's extra activities."

"What about the Antichrist? Do you know who he is?" Kelsy asked, sounding like she would rather not hear the answer.

Greg hesitated. He also appeared unwilling to hear himself say the answer aloud.

His poignant pause confirmed her fears. He must believe Allen Pyrit was the Antichrist.

Greg was ninety-nine percent positive that Allen was the Antichrist, but it was the other one percent that kept him from answering directly. "The Antichrist is someone who leads millions of the faithful away from Christendom," he explained, deciding to answer in a roundabout way. "Someone who suggests Jesus was simply a good teacher or one of the many prophets of history. Someone who removes Christ as the centerpiece of the faith."

"That's only true if you're a Christian. The Antichrist is solely a Christian figure," Sam pointed out.

"That is true, Mr. Dent," Greg agreed. "The Antichrist is a Christian belief. But other faiths of the world are being deceived and led astray, and those religions may not identify the deceiver as the Antichrist, but be assured, he exists in the form of Beliar, Mastema, Semyaz, Rahab, the Adversary, or Beelzebub; all under a different name, but all with the same purpose. Separate humanity from God."

"I don't get it, Sam said. "Someone like Allen Pyrit brings almost a billion people together in the name of God, but in the Christian world he's been branded the Antichrist. Is Allen Pyrit the Antichrist?"

Kelsy shifted uncomfortably.

"He fits the profile," Art said.

"Yes he does," Greg agreed, looking apologetically at Kelsy. He knew Kelsy liked Allen and at one time she herself believed in his New Faith Order, forgetting her Christian roots. But sometime during her journey, she rediscovered her true faith, which only opened her eyes to Allen's misguided teachings. Ironically, by helping Allen discover who he was physically, she discovered who he was spiritually. And it saddened her deeply.

"Could you be mistaken?" Kelsy asked.

Greg's eyes revealed the certainty of Allen's spiritual state. "He does possess freewill," indicating Allen did have a choice in the matter.

"Just like Carbon," Art's raspy voice added. "One day you're the False Prophet, and then one day you're not."

"Sometimes you feel like a nut," Sam mumbled. "Sometimes you don't."

"He, like everyone, has a choice," Greg said. "He needs to see himself for what he is."

"Well professor," Sam said. "We're going see Allen his afternoon. Would you like me to give him a message? Something like, Dear Mr. Allen Pyrit, you and your evangelic program are leading millions to hell. Sincerely yours, Professor Orfordis. P.S. You're the Antichrist in the Demonic Trinity."

"That pretty much covers it," Art grinned.

Greg stood. "Come here for a moment, Mr. Dent," he said, pulling a folder out from his desk. "Tell me, who is this person here in the photograph?"

Sam studied the picture. "Jordan Iblis, with black hair."

"That's correct," Greg said, moving his hand to expose the entire photo. "Notice who he's standing with?"

Sam chuckled. "Come on, professor. Are you trying to tell me Iblis is there with Hitler?"

"That's almost seventy years ago," Kelsy said.

"It's trick photography," Sam assured her.

"Look at this other photo," Greg said.

"I recognize Jordan," Sam said. "But who's he with?"

"A physicist named Robert Oppenheimer. The man that headed the Manhattan Project."

"The atom bomb guy?" Sam asked.

"The picture was taken in 1941," Greg said. "This other photo here was taken in 1999 with millionaire business man Charles Malefic, who, at the time, was running for president. Jordan called himself Luke DeMynn at that time."

Kelsy spread sixteen more photos across the desk, all of Jordan with significant figures throughout history, men who in one way or another influenced the future, and not in a positive way. Mao Zedong in China in 1949. Manuel Noriega in Panama in 1982, and Nixon in 1969. Mussolini in Italy in 1925. Libyan leader Gadhafi in 1968. And then, she saw a photograph that turned her stomach. An old faded black and white picture, but still sharp enough to see the faces clearly, taken in the 1860's by Mathew Brady. The picture appeared to be of seven actors posing on a theater stage. Jordan stood among the youthful actors, smiling with his arm around another actor, who Kelsy recognized immediately as John Wilkes Booth, the man who assassinated President Abraham Lincoln.

"The face is always the same," she said amazed by Jordan's appearance. "Sometimes he has facial hair, sometimes he has dark hair or long hair, but it's always the same face, the same eyes, calculating and devious eyes."

Sam examined the photos and was moved by the images, and for a split second he wondered to himself if it could possibly be true. But he convinced himself that the professor had mocked-up the pictures to use as props for his religious nonsense. "I'm sorry, professor," Sam said. "I can't believe one man, or whatever he is, goes throughout history spreading evil."

Greg closed the folder and placed it back inside the desk. "I can't make you believe; I can only show you the evidence."

"I believe Iblis is a corrupt man," Sam concurred. "Obviously, a highly intelligent and powerful corrupt man, but in no way can I believe he's the devil."

"I understand," Greg said, knowing if he believed Jordan was Satan, then he would have to believe in the existence of God. And therein lay the problem with so many, not wanting to believe in anything or anyone that may hold them accountable for their actions. Sam was God in his world and he'd rather not relinquish the position.

Greg handed Sam another file. "This is the document you dropped off," he said, changing the subject. "I interpreted the data from the old Greek and Latin to English."

"Anything new?" Kelsy asked.

"The document is a surveillance report," Greg explained. "From the 1950's. It appears our government was interested in a group of scientists in Cambridge, England, who were experimenting with crystallography."

"What is that?" Kelsy asked.

"X-ray diffraction," Greg answered. "It's when biological molecules are X-rayed. The process crystallizes the molecules and creates a complex pattern of its structure on a piece of photographic film. In 1952, a beautiful and brilliant young crystallographer by the name of Rosalind Franklin took an X-ray of a two-stranded molecule, which strongly resembled a double helix."

"DNA," Kelsy said.

"Back in the early fifties they called it deoxyribose nucleic acid," Greg explained. "They believed a group of molecules somewhere in the human structure held the key to the genetic code of life. Franklin's X-ray was the beginning of realizing the reality of that assumption."

"Scientists have been messing with DNA since the early fifties?" Art asked.

"Yes," Greg answered. "Strangely, after the discovery was announced in 1953, in a small journal called *Nature,* the talk of DNA stopped. It wasn't until 1959 a story surfaced about the research concerning genetics. The first human chromosome abnormality was identified, which later was discovered to be Down syndrome." He flipped a page on the document. "From there, the data records a few specific events. In 1970 researchers synthesize a gene from scratch. In 1972 scientists cut and splice genes to create the first molecules of recombinant DNA. In 1973 the first successful genetic engineering experiment was performed with an African clawed toad. In 1975 scientists met at the Asilomar conference center in California and called for guidelines regulating recombinant DNA research. In 1976 Genentech, a genetic engineering company became the first in the world. The years of 1977 and 78 scientists begin to separate and sequence DNA and cloned the gene for human insulin. In the 1980's they started transferring genes and introduced genetic engineered drugs, foods, and animals to the general public. If you have noticed, the sixties were very quiet. I believe the S.G. restricted any significant DNA research in those years. Of course, that didn't apply to themselves."

"I believe Allen was born in 1970," Kelsy said. "That's nearly twenty years of genetic engineering research before they successfully cloned a human."

"It looks like the S.G. was keeping tabs on the genetic scene," Art said. "It looks like they were always years ahead."

"Many years ahead," Greg added.

"Well," Kelsy said. "We'll just add it to the pile of evidence."

"Will you be able to bring charges against the people responsible for the conspiracy?" Greg asked.

"We don't know. It just keeps getting bigger and messier," Kelsy said. "It's like pulling a thread on a sweater; it just keeps unraveling. We're going to try to expose the organization and incriminate as many people as possible. We're hoping we get lucky and find the head man and some of the higher ranking names in the S.G."

"The evidence is good," Sam said. "But like Kelsy said, we need to find the main guy or guys."

"We know the S.G. experimented with human cloning and Allen appears to be a successful result," Kelsy explained. "But there were countless failures that the world won't take kindly to. We have evidence connecting them to the burglary and the stolen artifact. The S.G. also seems to be responsible for another dozen high profile international conspiracies. Once the world discovers the S.G.'s existence and their actions, it will be easier to expose them and hold them accountable. And it will be much easier if there's a name and a face connected to the crimes."

"Did you guys know Jordan Iblis was trying to take over the S.G.?" Art asked.

"We knew there was a civil war within the S.G.," Kelsy said.

"That's the only thing that makes sense," Sam said. "The operatives we've encountered have been sloppy, stupid, and desperate."

"It became obvious the new S.G. was attempting to take over," Kelsy said.

"With Jordan out of the picture," Art said, looks like it's business as usual for the old S.G."

"That's what we're trying to stop," Kelsy said.

"Hey professor, don't be surprised if you get a 'thank you' card from the old S.G.," Sam said. "For putting the squeeze on Iblis."

Greg grinned, hiding his concern. Jordan Iblis may be gone, but Satan lived on, and he was out there lurking in the hearts of men.

Sam and Art had started up the stairs, but Kelsy lingered back for a moment. "Professor, I've been wondering about something. Who is that man in the photo with you?"

Greg stood and pulled the picture from the wall. "His name is James Rood."

"I thought so," she said. "The homicide detective who saved President Moore's life."

"Yes," Greg said, returning the picture to the wall.

"He reminds me of someone I know," she said, thinking about James' warm brown eyes. "This guy who has been helping me throughout the entire Allen ordeal happens to call himself James."

"I'm certain it's not the same man," Greg assured her. "I went to his funeral."

"Right, of course," Kelsy said, turning to leave. She started climbing the stairs. "Hey, professor," she called back. "What was your friend's favorite music?"

Greg thought for a moment and then grinned. James loved classical, particularly Mozart. He would argue and try to convince Greg until he was blue in the face that Mozart was the greatest composer. "Classical," he answered.

"The James I know," she said, loves Mozart." She went up the steps. "I'll see you around, professor."

Greg spun his chair to face the wall. He stared at the photo curiously. He never did see James' body after the shooting. By the time Greg had reached the hospital, the doctors had pronounced him dead. Under the circumstances of his death, an investigation immediately proceeded, prohibiting all visitors. The following days were filled with red tape. The funeral was closed casket. Could he be alive?

Chapter 51

Crownsville, Maryland

The taxi pulled away from the curb, leaving Allen, Mary, and Buckler standing on a blacktop driveway in front of a fifteen-foot tall chain link fence with razor wire across the top.

Buckler looked at the fence curiously. "Are we at the right place?"

Mary's eyes followed the swirling razor wire along the top of the fence as far as they could. It was quite beautiful in the sun's light, glittering like silver garland on a Christmas tree. The scene reminded her more of a prison than a psychiatric hospital. "The fruit won't fall far from the basket here."

"Not without getting sliced and diced," Buckler added.

Ten minutes later Sam and Kelsy joined them at the front gate of the psychiatric institute.

"Where've you been?" Mary asked, impatiently. "You're late."

Sam kissed her on the top of her head. "You're so cute when you're upset."

"I'm about to get beautiful," she responded sharply.

"She's on time once in her life," Kelsy said. "Now she's Miss Punctuality."

"Where's your car?" Sam asked. "In the shop again?"

"It's cheaper to take a cab than pay for gas."

Kelsy could feel herself becoming uneasy around Allen. She wished she had the guts to confront him. Attempt to convince him to took a look at his teachings.

"What happened Al," Sam grinned. "Did your barber die?"

Allen's hair was longer than his usual short length style and his face had nearly a couple of weeks of growth on it. He hadn't cut his hair or gotten a shave since the assassinations in Florida. He subconsciously rubbed his beard and smiled. "It's my disguise."

"You got that *Jesus Christ, Superstar* look going on," Sam joked.

Kelsy found no humor in her uncle's comments, and she let him know with an elbow to the ribs.

They walked toward the gate.

"I heard you were in the CIA," Buckler said to Sam.

"That's right."

"Why did you leave, if you don't mind me asking?"

Sam stared at him. "Disability."

"Did you get shot or something?" Buckler asked, as if hoping for an exciting story.

"Carpal tunnel syndrome."

Buckler rolled his eyes. "All of you must be related."

After an hour of red tape in the administration offices, they made their way through security. A large gentleman with an entirely white uniform met them.

"Hello, I'm Chester, the head security officer," he said with a husky voice. "I'll be your tour guide for the day."

Chester was a very large man, about six-nine and easily over three hundred pounds, with skin as dark as coal. He made Sam look average and the rest of the group look like something out of Munchkinland. He led them down a number of white, unimpressive halls before reaching a quiet and isolated part of the building, just as white and boring as the previous sections.

"This is where we keep the harmless ones." Chester pulled a ring of keys that were attached to his waist by wire. He unlocked the large, metal door and took a peek through the small, wire-mesh window before opening it. The door opened to a wide and roomy space with four large skylights. The room, again, was painted white. "I don't think you're gonna get much outta Mr. Larson," Chester warned.

"Why is that?" Sam asked.

"He don't say much, and when he does, it's crazy stuff."

"How long has he been in here?" Allen asked.

"About ten years."

"What happened to him?"

Chester pulled the key out of the lock and the small metal device on his waist reeled the wire back in, leaving the keys dangling at his side. "His kids put him in here. They said he stopped going to work, stopped going out completely. He stopped talking, too, except for that crazy talk."

"Like what?"

"He would say he was doing the devil's work, and that he created the Antichrist," Chester said with a skeptical glance. "He says he's responsible for millions of souls going to hell."

"There seems to be a lot of that going around lately," Sam smirked.

Kelsy gave Sam a dirty look.

Mary rolled her eyes. "I can see this is going to be interesting."

"It should be fun," Sam grinned.

"Do you know what he means by that?" Allen asked.

"I don't got a clue." Chester shrugged. "He never really explains anything." He pointed across the auditorium-sized room to a man seated on a stool in front of an easel, alone in the corner. "That's him, painting."

Larson sat quietly, staring at a large canvas. He was positioned beneath one of the skylights in a way that appeared very surreal; the streaming sunlight from above gave the impression of an alien spacecraft preparing to transport him up in a beam of light.

Buckler looked around the room. "Cathedral ceiling, good light," he said like a man shopping for an apartment.

"Nice color," Sam added sarcastically.

Buckler grinned. "What, you don't like white on white on white?"

"All this white would drive me crazy," Sam mumbled.

"I heard Larson was a brilliant surgeon." Allen said.

"Was," Chester remarked.

The group crossed the floor, which stretched before them like a snow covered landscape.

"Good afternoon, Mr. Larson," Chester said joyfully. "You have visitors."

Larson continued to stare at the canvas on the easel.

"They would like to ask you a few questions."

Larson didn't acknowledge their presence.

Chester shrugged his shoulders. "Good luck." He turned to leave. "If you need anything or are ready to leave just wave at the camera." He pointed to a corner of the room. "If it gets weird, push this red button." He handed Mary a device the size of a beeper.

"Weird?" Kelsy asked. "What does that mean?"

Chester disappeared through the door.

"Maybe," Sam said. "Somebody might try to take our lunch money."

The five of them stood there watching a seventy-year-old man staring at a canvas.

"Well?" Mary asked, feeling anxious to get the interview over with.

"Mr. Larson," Kelsy asked politely. "Can you tell us anything about the burglary, artifact, or the experiments you were involved with?"

He stared blankly at the canvas.

Mary gave Kelsy a look and glanced at the camera, suggesting they leave.

Allen had maneuvered around so he could see what Larson was painting. His expression prompted the others to walk around to see what had intrigued him. They too, were captivated.

Sam whistled with amazement. "This guy can paint."

"That . . ." Buckler said. "That is . . . really good."

The painting was of a beautiful angel with wavy, golden hair dressed in white and silver armor, hovering weightlessly with his wings and arms extending outward invitingly. Below and to the right of the angel was a naked man kneeling in prayer over a crack in the earth. On the left of the canvas there was another nude man, who was reaching desperately toward the angel from turbulent waters. A golden metallic serpent was coiled around both of the men; the tail and the head of the serpent joined behind the angel's spread wings; the serpent united the three figures together in a triangular frame. In the center of the triangle was a burning wooden cross and the background was a stormy mass of clouds and lightning. The painting would be perfectly suitable in the Renaissance Age wing of any museum with its vivid and deep hues; the realistic and natural depiction of the figures could easily be mistaken for DaVinci or Michelangelo's work. Larson was a master surgeon in the sane part of his life, now it appeared he was a gifted and brilliant artist in his insane golden years.

"What do you think it means?" Buckler asked.

"It's definitely biblical," Kelsy remarked.

The four of them look at Allen, expecting an explanation as if he were the expert of the group on bizarre religious paintings.

Allen stared at the painting, finding it meaningful, somehow relating to the images. Larson's artwork had moved him, but he also felt uncomfortable. "It's the Demonic Trinity," he finally responded.

"The what?" Buckler asked.

"It's when Satan, the Antichrist, and the False Prophet come together," Kelsy explained.

"Escalating and intensifying the demise of the human race," Sam added, without realizing he sounded like a brainwashed zealot.

Mary and Buckler gave Kelsy and Sam an odd look.

"What?" Sam and Kelsy asked defensively.

"The two of you scare me sometimes," Mary said.

"Where did you get that from?" Buckler asked.

"The linguist who helped with the cryptic files also happens to be a theologian," Kelsy said. "He explained that Satan will position himself where he can attack the body, the flesh; and the Antichrist will be in position to attack the spirit, the soul; and the False Prophet will attack the mind, spreading the Antichrist's deceptions. Attacking humanity mentally, physically, and spiritually."

Allen started to ask Kelsy a question about the theologian, but suddenly, Larson mumbled something.

"Mr. Larson, did you say something?" Kelsy asked.

"We stole, murdered, and lied . . . we killed the Prime Minister's son," he said, his eyes never leaving the colorful canvas.

"Who exactly is 'we'?" Sam asked.

"Me . . . you . . ." Larson mumbled incoherently. "Us . . . them."

"Were the experiments human cloning?" Kelsy asked, wanting to confirm the evidence they had.

Larson's lips moved, but no sound was heard.

"He said, yes," Sam said.

"You were the surgeon."

"Yes," Larson answered clearly.

"What is the artifact?" Kelsy asked. "And why was it so important to the experiments?"

Larson pushed the painting off the easel to the floor, startling the occupants in the room, not to mention the rest of them.

"I think you upset him," Buckler said, moving behind Sam.

A large sketching pad took the place of the canvas on the easel. Larson started sketching with a piece of charcoal.

"Mr. Larson, the artifact. What was it and what did it have to do with the experiments?" Kelsy asked again.

Larson continued to sketch.

"I think it's time to go," Mary suggested.

"Wreath?" Sam guessed what Larson was drawing.

"What?" Mary asked.

"It's a wreath," he said again as if he were playing "Pictionary."

Larson continued to sketch, now drawing a head and a face. The person appeared to be wearing the wreath like a crown.

"Looks like an angel or a fairy," Buckler said.

Larson added a beard.

"It's a king," Kelsy guessed.

Larson lengthened the hair.

"King Arthur," Buckler guessed.

Larson altered the wreath into a spike and thorn-like texture. The unanticipated violent and dark appearance of the tormenting thorns silenced the group.

"A crown of thorns," Allen whispered. "That was the artifact."

"Jesus Christ," Buckler said.

"Exactly," Allen said.

"Hey, Mr. Archaeologist." Sam looked at Buckler. "Can something organic like a crown of thorns survive two thousand years in the ground?"

"Of course," he answered. "In the right circumstance anything can be preserved. Obviously, the artifact must have been protected from water, wind, the sun, and temperature changes. Any object exposed to any of these elements over the years would suffer a great deal of damage. The artifact was in a sarcophagus, sealed in a tomb, in a cave twenty feet below the surface of the desert. I believe those are good circumstances."

"It was a similar situation with the Dead Sea scrolls," Kelsy said.

"Yes, same concept," Buckler said, "but the crown of thorns was in a much better situation."

"What does the artifact have to do with the experiments?" Mary asked.

Larson drew two lines intertwined.

Sam grinned. "Snakes mating."

After Larson connected the two strands with prongs, the drawing appeared to be a twisted ladder, shaped like a corkscrew.

"DNA," Buckler said. His guess put an eerie silence in the air. "They had sweat, blood, and hair fibers from the crown."

"They have Jesus Christ's DNA?" Mary asked.

"Oh, my God," Kelsy blurted out. "They cloned Jesus Christ."

"Are you crazy?" Mary exclaimed.

"They stole the artifact, then extracted DNA from the hair and blood off the crown of thorns," Buckler explained. "Then, they used an embryo and implanted it into the woman known as Rosenberg, who in turn gave birth to the clone."

"And you knew nothing of this before now?" Mary asked Buckler.

"Mary," Buckler said sincerely. "I swear I didn't know where the DNA samples came from."

"If this is all true," Kelsy said amazed, "Then Allen is the clone of Jesus Christ."

They stared at Allen, finding it difficult to comprehend the fact that they may be looking at what Jesus truly looked like.

Larson sketched an identical image of the Christ figure. Now there were two, but he drew a circle around the second image with a line crossed through it, the universal sign for, "no" or "anti."

"What does that mean?" Buckler asked.

"She gave birth to the Antichrist," Allen said.

No one responded at first, but after a moment of silence, Kelsy finally spoke up. "They had the DNA of Jesus Christ, but the Antichrist was born instead. Why?"

Allen stared for a moment at the drawings. "Because you can't clone God."

"That's a fascinating yarn," Sam said cynically. "And it would make a great book, but we need physical proof of the experiments. We're here to prove the government was involved in unethical and pernicious practices, not religious myths. No one will believe Larson. We need him to tell us where to get physical evidence."

Allen put his arm around Mary. "So, how does it feel?" he asked, attempting to lighten the mood.

Mary looked at him confused. "How does what feel?"

Allen smiled. "To be married to the Antichrist."

"Very funny," she said.

"Let's go," Sam said. "We need to find Stainwick."

"Stainwick has all the answers within him," Larson whispered. They turned around.

"Stainwick is the key," Larson added quietly, staring at the pad.

"Where is he?" Kelsy asked.

"Not in heaven."

"Is he dead?"

"Everyone is afraid of Stainwick," Larson said.

"Why?"

"Because he has all the secrets." Larson turned his head and stared at them. "He has what they fear most . . . the truth."

Chapter 52

Washington, D.C.

Mary sat in front of her computer and waited for a fax from one of her former coworkers at the Bureau. Larson, from the loony bin, suggested Paul Stainwick was dead. If that were true, then there would be a death certificate, and if there was a death certificate, it would name the hospital at which he died. The hospital's morgue would have records indicating which funeral home he was released to, and the release forms and the funeral home records would have next of kin or friends who could be questioned.

The machine spat out the information at a painfully slow crawl. It belonged in the Smithsonian. She read the data as soon as it was visible; Stainwick died at Prince George's Hospital. She was out the door with fax in hand.

She left the hospital with the information she needed most, the name of the funeral home which had handled Stainwick's service. She called Kelsy to update her on the situation, and gave her the name of the relative who signed for Stainwick's body, hoping Kelsy would be able to locate and interview the relative.

Fifteen minutes later, Mary pulled up to the funeral home. Her cell phone rang. "Yeah."

"I talked to the relative," Kelsy said. "She's Stainwick's sister."

"Damn," Mary blurted out. "You already found her."

"Sure."

"It must be nice to have the most sophisticated equipment in the world at your beck and call."

"Actually," Kelsy said. "I found her in the phone book. I called her and interviewed her over the phone."

"Anything we can use?"

"I'll give you the highlights," Kelsy said. "She said her brother's will insisted his body be handled by his best friend, Joe Philips."

Mary glanced at the name of the funeral home on the front of the building. It read, "Philips' Funeral Home."

"Who owns Philips' Funeral Home," Kelsy finished saying. "Was there anything suspicious about Stainwick's death?"

"The report said he died of natural causes, if you consider a massive heart attack, natural. Why?"

"Stainwick also insisted that the burial be closed casket."

The thought of Stainwick faking his death entered Mary's head. An image of an old man living out his life on some tropical island sucking on banana daiquiris also crossed her mind. She quickly dismissed the thought for now.

"The rest is the usual," Kelsy said, "He was quiet, some friends, some enemies, you know the story."

"Thanks."

"Mary," she said. "I need to ask you something."

"What is it?" Mary could tell something was bothering her since the Larson interview.

"It's Allen," she said softly. "It's about . . ."

"I know Kell," Mary interrupted. "I think he's beginning to see. The Larson thing with the painting and the artifact may have been the last straw. He mentioned he wanted to quit and start over, get out of show business, go back to the way it was in the beginning."

Kelsy smiled. "That's good, right?"

"Yeah, his priorities were in order back then."

"I'll pray," Kelsy said, before hanging up.

Kelsy was a good friend, Mary thought, regardless of their opposite personalities. The two of them always seemed to understand and help one another. She thought about the conversation they just had and it brought a smile to her face. They had some sensitive and strange talks before, but this one was over-the-top. It wasn't everyday your best friend tried to help you rehabilitate your husband from being the Antichrist. Of course, Mary doesn't believe Allen's the Antichrist, or the Son of God or any other divinity, and hopefully Allen doesn't either.

Mary made a quick call to the funeral home. A woman politely answered the telephone. Mary asked for Philips, and the woman explained he was dealing with family members and was unable to come to the phone. She offered to take a message. Mary hung up and approached the funeral home. The last time she was in a funeral home was for her partner, but the memory didn't sting as badly now that his death had been avenged. There was a service being held in one of the parlors. Standing in the back of the room was a short, overweight, balding man with an unaffected expression on his face, which distinctly set him apart from the grieving relatives and friends of the deceased. She walked up to the man and stood next to him. He looked at her with a sympathetic smile, apparently taking her for one of the mourners.

Mary leaned in toward him. "Are you, Joe Philips?" she whispered.

"Yes," he whispered back.

"I need to ask you some questions."

"Are you with the Hartford party?" he asked, glancing at the grieving group seated in the room.

"No."

"Have you lost someone?" he asked with a caring tone.

"Yes, I have." She looked at the lifeless shell lying in the casket in the front of the room, encircled by hundreds of flowers. "His name is Paul Stainwick."

Philips' eyes widened. Mary's remark had left him speechless for a moment.

"Is this some kind of sick joke?" he asked, regaining his composure.

"You tell me. Is he still alive?" she asked, her voice far from a whisper.

"What are you talking about?" He looked at her as if the thought was simply absurd.

Friends and relatives of the deceased glanced over their shoulders at the two inconsiderate people in the back of the room. Philips walked away, heading toward an office. Mary followed.

"Where's Stainwick?" she demanded.

"Arlington Cemetery."

"Is that where he's supposed to be buried?"

"Why is everyone interested in Stainwick, suddenly?"

"Who's everyone?" She suddenly felt uneasy.

"Two men from the NSA."

"How do you know they were NSA?"

"They showed me I.D.s."

"What did you tell them?"

"Same thing I told you."

Mary walked over to the window and looked out at the cars parked in the street, wondering if she was being followed. She tried to remember when she last debugged her telephone and apartment. They must have gotten in again and placed a listening device somewhere in her home. Then it hit her, Kelsy's phone interview with Stainwick's sister. They must be only minutes ahead of her.

"I didn't see your badge." He looked at her like she was an impostor.

"Did anyone else come to see you?" she asked, now anxious to get the information.

"Yeah, a couple of other guys in suits."

She shook her head. "Who did they say they were?"

"FBI, and they were much more polite than you and the NSA thugs."

Mary turned around. "I guess you told them that Stainwick was buried at the cemetery."

"Sure. Now, who the hell are you?"

"None of your business."

"I'm going to call the police," he said, lifting the telephone.

"Put the phone down or I'll tell your customers that you remove their dear departed from the five thousand dollar coffin and bury them in a wooden box after the funeral," she threatened.

"Go right ahead, and I'll sue you."

Mary pulled out her weapon and pointed it at him without a trace of hesitation to shoot. "If you dial that phone, you'll be test driving one of your overpriced caskets." At this moment she had an 'I belong in a straitjacket glare in her eyes.'

Sensing her rancor, he replaced the phone. "Who are you?"

"Someone who hasn't had her morning coffee or a cigarette in days, who is sleep deprived, and has cramps."

"I can prove that he's dead," he said pulling a file out, eager to help.

Mary grabbed the file. "It'll take more than some paper work, Philips."

"We can dig him up if you like," he suggested sarcastically.

She gave him a look stating that suggestion was inevitable. After reading the file she threw it on the desk. "I got this crazy idea while I was driving over here. Would you like to hear it?"

"Sure," Philips said, sounding as if he didn't have a choice.

"Recently, I spoke to a man named, Howard Larson. Do you know him?"

"No."

Mary gave him a look that was asking the question again.

"No, I swear to God."

"Don't take the Lord's name in vain," she said putting her weapon away. "It's a bad habit." She was starting to sound more like Allen everyday. If she weren't attempting to be tough, she would have smiled. "Larson said that Stainwick had evidence. What do you know?"

"I have no idea what you're talking about."

Mary gave him the stare again.

"I don't know anything. I swear to . . ." He stopped. "I don't know anything."

She walked over to the window. "Larson said something that gave me an idea. He said Stainwick had the evidence within him," she said turning around. "I believe Stainwick wanted his best friend to handle the burial so he could perform one final request for him."

Philips appeared to be a little uncomfortable.

"I think the evidence is in Stainwick and you put it there during the embalming."

There was a flicker in Philips' eyes. "That's insane."

Bingo! I got you, she thought. That was exactly what he did. She leaned across the desk. "If you don't start telling me the truth,

I'm going to drag your short, round, butt up to Arlington, dig up
Stainwick, and when I find the evidence with him, you and your
buddy are going to be roommates."

Philips sat down at his desk. He put his hands on his head.
"He didn't tell me anything about his work and he certainly didn't
tell me what was on the microfilm."

"Microfilm. Did you tell the others about the microfilm?"

"The NSA guys."

"Great," she mumbled. "Is it in the casket or in his body?"

"In his body."

Her face cringed. "Of course, it would be. Where in his body?"

Philips smiled licentiously.

A mile away from the funeral home, Mary pulled her car over
and used a pay phone. "There are ten bombs placed throughout
the cemetery grounds," she said in a calm, dry manner before
hanging up and driving off.

She knew that the woman who had answered the phone would
call security, and Arlington Cemetery would immediately be
evacuated, grounds closed to the public for the remainder of the
day. Bomb units and other specialty forces would comb the area
all day, which was exactly what she planned on. Hopefully, the
media would get up there, too. Bad guys hated cameras. Maybe
her fake bomb threat would buy her time and discourage any
potential grave robbers.

Chapter 53

The White House

Walter sat alone, waiting to be removed from the Oval Office at any moment. The entire world had been told President Derrick Moore was alive. Alive, but in what kind of condition? Was he capable of performing the duties of office? Regardless of his current condition, Congress had been busy preparing Walter's dismissal since the accusations brought against Jordan hit the front pages. His fifteen minutes of fame were over, as they indicated in an earlier briefing. It didn't matter if the evidence linking him to Jordan was vague and insubstantial, they would remove him, and the President's health was irrelevant. Walter knew it was that brown-noser, Elliot Paste heading the lynch mob.

Paste was the president pro tem of the Senate, next in line for the Succession Act and undoubtedly had his eye on the presidency. Maybe Paste knew something already about Moore's condition. Maybe Moore was a vegetable. Walter hated Elliot Paste, always had. There they had sat, Paste and the other pencil necks, smug and arrogant with their little file of evidence in front of him. They'd waved it like a pink slip in his face, trying to intimidate him like some employee who feared for his job. Every wave of the file only fanned the flames of his growing spitefulness and hate for them. Now, he sat and waited, boiling with a single thought cooking in his mind.

He had six SEAL commandos on the roof of the warehouse prepared to defuse the hostage situation at his will. He felt for his cell phone in his pocket. One call and he could set forth . . . What? One of the largest catastrophes the world had ever seen. Or the boldest successful rescue mission conceived. Walter's cell phone rang, startling him. "Hello?"

"Hi, Walter," the voice said pleasantly.

"Jordan," Walter exclaimed, standing from behind his desk. "What happened? Where are you?"

"I'm fine," he assured him. "It appears I have some enemies."

"What do you mean?"

"Someone framed me," he said. "Someone didn't want the information concerning the hostages and the warheads released. Someone wants the terrorists to get their demands."

"What demands?" Walter asked, never hearing about a ransom.

"They want a terrorist leader released, twenty million dollars, and foremost, the United States government interests removed from all Arab nations. That's what this whole thing is about."

"What happened to the data you showed me?"

"It disappeared."

"My people have proof the hostages are alive and the warheads are hot," Walter said.

"All I know," Jordan said suspiciously. "Is there's something going on and the United States is getting the squeeze. I believe the UN and some of the more influential Arab nations are in bed together, and have some sort of hidden agenda."

"Why are you running?"

"I need time to prove they know the hostages are dead and the warheads are disarmed," Jordan explained. "Now, I also have to prove they have a hidden agenda and were afraid I was going to expose them."

"They said you framed Shelly and were responsible for the Air Force One crash."

"That's insane," Jordan said calmly. "I still love Shelly, and there's no way I could be responsible for bringing a plane down. Whoever framed me must have known I was talking to you and that I must have convinced you to rescue the hostages, which would expose and destroy their plan."

"Everyone is against me," Walter said, sounding defeated. "They plan to remove me, most likely by the end of the day."

"Walter, I have to go," he whispered. "I think they found me. Now you know why I'm running and what truly is going on. The United States is being deceived, misled into a treaty with terrorists. You're still the President of the United States, you can still . . ." The line went dead.

"Jordan," Walter said. "Jordan, are you there?"

No one answered. Nothing but silence, except for Jordan's last words lingering like a final encouragement; 'You're still the President of the United States.'

*　　*　　*

Tripoli, Libya: The airport

Two Libyan traffic control officers whispered to one another. They appeared somewhat puzzled and preferred to keep their conversation discreet.

A commanding officer approached and asked, "What is going on?"

One of the traffic control officers explained that an aircraft just requested clearance to land. The commander impatiently waited for the officer to elaborate. When the officer finally continued, he said the request came from Air Force One and the President of the United States, Derrick Moore.

The commander was calling his superior before the final words left the officer's mouth.

*　　*　　*

Air Force One

"Sir," an aide said to Derrick. "It appears someone forgot to tell traffic control we were coming."

"Can you imagine their faces when we came over the wire?" Derrick laughed. "Hi, this is Air Force One. We'll be landing at your airport in two minutes. See ya soon."

From the moment Derrick stepped onto the second Air Force One, the backup plane, everything began to evolve in a strange and unpredictable fashion. After the initial shock of discovering he was the President of the United States wore off, he started to get used to the position. An aide suggested he call his wife to assure her he was fine and would be back soon. He did exactly that and hoped she didn't suspect he had no idea who she was. He had no recollection of what she looked liked until he saw the framed photo of her and his child in the plane's version of the Oval Office minutes before he called.

After the call, he was briefed on the hostage situation during his medical examination, and that was where things started to get, well, out of character. He ordered the plane to fly directly to the warehouse in Libya. He convinced the entire security and military cabinets in a matter of minutes with an inspirational speech, insisting they must take control of the situation, and it must be done face-to-face with the terrorists. He inspired the crew and the staff with speeches of grand purpose and of the importance to seize the day.

The plane banked right and headed east over the Atlantic Ocean, where a KC-135 refueling aircraft joined Air Force One over the ocean for a midair refueling rendezvous.

Derrick read a dozen files attempting to become familiar with his own policies. He slowly discovered he didn't like some of his own opinions on political matters. When he returned to Washington he would see to it that some changes were made.

He couldn't believe how physically stronger he felt with every passing hour. But he felt something else . . . a blazing electricity in the center of his soul, fueling him with confidence. He had never felt this way before. The power was growing within him. He felt invincible. He continued to gain information on what had occurred in his personal past; things he should know and care about. He was told about his vice president's situation and the latest development with Jordan Iblis, but he couldn't recall either one. And it didn't concern him.

*   *   *

The Situation Room

Walter sat in a leather chair watching the thousands of military and media people gathered around the warehouse on the three large projection screens. It had become a circus. He wasn't the president anymore. Derrick was kind enough to call and relieve him of his presidential duties. The two secret service agents helped him out of the Oval Office and escorted him here, where he sat, surrounded by a dozen idiots whining about Derrick's little detour to Libya. Now, Walter had two things to smile about, Derrick in Libya and the six SEAL commandos. He may not be president, but he still had power. His hand tapped his cell phone gently. *One call away,* he thought.

*   *   *

Air Force One

In the infirmary, the two doctors discussed the results of Derrick's medical examination. Everything appeared to be healing properly and he seemed to be out of any immediate danger. But, while studying the test results, they found an odd and amazing discovery on the X-rays of his head wound. The doctors agreed the wound was so severe that a person could not survive after suffering such an injury. Matter of fact, the tissue surrounding the wound and the damaged brain matter indicated total shutdown of the body. In other words, it appeared Derrick was dead at some point after the crash. Not for long obviously, but dead all the same. Even if the victim of a wound of this nature lived, like in Derrick's case, there would be irreversible brain damage. What degree of damage was impossible to determine, but in no way should Derrick be walking and talking. He was a medical phenomenon. Since the doctors didn't believe in miracles, they had no explanation.

*   *   *

Tripoli, Libya

Derrick stepped off Air Force One with an entourage of staff members and secret service agents under the burning Libyan sun. The Libyan head of state, Moammar Gadhafi had started across the tarmac to meet him with his own group of men, but most of his men were heavily armed military soldiers.

President Gadhafi was still in shock from the phone call he received from the American president who supposedly had been in a horrible plane crash. He was taken aback to discover that Derrick, who apparently had survived the crash, had requested to meet him right away. It only became stranger when Derrick suggested they meet and negotiate with the terrorists personally as a sign of unity. It was only two weeks earlier, that he and the president were at odds, quarreling before a committee at the United Nations. Gadhafi found himself approaching a situation that had left him puzzled, curious, suspicious, and surprisingly, optimistic.

Derrick confidently crossed the airfield with his people. The hundreds of Libyan airport personnel and soldiers stood and watched with astonishment. The President of the United States was here and meeting with Gadhafi. The American President appeared intrepid and comfortable as if he just stepped onto the White House grounds.

Again, President Gadhafi was bewildered by Derrick's actions. He was approaching accompanied by a small army of armed men, but he was at the front of the group, in plain view, fearless, with no regard for his safety.

President Gadhafi placed his hands on the shoulders of the men leading him, and then parted them, taking the point.

Derrick extended his hand, smiled and spoke in Arabic. "Mr. President."

Gadhafi returned the smile. "Mr. President."

"Let us go and make peace," Derrick said.

He suggested they ride together in one limousine, no aides and no bodyguards. President Gadhafi was again surprised, but agreed, regardless of the protests from both security advisors.

In the limousine, Gadhafi divulged the information his intelligence agency had uncovered. He went on to explain how terrorists impersonated UN inspectors and smuggled a biological chemical weapon in from neighboring Tunisia. It was true, there were warheads in the warehouse and they were his, he admitted, but in no way was he going to use them for an offensive strike.

Derrick believed him and Gadhafi appreciated the trust.

The limousine and the convoy of twenty military and security vehicles pulled up to the restricted area surrounding the warehouse. When Derrick and President Gadhafi stepped out of the limo, the rumors were confirmed. President Moore was alive. He did survive the plane crash. And as for the other rumor, it was also true that the two leaders had joined to defuse the hostage situation. The international team of fifteen negotiators immediately took notice of the two men standing near the limo. They heard the leader of Libya and the United States were joining forces to resolve the crisis, but like so many others, they too didn't believe it until this very moment.

All fifteen members of the negotiation team encircled the two presidents and welcomed them the way one would welcome celebrities. Secretly, the negotiation team was beginning to crumble due to the extreme pressure and scrutiny of the world media. So, the emergence of Derrick and Gadhafi as chief negotiators was a relief, and to some on the team, an answered prayer.

Everyone, from the thousands of military personnel and the hundreds of the media people to the millions viewing the television screen were feeling an indescribable emotion. Witnessing two important world figures standing only a hundred yards from a potential biological catastrophe was uplifting. They were the only two humans in the restricted area not wearing some type of biological chemical protection gear. Watching two men, who were at odds with one another, come together and put aside their differences for the betterment of innocent citizens was moving. And every television programmer worth his or her salt was milking the event to its sappiest last drop.

Derrick saved his biggest shocker for last. He told the negotiation team he was going into the warehouse to discuss the terrorist's demands. After a quick and one-sided argument with his security advisor, he proceeded to convince the negotiation team that his life wasn't more important than the millions at risk. Plus, he could give them the one demand they wanted most, the United States out of Arabic nations. He was unable to convince President Gadhafi to stay behind, so the two men began the walk to the warehouse, and what a strange sight it was. Two men dressed in thousand dollar suits crossed the sun-beaten and barren land toward potential death.

While Derrick and Gadhafi made their way to the warehouse entrance, the head negotiator called the terrorist in charge and explained they were sending in two unarmed men to consider their demands. He also told the terrorist it was the President of the United States and the President of Libya that was coming. But the terrorist didn't believe him until he saw Derrick and Gadhafi twenty yards from the door. The other terrorists ran to the window and stared, astonished at the two men in suits.

"What do we do now?" one of the terrorists asked, as if Derrick and Gadhafi were an army of a thousand.

*   *   *

The White House was in total chaos. Staff aides were answering hundreds of phone calls from other world governments looking for explanations, Congressional members were flying in from all over the country for an emergency session, military and security staff were screaming at each other, playing the blame game. And in a quiet room somewhere in the White House, Derrick's wife prayed for her husband's safety. But one man was calm, and he had a grin. Walter slid his cell phone from his pocket, and dialed a number and quietly said, "*Veni, vidi, vici.*"

*   *   *

Tripoli, Libya

The SEAL team leader received the coded message from Walter. He positioned himself for entry to the warehouse. His men, armed and anxious, waited behind him. And then, he saw something that froze him in his tracks. He actually blinked his eyes to see if the image would go away. It didn't. He had been in the sun too long, he thought. The SEAL leader waved a member of his team to crouch beside him. "What do you see?" he whispered.

The second SEAL squinted his eyes and stared through the tiny opening in the retaining wall. Now, he also was struck with disbelief. He looked at his team leader and then looked back through the opening. "I see Derrick Moore, the President of the United States." He paused and stared at his team leader. "And Gadhafi."

The team was seconds from making an immeasurable mistake.

The SEAL leader ordered his men to hold. He returned to the listening device that was in the ventilation system. He would listen carefully and be ready to enter if the president was confronted with a threatening situation. The SEAL team had new orders: protect the president.

*   *   *

The terrorists finally decided to let Derrick and Gadhafi into the warehouse. After quickly searching them, they stepped away as if they had a contagious disease. They stared at the two well-dressed men almost fearfully, trying to decide if they really were the presidents or if it were some kind of trick.

The hostages also stared at Derrick and Gadhafi, amazed at their presence.

Derrick noted none of the hostages were dead, and surprisingly, they looked good. "Sorry it took so long to get here," he said apologetically to the hostages. "I had a little plane trouble." He returned his attention to the terrorists. "Do you understand English?"

The head terrorist answered "yes."

"You should read that piece of paper in your friend's hand," Derrick said.

The terrorist leader took the sheet of paper from his comrade, who had taken it out of Derrick's pocket when he searched him.

He read it. Derrick had drafted a resolution on the flight over. The
document met the demands of the terrorists concerning the
presence of the United States on Arab soil. it simply stated the
United States would remove all military and political influences
and interests from the countries in question. He could not hand
over the imprisoned leader they sought because he had no
jurisdiction over the matter, and he certainly didn't have twenty
million dollars for them. His signature was already on the document,
next to the embossed Presidential Seal.

After reading the document, the terrorists revealed their reason
and purpose for the hostage situation. The head terrorist started to
tell the story. They were from Tunisia, the small country neighboring
Libya's northwest border. The United States had established a
military base in their country, which brought a thousand power
drunk soldiers into their towns, who abused their women and
bullied their men, and imprisoned one of their religious leaders
for speaking out against them. The reason they took the warehouse
was to bring attention to the their country's situation, but someone
was distorting their demands to the media. Yes, they wanted the
United States out of their country, and yes they wanted money,
but not twenty million dollars. It was thirty five thousand dollars
for the damages caused to the town by the American soldiers. And
yes, they wanted the release of a leader, their leader who was in the
American military base's prison.

Derrick explained that he would order the release of the
religious leader immediately and remove the military base as soon
as possible. Jokingly, he asked if they would take a check for the
thirty five thousand dollars. Derrick also promised a new
relationship between Arab nations and the United States, and this
event would be the beginning of a new era of peace. He extended
his hand. "You have my word," he guaranteed, looking the young
Tunisian man in the eyes. "We can live together, or we can die
together."

The Tunisian man stared back into Derrick's eyes, feeling his
trust. He reached out and took hold of Derrick's hand. And just
like that, the hostage situation was over.

Chapter 54

Maryland

"Hello," Allen answered the phone.

"Hi, Mr. Pyrit," the voice said. "I'm—"

"Clint from Time," Allen interrupted.

"How did you know?"

"I'm physic," Allen said seriously.

"Really?" he asked.

Allen laughed. "No, I have caller I.D."

Clint laughed. "You got me."

"What can I do for you? Is it time for the exclusive?"

"Yes," Clint said. "But you might not want to do it."

"Why not?"

"All the healings were bogus," Clint explained. "Your producer and manager Robert Ward hired people to play the miraculously healed followers. But that's not the half of it. It gets real weird. Ward was being funded and supplied with people to pull his little masquerade off by an outside source. None other than the Secretary General of the United Nations, Jordan Iblis."

Allen was not surprised, nor was he upset. "Sounds like a great story."

"You're still going to do the story?"

"Sure," he said. "I owe you."

"There was one thing you should know about," Clint said. "The blind boy."

"What about him?"

"He was really blind."

After Allen got off the phone with Clint, the words, 'He was really blind' floated before his eyes like a ghost. Could it be true?

Did he truly heal a blind boy? Did it really matter? The thought triggered an avalanche of memories. When he was a young boy there had been the cardinal that suddenly sprang to life in the palms of his hands. There was the time he saved little Joey Brown from falling and the miracle of Frank's baby sister's recovery immediately after he prayed for it. The assassination attempt in Florida, how the gunman's weapon didn't fire for no apparent reason, and his ability to learn and speak numerous languages with incredible ease. A hundred memories flashed through his mind, all the little odd events he experienced. Things he simply became accustomed to or took for granted. But now he had the answer to the question he must have asked himself a million times since the age of six. Why were these things happening to me? Now he knew. The blood of God ran through his veins. He was different. He was special, just like his mother told him a million times before.

Also, Allen finally understood what the dreams of Captain Ahab and Moby Dick were about. In Melville's story, Captain Ahab was obsessed with destroying the white whale, which he believed embodied the evils of the world. When in reality, Ahab was the evil one, leading his crew to their deaths. Allen's obsession, or white whale, was the organized religions of the world, particularly the Christian churches, but like Captain Ahab, Allen was the problem, not the church. Tonight, he wouldn't dream he was walking the decks of the Pequod, consumed with obsession and insomnia, chasing evil, night after night. Tonight he would sail home, and not steer the ship and crew to a watery grave.

*   *   *

Tripoli, Libya

The newscaster on CNN watched the front doors of the warehouse along with the several billion viewers around the world. The doors of the warehouse opened and the President of the United States and the President of Libya walked out with the hostages following behind. The CNN news reporter quietly said, "Listen, you can hear the applause around the world."

*   *   *

Greg just watched two hours of CNN, all of it about President Derrick Moore and President Gadhafi. Over the past twelve hours Derrick had become a global hero. The world discovered the terrorists weren't terrorists, but a small group of men from Tunisia attempting to stop the juggernaut known as the United States from consuming their country.

The biological weapon in the warehouse was capable of killing a quarter of a million people. If the winds were blowing in the right direction, the death toll could have reached nearly a million. The Tunisians didn't have a clue what chemicals they had in their possession. Only that it was dangerous enough to give them the leverage and the respect they needed to negotiate with the world powers. When questioned about how they obtained the hazardous material and why they choose the Libyan warehouse, they explained a man approached them and suggested the hostage plot. He supplied the biological agent, the UN inspector uniforms, and transportation into the country. But he never said who he was and why he was helping them. But he did fit the description of the now former Secretary General of the UN, Jordan Iblis.

The CIA had already tracked the biological agent to Jordan Iblis through his chemical industry connections and linked him to the vaccine scam with the aid of Greg and Art's evidence. They were convinced Jordan was also behind the hostage situation, another crime to add to the growing list of charges against him.

Regardless of all of Jordan Iblis' careful conniving and manipulating, his plan for destruction had failed. Not because of Greg and Art, not because of the CIA's investigation, or the SEAL team leader aborting the rescue mission at the last minute, not even because of Derrick. The evil plot of Jordan's failed because the young Tunisian leader never wired the biological weapon to the warheads. He never intended to harm anyone, certainly not millions, so he decided to leave the hazardous material in its container. Jordan's biological weapon was designed to activate and explode when Walter's cellular signal reached the SEAL team leader's phone. When the bomb didn't activate, Jordan, who of course had a back-up plan, had the same signal and the SEAL team leader's number. He attempted to discharge the biological chemical agent himself, but unknown to him the device was never connected, leaving him helpless and a tad annoyed.

And so, instead of a global disaster, the newly united Arab nations and the United States had started the most aggressive peace talks ever attempted.

As Greg watched and listened to his friend Derrick speak to the world about the great strides that would occur in the future for world peace, he noticed something odd. His friend didn't sound like the same man, nor did he look like himself. Then, there was a statement made at the end of his speech that sent a warning in Greg's soul. Derrick mentioned the Arab leaders, the United States, and the Israeli government were planning to build a memorial, a temple celebrating the peace agreement between the nations. The site would be in Jerusalem.

Greg stood and paced the floor, upset. What had happened to his friend? Why was Derrick acting strange? Why was he fulfilling one of the signs of the Antichrist? Greg knew it is the Antichrist who built the new temple in Jerusalem and desecrated it. Why was Derrick building the temple? Maybe he was mistaken. Maybe he was wrong about Derrick. *God, please let it be a mistake,* he prayed. He turned the volume up on the TV. A doctor was answering questions at a press conference about Derrick's condition.

"A medical report filed on the Internet suggests the president's head wound was fatal and a body double has taken his place," one reporter remarked. "Can you comment on the rumor?"

The doctor smiled. "I assure you," he said. "The president is Derrick Moore." The doctor's weight shifted and he became serious. "But I will say this much. The president's head wound in most cases would be considered fatal. President Moore's surviving the head injury he received in the plane crash is nothing short of a miracle."

"Are you saying," a reporter yelled, "the president should've died in the crash because of the head wound?"

"I believe ninety-nine percent of people who suffer a wound of this magnitude would not live," the doctor said.

The questions continued and the doctor did his best to explain his answers to a group of medically challenged people.

Greg didn't hear the TV anymore and his eyes filled with tears. He opened his Bible and turned to Revelation 13:3. "And I saw one of his heads as it had been mortally wounded, and his deadly wound was healed. And all the world marveled and followed the beast," he read. "Why?" he asked out loud. "I don't understand. Why Derrick?" He fell into his chair.

Someone was coming down the stairs.

Greg straightened up in his chair and wiped his eyes, expecting Art, or maybe Kelsy and Sam.

The strong frame of a man materialized in the candlelight.

Greg stood and a slow smile of disbelief appeared on his face. "Hello, my friend," James said.

"Are you really here?" Greg asked, still not believing his own eyes. "Are you flesh or spirit?"

"Oh, I'm flesh all right," James answered, grinning and tapping his stomach. "I got a little extra nowadays."

Greg hurried around his desk, but stopped directly in front of James, fearing he might walk right through him.

James looked down at the little man and spread his arms.

Greg hugged him. "I missed you my friend."

Greg put on Mozart and opened a bottle of 1997 Ruffino wine. James explained how he'd become an agent for the covert organization, White Cell. First, he had to confess he didn't remember anything from the time he was shot, to the time he woke up in a sterile, white hospital room. After three days, a man named Gill approached him and asked if he was interested in joining White Cell. Gill was the person who had a White Cell ambulance and doctor attend to him. Gill explained he'd been watching James for a year and was going to recruit him, but he got himself shot. So, he asked if James wanted to stay dead and work against another secret organization called the Shadow Government. James said yes, figuring he would change his mind later. Later hadn't came yet.

"I guess Kelsy was correct," Greg said. "Her James is my James."

"She's a nice girl."

"I'm glad you're helping her."

"She's helping me."

"Did you see Derrick," Greg asked, stinging from the thought.

"Yeah," James nodded. "We're going to have to get close to him, and find out what's going on in his head. The plane crash changed him."

"Are you staying?" Greg asked, fearing his friend would disappear again.

"I have a feeling I'm going to be around for long time."

Chapter 55

Mary took a deep breath of the cool spring air. The sun felt warm on her face. She walked along Constitution Gardens and headed toward the Lincoln Memorial, which sat proudly on the west end of the Reflecting Pool of the Mall like an ancient Greek temple erected to a mythical god. To some, the memorial stood as a reminder of a country vehemently torn apart over a hundred forty years ago; a reminder of a good man murdered in the zenith of his political mission; a reminder of wounds still healing.

But to Mary, the Lincoln Memorial was a lighthouse, a brilliant beacon of light to that grand and noble ship called America, who suddenly found herself drifting too close to the jagged shore of self-destruction. We the people, when confronted by terrorism or natural disasters, pull together and become Americans, not Greek-Americans, not Mexican-Americans, not Italian-Americans, not Jews, Muslim, or Christians, just Americans. But when the waters and winds become calm, we drift apart complacently, weakening our unity, weakening our country. We must remain united at all times. Was that not what the Lincoln Memorial was about? Unity. That was what he died for. Wasn't it? We had lost sight of his vision. But it may not be too late, she thought. She was a closet optimist. We again could steer toward truth and integrity, away from the sea of corruption and deception, and land on the shore of equality and true freedom. Some said such a place didn't exist, but one day a future generation would find it. Maybe. One could only pray.

Mary reached the top step of the first plateau of the Lincoln Memorial and turned to face the Washington Monument. It's white, elongated reflection mirrored perfectly in the calm waters of the pool. She was saddened suddenly by a random thought.

Before her, standing over five hundred feet, was the magnificent geometric form, the Washington Monument, a memorial dedicated to George Washington, the founder of the government; a hero, a warrior, a gentleman, a sparking jewel in America's history. And behind her was Abraham Lincoln, an eminent gem in the proud crown of the country's past, the protector and the preserver of the government; the savior. What would they think today of their beloved country and government they passionately fought and died for? Mary could hear the disconcerted thumping in the coffins, the proverbial rolling over in one's grave. Not that the system wasn't corrupted or faulty in their time; Lincoln himself discovered that fact first hand when he was assassinated by the same government he so painfully fought to preserve. Another sinister deed in the Shadow Government's long history. But there was an immense distinction between the corruption of the government of today and the forefather's government. In the past they were dealing with carpenter ants, in comparison to the termite infestation of today.

Again, Mary felt an onerous sadness overcome her. A haunting voice rang in her ears from somewhere, but it was too distant to hear clearly. She stared out across the Mall grounds in a trance, listening . . . waiting. Then, she heard it, a ghostly whisper. "I have a dream." The hush of the words in her ear gave her goose bumps and a shivering chill down her spine. Her eyes dropped to her feet, realizing she was standing in the exact spot where Martin Luther King, Jr. made his eminent "I have a dream" speech on August 28, 1963. It was his voice she heard resonating in her head, loud and clear now. A voice she heard many times as a child in her home. Her father had an audio recording of the speech and played it often, especially in times of hardship, for instance, when the family encountered racism and injustices because of their nationality. Her father brought her to the Lincoln Memorial once when she was nine years old. Standing here must have triggered the memory from her subconscious. The voice spoke again sounding as it did that very day, amplified across a sea of two hundred thousand, a message still echoing decades later; a message still searching for realization and fulfillment.

"I have a dream, that one day this nation will rise up and live out the true meaning of it's creed, 'We hold these truths to be self-evident, that all men are created equal.' I have a dream that one day on the red hills of Georgia, the sons of former slaves and the sons of former slave owners will be able to sit down together at a table of brotherhood. I have a dream that one day even the state of Mississippi, a desert state, sweltering with the heat of injustice and oppression will be transformed into an oasis of freedom and justice. I have a dream that my four children will one day live in a nation where they will not be judged by the color of their skin but by the content of their character.

"I have a dream today. I have a dream that one day the state of Alabama will be transformed into a situation where little black boys and black girls will be able to join hands with little white boys and white girls . . . I have a dream today. I have a dream that one day every valley shall be exalted, every hill and mountain shall be made low, the rough places will be made plain, and the crooked places will be made straight . . . From every mountainside, let freedom ring. When we let freedom ring, we will be able to speed up that day when all God's children will be able to join hands and sing in the words of the old Negro spiritual, "Free at last! Free at last! Thank God Almighty, we're free at last!"

Mary's eyes were closed. Before the last words of King's speech faded, the image of him lying on his back with his life's blood spilling out of his head onto a balcony in Memphis invaded her mind. The image fueled an already blazing hatred for the S.G.

She moved to the rear of the Lincoln Memorial, now facing the Arlington Memorial Bridge. She peered through binoculars scanning the grounds of Arlington Cemetery. Her bomb threat had officially been deemed a hoax. All media outlets quickly raced to air the latest breaking news, hoping to scoop the other. She watched the police units break down their equipment, preparing to clear out of the cemetery. The sun would set soon and the cemetery would be empty, with the exception of the altruistic and brave residents. And then it would end, one way or another; it would end tonight.

*   *   *

A quarter of a mile away from the Lincoln Memorial, at the John F. Kennedy Center for the Performing Arts, was a man watching the events at Arlington Cemetery very closely. He, like Mary, was very interested in the cemetery and one of its occupants. He was waiting for his opportunity for a quiet and exclusive visit to the grounds.

*   *   *

Southeast of Arlington National Cemetery, a man stood at his office window watching the bomb squad and police pack-up. He was also interested in what was occurring at the cemetery. He focused his binoculars and continued to observe from the top floor of the Pentagon. He watched and waited . . . for the darkness to come.

*   *   *

"Arlington National Cemetery will resume its regular schedule tomorrow morning," the newscaster reported. "After eight hours of intense searching, the bomb squad pronounced the cemetery safe." The newscaster turned to the meteorologist. "It was beautiful today, but what about tomorrow, Don?"

The meteorologist turned to his map of the United States. "Well, looks like another nice one tomorrow, but it's going to get a little chilly overnight." The map of yellow, red, and blue arrows swooping and dipping across the country, indicating low and high pressures and storm fronts, was replaced by a detailed graphic of the Washington-Baltimore area. "We should reach a high of seventy-one tomorrow, but expect early morning fog and cool temperatures for the morning rush hour . . ."

*   *   *

The full moon illuminated the clouds a blue-gray, giving them the appearance of ghostly ships at full sail streaking across a sea of black sky. The warm day and the cool night had given birth to a creeping, eerie fog, the type seen hovering a few feet above the ground in low-budget horror flicks or tacky rock concerts.

Mary pulled her car off at Columbia Pike and parked beneath a group of pine trees near the service complex gate on the south side of the cemetery grounds.

"I'm assuming it's useless to ask you to stay here," Mary said, opening her door.

Allen got out of the car; he hadn't spent the last two hours persuading her to let him come along, just to sit in the car. "Are you kidding? I love walks through foggy cemeteries at midnight." He gave her a wink. "It's so romantic."

She smiled, and just for a second, she forgot the about danger waiting for them.

"It is our honeymoon," he added.

They met at the back of the car. She pulled out a gun. "Safety on, safety off," she said, handing him the weapon. "Remember what I said."

"I know, honey. Identify your target, two hands, take aim, squeeze softly," he said, rehearsed.

"And?"

He stared at her confused. He didn't recall any other instructions.

"Don't shoot me, or yourself. In that order." She popped the trunk of the car. There was a dozen various models of weapons and ammunition.

The large number of weapons and their malicious appearance shook Allen a little. A wave of fear and realization washed through him. "Do you think you have enough guns?" he asked, attempting to soften the cold image of death sitting in the trunk.

Mary stuffed handfuls of clips for her 9mm into her coat pockets. She also grabbed an extra 9mm out of the trunk and tucked it in the back of her pants.

Allen watched and his gut tightened with nerves. "Are you expecting company?"

She stuffed his pockets with ammunition and grabbed an assortment of other gear. She softly closed the trunk and turned to him. "There will be others up there," she said, looking deeply into his eyes. "And they'll kill us on sight."

Allen looked at her solemnly. "I know."

Mary kissed him; she kissed him the way a woman who was passionately in love kissed a man. She kissed him as if it were the last time.

They pushed through a barrier of shrubs and climbed over a black chain link fence. Followed by Allen, she darted across Patton and Jesup Drive, and then up an incline. They stopped under the cover of trees near a monument shaped like an Egyptian pyramid. This particular site was dedicated to the U.S. Coast Guard, but at the moment Mary and Allen were too uptight to care about what monument was dedicated to whom.

"What about Kelsy and Sam?" Allen whispered.

"They're late," she said, checking her map. "They know what to do. Do you have the vest on?"

Allen tapped his chest. "Check."

                    *   *   *

Kelsy turned off her headlights a quarter of a mile away from the rendezvous spot. She parked behind Mary's car and stepped out with a gun and a flashlight, but she kept the light off, not wanting to draw attention to her position. She stood near her car, listening carefully to the soundless night. It was incredibly quiet. So much so, she thought she could hear the fog pushing through the night air. She checked her watch; she was fifteen minutes late. She made one wrong turn in the city and it took her three one-way streets and one u-turn to get back on track. Slowly, she approached the driver's side door and discovered the car was empty, but there was a note from Mary. It said she and Allen went ahead and for her and Sam to follow the plan they talked about earlier. In the event someone else might stumble across the car, Mary didn't reveal anything in the note that may expose their strategy. Kelsy and Sam's part of the plan was to go to the administration building and retrieve the Stainwick file. Mary had a hunch Stainwick's body was disinterred and whoever ordered the exhumation must be the main man running the S.G.

A few hundred yards away and up the hill, flashes of light dotted the darkness. "Gun fire," Kelsy said to herself. *With sound suppressors,* her thoughts added. She pulled a map of the cemetery out of her pocket and looked around for a landmark as a point of reference. She guessed the shots were fired near the Miles Mausoleum, where Nelson Miles was buried, the general who captured the Apache chief Geronimo. *Where the hell is Uncle Sam? He should be here by now.* Her nerves were knotting up like old, tossed fishing line. She called Mary on the cell phone.

*   *   *

North of the gunshots, a 3rd U.S. Infantry guard continued the timeless ritual of honor at the Tomb of the Unknowns. The soldier paced twenty-one steps down the mat before the tomb, paused twenty-one seconds, and returned. The sentinel maintained the vigil around the clock every day of the year, in snow, rain, or hundred degree heat. The changing of the guard took place every hour.

The soldier heard the sound of suppressed weapons firing in the distance, but he wasn't sure what to make of the shots, if that was what they were. Could it be gunfire? What the hell is going on? He saw the unmistakable flashes of weapons firing in the fog below him. He rushed to the guard booth to report the bizarre activity. But before he reached the phone, a tiny dart struck him in the neck, rendering him unconscious.

A man dressed in black military garb appeared from the foggy shadows. He dragged the soldier to a safe, secluded spot, hidden from sight, where he could sleep off the sedative. "I think you should sit this one out," James said, removing the dart.

*   *   *

Two unmarked, dark blue vans parked in a lot at Fort Myer Chapel on McNair Road, which abutted on the west side of the cemetery. Ten men wearing trench coats scaled the wall and entered the cemetery grounds; they were FBI agents, who weren't FBI agents tonight. The man leading the group of nine moonlighters would be considered the most unlikely candidate for the illicit assignment taking place on this night; by day he was Assistant Director Amps of the FBI, but tonight he was nameless and off the Bureau clock. Tonight, it was personal business. Tonight was his redemption. They split into pairs and quietly disappeared into the thick fog.

*   *   *

The dark surface of the Potomac River had disappeared beneath the murky mist. A pair of eyes behind a scuba mask broke the glass-like surface; the fog was barely stirred. Eleven other black-hooded heads emerged from beneath the Potomac waters, gliding across the surface like Canadian geese in a V-shape pattern. The twelve dark forms silently reached the shore of the Boundary Channel and began shedding their scuba gear and wet suits. One of the S.G. agents adjusted his transmitter pack; the faint red light on the Global Positioning Satellite transmitter brightened on the green and black screen. He gave the group a thumbs-up.

The S.G. agents unfolded small, thin, wire-like headsets and placed them on their heads for continuous communications. They pulled their night-vision goggles over their eyes, but quickly discovered the night-vision and heat-sensitive goggles had been rendered useless because of the cool, dense fog. The odds had been evened slightly. The team leader ripped off his goggles and cursed God's involvement. Now, they too, would go into battle blind, like their opponents. The S.G. team made a final check of their submachine guns with stainless steel sound suppressors, and the map of the cemetery's terrain before separating into three teams of four. Wristwatches were calibrated, and a moment later, twelve dark forms vanished into the pale fog.

*   *   *

A little over thirty miles away at a small airfield in Bowie, Maryland, a single prop plane taxied into position for take-off.

Across from Arlington Cemetery on the opposite side of the Potomac River, an S.G. agent was positioned on the rooftop of the John F. Kennedy Center for the Performing Arts building. He ignored the glowing screen of a remote control mechanism in his lap; at the moment his attention was focused on a small, hand-held device, which was in the process of decrypting a transmission. After reading the message, he typed a response and ended the transmission. He lifted the remote control device. The glowing green display now had a single, blinking red dot.

The small plane waited at the south end of the airstrip.

The S.G. agent pushed forward on a tiny throttle on his remote control. A set of gauges and instruments appeared on the monitor screen that replicated the cockpit display of the small plane.

The plane sped along the pavement. Within seconds the wheels left the ground and the small plane lifted off the airstrip and started the journey west toward Arlington National Cemetery. Ironically, a hundred yards away, an enormous electric sign that spanned across four lanes of highway displayed the message, 'REPORT ANY SUSPICIOUS ACTIVITY. HOMELAND SECURITY.'

The stars were out and the temperature was cool. It was a perfect night for flying. A very enjoyable view of the Washington metropolitan area; that is, if one were alive to enjoy it. The pilot of the plane was a man named Alka Bin Rahm, who was a well-known terrorist from Syria, but he was unable to enjoy the ride. He had been dead for six hours now. But there was life on the plane; a small black box in the dead man's lap blinked with a steady, pulsing red light. The red heartbeat of death was wired to a box the size of a footlocker, filled with enough explosives to clear a city block. The flying coffin hummed along the star-filled sky, only a short fifteen minutes away from Arlington Cemetery. And the red light of death blinked on. Blink. Blink. Blink . . .

*	*	*

Surprisingly, Mary and Allen had made great time crossing the grounds of the cemetery, avoiding the shootout. They circled around to the west side of the cemetery and maneuvered through some of the thousands of headstones and memorials, stopping at the Spanish-American Nurses Memorial without incident. After a five minute rest against a large Maltese cross, they hiked up the hill leading to Memorial Drive. When they reached the summit of the grounds, the timeless white marble of the Memorial Amphitheater glowed brilliantly under the moonlight. The amphitheater was nothing short of amazing architecture. The double ring of columns and the wide, marble steps rivaled the coliseums of ancient Rome or the temples of the classical Greek era.

A fierce exchange of gunfire erupted below them. Stray bullets winged past their heads. Allen instinctively leaned up against the marble steps of the amphitheater. Mary took shelter behind a large oak tree. The discharge of weapons filled the foggy night, and flashes of light from the barrels of the guns blinked like lightning bugs in the dark woods. Bullets began hitting around them. They may have been spotted.

Mary's cell phone vibrated in her pocket. "Hello," she whispered.

"Where are you?" Kelsy asked.

"Getting shot at," she answered calmly. "I'll call you back." She ran past Allen yelling, "Come on!"

"Where are we going?" he asked, trailing right behind her.

"Not down there."

They sprinted up the steps of the amphitheater and ran in between the marble columns. Mary was the first to reach the north side of the memorial, and she was the first to trip over a pair of legs stretched out across the walkway, sending her airborne and face down on the marble floor. Allen managed to jump over the extended legs and side step Mary's body.

The legs belonged to a man seated against the wall, his eyes closed, his head slumped over. In his loose grip was a gun.

Mary had already rolled over with her weapon drawn and fixed on the motionless man.

Allen checked him for a pulse. "He's alive."

She looked him over and announced. "He's FBI."

"How do you know?"

"Check his I.D."

Allen carefully searched for his I.D., one pocket at a time, but didn't find one. He found nothing but a handful of empty clips. Mary continued to hold her weapon aimed at him.

"Standard issue weapon," she said, removing his gun from his limp hand. She grinned. "Plus, look at that haircut and suit."

"Hey, this is a nice suit," the man said opening his eyes. "Two hundred bucks."

"You got ripped off," she said moving closer, weapon extended before her. "Don't move."

"I have no plans to," the man said.

"Playing dead?" she asked.

"No," he grinned through his pain. "I thought I'd take a little nap." His body suddenly tightened with a wave of extreme pain, nearly causing him to pass out again.

"Where are you hit?" she asked.

"In the hip," the man said, pushing his trench coat to the side, revealing a dark red stain the length of his entire left pants leg. A small puddle of blood had collected under his hip.

"Who shot you?" she asked, glancing around.

"You can't see a damn thing out there, until it's too late."

"Who are you?" she asked.

"I'd rather not say."

Mary leaned over the man and unbuttoned and unzipped his pants. She pulled the side of the pants down far enough to reveal the bullet hole.

"No dinner and movie?" the man joked.

"The bullet hit the bone and came out the side." She searched through her coat and found six large gauze pads and antiseptic towelettes. She wiped the wounds clean before applying the gauze pads.

The man's face grimaced. "That feels nice," he said sarcastically, clenching his teeth together.

"Hold the gauze there," she told him. "Al, let me see that little bag."

Allen searched through his pockets, finding the leather bag she gave him back in the car.

She pulled out a roll of white, first aid tape and a pressure bandage. She also retrieved a syringe and a tiny vial.

The man gasped with pain. "Do you always carry first aid material around?"

"Just on the first date."

She inserted the needle in the vial and filled the syringe with a clear liquid.

The man's eyes locked onto the syringe. "Is that for me?"

"Something for the pain."

He smiled. "Bless your heart."

Allen kept an eye on the far end of the building. The gunfire had stopped.

"I know you," the man said, looking up at Allen. "You're the religious guy on TV."

"That's right." Allen turned to Mary. "Is he going to be able to walk?"

"I don't know," she answered.

The man looked up at him again. "Do you give last rites?"

"You're going to be fine."

Allen's words gave the man a strange sense of comfort.

"You need to relax and stay still," she warned. "And you need to think positive."

She taped the gauze down on the wound, then wrapped the bandage around his hip and leg as if it was the hundredth time she had performed the first aid treatment.

"I know you, too." The man pointed at her.

She glanced up from her bandaging work for a second to get a reading on his expression.

"You left the Bureau the same year I came in," the man said.

Mary stared at him. "So, you are in the Bureau," she said, catching him in a gaffe.

He grinned. "Oops."

She put the finishing touches on her field dressing, while Allen continued to watch for approaching trouble.

"I'm glad you got him," the agent said breaking the silence.

He was speaking about Jack Copper a.k.a. Ronald Conway, the S.G. operative, who had murdered her partner.

She avoided eye contact while tightening the bandage on his thigh to insure a slower blood flow.

"You have the respect of a lot of us at the Bureau, Agent Jopuez." There was obvious admiration in his voice.

Mary stopped, but didn't look up.

"Anyone who tries to take down the Shadow Government is either stone cold crazy or just plain stupid," he said, struggling to smile over the wave of pain.

"Just plain stupid," Mary whispered.

"A little of both, I would say," Allen added under his breath.

"Are you here with Amps?" she asked.

"Yeah."

They moved the agent into an office, which Mary broke into like a professional criminal.

"You need to lie down and not move," she said. "Keep the pressure on the wounds. I'll call for some medical help."

"I already did," he said.

They left the agent with his wounds, a loaded gun, and their prayers.

*   *   *

Kelsy spent a good ten minutes hiding against a headstone, while S.G. operatives moved through the woods twenty yards away from her. She spent the next twenty minutes trying not to get lost in the darkness and thick fog of the huge cemetery. By some astounding good fortune, she reached the National Park Service Administration Building. She slipped in through an unlocked door, which she found suspicious, and made her way down one of the dark hallways. She needed to locate the records room. She wished she had waited for Sam. She called him on her cell phone for the third time, but she got his answering service again. Why was it taking him so long to get here? She called Mary again and left a message. She worked her way along the hall with her weapon down by her side, but ready to fire. Her nerves were taut as a piano wire and her stomach was in knots. The same old insecure voice creep back into in her head. *What the hell are you doing here?* the voice ridiculed. *You're analyst—a desk agent.* She ignored the voice and kept moving. She glanced into a dark room, and then slid past the open doorway.

A crunching and grinding sound stopped her in her tracks. She looked down at her feet. "Damn," she said under her breath. She was standing on smashed glass that someone had broken out from one of the doors, and most likely that someone purposely placed it across the floor so that anyone approaching would be detected.

A few office doors away, a man stopped searching through a file cabinet after hearing Kelsy in the hallway. He put away his penlight and listened.

Kelsy moved again, attempting to avoid the broken glass.

The man in the room could hear her approaching. He maneuvered across the office and positioned himself near the open doorway. He silently slid a large military knife out, then waited for Kelsy to pass. She took a quick, careful peek into the dark room, then slipped past the open door. He repositioned the knife in his leather-gloved hand into a strong striking grip. His boot soles remained deadly silent on the floor.

Kelsy took two steps forward when suddenly a sharp cracking sound from behind sent her into a hundred and eighty degree spin. She was ready to shoot the first thing she saw, but there was nothing there to shoot, just a long, empty, dim corridor from where she came. Then, from the dark doorway a shadowy figure fell to the hall floor like a large oak tree cut from the base. The body hit the floor with a dead thump.

A knife slid across the floor from the dead man's hand. Kelsy had her weapon aimed at him, then at the doorway, then back to the dead man, then back to the doorway. Her mind was running a million miles an hour, not a single comprehensible thought in the lot.

"Don't shoot," a voice said from the dark room.

She recognized the voice immediately.

"Don't shoot, it's me. James." A black man, slightly over six foot with a medium build stepped out from the blackness of the doorway. He had a tight, military style haircut and a week's worth of growth on his face. He gave her a tight-lipped grin. "Hey."

"Hey."

"You can put the gun down. I'm one of the good guys."

Kelsy lowered her weapon. "That *was* you at the airport." She remembered his warm and trusting brown eyes.

He smiled. *"Sí."*

She looked down at the dead man.

"S.G."

"Thanks."

"I'm sure you would do the same for me."

She walked over and leaned down over the dead man. She pulled the black mask off his head, revealing his face. She lifted his eyelids and studied the S.G. agent's eyes. She would never forget those eyes that glared at her with cold blue emptiness. It was not the man who'd shot her mother. She dropped his head and threw the mask away.

"We'll find him," James assured her.

She stood and studied James like pen pals meeting for the first time. His eyes attested to the sincere and trustworthy voice she had become accustomed to. "Thanks again," she said, entering the office.

"Would you mind some company?"

Right now, she wouldn't love anything more. "Why, are you scared?"

James stepped over the dead S.G. agent. "Yeah."

*   *   *

Sam had cut through the fence of the north end of the cemetery. He took Custis Walk, a remote path that led directly to the Arlington House. He reached a secluded grove and heard rustling in the woods ahead, but because of the fog he couldn't see ten feet in front of him. Regardless, he pushed forward, prepared to kill if he needed to.

*   *   *

An S.G. operative had positioned himself against a large, thick oak tree. He unfolded a map that he had stolen from the administration building. This map had the name and precise location of every person buried on the grounds. After a quick update on his position he moved grave site to grave site, closing in on his objective, Stainwick.

A hard thump against his chest stopped him cold. The black cloth around his heart became warm and wet, spreading outward like an inflating balloon. He was dead instantly from the high caliber bullet exploding through his heart and exiting through a hole the size of a softball, out of his back. He leaned silently against one of the thousands of grave markers staring blankly at the city lights of the nation's Capital.

*   *   *

Mary and Allen had walked right smack dead into the middle of another shoot-out between S.G. operatives and FBI agents in the section of the Unknown Civil War Dead; a hundred yards from the Arlington House and Stainwick's grave site. Sixty yards away, the four S.G. men were positioned in a wooded patch on a hill near the Old Amphitheater, and the three FBI agents were hunkered down along the side of a ravine near an open field with no more than fifty yards between them. The FBI's position would be considered a death trap, in strategic military argot, 'sitting ducks.'

Mary and Allen's position, on the other hand, would be considered simply a stupid blunder. Strolling leisurely into crossfire certainly topped the list of bonehead moves. Mary wasn't sure if either side had taken notice of them. If not, it wouldn't be long until the S.G. did and started taking potshots at the new dummy targets. No sooner did the thought leave her mind, a bullet struck the tree a foot away. *Great,* she thought, *trapped twenty yards from any real cover.*

Mary pulled her cell phone out and fiddled with the options. She changed the ringer and increased the volume. Seconds later her phone rang. The steady annoying ring of her phone was surprisingly loud in the cemetery. The gunfire came to a halt almost simultaneously.

"Come on!" she whispered, and grabbed Allen's arm.

They made it to a safe distance before the gunshots resumed. She could picture heavily armed men instinctively reaching or digging for their cell phones, knowing damn well they'd either turned them off or had them on vibration.

Allen laughed. "Genius."

"Yeah," she grinned. "The same genius that put us there in the first place."

Suddenly, a figure with an automatic weapon appeared like a black ghost from behind the old Arlington House slave quarters twenty yards directly in front of them. Allen, without hesitation, leaped toward Mary, shoving her behind a large tomb. He fell short of any adequate cover. The gunman released a cluster of bullets, spraying across the ground and ricocheting off stone around Allen. The assault ended quickly. A layer of chipped stone and chunks of sod blanketed Allen's backside.

Mary's heart pumped with fear at the sight of Allen lying lifelessly on the ground. She jumped to her feet and circled around the building. She killed the S.G. with a single shot to the neck. Emerging from the darkness and fog, three armed figures opened fire on her with mindless decisiveness. She sprinted to the other side of the slave quarters, where she'd left Allen lying, but he wasn't there. *He's alive!* her mind concluded. *Now, get the hell out of here,* she said to herself as she ran toward the Arlington House.

*   *   *

The small prop plane continued westward through restricted airspace, carrying its dead pilot and a cargo of death. The plane hummed and blinked along the starry skyline of the suburbs of Maryland, minutes from giving Arlington Cemetery a new landscaping design, and adding a few new occupants.

*   *   *

An S.G. operative reached Stainwick's grave site, which was only fifty yards away from the Arlington House and Mary. He retrieved a homing monitor the size of a videocassette from his backpack. It was designed to attract a small plane with a big attitude. He placed the dull, black device at the base of the headstone and activated the homing single. He transmitted a message to the operative on the roof of the JFK Performing Arts Building. All systems were "go."

*   *   *

In the plane, a second blinking red light appeared on the small black box in the dead man's lap. This was the homing signal and it had locked in to its destination. The man on the roof gathered his equipment, turned off his remote control gadget, and disappeared into the city night.

The plane, with one dead terrorist and a whole lot of hurt was flying smoothly and determinedly on automatic pilot. Next stop; Stainwick's grave site. Arrival time, seven minutes.

*   *   *

Mary studied a hand-sketched diagram of the cemetery grounds. Joe Philips from the funeral home had been kind enough to depict the location of Stainwick's grave. This would be much easier if it weren't for the fog and darkness. She had no intention to dig up Stainwick's body, at least not tonight. But she did plan on installing a miniature cellular surveillance camera near the grave site. Pictures were worth a thousand words. Words like conspiracy, murder, guilty, and convicted. She shoved the map into a pocket and ran. An S.G. operative leaped out at her, knocking her to the ground with a vicious hit. Her gun slid across the gravel road. The S.G. moved in close so he could see her eyes when he put a bullet in her head. The only problem was he didn't expect Mary to recover from the blow he inflicted on her. She kicked his legs from beneath him and sent him crashing to the gravel, separating his collarbone and opening a gash in the side of his head. He jumped to his feet, searching the ground for his weapon.

Mary was burning with fury. Every inch of her body was pumping with the built-up hatred for the S.G. Thoughts of the S.G.'s victims fueled her body with strength. Lincoln, the Kennedys, King, her partner, her friends were there with her. Her hands became fists of rage.

Blood ran down the face of the S.G. operative from the gash in his head. He wiped his hand across his cheek and then licked the blood from his fingers. He slid a long knife out of his vest. "I'm going to enjoy cutting you up," he said, smirking at her. He lunged and took a strong swing with the knife. He missed her stomach by no more than a quarter of an inch. The blow to his head and the blood dripping into his eye had dulled and diminished his killing skills. The power behind the thrust put him in an unbalanced position, exposing his face.

Mary threw a crushing blow to the bridge of his nose. The sound of bone breaking was unmistakable.

He cried in pain as he dropped the knife, both hands clamped over his bloody nose.

Her eyes locked on his. "Are you enjoying yourself yet?" she asked, sounding like someone possessed by evil spirits.

He looked at her, shocked and blurry-eyed, holding his nose while blood flowed through his fingers.

Mary kicked him in the middle of his chest and sent him down the steep hill. He tumbled uncontrollably, crashing through the shrubs, finally coming to rest at the bottom of the hill, where his head collided with a slab of Massachusetts granite. His life's blood poured into the spaces around the granite slabs of the John F. Kennedy grave site. The Eternal Flame reflected in his dead, unblinking stare.

*   *   *

Two F-15 jet fighter planes left Andrews Air Force Base. They had orders to intercept a small, unauthorized aircraft that entered the restricted air space of thirty miles encompassing Washington, D.C. called the ADIZ, Air Defense Interference Zone. The plane would soon enter the fifteen-mile radius called the Flight Restricted Zone, also known by the local pilots as "The of Line Death."

*   *   *

The S.G. operative, who placed the homing device on Stainwick's headstone, prepared to hightail it out of there when two shots cut through the fog and pierced his upper thigh and wrist. He collapsed to the ground in agonizing pain, but within seconds he was rapidly dressing the wounds with bandages as best as he could. The blood flow slowed, but didn't stop. He looked at the homing device's red blinking light and then at his watch, and then back to the red winking eye of death. Suddenly, the barrel of a gun was pushed to the back of his head.

"Looks bad," Mary said, glancing at his wounds.

"It could be worse," the S.G. said calmly.

"Really?" There was something about his composure that had her curious, considering he had a potentially fatal wound in the leg and a gun pointed to his head.

"Sure." He looked at his watch. "In about four minutes *it* gets worse."

"What happens in four minutes?"

"Landscaping."

Mary waited for him continue.

The S.G. shifted his weight with a grimace. "About four acres worth." He nodded toward the blinking red light.

"What is it?"

"A homing device," he answered. "There's a plane loaded with explosives headed here. And we're at ground zero."

Mary stared at him, unsure if she should believe him. "Disconnect it," she said, pointing her gun at him.

"Sorry, can't do it. It doesn't have an abort option."

"Clip it," she said. "Or throw it in the river."

"Can't. It's got a mercury switch and level. A little tilt or bump . . . boom. Not a big boom, mind you, but enough boom to ruin our night. Plus, the coordinates are already programmed by now."

"It was nice knowing you," she said, backing away. "I must be going."

"Hey, don't leave me here," the S.G. pleaded.

"You're kidding?"

"I got two young kids," he continued, imploring. "Please, help me out of here."

"You had no problem blowing up a bunch of people a couple of minutes ago."

"Please, lady. I don't want to die."

Her heart and mind were having a screaming contest.

"Three minutes," the S.G. reminded her.

Mary looked out across the eastern horizon. Washington, D.C. shone beneath the star-filled sky with a quiet, artificial glow. A feeling of anxiety rushed over her with the thought of Allen still out there. She didn't know if he was wounded, dead or alive. Flashes of exploding light in the woods below caught her attention. Bullets hit the gravestones and the trees around her. She hit the ground and rolled for cover. "See ya," she said, leaping to her feet. "Good luck." She jogged down a path and disappeared into the darkness.

The S.G. man sat for a moment in silence staring out at the Potomac River and the skyline of Washington. The moon broke through the clouds for a second, bathing the surface of the river with a beautiful silver sparkling light. He pulled out a picture of his wife and two children, which he wasn't supposed to be carrying. The two-year-old little girl smiled happily and the five year old boy grinned with pride at him. He looked at his wife's eyes in the photograph and mumbled, "I love you." He touched the face of his children. "I'll miss you." His eyes welled with tears and his heart broke with the thought of never seeing them again. In the middle of cursing his life decisions, a pair of arms suddenly slid under his armpits.

Mary grabbed him from behind and lifted him to his feet. "Come on," she groaned, helping him down the path. "Those better be your kids."

*   *   *

Kelsy was searching through a file cabinet in an administration office. James went outside and helped two FBI agents trapped in the Arlington House by S.G. She heard something near the doorway. She scanned the room with her weapon. Her peripheral vision located movement on her flank, but she ignored her first impulse to look, and instead she dove behind a desk and antique cabinet that quickly became flying, breaking glass, and splintering plastic and wood.

While attempting to crawl toward more reliable cover under a stream of bullets over her head, she cut her hands and knees on the broken glass. She positioned herself against a metal file cabinet. The bullets stopped, and a blue cloud of smoke from the submachine gun raised slowly to the ceiling. Kelsy listened carefully to the sound of footsteps approaching her position. She fell to her stomach and looked beneath one of the office desks, which gave her a clear view of the assailant's black boots approaching her. She took aim and fired, hitting the S.G. three times, once in the top of the foot and twice above the joint of the ankle. He dropped like a sack of potatoes, grabbed his ankle and agonized in pain as blood poured profusely from all the openings in his boot. She fired again, hitting an artery in the leg. He fired his weapon randomly throughout the room, and while he did, Kelsy made her way to the other side of the room.

The roar of the gun stopped, but only because of the lack of ammunition. The gunfire was replaced by the sound of a man whimpering in pain. When Kelsy finally checked the position of the wounded man, he had disappeared. She followed a bloody trail to a back door, where he had dragged himself. She caught him attempting to unlock the door.

He turned and sat against the door, his eyes filled with pain. His black mask moved in and out where his mouth was breathing hard. He showed Kelsy his empty black-gloved hands in a surrendering gesture.

She stared at the blue eyes that peered from the masked face. Her heart sped up and her blood grew cold. She knew those eyes. Her mind flashed back to the day her mother was shot. With one hand guarding him with a gun, she pulled the mask off his head with the other. The hair was brown, the face was young, but the eyes were icy blue, like Windex, eyes so cold, beautiful, and empty she would never forget them. He shot her mother, there was no doubt in her mind. He appeared to recognize her and she watched his pain turn to fear. She took aim. The surge of revenge rushed toward her trigger finger. The thought of her mother in the hospital fueled her anger. Her blood burned for vengeance; the death of his man seemed to be the only way to quench the fire. The image of her mother slumped over and bleeding in the car appeared in her mind, quickly followed by the image of her in the hospital. Those thoughts brought her to the edge of murder.

She was burning with hate and death, but suddenly something from deep inside of her emerged like a cool breeze on a hot and humid day. Something truly beautiful and much stronger than her, something able to cool the smoldering abhorrence in her, something that could turn her away from the edge of pure evil. Forgiveness. She slowly lowered her weapon to her side. The S.G. took his last breath; his life's blood became a puddle around him in a black circular shape.

"Sorry, I'm late," James apologized, running into the room armed and ready. "Who's that?"

"The man I've been looking for."

James walked over and looked down at the dead S.G. "Good."

Kelsy grabbed the file the dead S.G. dropped. A file with burial and exhume records. They headed for the exit.

Outside the building, quickly approaching the same door, was a group of four S.G., and at the current pace of both parties, it appeared they would come face-to-face in ten seconds. The group of S.G. possessed enough weapons and ammunition strapped to their bodies to take on any small country's military. In a matter of seconds, Kelsy and James would be introducing themselves. If there was a bright side for Kelsy and James to the upcoming encounter with the heavily armed foursome, it would be the condescension and superiority the S.G. exuded. There was an overconfident mentality rooted deep in the minds of the men in this S.G. team. They had no fear and a narcissistic feeling of invincibility. And this type of arrogance made an agent slow, careless, and possibly dead.

Kelsy and James opened the door, and standing outside within arm's reach was a black wall of automatic weapons. Luckily, all the guns were pointing down. It only took Kelsy a second to lift her gun into shooting position, but that was slow-motion in comparison to James' reaction.

The S.G. team was frozen statue-like, almost in shock. Some of them couldn't believe they got caught in this humiliating position, and others were entertaining thoughts of a shoot out. But at the moment the team remained calm and silent under the hand signal of the team leader.

James guided Kelsy around the S.G. team. "We're just going to disappear," he said in a friendly way, like a man who wanted no trouble.

The S.G. team watched them carefully in their painful embarrassment, hankering for a chance to put a bullet in these two lucky nobodies.

James put himself in between Kelsy and the eyes of burning hate and itchy trigger fingers. "We'll just be on our way."

One of the S.G. had an Astra Cub. He secretly slid the compact 9-mm caliber pistol out from his sleeve and started to lift it for a shot, but his moment of grandeur was stopped short by one of James' bullets. The S.G. agent hit the gravel walkway with a dark hole through his stupid, and now brainless head.

The S.G. team leader barked out commands, maintaining control over the team, preventing an all-out blood bath. Somehow, calmness prevailed. The stares from the deceased agent's companions were as piercing as any real daggers.

James backed away, never taking his eyes off the S.G. team. "Anyone else want to be a hero?" he asked, but this time his voice wasn't passive and friendly. Now he sounded more like a man prepared to kill every last one of them, only needing a reason to do so, and it didn't have to be a good one.

The S.G. leader gave a slight nod, preserving the temporary peace treaty.

James quietly told Kelsy to start running down the path. "What about you?" she asked.

He laughed. "Don't slow down. I might run you over."

James instructed the group of S.G. to get in the building. He closed the door and headed down the path in a full sprint, disappearing into the fog.

Bullets shredded the door. The lead S.G. kicked the door off its hinges. They opened fire after seeing someone running down the path. The darkness ignited with gunfire, turning the grounds into a strobe-light show.

Instinctively Kelsy wanted to turn around and help, but bullets hitting around her forced her to keep running. She stumbled over a low-lying stone marker and hit the ground hard, dropping her weapon. An S.G. operative approached from another position. He spotted her and closed in. She rolled behind a large headstone, but her gun was ten feet away. The S.G. surprised her from behind. He grabbed her hair and pulled her up. He pushed her against the headstone and then leaned his body on her in a sexual manner. He stared into her eyes, trying to decide what to do with her. A second later the decision was made for him. Sam helped him make up his mind, by putting a bullet through it.

"Sorry I'm late, honey," Sam said. "These hills are killing me."

Kelsy hugged him, still shook up with thought of what could have happened to her. "Thank you."

"Anytime, sweetie."

Kelsy's phone vibrated. "Hello?"

"Where are you?" Mary asked hastily.

"Near the Arlington House."

Over six hundred acres of cemetery and she had to be there, Mary thought. "Get as far away from there as fast as possible! There's a plane loaded with explosives coming to that spot any second. Did you hear me? Get the hell out of there!"

"Come on," Kelsy said, grabbing Sam by the arm and explaining the situation.

"Follow me," Sam said. "I know the perfect place."

*   *   *

The two F-15 jets had a visual on the small plane. One of the pilots contacted his superior. The plane was leaving the city limits without incident, he reported. The jet pilot was instructed to engage the aircraft and escort it out of the restricted zone, or bring the plane down using any means.

The senior pilot kept asking himself why the alert was late. Why did Homeland Security wait so long? If this were a terrorist attack, they would have been too late. The plane flew over every significant building in Washington and easily could have reached the Pentagon before being shot down. His stomach sickened with the thought of what could have occurred.

The fighter pilot would never know the truth. He would never know that the radar security duty officer was approached by an S.G. operative with a special message, ten minutes before the small plane reached the restricted area. Delay the alert or his family would be killed. And he wasn't the only security officer who received the distressing message. Three others shared his dilemma, and apparently, they all must practice the same creed; God, family, country.

*   *   *

Mary had one arm around the waist of the young S.G. op while leading him down a sloping field of thousands of white headstones. An approaching sound stopped them for a moment. They listened to the hum of a single engine plane quickly drawing near. A plane loaded with explosives. They also heard the F-15 jets screaming into view. The young S.G. suggested they get moving, when shots started blasting at them from the woods. She took hold of his waist and he threw his arm across her shoulders and they ran for their lives. They looked like they were in a three-legged race. She pulled her weapon and attempted to lay down cover-fire. The S.G. man hopped and groaned in pain, but he also attempted to provide cover with his weapon. Bullets thumped and spattered into the moist ground behind them, some so close that the mud hit them in the back of the legs and head. The plane roared over their heads so close they could feel the back draft. *Where the hell is some cover?* her thoughts yelled. *We've been in the open too long.* She could feel the cross-hairs of someone's scope on her back.

Suddenly, a vibrating shock-wave of sound and light filled the foggy night. The cemetery grounds ignited with a blinding white flash that turned bright yellow and then became an orange and black plume reaching for the night sky. The ball of fire could be witnessed from miles away. The ground trembled with raw energy. The air was filled with earth. The heat from the blast was incredible, the sound, deafening. Two acres of cemetery was destroyed instantly. Headstones and grave sites were obliterated.

Unexpectedly, Mary and the young S.G. plunged down a slope into a fresh grave. Mary grabbed her wrist in anguish and the S.G.

yelled out a curdling shriek after crashing down on his wounded thigh. A burning wave of fire and smoke rolled through the cemetery grounds in every direction. The heat flashed across the top of the open grave. Burning ash, rock, and sod rained down from the night sky like a Fourth of July fireworks display. Orange and yellow flames flickered across the foggy cemetery grounds. Moments later an eerie silence replaced the echoing blast of the explosion. Things had become as silent as a graveyard.

"Hi." A voice warmly welcomed Mary and the S.G. agent to the muddy, dark grave.

"Kelsy?"

"And Uncle Sammy," he announced.

Mary flashed the penlight throughout the grave. There they were; Sam and Kelsy smiling back at her. The light caught another face in the corner of the hole. She sprung out of her sitting position and leaped across the length of the grave. "Allen," she cried, embracing him so tightly he groaned.

"Miss me?" Allen grinned through a muddy face.

"Who's your friend?" Sam asked.

"S.G.," Mary answered, her face buried in Allen's neck.

"Ex-S.G.," the young agent corrected.

"You know," Kelsy said. "You're a married woman now, you can't go out picking up guys."

Chapter 56

The fog from the night before had long burned away. The sun was warm and bright, and to a few people it was amazingly beautiful. A sunrise some didn't believe they would see.

"Officials are now saying the explosion was a terrorist attack on Washington, D.C. Some believe it was an assassination attempt on the President of the United States," the news reporter stated, standing on the grounds of the Lincoln Memorial. "Here behind me at Arlington National Cemetery, a small aircraft carrying explosives and flown by a known terrorist was shot down late last night while attempting to fly the craft into the city, kamikaze style. Special biotechnicians concluded earlier this morning there were no biological or chemical weapons involved. A White House spokesman announced the terrorist's plot was foiled by the combined efforts of the Secret Service, Homeland Security, and Air Force fighter jets." The news program showed a shot of the cemetery grounds. The image of a smoldering black crater the size of a football field filled the TV screen. "Authorities are saying it may be weeks before the official report is released. I'm Doug Patten of Fox News."

On another channel, a journalist was explaining the incredible events of the Jordan Iblis story. How he framed the vice president, manipulated the Speaker of the House, and contaminated the fuel on Air Force One. The reporter explained Jordan's plan to detonate a biological weapon to establish an international dependence for his product—a remedy for the biological substance, ultimately creating a leadership role for himself and the United Nations. The reporter went into detail about the hired, look-a-like vice president who opened an account in the Caymans and deposit five hundred thousand dollars of dirty money. Then there was the relationship with Walter Web, the Speaker of the House, who Iblis convinced to attempt a rescue mission that would have started a biological catastrophe. Also, there was the blackmailed chemist who stole a highly experimental agent, which he in turn used to contaminate the fuel on Air Force One by acquiring the company responsible for fuel deliveries to the Mexican airport. All in the name of power. Life could be stranger than fiction, the journalist concluded.

The local television stations were interviewing eyewitnesses of the cemetery explosion.

"Yeah man, it was cool," the witness claimed. "The plane flew right over my head."

"It was so low," another witness explained. "I thought it was going to hit the Washington Monument."

Stories in the media were already questioning the government's account of the incident. The media sources were claiming the terrorist's plane traveled from the east, flying over the city, not from the south as reported by the security agencies.

On the radio, the conspiracy theorists spun their over-imaginative views to whomever would listen. One of the paranoid specialists asked if the plane was shot down, why did it blow up on the ground? And if it did come from the east, why bypass Washington? These were very good questions, which may never be answered truthfully.

The cemetery had been sealed off from the public. Every federal law enforcement agency was on the scene, either investigating or watching the ones who were investigating. Of course, no bodies were found at the cemetery, with the exception of the ones who were there already.

*   *   *

Greg was in the garden of the church, pulling weeds and planting spring flowers.

Kelsy sat on the marble bench beneath a hundred year old oak tree. "Hello, professor."

"Hello, Kelsy," he turned to greet her. "I didn't hear you."

"I've only been here a second. Don't you get tried of pulling weeds? They just keep coming back."

"True," he said, wiping the sweat from his forehead. "But if I don't pull them, they will overrun the garden, choking the flowers and plants."

She turned to face the morning sun, yearning to feel the warmth of spring and summer again. "It's another beautiful day."

"What happened to your cheek and neck?" he asked, noticing her wounds.

She'd suffered several cuts, bruises, and burns from the night before. The burns she endured were from falling, burning debris. "I was at the cemetery last night."

"I was afraid you were," he said, concerned. "Did you find what you were searching for?"

"Yes, but it didn't help. Mary thought Stainwick's body was exhumed and there would be a record of who ordered it. Giving us a name. The file said the government exhumed the body. There was no mention of the person who ordered it. And Stainwick's body was blown up, as you might have guessed. So, whatever evidence was in there with him is now cremated. But we did find out what the artifact was."

Greg became very interested.

"It was the crown of thorns," she revealed.

The thought of the crown of thorns surviving two thousand years astonished him. The fact that the government stole and murdered for it also amazed him. "Why did they want it so badly? What did they want it for? What did they do with it?"

She explained how they extracted DNA from the blood and hair found on the crown, and how they used the samples to clone Jesus Christ, and apparently Allen was the successful clone.

To Greg, this explained Allen's ability to convince and seduce billions of people to follow him. He thought about Derrick. Strangely, Allen was turning away from the role of the Antichrist and his friend Derrick appeared to be fulfilling the prophecies. "Where is the artifact?"

"We don't know," she answered. "It may have been destroyed in the explosion."

"What's next?"

Kelsy took a deep breath. "Everyone just wants it to end—the spying, the fear, and the killing—we just want it to stop. We want our lives back." She longed for the way it was.

Mary, on the other hand, would never stop looking for the head of the S.G.

"I heard Allen left his evangelist career," Greg said.

"It seems he's back on the right path."

"How's your mother?"

A warm smile crossed her lips. "The doctor said she woke up twice. He thinks her chances are getting better by the day."

"That's wonderful," Greg said, handing her a flower from his garden. "I'll continue to pray for her."

"Thank you, professor," she said, looking into his kind eyes. "Thank you for being there for me and helping me through some tough times."

"We all need a little help from time to time. Sometimes we need someone to put us back on the path."

"Hey, guys," Art yelled, from across the garden. "What's going on?"

"Hi, Art," Kelsy said.

"Careful Kelsy," Art said, removing the cigar from his mouth. "If you hang around long enough, the professor will have you pulling weeds."

"What brings you to church on a Sunday morning?" Greg asked.

"I got something that may interest you," he said, handing him the Post.

Greg looked at the front page. The lead story read, "North Korea Begins Nuclear Testing." There was also a photograph of four North Korean political figures standing at a platform. Then, Greg saw something that got his attention. He pulled his glasses from his pocket and studied the picture more closely. "Jordan," he said, the words feeling bitter in his mouth.

Kelsy looked at the picture. There he was, standing in the background. The hair was different and some of his facial features had been altered, but the eyes were the same, eyes filled with eternal evil, calculating deceitfulness, and a devious smirk.

"Here we go again," Art said.

*   *   *

In the White House many changes were taking place. The relationship between the United States and the Arab nations had improved dramatically, but that couldn't be said for Derrick Moore's marriage. White House staff had overheard heated arguments between the President and First Lady. Everyone had noticed the changes in Derrick, but no one more than his wife. It was destroying their marriage, and Derrick didn't appear to care. He had become possessed with self-importance and power.

*   *   *

Mary, Kelsy, Buckler, and Sam stood on the sidewalk in front of a small, gray stone church under a perfect blue sky. Spring had arrived with gentle, optimistic breezes and colorful blooms, and the cherry blossoms on the Mall confirmed the seasonal change.

Mary had a soft cast on her wrist. She'd re-injured the same wrist from the Greece trip. Kelsy sustained cuts and burns from the explosion. Buckler still had the head wound from Greece. And Sam caught a cold.

Mary's phone rang. She answered and listened for a minute before she hung up. That was her insurance policy. She'd made a copy of all the evidence she had and placed it in the hands of a friend at an Internet service, who was one push of a button away from hitting the World Wide Web if something suspicious were to happen to any of them. But this arrangement she kept to herself for the time being. Her phone rang again. "Put the data where I told you to, and I'll pick it up later." She hung up and grinned.

"What was that about?" Kelsy asked.

Mary leaned into Kelsy. "I have the microfilm," she revealed.

"What?" Kelsy exclaimed. "How? When?"

"You have the microfilm?" Sam asked, very interested in the latest news.

"Philips from the funeral home told me something he told no one else," she explained. "Stainwick separated the microfilm, hiding half of it himself and having his good friend Philips put the other half in his body after he died."

"Where was the other half?" Buckler asked.

"In Robert E. Lee's personal traveling chess set, behind the checker board. Sitting in plain view in Lee's bedroom at the Arlington House."

"How in the world did he get it in there?" Kelsy wondered.

"Stainwick's sister specialized in garment and furniture restorations, giving her access to the restricted rooms twice a year. I'm sure she did her brother a little favor by slipping the microfilm in the chess set."

"Amazing," Buckler said. "And you got it? When?"

"Last night," she answered. "I went there first."

"Where's the microfilm?" Sam asked, loosening his tie.

"At a bed and breakfast in Annapolis called the 1908 William Page Inn."

"I hope you have it hidden in a good place," Sam said. "Who else knows about it?"

"Us and my friend at the B&B. It's in a pineapple vase in a room on the third floor." Mary started walking toward the church. "I called the professor and in about an hour we're going to make copies and figure out what's on it."

Once they got in the church, Sam excused himself and headed for the bathroom.

Mary, Kelsy, and Buckler joined the odd-looking congregation that had gathered in the tiny church. Seated in the back row of the church were two FBI agents with cuts and scratches on their faces. Seated across the aisle were two S.G. operatives with an equal amount of damage to their faces and hands, and one had a sling for a broken arm. Apparently, some people were out late last night and too close to their own Fourth of July show. She knew some of the S.G. men would show up. They were so deep in the system, you could have their fingerprints, photographs, or DNA, and you still couldn't identify them. There were a few other FBI and S.G. operatives in the crowd with bumps and bruises, Mary noticed. Assistant Director Amps gave Mary a short nod of recognition and respect. Mary returned the gesture with her broken wrist. More agents, good and bad were entering the church. Mary and the agents acknowledged one another with lingering stares and admired each other's wounds.

The church looked more like a military hospital than a congregation attending a place of worship. There were plenty of curious and inquiring looks from the regular church-goers attending the service today. Mary smiled to herself, thinking how it must appear to them. Twenty-some new faces seated among them, appearing as if they just returned from the front-line of a war.

Allen sat in the back room of the church and prepared to speak to the congregation. The church hardly held a hundred people. A dramatic change from the ten-thousand-seat church that he no longer pastored. No more television cameras, no more international broadcasts, no more worldwide radio and Internet programs, and no more front cover spreads on every magazine in the world. Today, he would simply preach the word of God, the Gospel of the Lord Jesus Christ at this small church on weekend mornings; the way it all started, the way he liked it, the way it should be, the only way it was. He stared into the mirror and felt a peace in his soul he had never felt before. He sensed a feeling deep in his heart that things were right. There was a comfortable gaze in his eyes as he studied his own reflection, a comfort that had never been there before, until recently.

He lifted a thin folder from a desk and looked at it for a moment before dropping it into the wastebasket. The file was on Sarah Rosenberg and how she and her husband had gone to a government clinic to take part of an experimental fertilization program. The file explained how Rosenberg had been artificially impregnated, and nine months later was told her child had died at birth. The file also noted her husband left her because she couldn't give him children. She moved to Florida to live, and eventually to die. Strangely, Allen felt nothing for his biological mother. He had no remorse, no sadness, no satisfying closure, just a sense of understanding.

His thoughts turned to the woman who raised him. The woman who taught him, nourished him, and above all, loved him. She would always be his mother.

Allen stood and put two airline tickets to Greece in his pocket. By tomorrow afternoon Mary and he would be enjoying wine, olives, cheese and calamari on the island of Santorini, watching the sunset on the Mediterranean Sea; honeymooning. He checked the clock on the wall. Today's sermon would be on "judge thyself." But laced within today's sermon would be a message for the special guest attending the service, a message of warning, a message of offering, and a message of accord.

*　　*　　*

Twenty minutes later Sam was in downtown Annapolis. He pulled up to the gingerbread wood-shingled bed and breakfast on Martin Street. He slowly entered the 1908 William Page Inn. There was no sign of the guests. He wasted no time and climbed the stairs to the third floor. Still no guests or the owner. He passed the Fern Room, the Templeton Room, the Wilber Room, and the Charlotte Room, and finally reached the third floor room called the Marilyn Suite. The sunlight poured through the dormer windows and skylight. He looked around, but he didn't see a pineapple vase.

"Looking for something?" a voice asked from the bedroom door.

Sam turned slowly and fearlessly. "Why, yes. I am," he said with a grin.

James leaned against the door-frame. "You have your Sunday clothes on, but you're not in church."

Sam's grin disappeared. "Where is it?"

"It doesn't exist."

"What?"

"Mary made the whole thing up," James revealed. "There is no microfilm. Your name appeared in a document Kelsy recovered from the warehouse. Actually, it was Professor Orfordis who found your name and told Mary yesterday. I told her you were S.G. a couple of days ago, but she didn't believe it. After the professor fingered you, she contacted me and set up this little meeting between you and me."

"White Cell can't touch me," Sam declared. "You're no different than me." The reprehensible and devious man surfaced above the cool and professional facade. He wanted to snap James in two with his bare hands. Then, the anger became shame. He sat down at the window seat, the sunlight streaked over his massive shoulders. "Does Kelsy know?"

"Yes."

The shame began to eat at him. "They know I had nothing to do with the attempts on their lives," he said quietly. "And my sister's."

"Mary and Kelsy know it was Jordan Iblis and his S.G. thugs who were responsible."

Sam stared at his hands. "Now what?"

"You know what we want," James said. "The name."

Sam laughed. "He's so covered, you couldn't plant a case against him."

They were talking about the head of the Shadow Government. The man, who could have presidents assassinated and make citizens disappear with a phone call. The man who could start wars and remove entire governments, only to replace them with a political system of his choice.

"So, it can't do any harm if you give me his name," James implied.

Sam stared at him for a long time. "I'll tell you who he is," he finally said, insinuating James would wish he never asked. "Frank Shapino, the Secretary of State."

James' eyes didn't waver from Sam's gaze. The name Frank Shapino pushed into his head like a hot branding iron. Not only did Shapino have the power of the S.G., he also had the power of the legitimate government at his command.

"You don't look happy," Sam said.

James smiled. "I've had better news." He would relay the information to Gill, the head of White Cell. Exactly one week later Gill would see to it that Frank Shapino had an accident. He wasn't sure what kind of accident yet; car, boat, plane, or maybe the bathtub, but he would have an accident.

"What about me?" Sam asked.

"That's up to you."

"What's that mean?"

James took a seat on the queen-size sleigh bed. "It's recruiting season," he said, grinning.

*   *   *

Mary's cell phone vibrated. She read the message and smiled. "I have a new recruit," James sent. She leaned toward Kelsy and told her that Sam had joined James and White Cell. Kelsy felt the heaviness on her heart lift and the sharp pain in her head stop.

A thin smile remained on Mary's lips. She thought about last night at the cemetery. She thought about when she was in General Lee's bedroom. She also thought about the microfilm she found in his chess set. The microfilm no one knew she had. The thin smile grew slightly wider when she thought about what was on the microfilm. Photographs of the artifact, detailed documentation of what the government did with the artifact, endless records of the cloning experiments, and a hundred fifty names of the people involved. And then she thought about the driving force behind the madness. Her smile faded when she remembered the paragraph of information that summed up the deranged premise of the total ordeal.

The government had cloned Jesus Christ, put him with foster parents, where he would be raised and programmed to be the president of the United States, believing he would influence and control the 2.5 billion Christians in the world. That way the government could manipulate nearly half of the world's population. The sheer concept of the plan was maddening. Within a week, the entire world would know what was on the microfilm. And that thought made her smile again.

Allen stepped out in a dark blue suit. He put his hands on the pulpit and surveyed the crowd. "What was once lost, is now found. From the shadows of darkness comes light," he started, with a mighty voice. "And the light of truth will expose the dark." One thing was certain. He hadn't lost his charisma. From the first words, he had people riveted; even the nonbelievers were in rapt fascination. The sermon continued. Allen stared at the S.G. operatives. "God knows your sins, God knows your thoughts. He has your names in His book of life. You can't hide the truth from Him." He searched the crowd for eyes of guilt, and there were many. "And you will be judged." His words fell like a mighty gavel.

Kelsy and Mary were astonished by Allen's conviction and transformation. He became a different person when he preached.

"Your sins will be forgiven," Allen stated. "Your sins will be in the past, dead and buried. Wiped away, wiped clean. But you must allow the light in, turn away from the darkness. He knows who you are. He knows what you have done. Leave the shadows of darkness. Or you will feel the wrath of God's judgment."

The S.G. operatives got the message. The evidence was coming like God's judgment. Every media outlet in the world would have the evidence. This was a fair warning. Judgment was coming, and the weight of the world would follow. The consequences would come in the form of relentless exposure.

The FBI appeared comfortable with latest developments.

The Shadow Government would do what it had done so many times before when conditions became intense. They vanished, only to resurface later like an anaconda in the Amazon River.

Allen continued preaching for another twenty minutes, occasionally dropping a message or two in the sermon for the S.G. But most of the sermon dealt with a "judge thyself" theme, and the best way to improve the world was to start with oneself.

"Regardless of one's beliefs, good and evil exists," Allen said, nearing the end of his sermon. "The war rages on and we are all on the field of battle. Casualties mount on both sides as battles are won and lost everyday in the physical and spiritual realms. Some souls know they are in a great struggle; some souls do not. Many know which side they are on; and others think they know. I strongly suggest that all of us take a long and close look in the mirror and make sure that we don't see . . . *the reflection of evil.*"